REFRACTIONS

M V MELCER

Storm
PUBLISHING

To request permissions, contact the publisher at rights@stormpublishing.co

Ebook ISBN: 978-1-80508-276-7
Paperback ISBN: 978-1-80508-278-1

Cover design: Phil Dannels Design
Cover images: Phil Dannels Design

Published by Storm Publishing.
For further information, visit:
www.stormpublishing.co

To my parents, for all their love
Rodzicom, za ich miłość

CHAPTER 0

DEPARTURE DAY

The Feidi is still burning as my cab winds its way towards the elevator terminal, the enclave's empty streets littered with shells of riot gas and abandoned picket signs. Ahead, a food depot has been reduced to a charred husk, smoke drifting from the broken windows. A truck, half loaded with salvage, sits by the side of the road, surrounded by forlorn workers like a circle of mourners.

I wince as something scrapes the roof of the cab: a sheet of red and yellow tarpaulin, like those covering the market stalls. How far are we from The Two Horsemen? Is anything left of that bar?

I close my eyes. I don't want to know. In an hour I'll be in the elevator, away from Kenya and away from Earth for close to a century. By the time I return—if I ever return—nobody will remember what I've done.

On the cab's windscreen, the newscast flickers soundlessly, a mirror to the devastation outside. Seventy dead by now, three hundred wounded. The investigation's already starting, angry faces calling for the leaders of the riots to be brought to justice. Justice. A hollow chuckle shakes my frame, even as some part of me demands that I stay here and face them, that I tell them why I did it and demand they prove me wrong.

It won't work. They'll find a way to hide the truth.

I clench my fist, the warmth of Jason's tiny fingers imprinted into my flesh. *Where are you going, Auntie? Will you bring Mummy back?*

Sorry, kiddo. Nobody can bring your mummy back, nor your daddy. They're dead, and it's all my fault.

You can't take care of that kid from jail. I shudder as the memory returns: the words, barely louder than my heartbeat; Stepan's closing eyes; the smell of his blood on my hands. The sound of my footsteps as I run away, broken and numb.

I'm doing the right thing. Jason's grandparents will take care of him. He doesn't need *me*; he needs money to give him a good start. My fee will pay for the best schools. And this mission—it's about saving lives. I'm no use to anyone in the Feidi, but out there I can still do something good.

My hands shake as I reach for the wan-kong and swipe through messages, hurrying before my doubts return and I see Jason's face again and hear the promise I made to my dying sister: *I will take care of him.*

I press the play button. 'Welcome on board *The Samaritan*, Nathalie. We're lucky to have found you at such short notice. Thousands of lives depend on your mission: not only the colonists on Bethesda, but also those still en route to their destinations. I congratulate you on your courage—not many have volunteered to give up their lives for a mission of such duration. Thanks to you, the launch can proceed as planned. Captain Chen Xin will meet you and the rest of the crew—'

I stop the recording; I've heard what I needed to hear. This is why I'm going: for the settlers on Bethesda, the first colony under a different star, gone silent after barely a decade. For the other ships, each carrying thousands. Real lives I'll be helping to save. And if I can save even one, that may just repay...

I can't finish the thought, tears welling in my eyes again. My heartbeat booms in my ears, drowning all sound as darkness tightens around the edges of my vision. I clench my fists against the tingling in my fingers. Not now. Please, not now.

Ahead, the Kilimanjaro Space Elevator glistens in opalescent blue, the glass terminal untouched by the riots as if it belonged in a different world. The tether shoots up into the cloudless sky, thin like spider-silk, all the way to the tranquillity of the Yun Ju's stations. I draw in a breath, grounding myself in the moment. I can do it. For all those people. For Jason.

CHAPTER -5

4 MONTHS BEFORE DEPARTURE

I'm on my feet the moment the elevator cabin hits the atmosphere. My muscles protest, still readjusting to gravity, but the discomfort vanishes after a few steps. The altimeter above the door perks up, the digits brightening as we pass the fifty-kilometre marker. Not long now.

I press my earbud as I make my way to the luggage locker. Still no answer. Damn! They must be at the clinic already. I shouldn't feel guilty, really—I did my sisterly duty when she was having Jason. And let's face it, bodily fluids are not my thing. Still, Anna will always be my kid sister, even if she's having her own children now.

'No point rushing,' someone behind me says, the tone both patronising and annoyed. 'It'll be at least an hour before they let us out. And that's if the zhu-yuan don't take too long.'

Not if I reach the exit before all the orbital officials. I bite my tongue before I say so aloud. The last thing I want is the rest of the economy level following me out. Not worth it.

The locker spits out my over-stuffed rucksack, stretched into the shape of the gift package inside. I throw it over my shoulder, then change my mind and pull out my uniform jacket.

The captain's bars and the Orbital Logistics golden insignia may come in handy.

It works immediately, as the voices behind me hush to embarrassed silence.

'Is it true the zhu-yuan are too scared to come ground-side —' somebody starts, but the door closes behind me before I can hear the rest of the question. Good, because the feelings of the orbital elites are way beyond my pay grade.

The corridor is empty as I sneak down the service staircase to the premium level. The elevator's like a mobile hotel, each floor with a different price tag—cargo on top and the upper class at the bottom, the closest to the exit. I could have afforded the mid-level if not for the fortune I've spent on Jason's present, but hell, the smile on his little face will make it worth it. He's only got one auntie.

I check my messages again. Nothing. But just as I reach the red-upholstered corridor, my wan-kong finally vibrates.

'Nathalie! Where are you?' Stepan's voice crackles with excitement. 'Anna's in labour!'

'Almost there...' I speed up, as if that would bring the elevator down faster.

'Don't be long. She's got everything, but... she needs you.'

He hangs up, leaving me with my heart pounding like during those not-so-long-ago days when Anna ran back from school crying, and I hugged her and told her that being a foreigner was nothing to be ashamed about. My kid sister.

I round the last corner, hurrying towards the exit. The duty tech's already prepping the door, safety locks beeping with annoyance as he keys in the docking codes. He glares as I approach, but his frown relaxes at the sight of my uniform. That was a smart move.

Still, he cocks an eyebrow. With his pencil moustache and a buttoned-up yellow livery, he looks like a bellboy from some period drama. Well, this is an elevator, after all...

'In a hurry, are we?'

I put on my best smile. 'Yeah. I need to get to the hospital.'

The man jerks away, his mouth open and his skin paling to tawny brown. What the hell?

I make my smile wider. 'My sister's having a baby!'

'Ha! You had me scared for a moment!' He starts to laugh, relieved, but then his eyes narrow again. 'It's that new plague, you know? They say it's nothing, but... that's what they said the last time.'

He tilts his head, the statement turning into a question. His fear is real, even if misguided, and it seeps into me like a fever. The 2200s influenza killed two billion people, even if it was over a century ago. The second Horseman of the almost-Apocalypse.

'Nah, that's just gossip,' I say. 'I've seen nothing at the Yun Ju, and the last two weeks I've been to all the big stations. I mean, they quarantine you for sneezing. A whiff of a plague and they'd be in lockdown!'

The man doesn't look convinced. He runs his fingers over his thin moustache, his brows tight. Well, that's his problem. Just as long as he doesn't send me back to my cabin.

I wait for the altimeter to chime the three-hundred-metre warning. Disembarking instructions waft out over the PA system, first in Mandarin, then in English and Swahili. Almost there.

The man straightens, his confidence returning like a hyena to a watering hole. He leans closer, a new spark in his eyes. 'I'm off for three days now. If you get bored babysitting...'

I manage not to roll my eyes. 'I doubt my sister will let me go before the kids start school...'

'If you change your mind, I'll be at The Two Horsemen, in the east quarter.'

'I'll remember that,' I say, but neither of us looks convinced.

The floor shakes as we touch down. Locks clunk into slots,

and the PA chimes our arrival. I sidle closer to the door, willing the blinking amber light to settle into green.

The sounds of footsteps and the chatter of conversation drift in from behind me. Something about them feels off. I realise what when I turn to look: in place of the usual crowd, only a dozen passengers approach the exit, most in the functional garb of the bottom ranks of the zhu-yuan. That's odd. In all my previous trips, the elevator's been packed with them; from the low-level support staff to the highest ranks of business managers, all wearing tailored suits and impatient expressions as they hurry to make new fortunes for their orbital bosses. Why the sudden difference?

The elevator tech follows my glance, his grin fading into a worried frown.

I turn away, my eyes on the door. I've got no time for this. Whatever their number, any zhu-yuan will get bumped to the front of the queue unless I get to the checkpoint way ahead of them.

The door shudders and begins to slide open. I squeeze through the widening gap, out into a long tubular passage with iridescent walls. Signs in Mandarin, Swahili, and English blink into existence as I run past: 欢迎来到肯尼亚的中国飞地, *Karibu Fei di, Welcome to the Chinese Enclave in Kenya.* I emerge in the glass-walled terminal, blindingly bright in the midday sun. Air coolers up in the solar roof wheeze with the effort of keeping the temperature tolerable. The rest of Kenya is barely habitable, the whole continent little more than a desert, but Chinese money keeps their Feidi enclave going as if they could turn back time.

I reach the checkpoint in a record-worthy five minutes— then gasp at the sight in front of me. Most of the arrivals hall is gone, given over to departures. Behind the glass wall separating the two sections, a throng of departing passengers shuffle in snaking lines towards a row of blue booths that have replaced the exit gates. What the hell?

I slow down, uncertain. Ahead, the passage funnels towards just three arrival gates. A red sign flashes above: *Priority Passes Only*. Wou kao!

A single border guard watches over the checkpoint, her arms folded and her expression sour. She doesn't need to see my chip to guess I'm not a zhu-yuan. And I'm white, too, not Chinese and not even Kenyan. I may be a registered ji-gong, but I'm still a third-rate citizen here, a foreigner.

Her scowl deepens as I approach. 'You need to wait—'

'Please. My sister's having a baby...'

The woman's expression softens, so I continue, my best puppy-face on. 'I'm like a mother to her... Our parents lost their visas... had to go back to Canada when we were still kids.'

She starts to nod, then notices my bulky rucksack. 'What have you got there?'

Damn! I struggle to pull it open, my hands shaking as the first of the zhu-yuan appear at the back of the hall. 'It's for my nephew. One of those 'zero-g' gizmos—you must have seen the ads.'

The guard hesitates, her eyebrow rising in suspicion. She hasn't seen the ads; she has no clue what I'm talking about.

The footsteps behind me draw close.

'Please...'

'Go,' she says. 'But make it quick, okay?'

'Thank you!'

I'm at the controller before she can take another breath. The sensor blinks as it scans the chip in my wrist, then the door on the other side opens, and I'm through.

I'm almost at the taxi rank when my wan-kong's display lights up with an incoming call.

Stepan's grinning face stares at me from the screen. 'She's

here! All healthy and as cute as her dad! Say hello to Nadia Stepanovna!'

He pans the camera to let me see Anna, pale and exhausted but smiling at the blanket-wrapped bundle in her arms.

My chest tightens. They look so happy together. So fragile, so loving, and so, so perfect.

The image shifts, and I stifle a chuckle as Jason's blue eye fills my view, then retreats to show the rest of his face, rosy-cheeked and hyperventilating with excitement. 'Tyotushka! U menya sestra!' *Auntie! I have a sister!*

The picture tilts up, the camera pointing at the ceiling as excited voices coo over baby Nadia.

I wipe my eye and cut the connection. I'm grinning so hard my cheeks hurt. Twenty more minutes and I'll get to hug them, and everything will be perfect.

CHAPTER 1

Cold. So cold.

A million icicles burrow through me, needle-sharp. I shudder, gasping for breath, but the air in my lungs is frozen solid.

What happened?

Something viscous and cold worms its way down my throat. I gag, my body spasming as a thousand knives pierce my every cell. My heart flutters, frantic and irregular, propelled only by fear.

Where am I?

I force my eyes to open, squinting through the sticky powder that clings to my face. The air around me flickers red, pulsating in the rhythm of a shrill blare.

The cold-sleep pod.

My memory congeals into a spike of pain sharper than the ice that froze my body. Anna's dead. And so is Stepan. And baby Nadia. All of them gone.

I heave, choking on tears that won't come. If I could just keep my eyes closed, drift back into the cold. Oblivion's just a breath away.

No.

My mind snaps into focus. I'm on a ship, heading to Bethesda... The rescue mission! The sound—it's the alarm. This is emergency revival kicking my brain and body back to life with no regard for comfort or safety.

Something's gone wrong.

The breathing mask drifts away from my face. The cryo-fibres have almost evaporated; only blue dust motes still float in the air around me, clinging to my arms and my underclothes. I yank the electrodes off my chest and limbs, then shove the door open. Stale air rushes in, and the shriek of the alarm assaults my ears.

I push myself out with a groan. 'Ship, re—'

My voice disintegrates into a coughing fit, each heave tearing at my diaphragm.

'Ship?' I try again, breathless.

No answer.

'Anyone receiving?'

Nothing, just the dead wail of the alarm.

I try to focus, but my mind's a ball of fuzz, my thoughts slow and disjointed. I'm floating in zero-g—so we're en route, no longer accelerating and not yet braking. I'm breathing, too, so no decompression, at least not here. I glance around. Blue-lit cryo-pods stand in a semicircle facing the door. Status data scroll over the lids in Chinese characters, the details too complex for me to decipher, but their steady green hue is all I need. At least three blink purple to signal emergency revival. Good, I'll need help.

I rotate, scanning the area. We must have a manual console somewhere... There, next to the door, the display blinking with nervous urgency. At least it's still working.

I swing towards it, bracing my legs against the top of the pod. My aim's poor, one leg stronger than the other. I drift side-ways, stretching to catch the soft handgrips dangling from the ceiling like tentacles. I catch one, my wrist burning with searing pain—the injury that never healed. I grit my teeth and pull myself to the console. On the screen, Chinese characters scroll up in flashing red. Shit! I punch the corner to change the language, but the familiar icon is greyed out, disabled. Why? This part of the ship isn't supposed to be restricted!

I stare at the screen, willing my brain to speed up. My Mandarin's okay on a good day, but now I can barely recognise the characters.

'Zǒu kāi!' someone croaks. *Move away.*

A man is floating behind me, lean body ghostly in the flashing red light, Asian features, black hair dusted with blue cryo-fibres. More fibres on his shirt obscure his name—but not the red and gold of the Chinese flag. I breathe with relief. If he's part of the Chinese group, then he's engineering. Or at least his Mandarin's better than mine.

I shift to the side of the console. 'Switch it to English.'

The man ignores me. He taps a command and the blare of the alarm fades to a drone.

'Fāshēngle shénme?' I try. *What happened?*

I get no answer—but the man's frown deepens as he studies the screen, a trickle of blood on his lips.

I grab his arm. 'What's our status?'

He looks up, as if only now remembering my presence. His eyes focus on the maple leaf on my chest. 'Who are you?'

'Nathalie Hart. Pilot.' *Second in command*, I almost add, but there's no point. 'Do you know what happened?'

'Not yet.' He blinks, something metallic glistening behind his iris. 'The bridge is intact. You'll do better from there.'

He's right. I need access to the command consoles—I can't do anything with engineering controls, even if they spoke my language. And the captain may already be on the bridge.

I push myself away. The door opens as I approach, but slowly, as if it needed to consider the action. A chill runs down my back. This doesn't bode well for the rest of our systems. I float into the corridor, sucking in air as I turn towards the bridge. My inhalation turns into a cough, the air thick with something sharp and sour.

The smell of an electric fire.

I glance around, increasingly frantic, till my eyes find a thin blue line of smoke drifting from a door further down. The third cryo-chamber.

Good God. My breath catches, my throat dry and numb.

Fire in a cryo-chamber. Is anybody awake there? Or are they all asleep, about to burn alive?

My insides turn solid at the thought—but no, somebody will be there. The system's set up to revive two people per chamber. And the extinguishers will take care of the fire. My duty is on the bridge; the entire ship may be at risk. And the people on Bethesda, they may still be alive. We're their only hope. This must be my priority.

And yet I linger, paralysed by the vision of cryo-pods swathed in flames, sleepers waking up to searing death. My vision clouds, and all I can see is Anna's pale face and Stepan's blood on his white shirt. Tears sting my eyes, unable to escape without gravity.

No more death. No one will ever die again because of me.

I scream as I swing around, back past the room I just left, my arms throbbing with every pull on the handholds.

How many pods here? Thirty-six crew spread over three chambers. Twelve per room. I touch the half-open door: warm but not hot. Orange glow spills from behind, the smoke tinted red with the flash of the alarm. My eyes burn as I slide inside. I cover my mouth with my hand, struggling to breathe.

The semicircle of pods faces the entrance just like in my chamber—but here, all the lights blink in panicked red, some irregular, as if the machines themselves convulse under the strain. On the right, where the smoke is the thickest, balls of gravity-free flame flicker in yellow and blue.

I stop, gasping. I don't know what I expected, but not open fire. Not on a spaceship with a dozen redundancies for every eventuality. The safety systems should have kicked in. If those have failed, what else...

I bite down on the fear. Manual extinguishers, that's what I need. Images flash through my mind: the ship's specs I've committed to memory. Emergency equipment panel, right outside...

A figure glides towards me from the other side of the chamber: an athletic woman with blonde hair and white skin glistening with blue cryo-fibres. I recognise her even before I see the name tag and the Cross and Stripes on her chest: Amy Price, the chief of the American security contingent.

'Where are—' she starts, her voice hoarse.

'Out in the corridor,' I call back. 'Wall panel, left of the door.'

Price is on the way out before I finish the sentence. I turn back to the pods and force myself to acknowledge the blackness inside those on the right, the glass lids charred and cracked. Too late. Death's closing in on me, stretching his hungry fingers for more, always more.

Not again.

Another pod lights up, red filaments erupting into ghostly sparks as the cryo-fibres melt and burn. I dash towards it, my teeth clenched—when the whole thing erupts in a zero-g fireball, the heat smashing into me like a fist.

Too late! Too damn late!

At the base of the next two pods, blue sparks flicker, intensifying into a frantic dance. I push myself towards them, gasping in the heat. Something, no—someone—thrashes inside the right pod, limbs jerking as the fibres cocooning their body turn to ash. Another movement catches my eye: hands pressed against the inside of the next pod, straining to pry it open.

I can't save them both. The realisation comes with ice-cold clarity that freezes me in place. I have to choose.

My eyes flicker between the pods, my heart beating the seconds away, each as long as a lifetime. I must decide, must choose one life over the other.

A cold, detached part of me knows that the right pod is too damaged, but the left still has a chance. I move, acting on logic alone, turning my guilt into focus even as my heart splinters in pain.

I punch the control panel; most of the lights are dead but the emergency release icon still flashes weakly. The door shudders. It moves an inch, then stops as the last light on the panel flickers out. The cryo-fibres at the bottom of the pod are starting to glow. Behind the glass, the woman stares at me in horror, the breathing mask heaving with the rhythm of her gasps.

I grasp the edge of the door, pulling. My wrist sears in pain, flaring up like the flames burning the pod. The woman pulls from the inside, our fingers touching, hot and desperate. The door slides another inch. Not enough. I tug again but lose my purchase, my legs flailing as I kick for something to brace against. The ceiling spar. I rotate, head down, then push my fingers into the gap in the door, into the heat inside.

The woman's arms drift away, lifeless. The cryo-fibres around her are turning grey, then black. Her head rolls back. Another moment and she'll be gone. I can't let her.

I scream as I pull, another inch, then another. Something soft and sticky erupts around me, smothering my face and my mouth. I gasp for air and choke on the sticky dust—but I thrust my arm inside the pod until my fingers curl around the woman's hand. I pull and howl and pull until another arm latches on to me from behind and drags both of us out.

I come to a stop on the other side of the chamber, shaking and sucking in air in great gulps. It takes me a second to release the woman, my desperate gaze sliding over her figure: unconscious and covered in scarlet burns, but breathing, breathing!

My elation shatters as my eyes turn back to the pods. Price is back there, she and a tall black man spraying yellow dust from handheld extinguishers. The fire's gone, smothered by the dust —but at least five pods are charred black, and several others show no signs of life. How many dead? Who?

Price lets go of the extinguisher and glides towards me, her hair like a halo around her head. 'Are you all right?'

I follow her gaze to my hand: a blooming blister on my palm, my wrist red and swollen. The pain finally registers, as if it needed time to punch through the shock.

'It's nothing. The fire?'

'We got it. At least what we can see here.'

I pull myself out of my despair. This isn't over. I must get to the bridge and figure out what's going on.

'Check the other chambers,' I say, turning to leave. 'There's an engineer awake in chamber two. I'll be on the bridge. I've got to find the captain.'

Price's eyes widen. 'The captain's gone, sir.'

I frown, not understanding.

Price glances at the charred pods, then back at me. 'He's dead. You're in command now.'

I stare at her, my mind blank. This can't be happening. Not the fire, not this accident. Not Anna. Part of me wants to laugh because surely in a moment I'll wake up back in the Feidi and everything will be just fine.

Price's gaze fixes me in place, unrelenting like the pain in my wrist. I swallow through the lump in my throat and point to the burned woman.

'See to her,' I say, and head for the bridge.

CHAPTER 2

I try to keep my mind blank as I glide down empty corridors, eerie in the pulsating glow of the alarm lights. How many years has it been? How much longer to Bethesda? Is anybody even alive out there, or are we risking our lives for nothing? Not risking, I correct myself, the smell of smoke still burning my lungs— for some in that chamber, the risk is already run.

I push the thoughts away. For now, I just need to keep the ship from blowing up; everything else will come later.

The bridge is crescent-shaped, the leading wall tiled with screens, each with a function console directly in front. Now all but one of the screens are blank, only the leftmost engineering display blinking with rows of Chinese characters. In the middle of the room and set back slightly, the captain's chair rotates slowly as if rocked by the hand of a passing ghost.

I glide inside, forcing my gaze away from the empty chair. I'm not alone: a small, dark-haired woman with ochre-brown skin and bird-like movements leans over the communications console on the right. I recognise her, even though I don't remember her name: she's Kenyan Chinese, one of the 'elevator babies' the construction crews left behind in the suburbs of the

Feidi—but she's the first dual-national I've seen in an officer's uniform. At least, that's what she was wearing during the hurried briefings before our departure—now all either of us has are white underclothes dusted with the remnants of blue cryo-fibres.

The woman looks up as I approach. 'What's happened?'

'We... we've had a fire.'

I ignore her unspoken question and float to the systems console. I slide my legs into the harness. The screen lights up with a string of Chinese characters requesting authorisation. I punch in my codes. The display flashes the New Horizons logo, then aligns into my personal configuration. The indicators blink orange and red, but most of those are secondary functions. The vitals are green; we're not leaking gas, and the hull integrity is at a hundred per cent. I let out a long breath. It seems we're not going to blow up just yet. Or at least until whatever woke us up happens again. Was it the same thing that caused the fire?

If I only had a clue what it was. I scan the alerts. Most of the error messages point to the engines, but the signifiers tell me nothing.

'Can you read the engine data?' It's a stretch, but I have to ask.

She shakes her head. 'I only have comms access. I'm digging through the logs for whatever I can find.'

Kao. Of course, the comms officer wouldn't have access to any other console. Never mind safety, industrial secrets always come first.

I curse under my breath as I slide out of the harness and towards the engineering station, wondering if my codes will even work there.

Limited interface appears on the panel. *Main systems access only.*

For fuck's sake. That damned trade war is going to kill us. All the long-distance vessels in existence are Chinese. Deep-space propulsion was a Chinese invention, one the Americans have been trying to crack but never managed. A sad irony for them that their dream of a new world in outer space had to be attempted with leased vessels. The Americans would kill for a good look at the engines, and the Chinese would die to protect the secret. And now we're stuck with consoles that will only speak to the people with the right papers.

'At least it's working,' the woman says. Ten points for optimism.

'Can you...' I start, but she's already at it, scrolling through submenus with bloodstained hands. I frown but leave her to it. The injury doesn't look life-threatening, and I need her here, at least for now.

I glance around the empty bridge, the captain's chair still swivelling in an unseen breeze.

The captain's gone, sir... You're in command now.

My breath catches. No, I can't let myself think about that now. I must focus on the ship. Find out what's happened before it happens again.

Many things could have caused a fire in the cryo-chamber— all unlikely, but not impossible. But none of them should have affected the suppressants. That means the problem must be deeper and somehow linked to the control systems. I return to my station and reconfigure the display, hoping to piece together a broader picture from the scraps. The numbers scroll up the screen. We're at cruising speed, engines idle, position and velocity in the green. On track to reaching Bethesda in thirteen years.

Twenty-two years since we left.

I shiver, my wrist throbbing as my fingers clutch the edge of the console. Jason's twenty-seven now. Does he even remember his parents? Remember what I've done?

A noise from the entrance snaps me back to the present. The Chinese engineer glides inside. His head is down and his hair hides his face, but what I can see of his expression sends a chill through my bones.

Price and the man who helped with the fire, brown-skinned and built like a brick, appear behind him. All three are in their undergarments, but Price and her man, both with the Cross and Stripes on their shirts, carry emergency radios and ship-safe guns tucked into holsters across their chests. My brows rise—in worry or confusion, or maybe both at once. Are they planning to shoot their way out of this? Whatever. I'm just glad the engineer is here.

He moves straight to the engineering console, barking something in Mandarin to the comms officer still working there. The woman retreats back to the useless comms station.

'Two of Zhang's crew have suited up to check the engines,' Price says, floating towards me.

So the man is Zhang Min, our chief engineer. I nod, the relief like a breath of fresh air. He'll have all the access codes—and know what to do with them, too.

Price's drawn face brings me back to reality.

'How many...?' I start, but cannot finish.

'Seven dead. We're still confirming the names.'

A fifth of the crew gone. Twenty-nine of us left. I clear my throat. 'How many awake?'

The key crew from engineering and operations should have been revived, per the emergency protocol. Ten people—if they are still alive.

Price starts to answer when a jolt shakes the floor.

I hold on to the console, but the impact sends a searing pain up my arm. The alarm reawakens with a mind-piercing wail. I swing back to the console: pressure indicators blink into yellow, warning icons flaring.

'Gas leak at engine three,' I yell. 'Bulkheads not responding.'

Zhang's face twists into a grimace. 'I can't reach the controllers... Go for manual!'

He lifts his hands to his face, his expression pained—yet he does nothing, just stares at the red light flashing on his console.

Damn! What's wrong with him? No time to wonder. I can't help him with the engines; I wouldn't know where to start, even if I had access. But the bulkheads have manual overrides—is that what he meant? My heart thumps an urgent tattoo as I open a chain of system menus, searching. There!

The window flashes open, and I punch the command with my fist. 'Sealed!'

Pressure numbers stabilise, then climb back to green. I can't see the engine data, but the peripheral systems are still orange. And Zhang's still staring at his console, feet pushing against the harness, motionless.

I'm about to call him back to his senses when I realise: Si-Lian. Mind-Link. He's interfacing with the system directly, issuing commands to the ship's central computer straight from his skull. All the Chinese crew will have the tech, and probably some of the others. I should have realised. The captain would have known. He was Chinese himself; he'd have been able to link up with the engineer and assist him. I'm not the captain.

I return to my console, feeling out of my depth. Whatever Zhang is doing is having an effect, as one by one my indicators pale to green. The alarm withers and dies.

I allow myself three seconds of relief, then call up the logs. It's just a hunch, but—yes, right there, an identical pressure drop two hours ago, with a source near engine four. That has to be the initial malfunction, the one that caused the fire. Are we done now, or are more on the way?

I turn to Zhang. 'What was it?'

The engineer doesn't meet my gaze, his frown tightening as he peers at something on his screen. 'Maintain coolant pressure!'

I wince. Does he mean me? No, he's glancing at the comms officer. She blinks, flustered, her lips moving soundlessly.

Mind-Link, again. She has it, too. But they're not supposed to use it on the bridge, precisely because it leaves the rest of us out of the loop.

'Speak aloud,' I snap. 'What do you need?'

'I need someone to check the coolant pumps. I can't hold it all myself, there's too much—' He looks away, his attention already back to the strings of symbols flashing on his screen.

The comms woman glances at her useless station, then at me, distraught and confused.

I wave her to my console. 'Can you do it from here?'

'I'll try.' She's there in an instant, her fingers flying over the glass, rifling through navigation panels and menus. It'd be easier if either of us had engineering access, but even so, she's pretty amazing with the general systems.

I look at her chest, but her name tag is lost under a fold. I shouldn't need to check. The comms officer is part of my team. I should have made the effort to learn their names, even if my appointment came through at the last moment. My eyes fog, from memory or pain, or the vision of burned pods and the crew I'll never get to meet.

I pull in a grounding breath. *Not now.* I've got to hold it together.

'What's your name?' I ask.

'Lim Firyali.' She gives her surname first, the Chinese way.

I consider introducing myself, but she strikes me as someone who'd have done their homework.

'Thank you,' I say, and push myself towards Zhang.

The engineer seems about my age, mid-thirties or maybe a bit older, his frame trim and rather short, though it's hard to say when we're floating in zero-g. Black hair, slightly longer than practical, sways like seagrass when he turns to face me, his jet-black eyes intense. His frown hasn't eased, his expression hard in a way that worries me more than the red lights on his display.

'Do you know what happened?' I ask.

Zhang rubs his forehead, then grimaces at the blue fibres that have peeled off his brows. 'I know what. But I don't know why. We ruptured a power cell, and it overloaded the system. The malfunctions cascaded from there, sweeping everything on that node.'

'And this just now?'

'One of the subsystems failing as a result. My people are checking everything they can reach.'

This doesn't make me feel better. 'Can it get worse?'

Zhang snorts, the sound sharp and bitter. 'Overflow circuits are holding. We're testing the remaining power cells. But I can't—'

Something beeps on his console. He glances down, his frown returning. 'What's up with those pumps?'

'I've got the readings,' Lim says, her voice uncertain. 'The values... seem within parameters.'

Zhang groans. 'Useless. Send it over.'

The numbers pop up on the screens. When I look up, Zhang's eyes are closed, and his lips move as he subvocalises the commands for his crew. This time I don't protest at his using Mind-Link; he's much faster without having to go through the comms.

'They'll recalibrate all the power cells,' he says eventually.

I don't like the way he says it, his face drawn and his voice cagey. 'Will that fix it?'

'We're working on it.'

It's not exactly an answer, but it's clear the engineer's done talking, his focus back on his console. Better leave him to it; it's not like I can give him any advice.

Behind me, Price clears her throat. She's been waiting to finish our conversation.

I draw in a grounding breath and signal for both her and her man to join me at the system's console. 'Key crew?'

'We've lost Captain Xin, Erik Smith, the second pilot, and Kuang Jin, junior engineer.'

Erik... Blue eyes, wide, carefree smile. He said he was looking forward to learning my tricks. Was he the one thrashing, the one I failed to save? The one I chose to let burn?

'We'd have lost eight if you hadn't pulled that woman out,' Price says.

She probably means it as reassurance, but it's too little, too late. *Seven to death.*

'How is she?' I ask, because I have to say something.

Price juts her head at the man next to her. 'Moses took her to the infirmary.'

Moses Miller, according to his name tag.

'She's stable,' he says, his voice a warm baritone. 'Some nasty burns but nothing life-threatening, at least according to the em-kit.'

'Two pods were showing warnings, so I set them to revive,' Price says. 'Michael Lee from my team, and a nurse. I wanted to defrost a doctor, but since we're getting a nurse...'

Her gaze is a question, so I nod. 'Keep checking the pods. I'll ask the engineers to inspect them as soon as the rest of the ship's in order.'

'What do you want to do with the bodies?' Miller asks.

The question catches me unprepared. I tremble, the image of the charred corpses blending with the vision of blood-covered ones, Sunday-best clothes smeared with red dust, Stepan's white shirt and Anna's closing eyes. All my fault.

I chose this mission to help the living, but death's creeping in behind me, laughing at my guilt.

I clench my fist, the pain in my wrist fixing me in the moment. 'We need to move them,' I start, then stumble again. Do we even have a morgue?

'We'll find a place,' Price says. 'Leave it to us, *sir*.'

She articulates the title, her gaze shifting to something

behind me—to the engineering console, where Zhang's watching us, his lips pursed and his brow furrowed.

Things fall into place. Of course. The captain's death technically puts me in charge—a laowai, a non-Chinese. He's not going to accept that—and Price won't let go either, especially with Erik Smith, the only American on the bridge, now also out of the picture. But this is not the time for this discussion, not when we're all bundles of adrenaline on a ship that may give up on us at any moment.

'You need to inspect the pods for damage,' I say to the engineer. 'As soon as the ship is secure.'

A shadow crosses Zhang's face. He turns to Lim, rattling out something in Mandarin. I don't need my language skills to know he's ordering her to the pods.

'She can't do it,' I say.

'Useless.' He growls the words like a curse.

Something inside me snaps. I swing towards him, my voice caustic. 'She's a comms officer, not a technician. Also, she's my crew. You want something from her, you go through me.'

Zhang glares. His mouth opens in a retort—but then a tremor runs through his face, rearranging his anger into something fragile. He lets his head drop, eyes half-closed, shoulders hunched. When he lifts his head again, his eyes are moist. 'This would be Officer Kuang's job. He... he was a... friend.'

Kuang... The junior engineer. Another charred corpse thrashing inside the spider-web of scorched cryo-fibres. What a way to lose a friend. And from the way Zhang's voice cracks on the word, I guess Kuang must have been more than a friend.

The engineer sucks in a breath, his composure returning even as his lips stay pale and his fists remain clenched. He turns to Lim. 'I was out of line. I apologise, officer.'

Lim nods in acknowledgement; I can tell the apology means a lot. She's still trembling, both of them are, faces drawn from pain and shock as they face each other for a long moment before finally returning to their work.

We're all broken, I realise. Every one of us. Why else would anyone let themselves be frozen for a seventy-year trip there and back in a mission with such slim chances of success?

Bethesda, our destination, was humanity's first and only extra-solar colony, settled by American missionaries to spread the glory of the Lord—and to find purpose for the millions displaced when the seas rose, and hurricanes made coastal states uninhabitable. At first, it appeared to be a great success, documented with a string of exuberant messages. New Horizons, the company behind the whole endeavour, promptly launched three more ships with just enough fuel for one-way trips to new destinations. But then Bethesda fell silent, with no explanation of what had gone wrong. Years passed while executives argued about the levels of risk and desperate calls crawled through space—six years for the radio signal to reach Bethesda and another six waiting for answers that never came—until it was too late to turn back all the other ships.

Our mission was billed as 'rescue', even though few believed we could make a difference to Bethesda. The colony will have been silent for decades by the time we even get there. From the way New Horizons handled the whole thing, it was clear they saw it only as a PR exercise to appease the media and avoid litigation. And yet, here we are, all volunteers. Running away from our pasts or searching for redemption.

For a moment I wonder what it was that brought those two here. One thing I know is that I'll never ask.

Price and Miller are off checking on the new revivals when the two engineers surveying the ship's guts deliver their report. I watch Zhang conduct a silent conversation with his people, eyes half-closed and only his chin twitching. Colours from the screens on the leading wall of the bridge play on his face. I've turned on all the displays in the hope that seeing the data in one place will make me notice something I may have missed. So far, I've got nothing.

'They've recalibrated every power cell and checked the peripheral systems,' Zhang says eventually. 'Everything's working to specs. Some circuits will have to be replaced, but nothing critical. I've sent them now to inspect the pods.'

'Do you know what caused the initial malfunction?'

'No idea. Nor why the safeguards didn't kick in. We've checked them again and they are fine.' Zhang's lips curl into a grimace. 'As much as I hate to say it, this looks like a random anomaly, a one-in-a-million chance of a build-up inside a cell.'

I shake my head, returning his scowl. This is a bad answer, and we both know it. We have another thirteen years of travel ahead of us and not enough food or air to last that long, even if we wanted to sit it out. We have to go back to the pods. If this wasn't a random anomaly, the rest of us may be waking up in flames.

I glance at the screens, the kaleidoscope of flashing digits and status bars like the ship's own intimate language. The problem must be hiding somewhere in those scrolling numbers, but it's hidden too deep for me to see.

I turn to the comms officer. 'Lim, you're a programmer, aren't you? I've seen you work the system.'

The woman nods, uncertain, as if I might hold it against her. 'Yes, sir. That's my core skill. I mean, comms, too, of course.'

'Good. I need you to write a filter to check the raw data for all the systems, tracking back to when we launched. I want to see any deviation from standard, even if it's still in the green. Can you do that?'

She nods, her fingers already on the console.

'It's all in the reports,' Zhang says from behind me.

'The system logs only the readings that tipped into yellow. I want to see any fluctuations—'

'Fluctuations don't matter, not when they're still in the green.'

I swing around to face him, the motion making me spin in zero-g. My vision sways from the sudden movement. 'Maybe. But since we don't have a clear answer, why don't we try?'

Zhang's reply dies on his lips as voices approach from the door. Price floats in, followed by Miller and the two people they defrosted. Judging by the gun in his holster and the New Union's flag on his chest, the first one must be Michael Lee, another of the American security team. He's a tall, Asian man with a square jaw and the deliberate air of someone aware of his presence. Behind him is a brisk, chubby woman, her golden brown skin and short, ruffled hair glistening with the remnants of blue fibres. She clutches a first aid pack under her arm, the patch on her chest showing the Australian white stars on a navy background.

'Katy Chao, nurse,' she says, then points to my swollen wrist and red, blistered fingers. 'Let me see your hand.'

'Have you checked the patient in the infirmary?'

The nurse shoots a glance at Price. They've had this conversation already.

'We've got to have you looked at first,' Price says. 'The commanding officer—'

'My injuries are minor. That woman almost died.'

'Sir—'

I turn to the nurse. 'Go to the infirmary. If you need help, we'll revive a doctor.'

The nurse seems relieved, but then her eyes narrow and she peers at me with new interest.

Whatever she's noticed, I don't want to hear it. 'Go.'

'Yes, sir.'

Price purses her lips but says nothing. Her gaze shifts to

something behind me, and she squares her shoulders and pushes out her chin in come-get-me defiance. She's staring at Zhang—and I don't need to turn to know he's glaring back at her.

For fuck's sake. Here we go. The New Cold War reduced to the microcosm of a ship, with me stuck at its centre just because I happen to be Canadian.

Ever since it emerged from the worst of the climate disaster, America has been fighting tooth and nail to reclaim its former glory—but by then China was too far ahead technologically and economically. The Americans responded by refusing to acknowledge the fact and instead insisting on their God-given place in the universe. The result was spiralling tensions and both countries accusing each other of plotting their demise.

This ship, like all the others, is Chinese—but our mission, and the rest of the colonisation business, is funded and run by the Americans. Crewing agreements are a delicate affair, with Canadians in high demand. The Yanks have always treated us as the younger sibling, and the New Union's no different. They choose us because we're *almost* American—the rest of the world choose us because we're *not* American.

Zhang makes the first move. He swivels towards me, slowly, his voice cold and heavy. 'The captain's dead, but that doesn't put *you* in charge. We all know you only got the rank because they needed a Canadian.'

'That last part's true,' I say. 'I'm a pilot, and a good one, but no one ever expected me to command.'

Zhang's eyes narrow. Not a confession he anticipated. 'What do you suggest?'

Out of the corner of my eye, I see Price tense. Behind her, Miller and Lee stretch to their imposing heights, shoulders squared and elbows jutting out.

With the Chinese captain out of the way, the Americans will jump on having what they think of as 'their man' run the show. I wonder how far they're willing to go to make that happen, and if that's what the guns in their holsters are about.

I thought my job was to keep this ship from blowing up. Now it seems I've got to stop it from tearing itself apart.

I raise my arms—and the pain in my burned hand makes my stomach heave. Damn. This is a bad time to puke, even if zero-g vomit is guaranteed to get everyone's attention. 'I suggest we table the discussion until we're sure we have a ship to argue about?'

Zhang glances at Price, then back at me. He's not done yet, I'm certain. But I'm even more certain that Price is not going to let him win, not when she's the one with the gun.

I turn to Lim. Maybe a reminder of why we're here will help bring them to their senses. 'Officer, as soon as you're free, check the logs for mission updates.'

She bobs her head, birdlike. 'Yes, sir. But first, I think you need to see this. From the search you asked me to run.'

'What have you found?'

Lim casts a nervous glance towards the engineer, then fixes her gaze on me. 'The power auxiliaries in the left generator started fluctuating two years into our journey. Still in the green, nothing alarming, but not normal either.'

'If they're in the green, then they *are* normal,' Zhang says flatly.

Lim shrinks as if she wants to disappear into the console.

'Thank you, officer,' I say to her, then rotate to face the engineer. 'We'll inspect these ASAP. Chief Engineer?'

A hot wave passes through me. My stomach heaves, painful and empty. I haven't eaten in twenty-two years, I realise, and one half of me wants to laugh while the other is too exhausted to move, too exasperated with the politics and the pain in my hand.

I make the effort to speak again, pronouncing the words

slowly, one by one. 'We can't take the risk. Something may be off. Have your people check the auxiliaries and the generator.'

Zhang holds my gaze. 'As you wish.'

He closes his eyes to let me know he's communicating with his people, then nods when he's done.

'Thank you, Chief Engineer.'

I reach for a handhold to push myself back towards my post —but the world ripples around me like a bootlegged vid-game. I pause, and then Price is next to me, her hands on my shoulders.

'Are you all right?'

I try to nod but think better of it. 'I'm fine. Just a bit dizzy. Probably the smoke.'

I let her take me to the captain's chair, belatedly realising she may have a bigger agenda than just getting me secured. I'm not sure I care. Keeping my eyes open is hard enough.

The next moment, the nurse is there, testing my blood and applying patches to my hand. The pain eases off almost immediately, then the fog I didn't even realise was there begins to drain from my mind.

The nurse, Katy Chao, looks up from her work. Crow's feet crease the skin around her eyes, her gaze bright even though her smile is troubled. 'Smoke inhalation and cold-sleep side effects. Everyone reacts differently, especially to emergency revival. You've pulled the short straw.'

'Will she be all right?' Price asks from somewhere behind me.

'Eventually.' Chao says nothing more and returns to dressing my hand.

I close my eyes. I need a moment to think, and this is as good an excuse as I'm going to get.

The state of the ship remains a puzzle. The engineers have checked all they could, though. Maybe Zhang's right, and we were just one-in-a-million kind of unlucky. If that's true, then it's not likely to happen again, or we've struck a galactic-scale dose of bad luck.

Then there's the command issue. I'd be perfectly happy leaving the job to Zhang, if that's what he wants. I couldn't care less. I signed up to make good for the mess I made, and for the money to give Jason a good start.

The memory makes me shiver. Jason's twenty-seven now. Is he back in the Feidi? Does he have a girlfriend? Boyfriend? Will I even know?

I squeeze my hands into fists—then groan at the pain.

'Easy, there,' Chao says. She puts her hand on my arm, warm and grounding. At least she doesn't seem to have an agenda.

I reach out for the pouch of forti-fix the nurse brought and suck in the sweet liquid. Price floats at my side, her body taut, her attention flicking towards Zhang's console whenever he's not looking.

Damn. This really isn't going to be easy.

'Did we get any updates?' a male voice asks—American accent but not Miller's warm baritone. Must be Lee.

I screw my eyes shut, trying not to think of twenty-two years' worth of personal messages that may be waiting for me on the server.

Has Jason forgiven me? Or has he found comfort in forgetting I ever existed?

'No change to our briefing,' Lim says. 'Bethesda's still silent.'

Chao's sigh sends a gust of warm air over my arm. 'Twenty-two years and they're still dead.'

Price grabs the edge of my chair and scowls at the nurse. I didn't expect such an emotional response, not from her.

'Their transmitters could have failed,' she says.

'All of them?' Zhang asks, then answers for himself. 'Unlikely.'

'It's possible,' Price snaps. 'Nothing's ever unbreakable. Not even if it's Chinese.'

Their voices have risen in pitch, their postures tense, shoulders rolled forward, one mirroring the other.

Zhang tilts his head, brows rising with incredulity. 'Whatever you say.'

Price stiffens. 'I'm not expecting *you* to care. It's American lives. You're only here to make sure your precious tech doesn't fall into the wrong hands.'

I sit up, loosening the restraints so I can spring out of the chair if I need to. Price is taking this too far, New Cold War or not. She glares at Zhang, her body taut, her posture challenging. Behind her, Lee and Miller watch the engineer's every move.

Zhang rotates, his hands moving towards the console—for support? Or for something else? He's alone against the three of them, no wonder he feels threatened. He'll want to protect himself as much as the technology. How far will he go?

My mind races as I circle through scenarios. Whatever he decides to do, Zhang doesn't even need the console. With Mind-Link, he can issue commands directly. And do what? Decompress the bridge? Release some nerve agent the Chinese crew have been inoculated against, exactly for such an eventuality?

Some rational part of me insists that it's not possible, that it's just paranoia fuelled by exhaustion and nerves. Maybe. But nobody here is thinking straight. Once the guns are pointed at him, he'll find a way to defend himself one way or another.

No more death.

I grab a handhold and push myself between them. 'Enough! Stop it right here. We're all exhausted and dizzy from cold-sleep. This is not the time to have this argument.'

Price and her men scowl, mouths pinched in frustration. I know what they are thinking: *Stay out of it. Let us handle this.*

No way.

I turn to Zhang. 'Chief Engineer, do we have a report on that generator?'

His eyes drill into me. I hold his gaze. Decision time, Zhang Min. Make the right choice.

His lips quiver. He's got the message. 'We've recalibrated the buffers. This will take care of any future fluctuations... *sir*.'

'Thank you,' I say with the tiniest of nods.

I rotate slowly, my eyes on Price. Her posture has eased; a satisfied smile twists the corner of her mouth.

It's done. I let my shoulders relax, only now noticing the frantic tattoo of my heartbeat. I take a slow breath—but no, I'm not relieved. I'm angry.

I don't want to be their commander. I don't want the responsibility, or the burden of mediating between the two sides, their constant bickering and accusations. That's not what I signed up for. I'm a pilot, not a damn politician.

But if I am the only person who can keep them from jumping at each other's throats, then that's what I'll do.

No. More. Death.

We're ready four hours later. We've done what we can. Replacement pods have been brought online and the rest thoroughly inspected. The engineers checked all the systems they could access, but as Zhang has cheerfully informed me, there are no guarantees.

The other two engineers are the last ones to join us after completing the final round of checks. Both are women, one wearing an elbow-length silver glove that probably covers a bionic arm. We float together in the corridor between the cryochambers. Lee's trying to joke, but the laughs he gets sound forced and die in seconds.

I turn to the engineers. 'Thank you for your work. All of you.' I shift to the others, looking at each face in turn. 'We've checked everything we could think of, so let's just get this over with. See you in thirteen years.'

I motion for them to move. They part reluctantly, gliding in silence towards their chambers. Zhang stays next to me. I haven't asked him to, but I'm glad he's here. We follow each group in turn, watching them climb into the pods. Price shoots me a lopsided smile as the lid closes on her. The glass in front of her fogs, and her eyes roll back.

We wait till the web of cryo-fibres coats the sleeping figures, creamy white at first, then congealing into blue gauze. The control lights settle into green.

I look at Zhang, and he nods.

We retreat the short distance to our chamber. Lim and one of the engineers are already asleep, cocooned in blue, the lights shining steady green.

Zhang heads for his pod without another word, as if everything has been said already. Maybe it has. I watch him for a moment, his movements fluid, his eyes focused on the task, then slide into my pod. I put on the breather mask, push the activation button. The lid puffs gently as it closes, the glass fogging with the warmth of my body.

There's something on the glass. Symbols materialise out of the fog, as if scribbled with an oily finger. I squint, fighting drowsiness that clouds my vision with every inhalation. I know these symbols. Not symbols—letters, in the Cyrillic alphabet I learned to impress Stepan a lifetime ago.

Cold seeps into my bones and into my brain. I must focus, must understand. Consciousness fading, I force myself to read the letters again, one by one.

Саботаж.

Sabotage.

CHAPTER -4

2 MONTHS BEFORE DEPARTURE

Anna's eyes still have that bright, mischievous spark despite the deep shadows circling them now, greenish grey against her chalk-white skin. My sister leans towards the camera, her face growing on my cockpit screen. The crack in her lip glistens in bloody red as she makes herself smile. 'I don't feel so bad, really. Just some post-natal complications. Nothing serious.'

Her voice breaks under the lie. She's never been good at those, always betrayed by this very expression: half-guilty and half-relieved, unwilling to be a burden but desperate for help from her big sister.

I put on a smile. 'Sure. More stories to tell Nadia when she grows up: how she made her mum suffer!'

We both fake a laugh, but neither of us can keep it up. Anna glances away, her hand moving to stroke Jason's head. He sits in a low chair by her hospital bed, his tongue between his lips as he labours over a drawing on his pad.

'What have you got there, Jason?' I ask, grateful for the distraction.

He lifts the pad to show me, his eyes sparkling with pride. 'Raaaaawrr!'

There's a creature on his screen—an animal, I think, with four sticks for legs and black dots as eyes peering from inside a tangle of orange lines.

'Impressive!' I cast Anna a pleading glance. *Help?*

'A lion! Well done, honey.' Her voice trembles, but her face comes alive with pride and joy. That's how she always looked, until a month ago.

I clench my fists out of sight of the camera. 'A lion. Of course!'

'They have one in the reserve,' Anna says. 'Supposedly the last in existence. All Jason's been talking about. I'm trying to get Stepan to take him...'

Her voice breaks again. She smiles, not meeting my eyes, but I can see her fear as clearly as if she were screaming.

I lean into the screen. 'Well, that's what aunties are for, right?'

Anna's eyes widen, incredulous. 'But I thought—'

'I'll find a way. I mean, who wouldn't want to see a lion?'

Her shoulders relax, her relief so evident it makes my chest hurt. 'Did you hear that, Jason? Auntie Nathalie's coming. Everything will be fine now.'

I keep my smile on, already inventing the arguments to persuade my boss to give me extra leave. I don't want to lose my job—but I've got no question about what I'd choose if he gives me no choice.

Logan meets me by the giant window that takes up one wall of the Orbital Logistics HQ reception. Outside, Earth rotates slowly, filling the view with its blue majesty. It's not actually a window, I remind myself, only a screen projecting the outside vista. We're deep within the bowels of the station, far below the luxury of the outer rings where the owners and their staffers reside. Even so, I'd prefer to see him in our usual dugouts by the shuttle dock. No gravity to worry about, in all senses of the word.

'Thank you for coming,' Logan says. He's wearing a proper suit, though nothing as fancy as the zhu-yuan crossing the lobby behind us. He seems aware of it, too, his manner self-conscious even as he's trying to put on a good show. 'I'm caught up in meetings all day but wanted to chat in person.'

I nod, my expression neutral. I made Anna a promise and I'm going to keep it, even if it gets me fired.

He leans on the window, his face troubled. 'If you go groundside now, you'll get stuck there.'

'Because of the 'plague'?' I snort, hoping to convince him with my bluster. 'You know it's not the real thing. All the credible sources agree.'

Logan shrugs. 'The truth doesn't matter. If enough people believe the plague's back, the effect's the same. No society can lose two billion people and maintain anything approaching rationality on the matter.'

That was a century ago, I want to say, but no, he's right. A century's not enough, not when the last of the survivors are still alive to tell the story.

The Two Horsemen, the almost-Apocalypse. The time of global collapse that started when the effects of climate change hit for real, with all the flooding, drought, and mass migrations that followed. And when the world was on its knees, the second blow came with a pandemic that wiped out two billion people. For a moment it seemed that that was the end, one more disaster and civilisation would collapse. But the next Horseman never arrived. Humanity clawed its way from the brink. China, the relatively least affected, led the global recovery—and made sure they stayed in the lead.

I look away, at the planet outside the 'window,' the blue marble festooned in lacy clouds. Out there, Kenya is just a yellow patch, lost in Africa's brown and ochre. For a moment I think I can see the silk thread of the elevator—but it's just the thin line of the once-mighty Nile labouring its way through the parched land.

Logan scans the lobby, then leans closer, his voice low. 'It's not official yet, so keep it quiet. We won the contract for that new American station. But the damned thing's still under construction and will stay so for much longer than they'll admit. With all the assemblers still whizzing around, that'll make for some tough flying. I need my best pilots for the job. I need you.'

Right. So this is why he's here, all fancied out. That new station—it's the first American outpost in the Yun Ju, and they're as proud of it as if it were the only one in existence. If we do well, this is bound to open up new opportunities—provided no one crashes into the assemblers or the construction crews.

'I won't be long. Just a few days.' I make my voice soft, pleading. He knows me well enough to realise that I will go whether he lets me or not, but I'd rather keep my job. 'The baby's only two months old. Anna's not well, and the hospitals are clogged up with alarmists mistaking a cough for the plague.'

'And how are *you* going to help?'

I open my mouth, then close it.

Logan snorts. 'You're just hoping something will come to you, right?'

He knows me too well. 'She's my kid sister. I can't—'

'She's got a husband—'

'Stepan's freaking out. He's a scientist with the practical skills of a three-year-old.'

Logan cocks an eyebrow, ready to challenge me, but I won't let him.

'I'm going, Logan. If you want me back, figure something out.'

He considers me for another moment, then sighs, a little too theatrically. 'You're my best pilot, Nat, but I'll go with the second best if they're actually here. You have a week—and not a minute more.'

The elevator's almost empty, so I get a free upgrade. I could splurge for first class, probably my only chance ever, but all money's worth saving now. I do intend to return to orbit when the week is up, but you never know.

On the way to my cabin, I spot Mr Pencil Moustache, the duty tech from the last time, but luckily he's too busy with equipment checks to notice me—or so I think because an hour after departure he knocks on my door.

'It's not what you think,' he says pre-emptively. 'I just want to ask you something.'

I should send him away, but there's something dogged in the way he rocks on his heels, thumbs sticking out of his pockets as if he was holding on to his uniform for support. 'What about?'

He leans closer, his voice conspiratorial. 'What are they saying up there? About the plague?'

So this is what it's about. He's panicking, like everyone else.

'There's no plague, that's what they're saying. Yes, there's a bug going around, but it's treatable and not very contagious. That's all it is.'

'Really?' He gestures to the space around us. 'Why have *they* stopped coming?'

'Because they don't want to get caught in the chaos?'

'That's the official line. But there's more.' He wipes his forehead, shifts his weight from right to left, exasperated. 'Can I come in?'

I wave him in, then stand with my back against the door, arms folded.

He slumps in the chair, his elbows on his knees. 'I just don't know. I watch the news and it all makes sense, like you say. But then, all the elevator staff—we're not allowed to go home in between shifts anymore. Supposedly so we don't get caught in the "disruptions".' He shakes his head, unpersuaded. 'They've turned an office block into a dormitory for us, all sterile. Even the air is filtered.'

A lump settles in my stomach. 'Is it just you they keep here? Or all the terminal staff?'

He gives me a lopsided smile that says I've hit the bull's-eye. 'Only the people who physically travel into orbit.'

I shuffle to the other chair, my legs soft. Anna. What... what if it's not just post-natal complications?

'They've got those new bio-scanners now,' he continues. 'All the passengers going up get a full medical. Any doubt, it's good-bye, visas revoked on the spot. Even the zhu-yuan can't go back, they must stay in quarantine.'

I shake my head, as if that could repel the doubts. 'Okay... Everybody agrees that there's a bug going around. It's nothing like the plague—but that won't stop the panic, not after what happened last time. The mayor worries the unrest will affect the business, so he goes into overdrive to put everyone at ease. Especially them.' I point at the ceiling as a substitute for the Yun Ju— the conglomeration of orbital stations owned and inhabited by the world's super-rich. 'It makes sense, right?'

'Yeah. Maybe.' He shrugs, the pinch in his face denying his words.

What if he's right? What if the experts are wrong and Anna is infected with the new bug?

I left it too late. I should have come down the moment she said she was unwell. If something happens to her...

'I'm going to go home this time,' he says, rising. 'I've got to check on my folks. And you? How's your sister?'

I swallow, my throat too dry for speech. My words come out scratchy. 'Not so well.'

He says nothing, and I'm grateful. I look up again when I hear him opening the door. 'What's your name?'

'Joseph. Jo.'

'I'm Nathalie.'

'Good luck, Nathalie,' he says, and closes the door behind him.

CHAPTER 3

'Easy there.'

I stop moving. Have I been moving?

'That's better.' The voice is deep and melodic, the accent oddly familiar.

I open my eyes, struggling against the weight of my eyelids. Patches of colour sharpen into a face: blue eyes in a pale, round visage, unshaven and shrouded with curly, greying hair.

Pink lips stretch into a smile. 'What's your name?'

'Natha...' I pause, startled by the hoarseness of my voice, then try again. 'Nathalie Hart.'

The man shifts. He's standing, not floating. The realisation comes with the awareness of my own weight pressing against a padded surface. We've started decelerating. No, have been decelerating for years, now probably approaching wherever it is we're going. Bethesda.

I glance at the tag on the doctor's green uniform. *Anatoly Yefremov* and Russian white, red and blue. 'It's okay, doc. I'm all here.'

'Ha!' Yefremov's laugh is a deep rumble, like a blanket on a cool night. 'If I had a yuan for every time I've heard that...'

A memory tugs at the corners of my mind. There was something... something I needed to remember. Something important and somehow related to the man standing next to me.

I lift my head. This isn't the cryo-chamber. I'm in the infirmary, in one of the treatment cubicles separated from the rest of the bay with semi-transparent panels. A plump woman with a mop of unruly black hair smiles at me from behind the doctor.

My thoughts screech to a stop. Katy Chao, the nurse.

The accident.

It seems we've made it through without another mishap. I should be relieved—but then I remember that I'm now in command, and how I got there. Damn. At least they're alive. Most of them.

The thought morphs into a question. 'How's everyone?'

'Well enough.' Yefremov flashes his teeth again. I get the feeling his grin is a permanent feature. 'We're keeping Wang in a coma for now, but she'll be fine, too. You got her out just in time. I heard there were some heroics involved...'

How wrong he is. Didn't they tell him about the one I left to die?

The doctor is watching me, his eyes narrowing. He points to my right hand, the wrist encased in a stiff dressing. 'You seem to have a recent—'

'An old injury. Never healed properly.' I look past him, to the nurse who approaches with a cup of forti-fix. I whisk it out of her hands. The drink is orange flavoured and cloyingly sweet, sliding down my throat in thick, velvety draughts. I've forgotten how delicious sugar is. 'Can I have more?'

'In a moment, or you'll puke. Trust me.'

'I don't seem to have a choice, do I?'

He guffaws, then turns at the sound of a panel sliding open behind me.

'Is she up yet?' a familiar voice asks. Price.

I crane my neck, but the angle of the recliner has me facing in the wrong direction. 'Don't tell me I'm the last one up...'

'You needed some extra time.' Yefremov gestures at the nurse. 'Katy tells me you've had a rough ride. Emergency revival doesn't go well with smoke inhalation. I'd have preferred to keep you under for another day, but Sergeant Price here wouldn't let me.'

'Cut it, doc,' Price drawls, the bright note in her voice contradicting the words.

She slides past the doctor to stand next to my bed. She looks even taller now that she's standing straight, her shoulders taut inside a velvety black uniform, shiny with a protective coating that looks almost liquid. Some new material I've never seen before.

She smiles, but there's an impatient pinch to her face. 'Good to see you're well.'

'What's our status?' I ask.

'We've completed the first two slingshots. Everything nominal, as far as I can tell. Zhang hasn't exactly gone out of his way to keep me informed. But he's doing the job,' she concedes. She leans on the edge of my bed, her fingers drumming on the frame. She's trying to appear relaxed, but it's not working.

'Anything else?'

'There's an urgent message for you in the system.'

I stiffen. Has something happened to Jason? Or... or have they found me? Realised I caused the riots? But if they did, they wouldn't be sending me a message—they'd be telling Price to lock me up. 'A message for me?'

'Well, for the captain,' Price says, hesitant. 'But now that he's dead, it's for you. Or a version of it.'

I'm not sure I understand, but I'm too relieved to care just yet. My head drops back on the pillow. It's not Jason. He's all right, back with his grandparents. Well, not really; he's a man now, maybe with his own family.

Out of the corner of my eye, I see the doctor studying me as if I've just transitioned from a patient to a specimen. Damn.

I push myself up with my good arm, my muscles aching with the effort. I'm still in my underclothes, the same I wore in the pod. At least I hope they're the same. 'I need my uniform.'

'Not so fast,' Yefremov says. 'You need—'

'My uniform please.'

The doctor crosses his arms. 'You can view the message here. That's—' He stops as Chao hands Price my clothes. 'Et tu, Brute?'

The nurse shrugs. 'Like she was going to listen...'

He glances at Price, but the woman's grin offers no support.

I reach for the white packet of clean underwear. 'Do you mind?'

Yefremov throws his hands in the air as Price and Chao lead him out of the enclosure. They continue to bicker outside, like old friends over a drink. I wonder how long they've all been up. What else have I missed?

My muscles twitch as I slide down from the bed. I pull on my underwear, then the light blue uniform T-shirt. I've got to pause before the rest of the outfit, navy trousers and jacket without any of the protective coating of Price's uniform. Finally, I slap the wan-kong over my left wrist. The display comes to life, the message icon blinking.

I do my best to conceal the trembling in my legs as I head out of the enclosure and turn towards the exit, down the aisle lined with medical stations and the curious glances of green-clad personnel.

'Any problems, you let me know, right?' Yefremov calls behind me, his Russian accent clearer than before. 'And try to avoid stress, will you?'

I stop. The giddy feeling that I've forgotten something important returns like vertigo. What could it possibly be?

Price pauses behind me. 'Sir?'

Oh, hell. It'll come back to me, sooner or later. 'Nothing. Let's go.'

We start along the taupe-walled corridor, my steps bouncy on the padded floor. The ship is decelerating, which gives us enough 'gravity' to walk with ease. I glance at Price. The ship-safe gun pokes from a holster on her right thigh, along with something long and narrow, like a truncheon. Before here, I'd never seen weapons inside a spaceship. On the stations, yes, all of the Yun Ju is crazy about security. But never on ships. Somehow, they make me feel just the opposite of secure.

'Has Zha—' I correct myself. No point fanning the flames. 'Has anyone given you reason to think you might need those?'

Price follows my gaze to her arsenal. 'My instructions are to carry weapons at all times.'

That gives me pause. Who would issue such instructions— and why? Is this just the Americans being paranoid, or do they have a reason they haven't revealed?

'This is a rescue mission,' I say. 'We're all here for the same purpose...'

I trail off. I know nothing of the others' motivations. I joined up to atone for what happened in the Feidi, but if I had to be honest, it was as much about escaping my past as hoping to save anyone on Bethesda. What are the others escaping?

Price shakes her head. 'Bethesda was an American colony. A Christian colony. Not everyone's invested in our success. I'd say some may have interests to the contrary.'

I stop. 'You can't mean—'

'If I hadn't had the gun, we wouldn't be in control of this ship anymore. You know that.'

There's a lot to unpack in this sentence—who does she mean by 'we', and how much control do 'we' really have if we can't even access the engines? I recall Zhang's expression when Price and her men cornered him. He didn't look helpless. Frustrated, yes, but not helpless. Price's bosses had to have a reason for arming the security team. Did they expect the Chinese engineers to have secret weapons of their own? But why would they? My brain erupts with possibilities, guesses, and counter-guesses until my head's spinning. This is pointless. I'm thinking myself into a corner, and without a shred of evidence.

'All I know is that people don't react well to guns. You may just start the very thing you're hoping to prevent.'

Price shrugs, her gaze not meeting mine.

I hesitate. I know what I should tell her, but will she listen? 'I want you all to remove your guns.'

Price scowls.

'Do you want to find out what happened on Bethesda?' I pause long enough for her to nod, then continue, 'Then we need everyone focused on this, not feeling like they're a suspect.'

'But what if—'

'If there's ever a reason for guns, I'm sure you'll find them fast enough.'

An odd smile plays on Price's lips. 'As you wish, *sir*.'

Damn. They're just going to conceal their guns, not remove them. Still, that's better than carrying the lot out in the open. For a moment I wonder what she'd do if I ordered her to lock the guns away, then decide I don't want to know the answer.

I move on again, down the corridor leading to the captain's office. 'Tell me about that message.'

'I don't know the contents, obviously, but I have a strong guess what it's about. Zhang and Khan agree.'

The name sounds familiar, but it takes me a moment to remember: Amal Khan, our chief scientist. I've only ever seen the name on the manifest as the company didn't see fit to introduce me to the science team.

'So, what is it?'

'There's another ship here. We're too far to be certain, but we think it's *Gabriel*.'

'Impossible. It must be *Messenger*. They must have failed to disassemble it completely.'

Messenger, the ship that brought the colonists to Bethesda, was built to be cannibalised on arrival. Most of the modules would descend to the surface to create a habitat, and the remains would form an orbital base from which the assembler drones would later spin a space elevator.

Price shakes her head. 'No, *Messenger*'s still in orbit, or what's left of it.'

I slow down, considering the implications. After *Messenger*, three more colony ships had departed before the news from Bethesda—or rather the lack of news—halted further launches. Two headed to New Jerusalem, a planet in another star system. *Gabriel*, the second one to leave Earth, had aimed for Bethesda, but the company managed to remotely change its destination to join the other two. Or so they said.

If *Gabriel* is really here—what has happened to the five thousand people it carried? Have they joined the others on Bethesda and met the same fate? Or are they still frozen and waiting?

I keep on walking, though my vision has narrowed to a grey tunnel and all I can hear is the thud of my heartbeat. Five thousand lives.

No more death.

The colony ships had fuel for only a one-way mission. We are too small to carry the five thousand of them back. *Gabriel*'s passengers will have to stay on Bethesda. And it's up to us to find out what happened to the colonists already here and make sure the same won't happen to them.

By the time we reach the office, I'm out of breath. I try not to show it, sucking in air through clenched teeth, waves of hot and cold coursing through my flesh. Focus. Nothing will bring Anna back.

My hand leaves a wet imprint as I push the door open. A

desk with a large screen sits on the right, the message light flashing urgently. I lean against the chair and allow myself three slow breaths before I touch the input pad.

Nathalie Hart, Commander, appears on the screen in both English and Mandarin.

'Confirm, Nathalie Hart,' I say.

'Audio interface is still out,' Price says. 'I told them to fix it, but Zhang claims it's low priority. I guess it is, if you've got Mind-Link.'

'Right. Call them both in, Zhang and the scientist.'

I can almost hear her brow scrunch. 'I'd advise against it, sir. Not till you hear the message.'

'They need to know.' I crane my neck to meet her eyes. She's more than a head taller and all compact muscle. 'It's just us here, Amy. Light years from the squabbles back home. We need the engineers. We need them to feel a part of this team.'

She pinches her lips, fingers drumming against the side of her leg. 'I don't trust them.'

I stifle a sigh. 'We'll keep an eye on them. But let's not assume the worst before we have proof, okay?'

'Yes, sir.' Price nods, her tone the opposite of convinced. 'Should I call the reverend as well?'

The reverend? Of course. This is an American mission; we'd have one even if it didn't concern Christian settlers. The New Union emerged from the almost-Apocalypse as a Christian theocracy, convinced they survived due to the strength of their faith. I need a missionary like I need a toothache, but I don't see how I can refuse them without Price staging another rebellion. 'Yes. Yes, let's have them all here.'

She heads out, and I drop into the chair, my knees shaking. I came here to save lives—but the idea had always been abstract, a worthy concept rather than the cold reality of five thousand human beings locked in ice, depending on our success for their very existence.

I rub my face, then lean back, forcing my focus outward, into the room around me. The office is surprisingly large, probably six by four metres, and tapered on both ends, like an egg. The terminal takes up one side; a meeting table with seven chairs and another, larger screen fill the rest. Two doors face each other, one opening onto the corridor, the other leading directly to the bridge. The walls here are a lighter shade of taupe, with lighting strips skirting the edges where the wall panels meet the ceiling. A programmable picture next to the table displays cloud-shrouded Earth and the Yun Ju stations sparkling around it like fireflies.

Price returns a moment later, Zhang entering behind her. Despite the frown cutting his brow he looks rested, his hair smooth and his cheeks clean-shaven. I notice again the metallic glint behind his eyes—Mind-Link lenses, implanted directly over his retinas.

He nods a greeting. For a moment, I half expect him to challenge me again, but his face is impassive, businesslike. Either Price's tactic worked, or he realised how close we came to a disaster—whichever it was, I'll take it.

I show them both to the table, but we remain standing. 'Price says you believe the ship to be *Gabriel*?'

'That's correct,' Zhang says. 'It had similar specs to *Messenger*, and that's exactly what it appears to be.'

The corridor-side door opens to let in a woman: medium height, small-boned, with shoulder-length, straight black hair, light brown skin, and bright, focused eyes. She wears the blue uniform of the science team, the jacket zipped up to her neck, the European Alliance flag on her chest.

She extends her hand, then pauses at the sight of the cast on my right arm. She gives me a nod instead. 'Amal Khan, chief scientist. I hear you wanted to see me?'

British, or at least that's what she sounds like, and with a sophisticated, if slightly haughty accent.

I start to answer when the door opens again to let in the reverend—though 'political officer' would probably be a better term. The man is picture-handsome: a well-built thirty-some-thing, with thick black hair and long lashes over bright, honey-brown eyes. His smile is perfectly cheerful, his tan skin flawless, perfectly complemented by the sky-blue shirt he wears in place of a uniform. Too perfect. It's like they cloned him from some image of what a reverend should look like. The effect makes me instantly suspicious.

'Pete Sanchez. Or just Pete. I don't think we've had the pleasure.'

'Thank you for coming. I want us to hear the message together.'

I wait for them to take the seats around the table, then punch my codes into the pad on the desk. The screen flashes the New Horizons silver logo, which dissolves into the image of the company's CEO, Daniel Williamson, seated behind a glass desk. Behind him is a floor-to-ceiling 'window' overlooking the Earth, just like the one where I met Logan an eternity ago. Unlike Logan, though, this man inhabits his space with every inch of his body—from his tailored, sage green suit to the chis-elled contours of his face, so immaculate you want to punch him just to see if he could even develop a bruise.

Williamson flashes his teeth in a smile. 'Hello, and welcome to Bethesda. I'm glad you made it safely to your destination.' He pauses, allowing his face to recompose into an expression of studied concern. 'By now you have undoubtedly spotted the other ship in the system. I can confirm that it is *Gabriel*, the second colony ship. You're well aware that we have told everyone the ship had been diverted—obviously, that's not the case. Unfortunately, *Gabriel* never had enough propellant to reach New Jerusalem.'

Khan snorts, then tries to cover it up with a head shake. Zhang doesn't look surprised, but Price is frowning, upset or incredulous. The reverend's face is a cipher; I get the feeling this is not news to him.

'After much agonising, we decided not to release this news to the public,' Williamson continues. 'We're very sorry about the lie, but it serves the greater good. We can't change the facts, so why cause more grief to the relatives the colonists have left behind? They've had enough of it already. More than enough.'

I try to keep my face neutral, though the man's fake concern makes my stomach churn.

'At the time of this recording, *Gabriel*'s transmissions confirm that it's performing according to expectations. As with all the vessels currently en route, we've reprogrammed the computer to put the ship in a safe orbit and keep the passengers in cold-sleep until it's safe for them to disembark.'

This time Khan snorts out loud. I shake my head. Disembark? He makes it sound like it's only a matter of logistics—not the fact that, in all likelihood, five thousand of their predecessors have perished on the planet.

Williamson sighs as he leans against his desk, silent for a drawn-out moment as if he needs to compose his thoughts. I'm sure he's reading off a prompter. 'The passengers can be kept in stasis for a long time. The ship has its own power supply and will use solar to replenish. However, it was never built for a return trip. You must identify what happened to the colony, and make sure *Gabriel*'s passengers avoid its fate. I wish you strength and wisdom. God bless you in your endeavours. *Gabriel*'s lives are in your hands.'

My hands are shaking, my breath like a flutter of wings in my chest. I tug the cuffs of my jacket, chasing off images of rows upon rows of cryo-pods, thousands of frozen people waiting for the sentence we will pass over their lives.

Williamson gives an encouraging smile, then the image blinks out.

'Fuckers.' Zhang shakes his head. 'They knew that all along.'

Price leans back, defensive. 'What were they supposed to do? You heard what he said. They couldn't divert it, so why make it harder for the relatives?'

'They could have told us,' Khan says coldly.

'It could have leaked,' Price says. 'And it wouldn't have made any difference.'

'It would, if they told *us*,' Zhang says. '*Gabriel* could be retrofitted. We could have brought a new engine, new fuel cells. We could have given them a chance.'

But that would have got the news out. And the other ships, the ones en route to New Jerusalem, wouldn't get that chance— not now, and maybe not ever if the cost proved too high.

I squeeze my fists into balls, struggling to calm my breathing. Anyway, it may be best to just watch the rest of them. I'm walking on a thin ice of loyalties; it helps to see which way they lean.

Price crosses her arms. 'Maybe they tried, and your government refused. It wouldn't have been the first time.'

The engineer snorts. 'They never tried.'

'How do you know? Maybe they didn't bother. It's just American lives, after all.'

Khan winces. 'That's a harsh—'

'They are people,' Zhang speaks over her, his eyes on Price. 'But if that's not enough for you, consider this: that ship has Chinese engineering crews. Just like *Messenger* had. And other volunteers: a total of three hundred Chinese citizens on each ship, all of them Christians.'

Price's eyes widen. She stares at the reverend. 'Is that true?'

Sanchez clasps his hands, his face a study of concern. 'That was part of the deal, yes, for all the ships. They needed crews, and it'd have been cruel to send only a handful of engineers on a one-way trip. So, we recruited Christian volunteers, enough of them to establish a population that would fit well with the other settlers.'

Price is still frowning, incredulous, but she's out of arguments.

I join them by the table. 'It makes sense. I never thought about it, but it does. Anyway, that doesn't change our situation.' I lean on one of the chairs, my fingers digging into the grey velvet. My legs tremble, either from the remnants of cold-sleep or from the weight of five thousand lives that has just landed on my shoulders. 'Our mission hasn't changed, it's just become a whole lot bigger. We came here to find out what happened on Bethesda—now we have to make sure the same won't happen again. *Gabriel* can't go back. If we fail, they die.'

'We won't fail, sir,' Price says.

Khan steeples her fingers. 'I'd like to share your optimism. But I've lost a third of my team. Our skills overlap, but it's not the same.'

Damn. I haven't even asked about the dead. My heart resumes its tattoo beat. What am I doing here? I should have let Zhang take the job—I only got it because I'm Canadian. At least he's used to leading people—the last time I thought I could make a difference I got everyone killed.

I clear my throat. 'Do we have... a list?'

Price seems to guess what I mean. 'It's in the system—'

'I've got it,' Zhang interrupts. 'May I?'

I nod, not sure what he means—but then the screen lights up again, displaying seven names. All without as much as a blink from the engineer.

I've seen Mind-Link in action before, but only in passing, an occasional glimpse from someone in the Yun Ju. Most of my employers have been American, and their religious leaders have decried the technology as a gateway to temptation. That has meant those of us wanting to stay employed have had to steer way clear.

Khan doesn't seem impressed, Sanchez's face is blank, but from the way Price's jaw tenses, I can tell she's hiding her reaction. I do the same, focusing on the names on the screen. We've lost seven out of thirty-six. The captain, the second pilot, the junior engineer. The science team, the most numerous to begin with, took the heaviest loss.

'A couple of my people are licensed pilots,' Price says. 'We won't be as good as you or Erik, but we'll do.'

I nod and turn to Khan. 'How bad is it for you? Can you do the work?'

Khan takes a moment to answer, her eyes on her steepled fingers. 'It all depends on what we find on the ground. As I said, our specialties overlap, but not entirely.'

'Can we find help on *Gabriel*?' Zhang asks.

'I doubt it. They're colonists. They'll have scientists, but not of the specialties or the calibre we need.'

Nobody speaks for another moment. I search my mind for something reassuring to say but come up empty.

'How long till we're in orbit?' I ask eventually.

'Two days,' Zhang says. '*Gabriel* is at geostationary, and I suggest we stop there to check on them.'

'I agree. Have we found anything useful in the scans?'

Khan shakes her head. 'Nothing on my side. All in-system bodies are just as the colonists reported. The assembler drones seem to have harvested a couple of small asteroids, but that's also exactly as planned.'

I turn to Zhang. 'The elevator?'

'We're too far to be sure, but it seems operational.' His voice takes on a heavier tone. 'That would make sense if the assemblers had no other demands on their production.'

The assemblers should be busy servicing the habitat modules on the surface of Bethesda. *No other demands* can only mean no communication with the colony. And no one to communicate with.

'Do you think...' My voice breaks, but I push on. 'Can anybody still be alive there?'

The silence is icy. Even Price says nothing, her fingers clenched over the side of the table.

'We can't exclude the possibility,' Khan says slowly. 'Whatever happened, some may have survived. Maybe they couldn't rebuild the transmitter.'

'Or don't have enough power,' Price adds. 'Not for long range.'

Zhang nods, but without much conviction.

I want to ask more, pry hope out of them as if they were hiding it from me. No point.

'Prepare the drones,' I say. 'Launch as soon as we're in position. Let's take a look for ourselves.'

CHAPTER 4

The zheping pad in my hand trembles no matter how I try to keep it straight. The screen shows the default image: the New Horizons logo superimposed on the silhouette of our ship, the proudly named rescue vessel *The Samaritan*. My fingers hover over the glass, their shaky reflection approaching then drifting away from the message icon.

I've got to do it. I've got to know.

I close my eyes and punch the symbol. When I look again, the screen has shifted to display my personal messages. Only ten of them, the last one dated almost two decades ago. All from my parents. None from Jason. I stare, my whole body shaking now, tears obscuring my vision. What happened?

I open the messages one by one. The first one has the three of them, my parents watching tenderly as Jason explores his new surroundings. Only a month after my departure. The next video is dated five months later—still cheerful, but more forced, like they know they're speaking to a ghost. The third one is a year later, then a two-year gap. Then it's just my parents, Jason apparently busy at school or out and about. I watch my parents age before my eyes, their faces sagging and their eyes colder with every message. The ninth one is just a birthday card. The tenth has only a text informing me that my parents passed away a short time apart, seventeen years into my journey.

The zheping slides from my hand as I roll into a ball on the floor of my tiny cabin. My parents are dead. Not surprising, really, my father was almost eighty. I never expected to see them again. But I hoped... I hoped they wouldn't forget me so quickly. That Jason... But really, what did I expect? He was five when I left him.

I hope he's alive. I hope he's well. It doesn't matter if he's forgotten the aunt who abandoned him thirty-five years ago.

I wrap my arms around my knees and rock silently. My eyes are almost dry when a low chime calls all crew to the bridge for the funeral.

The pods drift away from the ship, silver sparks against the blackness of space. The lights dim, the bridge lit only by the faint glowing of the consoles. Then even those blink out, only the main screen illuminated by the archipelago of stars stretching out to infinity. In the distance, a new star appears and dies, then another and another, seven diamonds lighting up one last time.

The reverend reads the names of the seven who died in the fire, their bodies returned to the stardust they were made of. The smell of incense drifts from the Chinese group. Zhang stands among them, his face as pale as the white mourning band on his arm. He closes his eyes when the reverend calls out Kuang Jin's name.

Two figures step towards the screen: Miller and Chao, their faces glistening in the starlight. They stop by the navigation console, as if in tribute to the ghost of the pilot who will never get to use it. I gasp as they start to sing, their voices hesitant, then gaining strength as they unite in haunting harmony. It's a hymn—a melody I recognise in an instant, the very one I heard at Anna and Stepan's funeral.

The memory returns in a flash of heat: two white coffins laid side by side, and the third one in between them, so tiny it's almost invisible under the cascade of white flowers. Jason's rapt face as he keeps asking for his ma and da, and why we keep them in the boxes for so long, they surely must want out by now. And baby Nadia, isn't she hungry?

I hide my face in my hands, shaking, the world around me collapsing again, shrinking into an icicle, sharp and dead. I float above it, trembling, distant and unreal as all the senses retreat, all perception gone till the music disappears as well, and I'm alone, finally and forever.

And yet a note breaks through, resonant and insistent. The song nears its crescendo, the voices unskilled but even more compelling because of it. I pull in a breath, sensation returning to my tingling fingers. This is bad. I haven't had a panic attack since... since after I buried them and decided to search for redemption somewhere else. To get a job that would give Jason the best start.

To bribe him for leaving him parentless.

The pain returns, but this time it's real, defined and concrete. I came here for a reason. For the colonists. For *Gabriel*.

I take deep breaths, counting slowly in my mind. I can do it.

By the time the lights come back up, I'm almost back to normal. It helps that everyone around me looks equally glassy-eyed and shaken.

I should say something, I realise. Something motivational and encouraging. I can't. Instead, I lead the way out, voices rising behind me as the twenty-eight remaining crew follow slowly towards the mess.

· · ·

On the screen, Bethesda looks like a bleached-out version of the Earth: a slate-grey ball sprinkled with pearly clouds and silver blots of lakes and inland seas. It looks ominous and mysterious in equal measure, an invitation to enter and explore the promise within. I wonder what the colonists saw when they first glimpsed this world: an opportunity? Hope? Challenge? When did they first realise that was only a mirage, a death trap camouflaged by wishful thinking?

The image flickers, then turns to grey.

'Entering communications blackout,' Lim says, perched like a kingfisher over the comms console, the flaps of her uniform jacket floating loosely by her small frame.

We're back in zero-g, deceleration complete, now slowly drifting towards our rendezvous with *Gabriel*. We have another day before we reach its position, the time we can use to get our first glimpse of the planet.

I'm in the captain's chair, still not used to the position, but at least I'm getting better at pretending. 'Time?'

Lim flicks the counter onto the screen. Nine minutes, thirty seconds before we hear from the probe again, and then another ten for the drones to reach the settlement and give us the first glimpse of the site.

Behind me, people stir. Everyone not on active duty is on the bridge for the big moment, except for the science team who chose to watch from the lab to avoid distraction. The murmur of conversation rises to an excited buzz, the hopeful and the pessimists uniting in anticipation.

I loosen the straps and turn to glance at the small crowd gathered behind me. The sight is oddly amusing: about twenty people floating in various orientations and poses, some upside down, others sideways to my frame of reference. The absence of gravity does allow for efficient packing.

The babble of conversation withers to a breath as all eyes turn to me.

'Sir?' Price asks from the edge of the crowd.

'Just checking that everyone's all right.'

I return to my seat. Damn. I read a story once where a junior officer had a general implanted into her head. Back then it seemed like a terrible idea, but now I wouldn't mind some advice on that whole 'command' thing.

I call up the archive map of the settlement on my personal display: the modules that used to be *Messenger* sit in a tight, geometrical pattern inside a spider-web of connecting passages. A large lake lies just a kilometre to the east. From its edge, a rotund purifier station feeds the water to a long row of manufactories and greenhouses with steep, triangular roofs of solar-glass.

'One minute,' Wang You-Yan says, back on duty at the system's console. Her burns are still covered in healing patches poking out from under her uniform sleeves despite her attempts to conceal them. Chao told me Yefremov refused to discharge her, but Wang slipped out the moment he left the sickbay.

The main screen flickers. Patches of red pop through grey static, settling into a grainy image bordered by the glow of the lens mount.

'Communications re-established,' Lim says.

'Telemetry as expected,' Tam Chau Yin, the senior engineer, says. He swings towards me, quick and agile, with a heart-shaped face and a permanent frown that seems to mirror his boss's. But unlike Zhang's implant lenses, Tam has opted for full automation with bright green bionic eyes that send a shiver down my back as I meet his gaze. 'Drones ready for deployment.'

'Proceed.'

The image on the screen vibrates as the probe opens the flaps of its cargo compartment. Two objects detach, instantly disappearing from view.

'Drones on own power,' Tam says. 'Autopilots responding.'

'Switching to drone cameras.'

Lim taps the console and the image feed from the probe shifts to a side monitor. The main screen splits in two, half for each of the drones. For the moment, the images are identical: calm, steel-coloured water and the distant line of the shore. We're approaching from the east, elongated shadows preceding the drones like lances hurled by the rising sun.

'Four hundred metres to shore,' Wang says.

On the side monitor, the image flickers and dies as the probe's main body hits the water.

'We got the water sample,' Lim confirms. 'Data transferred to science.'

I lean forward, peering into the screen. Ahead, I can just about make out the narrow line of the landing strip and the bulbous purifier station, and beyond it, the characteristic shapes of the greenhouses. Triangular roofs gleam with scattered light as the drones move closer, opalescent blue and almost alive with mirror reflections of drifting clouds.

I grip the armrests, then wince at the pain in my wrist. I'm free of the cast, but the pain's still there, like a memory.

'Zoom in on the glass.'

The image from the right drone flickers to maximum magnification. It's still hazy with distance, but clear enough to show the solar panels: undamaged, and still emitting the telltale glow of energy capacitors.

'They seem to be working,' Zhang says from his console on the left, his tentative tone a perfect echo of the flutter in my chest.

The image sharpens as the drones approach. No sign of damage, at least on the outside.

'Hundred metres,' Wang says.

Behind the greenhouses, the grey line of the settlement resolves itself into the familiar shapes of the *Messenger*'s modules: slate-grey blocks laid out flat, their walls a rough pattern of protrusions and recesses that once ensured that the modules slotted tightly together. Collapsible, tubular passages connect the modules, most still in place though several appear retracted or still waiting to be deployed. The place looks just like the plans on my console: ready and waiting. And empty.

On the screen, the two halves of the projection diverge as the drones separate to complete the flyby. One moves deeper into the base while the other circles the border towards the west, where the blueish wall of the dome stands some fifteen metres tall. This was going to be their future, an enclosed city where they could walk outside without breathing equipment. It's still far from completion but also much further along than expected.

'How can it be so high already?' I ask, the weight of the implications settling in my stomach even before I hear the answer.

Zhang's voice cracks as he answers. 'Plenty of raw materials. Nothing else for the assemblers to do, so they continue with the last task they've been given.'

Just like with the elevator, by now fully functional. Nothing else for the machines to do...

I see them now, worker ants crawling up the threads of the scaffolding, barely discernible from the distance. Printing the dome layer by layer from the materials their brethren process by the lake shore.

'Look!' someone cries.

In the image from the first drone, one module stands out from the rest, its walls shimmering with colour.

'Tam—' I start, but he's already at it, the drone banking in a tight turn.

For a moment, the building is behind us, even though the camera turns close to a hundred degrees. I hold my breath. The rest of the crew shift closer, crowding the space for a better view.

The turn completed, I search for the painted module—but

they all look the same from this angle, all grey and carbon-solid. And then I see it: a yellow cross painted next to a connecting pipe, and above it some lettering.

'Zooming in,' Lim says.

An insert window appears in the corner of the screen. On it, the yellow top of the cross and red, hand-painted letters reading, *THE HOUSE OF PRAYER*.

Someone gasps. I wonder if it's Pete Sanchez, our chaplain, but it could have been anyone: Christian, American, or just human.

The side of the module comes into view, hand-painted with clumsy renditions of green trees and blooming flowers. Child-like but too assured to be by children. *For* children, maybe. For children who'd never seen a tree or a flower growing in the wild.

I swallow, my breath stuck in my throat. They were people. Of course, I knew that, but now I feel it in my bones, with all their fragile humanity. Five thousand people. Crazy, devout, or desperate, but human. Brave, for sure, to have set up in a world so alien and tried to make it home. What happened to them?

Behind me, nobody speaks. Nobody seems to breathe, either, though that must be an illusion. A muffled noise breaks the silence—is that a sob?

'Resume flyby,' I force myself to say.

The drones dart across and along the settlement. We find another painted building, then one with something like a banner on the roof. It flaps in the wind, its Chinese inscription impossible to read. The drones snap photos and move on, searching.

Scattered detritus has blown into dead ends between some buildings: items of clothing, abandoned tools, odd-shaped objects like fragments of broken furniture. But no sign of the people.

They were here, and long enough to build the settlement. Long enough to paint buildings and try to make it a home.

That's no surprise; they'd been sending happy messages for years before they suddenly stopped. Why? The settlement seems intact.

I sit back, defeated. A tiny part of me hoped to find the colonists alive and well, waving flags from the rooftops and pointing to a failed communications array. I've always known this was unlikely—even if we had to try, had to come here and see if we could save them. Still, painful as it is, the bad news is not unexpected.

But this is not just about Bethesda—it's about *Gabriel* and the other ships now waiting at their destinations, unable to return. For their sake, what we need the most is an explanation: something easy to understand, even if not easy to prevent. A volcano, a hurricane, or even a reactor explosion that wiped Bethesda out in one violent blast. No matter how bad, it'd give *Gabriel* hope. They could study the events and prepare better, move to a different region, reinforce the walls, anything.

I watch the drones circle over the settlement once again, filming everything with cold efficiency. Nothing more to see. No easy answers to find.

'Proceed with sample collection,' I say to Tam Chau Yin, then tap the intercom button. 'The drones are yours, Doctor Khan. I'll see you all in my office at fourteen hundred hours.'

I wait for them in the office, feeling surprisingly calm and detached. Maybe it's the five thousand dead on the planet, or maybe just this office: too prim, too official, and too captain-like. Too not-me. I considered personalising it somehow, but the only pictures I have are those of Anna, and that won't do much for my sanity.

Price arrives first, as always, then Yefremov, his hair ruffled, a smile glued to his face even though it's more laboured than usual. It drops off his lips entirely the moment Khan steps into the room. She, too, stiffens at the sight of him, her chin jutting out and her gaze carefully averted. These two have a history, that's clear. I wonder if it's something that happened on the ship or if they brought it over from Earth.

I make a mental note to check on their backgrounds when the door opens to let in Reverend Sanchez, this time in a creamy shirt, one button opened to reveal a glint of a gold chain on his neck. He gives me a sad smile, then takes the chair opposite. Probably trying to be inconspicuous, but he is, in fact, placing himself at the other head of the table.

The others follow his lead and strap themselves into the chairs, Khan sitting as far away from the doctor as possible. Price pulls up the cuff of her black uniform, stealing a glance at her wrist. Still a minute to go; I've checked already. I consider placing a call when Zhang appears in the door.

'My apologies. I've run a consultation with my team.'

I motion him to the table. 'And your conclusion?'

The engineer grimaces. 'Hard to be sure from just a flyby, but we couldn't see anything wrong with the buildings or the equipment. The opposite, actually. Everything seems intact, and as far as we can tell, the solar cells are still pumping out minimal power, even through the dust. The hub's computer is not responding, but it wasn't designed for any form of autonomy.'

Yefremov puffs out his cheeks and exhales loudly. 'So, it's like the base is still good, but the people...'

He doesn't finish. For a moment, nobody speaks, as if not saying it out loud could change the facts.

'They're dead,' Khan says, her face impassive. 'All of them.'

'Could some...' The reverend's voice comes in soft and hesitant. 'Maybe a few could have survived...'

Zhang shakes his head unhappily. 'At that distance, we'd have picked up even a weak transmission. Like a suit radio. We got nothing—and all the equipment seems to be functioning.'

'So, what happened?' I ask. 'We haven't seen any bodies, have we?'

'They're probably inside,' Price says. 'Which means they weren't trying to escape or fight whatever was happening.'

'Or it was too sudden for them to try,' I say.

'True. Which rules out the plague, because then they'd have had time to send a message.'

I shiver, hot and cold at the same time. Not the plague. Not again.

Price leans back, pushing against the seat restraints. 'Did we find anything useful at all?'

'We haven't had time to go through all the data, but everything we've seen so far confirms the colonists' reports.' Khan taps her finger on the table, a jab for each point. 'Atmospheric composition, temperature, water minerals—all exactly as reported. Soil composition inside the camp shows nothing out of the ordinary. We're still studying the local organics, but again, so far everything's exactly as expected.'

Price huffs. 'So, we got nothing.'

'We've seen enough to know they felt settled here,' Sanchez says. 'We know from the messages that they started having children. The decorations seem to confirm this.'

I turn to Zhang. 'The characters on that banner—that was a Bible quote, right?'

'Yes. Psalm twenty-three, from what I've been told.'

'*The Lord is my shepherd; I shall not want...*' Sanchez says, his voice breaking at the end of the line.

'So much for green pastures...' Yefremov mutters, luckily too low for the reverend to hear.

I pull in a heavy breath. 'We'll have to wait for the field team to find out more. I'd like the initial group to be as small as possible. We haven't seen any imminent danger, but something down there killed the colonists, and until we know what, we'll need to be extra careful.'

I look from face to face, and they all nod agreement.

'Two people from my team,' Zhang says. 'That's less than optimal with all the equipment that needs checking, but it leaves only three on the ship.'

I hold his gaze for a moment, the unspoken grief clear behind his eyes. 'Two's fine. Doctor?'

Yefremov pushes his fingers through his hair. 'It'll be me and—'

'You're staying here,' I interrupt. 'None of the key crew are going. We need to mitigate the risks, and we need resources here to analyse whatever the ground team finds. And to treat them, if the worst happens.'

Yefremov sighs—but it sounds more like relief than disappointment. 'Okay. It'll be the medical scientists, then: Gonzales and Raji, the pathologist.'

'Good. Doctor Khan?'

'I need three. Should be more but... well, we don't have many left.'

She pulls a zheping from her uniform pocket, unfolds the screen, and syncs it with the monitor. The faces of the six remaining scientists pop up on the screen. Khan circles the names with her finger, and a corresponding red line appears on the screen. 'I want Johansson for exobiology, Berry for planetology, and Mwangi for chemistry.'

I watch her finger slide over the pad—and suddenly, I remember.

The writing on the glass. The finger-scribbled warning.

Sabotage.

Blood drains from my face. I'm floating, light and unreal, not just in zero-g but in a dark tunnel that tightens around me like an accusation.

The 'accident' that killed seven of the crew—it was sabotage. Or at least someone thought it was. Who? Why didn't they warn me directly? And why haven't they contacted me since?

I force my attention to the present. My head spins with questions—but they'll have to wait till the meeting's over. One of the very people in front of me could be the accuser—or the accused.

Khan's looking at me, and so is Yefremov, the doctor's eyes narrowing in a question.

'Okay, so that's seven for the away team,' I say, my voice hoarse.

Price raises her hand. 'Plus three from my team.'

Khan tilts her head in a scowl. 'Why would we need security on the surface?'

Price scowls back, her tone deliberate and her twang more pronounced. 'Because we're not just security. We're your fire brigade and your ambulance service. And your morticians, though I hope it won't come to that. Are your people going to put out fires or disarm explosives?'

'Do you think that's what we'll find there?' Khan asks.

'Are you certain we won't?'

I hesitate. Price has got a point, but so far, her team has caused more tension than solved problems. 'We'll send two. But make sure they understand they're there to help *all* the team members, not police them.'

A small smile plays on Price's lips. 'No worries. I'll brief them personally.'

A sigh escapes my lips before I can stop it. Zhang's mouth twitches in a ghost of a smile, but Price pretends not to notice.

'We also need to confirm the team to inspect *Gabriel*,' Zhang says.

The signals from *Gabriel* confirmed it was operating within 'mission parameters,' but nothing about its power reserves or the status of the cold-sleep pods. We considered accessing the systems remotely but decided against it in case the action tipped some internal power balance, or worse, triggered the computer to wake up the crew. Best to go there and check it in person.

'I'd like to be part of it,' Yefremov says. 'I assume you don't expect any risk on *Gabriel*?'

His Russian accent makes me wince. I rub my face to hide my reaction, but my hands are shaking. The sabotage message was in Cyrillic—but the doctor was asleep at the time. Why then? Was the language part of the message?

I shake my head, both to my circular thoughts and in an answer. 'No, that's fine, Doctor. We'll go as soon as the field team departs.'

'*We?*' Price asks.

It takes me a moment to realise what she means. I'm not the pilot anymore, I'm the commander. I shouldn't be leaving the ship. But I'll be damned if I'll just sit here and wait.

'Just as with the doctor, there's no risk in me going.' Price wants to protest, but I make my tone definitive. 'I know you're a licensed pilot, but these shuttles aren't the standard type. You may need me. Chief Engineer, I want you to come as well.'

'Naturally.' Zhang nods.

I release my seat restraints to show that the meeting's over. My wrist hurts again, and I can't wait for them to leave so I can think in peace.

'Commander, if I may?' Sanchez says.

'What is it?' This comes out snappy, so I cover it up with a smile.

'I'd like to offer a prayer meeting for the field team. For those who want to participate, of course. And personal counselling, if anyone finds it useful.'

'Of course. Please inform your crews.'

The others nod, all but Price trying hard not to roll their eyes.

'And one more thing,' Sanchez says again in his soft, melodic voice that could be intoxicating if it wasn't so damn annoying.

I nod for him to go ahead, even as the others continue releasing their restraints.

'We've already scheduled regular meetings for the Christians on the ship, but I'm sure more of us would benefit from prayer. I'd like to offer a multi-faith gathering for all the crew. The first one will be the day after tomorrow. At lunchtime, so as not to interfere with our duties.'

Khan pushes herself out of her chair. 'So, the multi-faith meeting happens to be on Sunday?'

Sanchez opens his mouth then closes it again.

Yefremov snorts. Price glares. Zhang doesn't say anything.

For a moment I wonder why New Horizons didn't recruit only Christians. They were nominally a Christian corporation, like everything coming out of the New American Union. They didn't have a say with the Chinese crew, but they hired the rest of us themselves. Probably didn't have enough candidates. Not many volunteers for a seventy-year mission, no matter how good the pay.

Sanchez stares at me, half-dismayed, half-pleading. I really don't need yet another issue to divide them.

'I think we can agree the calendar is something rather hypothetical here? Reverend, I appreciate your gesture. With your agreement, we'll hold the multi-faith service on a day of the crew's choosing.'

Khan raises an eyebrow, but I ignore her, my eyes and my plastic smile focused on Pete Sanchez.

'Of course,' he says, his smile miles more genuine. 'I'll be waiting for your word. Thank you, Commander.'

I try not to wince at the title. No way I'll ever get used to it.

The smile stays fixed on my face as they slowly float out of the office. I wait till the door closes behind them, then glide to my terminal and open the personnel files.

CHAPTER 5

The system shows me the crew grouped by department. Seven pictures are greyed out: those who died in the fire. Not likely any of them were the saboteur, unless things went spectacularly wrong. And why would they do it? Why would anyone sabotage a ship they were on?

Unless it'd been done before we left. In that case, it could have been anyone, from commercial rivals to anti-colonisation protesters. Even some Americans believed that Bethesda was a sign from God that we should have never left Earth. Could Price or any of her people be one of them?

I stare at the faces as if expecting the pictures to speak. Someone wrote that warning on the lid of my pod. Could it have been there before we left? It'd have been easy to miss in the commotion, with all the others entering cold-sleep and all the support technicians. But why a warning on the *inside* of the pod, something I could only read when I was no longer able to do anything about it? Unless they knew I wouldn't be affected. In which case, the sabotage was not intended to damage the ship but to attack the crew. Who? The captain?

This is hopeless. I'm working myself up into a Möbius strip

of doubt. If anyone'd known about the sabotage before we left, they could have stopped the launch, not left a useless warning. No, it had to be someone on board, and only nine of us were awake at the time.

I close my eyes, trying to remember the way the letters appeared on the glass. Cyrillic characters. Why? Mandarin would be a giveaway. And everyone on board speaks English.

That's my clue: not just that whoever it was knew enough Russian to write the warning, but that they realised I, a Canadian, could read and understand it. A chill runs down my back. That's not a casual piece of information. I've only revealed the most basic of personal details to the recruiters. They didn't ask, either, focused only on my skills records, my nationality, and the glowing recommendation from Logan, my boss at Orbital Logistics. I definitely didn't mention Stepan, or my attempts to learn Russian.

I push myself away from the desk, even more confused than before. My left hand wraps around my painful wrist, fingers clammy with nervous sweat. Somebody here knows me better than I thought possible. And if they know about Stepan, then they may also know about his death.

And the incident at the warehouse.

And everything that followed from there.

Pain shoots up my arm as my fingers squeeze my sore wrist. Wou kao, I'm only making this worse.

I return to the screen and open my own personnel file. The system requests verification codes—odd, as I typed them in only moments earlier, but whatever. I punch in the string of signifiers, careful that my shaking fingers don't slip.

Code accepted appears on the screen. *Configuring content.*

I frown. What is that supposed to mean? Is it changing the content because I'm not supposed to see my own file?

Document icons pop up on the screen and I open them one by one. My service record, just as I submitted it, with a high-lighted section relating to my space hours and the three Jupiter missions. Logan's recommendation letter, again with high-lighted sections that call me 'an outstanding pilot,' 'level-headed' and a 'team player.' Nice of him. I scroll through the content list: my medical checks, last will, financial arrange-ments. All my money goes into a Feidi branch of a Swiss bank; they handle the transfers to Jason's trust in full confidentiality. This can't be the leak.

Another file catches my eye—not really a file but an in-document link bolded for appended text. When I touch it, a title appears: *CCM*, but it's greyed out, inaccessible.

'Computer?' I ask, unsure. Zhang said the audio was 'almost' fixed, whatever that meant.

'Awaiting instructions.' The voice that answers is bland and inflectionless. Basic interface only. Better than nothing.

'Access personnel file for Nathalie Hart.'

'Accessing.'

'Open sub-document called "CCM".'

'Document not found.'

'Find any document, tag or file with that name.'

'No document, tag or file with the name "CCM" exists.'

I stare, the greyed-out link still on the screen right in front of me. 'Search the file for any occurrence of CCM.'

The screen lights up with the page I was watching.

'Open the link.'

'The link is inactive.'

Okay, so it's nothing. A deleted file or a bit of dead code, a remnant left behind by a hurried programmer. And yet...

I rub my forehead, furrowed and glassy with sweat. Too many coincidences. The accident, the warning, and now this.

On a hunch, I open Price's file. There it is again, in the same corner of her service record, a dead link to a CCM. I check the others. It's everywhere, in every file I open. One more try—the dead captain's record.

Authorised personnel only appears on the screen.

Not *that* odd; he was my superior, even if he's dead. Still.

I push myself off the desk, floating towards the ceiling and then back to the floor in the weightless equivalent of pacing. It doesn't help—not enough muscles involved in the process.

I can't do this alone. I can't trust anyone with the sabotage, but that CCM file, if it really exists, could give me something to hook on to.

'Computer, send a voice message to Lim Firyali: "I'm having some computer trouble. Nothing urgent, but I'd like your help when you have a moment".'

'Message sent.'

This time when my glide path takes me past the desk chair, I pull myself in. I manage to fasten the restraints when the computer's dead voice announces that Lim is requesting entry.

'Let her in.'

I arrange my face into an expression I hope looks mildly annoyed. 'Thank you for coming so quickly.'

Lim glides inside, slightly hunched, head lowered, a shy smile barely visible on dark red lips. 'How can I help?'

I point to the screen. 'When I put in my codes, I got a message that it was "configuring content." As if something needed changing because it was me and not the captain. I don't know, but it seems odd...'

I trail off. I know little about command, not at this level. Maybe it's standard procedure; maybe my jumped-up rank doesn't entitle me to pry into the crew's personal lives. But from the expression on Lim's face, I can see she's as surprised as I am.

'And then there's this.' I wave her over to the terminal and open her personnel file.

Lim anchors one foot in a soft hoop attached to the floor for this purpose. She leans in to the screen, her curiosity more than just professional. It's her file, after all. Mine was the first one I checked.

I touch the greyed-out CCM link to show it's inactive, then repeat the procedure of asking the computer to locate the file, with the same effect. Lim's frown gets deeper with every attempt.

'I'd say it's some vestigial code that makes the link show up while the actual file's not there...' She puckers her lips, her eyes narrowed. 'May I?'

I let her take my place, and she types a string of commands. The screen flickers to something I recognise as the operating code, but that's all I can tell. I watch her work for a moment then give up. This is out of my league. I'd rather be flying.

'Ha!' Lim stares at the screen, her expression somewhere between triumph and surprise.

'What?'

She points to the monitor, then flicks it back to its normal configuration when my blank face makes her realise I can't read code. 'It's gone.'

The place where the CCM text used to sit is now blank, no sign of the link.

'What did you do?'

'Nothing.' She shakes her head. 'I mean, what I did shouldn't have made it disappear.'

'What *did* you do?'

'I asked the system to scan for cruft, links without destination, or destinations without links. But—I asked it to show them to me, not to do anything about them.'

I look at her face, so eager and confused. Lim was one of the people awake during the accident—and she got into her pod first, while Zhang and I were inspecting the other chambers. Could she have been the one to leave the message?

And yet... The way she studies the lines on the monitor, eyes narrowed, tip of her tongue showing as she moistens her lips—it's not the face of a master conspirator. Unless she's really, really good.

'Vot zagvostka,' I say, pretending to look at the screen while focusing on her reflection.

Lim cocks her head. 'I'm sorry?'

'Oh, it's Russian. Something my brother-in-law used to say when he couldn't solve a problem.'

She sniffs. 'Ha, I may have to learn this.'

Her eyes don't leave the screen, her expression darkening as she follows the lines of the code. She's not acting, I decide. Because if she's that good, I may as well give up trying to ever crack this puzzle. Also, I need someone to trust.

'Can I ask you something?'

'Sure.'

'Answer only if you want to, okay?' I add.

Lim looks up. Her focus shifts away from the screen, her expression morphing to suspicion and... fear? 'Okay...'

'What made you join this mission? I mean, you're young, you had your whole life ahead of you. Who knows what the world will be like when we get back?'

Lim grins, relieved. 'Hai la! That's a risk. But I figured it was worth it. I was apprenticed to New Horizons, only four years in. So, it was like, spend another sixteen to pay off my debt or take this job and come back clean and with savings to spare. A win-win. Though my mother wasn't too happy...'

Her smile disappears for a moment, then she shakes her head. 'But she understood. And I've got siblings, so she'll have grandchildren enough. Had. I'm probably a great-aunt by now...'

I freeze, my chin trembling. *Does Jason have a family now? Am I a great-aunt? Why didn't he send any messages?*

Lim must notice something in my face. She tilts her head, her mouth opening in a question.

I laugh aloud before she can ask it. 'I've just realised that, objectively, I hit seventy this year.'

'Ha. I'm almost sixty...' A shadow crosses her face. 'I wish they'd sent more pictures.'

I thought I was the only one without much mail. I guess we've all been forgotten after thirty-five years without contact. They won't even know we made it here until our confirmation ping arrives, another six years from now.

I point back to the screen. 'Do you think...' I start, then hesitate. How can I word it without saying too much—or having her think I'm insane? 'I'm not happy something like that could happen.'

Her face brightens. 'Do you want me to poke around?'

'Yes, I think so. But discreetly. I don't want anyone to think there may be a problem.'

'Of course. I know what you mean.' The way she's grinning you'd think I've just handed her a bag of candy.

'Can you do it without access codes?' I hesitate again. I can't give them to her; I don't trust her that much.

'The codes are there to protect the contents of certain files and to prevent unauthorised commands to the ship. I don't need them just to check the architecture.' Lim's smile widens. 'Besides, I helped design similar systems. I can get pretty deep without triggering the defences.'

She winks, and suddenly I see a fearless adventurer concealed under the hunched facade. What makes her want to hide? Or need to hide? A question for another time.

'Thank you,' I say. 'Let me know what you find, no matter how minor.'

'Yes, sir!'

My personal cabin is a luxurious two-by-two-by-two metres, which for now I can use in all three dimensions. This will end very soon, when we shift to our permanent orbit, split the ship, and start it rotating. That will be better for our muscles and stomachs, but even so, I'm not looking forward to that collapse of my living space into floors and ceilings.

I yawn and pull on the straps to release them. My bed remains stowed against the wall; I haven't needed it so far for the little time I managed to sleep. I glance up at the pictures pinned to the ceiling, flat memories of what used to be: Anna splashing in the pool among inflatable toys while I sit at the edge, pretending to be all grown up. Our last family Christmas, the smiles strained after Dad learned his contract had expired and he had to return to Canada. That was the day we decided that Anna and I would stay in the Feidi. I was sixteen and Anna just ten, but I had already secured a scholarship, and the opportunities Chinese education would give us overshadowed anything we could find back 'home,' the place I left when I was four and never saw again.

The next one has Anna grinning as she points at her *I love soya* T-shirt. She made it for a laugh, or to make me feel better after a month of feeding her soya-laced meals I scavenged from the work cafeteria to stretch our meagre budget, not realising she was allergic. She never complained, just thanked me and stealthily disposed of the meals when I wasn't looking.

My eyes stop at the last picture, the one I took the day Nadia was born. I'd missed the birth but got there in time to see them all together, happy and excited. Stepan's got his arm around Anna, his eyes on the little girl in her arms. Jason is a blur, jumping up and down in excitement, a big brother now to his baby sister. I'm not in the image and yet present, my shadow falling on the edge of Anna's bed.

I wipe my eyes. I hate crying in zero-g. The tears just stay there, attached to your eyes like an extra lens, one that stops you from seeing anything but your grief.

I move to the basin and wipe my face with a wet cloth in the hope it'll make a difference. My hair sticks out in all directions, but I can blame that on zero-g. The captain's cabin has its own bathroom, but I've refused to move there. I'm not superstitious, but that place is haunted: the pictures, the clothes still in a travel bag, a uniform jacket with its shiny epaulets. Nope, I'd rather stick to my own ghosts.

My wan-kong chimes five to seven. I glance at the mirror again, but it's a hopeless cause, and I don't want to be late for breakfast. The away team leaves right after, so it's our last meal with the full complement. Or what's left of the full complement.

I glide out of my cabin, almost bumping into Chao. She smiles as we exchange greetings, but then her brows furrow as she inspects my face.

'I can give you something if you're having trouble sleeping,' she says.

Kao, is it that obvious?

She seems to read my mind. 'It's perfectly normal. We've been giving out sleeping pills like candy.'

'Are you saying most of my crew's sleepwalking?' I stretch my lips into a smile to let her know that's a joke.

'It's not that bad. And the pills are short-acting.' She grabs a handhold, her eyes on my jacket. 'May I?'

I nod, unsure. Chao adjusts my collar, and now I realise it was bent inward, poking into my neck.

'That's better.' She grins, her eyes warm like charcoal.

'Thanks,' I groan, stopping myself before I add *Mom*, the way Anna did when I prepped her for school.

And there I go, tearing up again. I look away, embarrassed. I'm really not cut out for this job.

'You're doing great,' Chao says. A mind reader or what? 'People like you. Even the Chinese crew.'

Now I just stare. They like me? Not that I care how they feel as long as they stay alive, but... the possibility hasn't occurred to me.

I force a smile. 'Let's go before they eat everything.'

We join the others in the common room, which doubles for the mess, the chapel, and the dance hall, if we ever decided to have a dance. The space is tight for all of us, but in zero-g we have the entire volume to play in and no furniture to worry about. The walls are a warm shade of brown, almost orange, probably following some psychologist's suggestion. It's not helping now, the voices subdued and faces solemn. I don't think many expected us to find good news on Bethesda, but it's different to know for sure. And in three hours, nine of them will be heading into the elevator and down to the planet that killed five thousand.

Only the security team seems unaffected, hovering in their usual spot by the ceiling, faces eager and voices booming in the silence around them.

Moses Miller floats in the middle, waving something with pride in his eyes. 'Did you see that? Nine titles! Go, Sox!'

'That must be some special pair of socks...' Chao murmurs behind me.

'In your face, Mo!' another voice chimes in. Michael Lee, the Asian American from Price's team. He's as tall as Moses and equally athletic, with strong, regular features and a supply of confidence that would last a standard human two lifetimes. He glides from behind the food dispenser, a predatory grin on his face as he pulls something from his pocket and slaps it on his head. A baseball cap, with multiple rows of shiny silver pins. 'How about twelve for the Yankees?'

I stare, astonished how decades-old sport results could possibly hold any significance for us here—but Lee and Miller are the two from security heading down to the planet, and I can't help feeling that their enthusiasm is just that little too ardent... If that's what it takes for them—go, Sox!

The voices around me grow louder, feeding on their energy. Wang gives me a broad smile when our eyes meet. Her face is almost healed; the last of the patches cover the burns on her neck. She's with the engineers, floating between green-eyed Tam Chau Yin and Sheng Jing, the woman with a bionic hand.

All the others float in their usual function clusters—all except for bridge crew, which is now only me, Wang, and Lim. I look around, my heart accelerating. Where's Lim? I haven't seen her since our chat. She's not on active duty, either; I remember the roster. Has she found something?

I follow Chao to the food dispenser. Yefremov's last in line, his eyes red and his hair making mine look coiffured.

'Rough night?' Chao asks as she moves in behind him.

Yefremov huffs. 'Humans don't belong in space, I tell you. Our stomachs need gravity. At least mine does.'

'Maybe you should see a doctor?' I suggest innocently.

Chao chuckles.

Yefremov scowls. 'Did you know this ship can split and rotate?'

'I may have heard about it.' I tap his shoulder. 'Not long now. Do you think you'll survive?'

The doctor sighs theatrically. 'Ha! Nothing's guaranteed, I tell you.'

Finally at the dispenser, I press the button for a cold mix, then insert the nozzle into my squeeze bottle. The machine rumbles as thick, oatmeal-coloured liquid inflates the pouch. We get the 'soup' three times a day: dry protein and nutrients liquified with hot or cold water, and with a flavour pack of your choosing. The afternoon meal, what we call dinner, consists of solid food, if the rehydrated rations can be called that. It's not horrible and it's got everything our bodies need, so I don't complain. Never been a foodie anyway.

I fill my bottle to the halfway mark, then select the banana flavour for taste. I glance at the door. Still no Lim.

Yefremov's staring at the options, face puzzled. 'Chocolate or tuna? Or both?'

'And you complain about an upset stomach? Just choose already. The reverend's waiting.'

The doctor makes a circle with his finger, then jabs a flavour selection. His eyes narrow as he peers at the flashing button. 'Strawberry! Didn't know we had that. Anyway—it's not me they're waiting for.'

Wou kao. Of course, they are waiting for *me*. I'm the damn commander.

I turn to Sanchez—just when Lim appears in the entrance, her face troubled. She frowns as she catches my glance. Damn. I'm dying to talk to her immediately, but that would raise too many questions.

I put on a smile that I'm sure looks perfectly fake and turn to Reverend Sanchez. 'I think it's all of us here.'

'Thank you,' Sanchez says.

Voices hush, some eager, others reluctant, as he lowers his head and begins to pray.

I wait for him to finish, then saunter towards Lim with forced ease. 'Have you found anything?'

Her lips twist in what's neither a 'no' nor a 'yes'. 'Nothing certain. But I'll keep looking.'

'So you think... there's something to find?'

'I can't be sure. I've seen some odd stuff. Nothing bad, just... odd.'

'What do you mean?'

She hesitates. 'The way the programming's organised—I've never seen anything like that. Nothing's wrong with it; it's perfectly functional, just why would it be so different?'

Not a question I can answer. 'Have you worked with ship computers before?'

'Not exactly. But a computer is a computer, if you know what I mean.'

I don't. I suck a gulp of my food, momentarily surprised at the banana flavour while Yefremov's strawberry sticks in my mind. That's not an answer I expected. I want clarity, good news or bad. The fact that she can't give me straight good news makes my stomach tighten. It's the ship's brain we're talking about, the thing that keeps it going—and keeps us alive.

And that's just one of my problems. The crew around me— at least one of them is a saboteur, responsible for killing the captain and six crew. Someone else knows about it, but for some reason refuses to identify themselves.

I draw in another mouthful. The liquid stays on my tongue, my appetite gone as my insides feel like tangled wire. One thing at a time, or I'll lose focus.

'Keep looking,' I say to Lim, then check the clock. Three hours till the field team boards the elevator for a three-day journey down to the planet.

Two more hours, and I'll be in the shuttle, flying to inspect *Gabriel*.

CHAPTER -3

7 WEEKS BEFORE DEPARTURE

I know we've entered the upper city when the ochre clumps of elephant grass and wilting agaves outside the cab window give way to thin strips of lawns. With water so precious, even these yellowing bands must cost a fortune. I've seen real parks up in orbit, but never in Kenya. And yet, the deeper we push into the Chinese quarter, the greener it gets. The strips broaden into carpets, sparkling like emeralds against the copper-red soil. Spillover water evaporates from overheated pavements, the petrichor seeping through the car's air con.

I've always known Chinese money kept the Feidi alive, but the reminder couldn't be timelier.

Next to me, Stepan finishes an anxious phone call. He speaks in Russian, too fast for me to understand, but all I need is the tone of his voice, breathless and abrupt.

More bad news.

He taps his wan-kong to disconnect, his mouth pursed into a pale line, his gaze unfocused, as if he were somewhere else entirely.

'And?'

Stepan's tone is as blank as his face. 'He says not to worry, it's not a real plague. People will soon realise and stop panicking, and then we'll get the meds.'

We've heard that many times before, the same story repeated by all the doctors we've seen. A 'fake plague' they call it now, not the real thing. It makes no difference. The antivirals disappeared from the stores and the dispensaries at the first signs of the disease. By the time I returned Earth-side, the supplies were gone, no matter how much I was offering to pay.

Most doctors laugh when they tell us the story—aren't people gullible? Hahaha. Except then we tell them about Anna and Nadia. Post-partum complications, compromised immune response. The doctors' faces turn grim, and they admit that yes, the infection is mild and treatable to most, but not to all. To some it's deadly.

But still, no antivirals. Maybe tomorrow. Or next week.

No one will tell us how much time Anna and Nadia have left.

I smile at Stepan, my back straight and my eyes opened wide in a practised simulation of optimism, even though I suspect I'm fooling no one. Yet he needs the pretence, and probably I do, too, because there's not much else we have left to keep our hopes alive. Stepan nods, as if to acknowledge my effort, then the muscles in his jaw tighten and he turns towards the window, hiding his face.

His wan-kong chimes again and he jerks his hand up. His mouth quivers, a smile fighting for life but dying, crushed under his grief. He lets his arm drop—just in time for me to glimpse the picture on the screen, yet another clumsy orange lion forwarded by Jason's sitter.

The lion I still haven't taken him to see.

I make myself point at the screen. 'I think he gets his drawing skills from you...'

Stepan's lips smile, as if separate from the rest of his face. 'He'll get better.'

'True. I mean, he can't get worse...'

He snorts, then squeezes my hand. 'Thank you for being here.'

I turn to the window, my throat too tight to speak.

The cab climbs up a hill towards a scattering of low buildings, each with a roof garden and walls of blue solar-glass, like truncated versions of the business district office blocks. A tall fence surrounds the entire complex, its filigree design deceptively decorative. It was probably electrified even before the unrest. Now two armoured vehicles wait beside the gate. Security guards patrol the perimeter. At least here they seem mostly bored, with just a couple of cars ahead of us. The lower-city hospitals are pretty much inaccessible by now, blocked by anxious crowds.

A guard checks our names against the appointment roster, peers into the cab as if to confirm we're not smuggling sick people into the hospital, then waves us through.

We pass a sprawling garden with bamboo groves, hill stones, and flowing water, and finally arrive under a columned porch, a valet waiting to receive us. Inside, it's plush sofas, fountains, and soft music, and not a white coat in sight. A receptionist meets us at the entrance, her hair in a formal up-do, her chestnut skin warm against her steel-grey business suit. She smiles, but I can see a hint of confusion in the way her brow lifts ever so slightly. Not used to Caucasian customers in this upscale clinic.

'I've been told you have an appointment with Doctor Huang?' she says in perfect Mandarin.

'That's correct,' Stepan answers in English.

The woman's brows twitch again, but her smile doesn't fade. Her gaze loses focus the way I've only seen in orbit with people using Mind-Link or contact lens projectors.

'Doctor Huang's expecting you, Mr Nevsky,' she says in English. 'This way, please.'

She ushers us to a wooden door with the Feidi emblem of

elephants and dragons carved in detailed relief. The man who opens it is young, maybe mid-twenties, with a round, pale face and wide-set eyes. He's wearing a fitted, light blue jacket buttoned up to the collarless neck in a look that sits perfectly between medical professional and boardroom formal.

He greets us with a bright smile. 'Delighted to meet you, Doctor Nevsky. My brother's such a fan. He says your research is ground-breaking.'

'I'm sure Huang Wei will produce even better research in due time.'

'Nathalie Hart,' I say when he looks at me. 'Anna's sister.'

'Anna? Oh yes, the patient.' Huang points to the two armchairs facing his desk. 'I'm sure we can get it sorted out. I'll be honest, we've had dozens of people calling in with complaints, but this new virus is hardly worse than the common cold. It just takes a bit longer to recover.'

Stepan tenses. It's the same story all over again, but we have to go through it.

I put on a smile. 'Maybe you can look at the file and decide for yourself?'

'Yes, that would be best.'

Huang reaches out his arm, and Stepan lets their wan-kongs touch. It takes a moment, and then the doctor's eyes lose focus, his attention on the data playing inside his head.

I lean forward, expectant. Stepan is licking his lips, his hand pressing down on his leg as it starts to tap nervously.

Huang's brows twitch, then the corners of his mouth pull down. When he looks at us again, his smile is gone. He rubs his forehead, tired and deflated.

'I know it's bad,' Stepan says. 'But I also know it's not hopeless, with the right medication.'

Huang leans back in his seat, his face sombre. 'You're right. But... you know of the supply issues, or you wouldn't be here.' He looks at us, and we nod. 'This is worse. You need the HDCspecific antivirals, but also the drugs to control all the secondary issues. These are just impossible to get—at least here in Kenya.'

Stepan gasps, pale as a ghost.

I lean forward even further, my chest so close to the desk it feels like my heart is thumping against it. 'You're saying *you* don't have them? In *this* hospital?'

'I'm afraid not.'

'I don't believe that.'

Huang winces. 'Are you accusing me of lying?'

'I'm sure Nat didn't mean—' Stepan tries, his voice frayed with panic.

'No, Doctor, my apologies.' I give him my best smile. I can't alienate this man; he may be our only hope. 'I'm sure you're telling the truth. I just can't believe that your customers would accept this when they can have the meds shipped from anywhere in the world.'

Huang snorts. 'You are right—and wrong, Ms Hart. Our clientele, they are precisely what you say. Won't accept anything but the best of the best. And so, when they have a real problem, they don't come here. They go straight to China. Or up to the Yun Ju, if they can. They don't trust us to handle more than routine treatments.'

I blink at the dissonance in his words—we're in the most exclusive hospital in the Feidi. But he's right—this may be a Chinese enclave, but by the mainland standards, it's only a poor cousin. Of course his rich customers would rush back home for any serious treatment.

Huang glances from me to Stepan. Somehow, I know what he's thinking: *Is there anywhere else you can take her?* We're both registered ji-gong, international workers. We're allowed to travel, but only for job contracts. We could go back 'home', but that's not going to help. Russia's never recovered from the wars they started even before the collapse. Canada's better, but not by much. Nowhere near as good as this clinic here in the Feidi.

I don't know if I should cry or laugh. Travel restrictions were a consequence of the 2200s plague, an attempt to control the spread of any future contagion—but now they're holding us here, unable to reach any place that still has the meds.

'Can you get her up to the Yun Ju?' Huang asks. 'I know they have supplies.'

I shake my head. 'I don't think they do. Nobody even mentions the plague in the stations.'

'Nobody mentions it to *you*. You're not the target, nor am I. None of us are rich enough for the scheme they're running up there.'

'What do you mean?' Stepan stutters.

Huang considers us for a moment, then makes up his mind. He taps his desk, and the top changes into a display showing a serious-looking publication with graphs and figures. It's in Mandarin, but I can clearly see Huang's name bolded as the lead author.

'I published this a month ago. This came out four days later.'

A new image appears, screenshot of a video publication called Citizen's Exchange with a headline in big red letters: *Four patients dead as 'Doctor' W. Huang avoids litigation.*

Huang points to the name. 'Not me. Nor any other Huang I could find.'

I stare from the screen back to him. 'What are you saying?'

'Every time a medical professional comments on the virus, immediately a report pops up about some corrupt researcher exposed for manipulating data. It's happened too often to be a coincidence.'

My head's spinning. 'Who's doing that? And why?'

'Whoever it is, they must be connected to the orbitals, because the worst disinformation has been in all the elevator cities. It's like they want people to panic. And this virus is perfect for that: just enough symptoms to make it look like the plague without actually being dangerous.' Huang casts an apologetic glance at Stepan. 'To the general population, I mean.'

He reaches for a water carafe on his desk and lifts it towards us with a questioning gesture. We both refuse, too anxious to drink. The doctor fills three glasses anyway, probably guessing we're not thinking straight.

'As to why,' he says after he takes a sip from his glass, 'my guess is they smelled a business opportunity. Scare people into believing the virus is another plague and they'll rush to buy meds, any meds, no matter what the doctors tell them. And if you want to make a fortune, you target those with fortunes to spend.'

I shake my head in stubborn denial, too stunned to speak.

'One more thing.' Huang bends forward, his voice tinged with anger. I lean closer, our faces near enough to feel the air of his words on my cheek. 'We keep ordering resupplies, meds for the vulnerable patients. Supposedly, full containers arrive in the Feidi, yet never make it to the hospitals. Guess where they are going?'

He points his finger up at the ceiling. The Yun Ju.

My breath snags in my throat. The ground feels soft, receding into a dark chasm. It's all for money. The fabricated panic, the stolen shipments. The drugs diverted to the rich over-lords laughing at us from their orbital mansions.

Nadia, only two months old. Anna, my kid sister, dying.

I promised I wouldn't let her. If I had to beg or steal or fight, I wouldn't let her.

I'm done begging. It's time for the stealing and the fighting.

CHAPTER 6

On the shuttle's screen, *Gabriel* sits suspended only an arm's length away: a long hexahedron, like a super-stretched shipping container composed of smaller blocks slotted together to form a solid whole. Only the engine exhausts indicate this thing can move at all, let alone traverse light years.

I glance at the timer in the corner of the navigation display. Twelve minutes till we reach the ship, another fifteen before we can dock and access the interior. How long to determine the fate of the passengers?

Not long, if they're all dead.

I clamp down at the thought. It's not helping. We'll know the truth soon enough, good or bad.

'All systems nominal,' Price says from the pilot's seat. I let her fly; checking her piloting skills is my excuse for coming along. She's flying manual, for exactly that reason—and from what I've seen so far, she's more than adequate.

'Telemetry nominal,' Tam's voice says over the intercom. 'It's all looking good from here.'

The bar-shaped vessel ahead of us grows in size till it becomes impossibly big, like one of the Feidi skyscrapers laid on its side. It's got nothing of their slickness, though, just layer upon layer of grey blocks. We move closer still, and the blocks resolve into individual modules, so familiar after the hours I've spent reviewing the drone footage of the colony.

The engine fires briefly as Price steers us around the stubby cupola covering *Gabriel*'s bow to take us to the other side of the ship.

'The hull looks fine,' Zhang says from behind me. 'Traces of micro-impacts but so far nothing above the expected.'

So far, so good. I let out a breath—then choke as I inhale.

A shadow cuts the steely-grey surface, probably a metre across and rough around the edges.

Not a shadow. A puncture.

'What's that?' Price asks.

My fingers are already on the console, taking over control. I swing us around, focusing the shuttle's headlights on the breach. Someone, probably Zhang, inserts a grid over the viewscreen. Red indicators appear, displaying the hole's dimensions.

'Looks like a micrometeoroid collision,' the engineer says. 'A piece of dust at hypervelocity could do this.'

'Is this a passenger module?' Yefremov whispers.

'In-transit storage,' Wang's voice says from the ship as the module number appears on our screen. 'Pressurised but not occupied.'

'It's okay,' Zhang says. 'The leak was contained and sealed automatically. No significant pressure loss to the rest of the ship.'

'How can you be sure?' I ask, not allowing myself to be relieved, not yet.

'I've made contact, Commander.'

Mind-Link, of course. He can talk to the ship even from the outside.

'Can you check on the status of the pods from here?'

'All I can see is that there are no alerts. But that's not enough to be sure. The reporting systems could be compromised.'

Price rotates to glare at the engineer, her voice cold and suspicious. 'How did you get access?'

Zhang's shoulders move up and down under his spacesuit.

'Why didn't you tell us you had command codes for *Gabriel*?'

She's always been suspicious of the engineer—but now she seems outright hostile, all reserve gone from her voice.

'I don't,' Zhang says flatly. 'I can talk to the systems, but I can't change any of the programming.'

'Which we won't be able to verify, at least not those of us without Mind-Link.'

That would be all the Americans, and those working for them. None of us can monitor his actions or know for sure if he's telling the truth. But what reason in the world would he have to lie?

Price turns to me, a desperate glint in her eyes. 'How can we know what else he's doing?'

'What I'm doing is telling the computer not to initiate emergency alarms when we dock,' Zhang says. 'I can only do this by Mind-Link. Or would you rather risk it waking up the passengers?'

He's right—even so, Price's suspicion makes me hesitate. But if Zhang had some other agenda, he could have done it all without any of us realising. No, this is a wrong tree.

'Mind-Link is a tool,' I say slowly. 'For the passengers' sake, we must use the best tools we have.'

She shifts reluctantly back to the controls. Unconvinced, I'm sure, but at least playing along. We continue the flyby, passing an endless parade of identical modules, all apparently untouched. Five minutes later she docks, again surprising me with her skill. Good to know I'll be able to rely on her for backup.

'Airlock secured,' Zhang says.

I float up from my seat and lower my visor. 'Seal up, everyone. Ship, we're going in.'

'Switching to imager-projection,' Lim says.

The imager icon pops up on my visor as the ring of tiny cameras in our helmets transmits the combined feed as full VR for those back on the ship.

I lead the way into a dark passage, the beam of my helmet light flanked by three thinner beams further back. Their even breathing rises and falls in my ear, almost hypnotic against the featureless background. Twenty metres in, the passage expands into a small cavity with round hatches spread evenly around. On each door, a Chinese label flares yellow with reflected light.

I float towards the biggest hatch, a red glowing seal around the edge marking it as the inner airlock. For an instant, the lever seems stuck, but then the servos kick in and the hatch swings open. I glide in first, then Yefremov and Zhang. Price comes in last and seals the door behind her.

We emerge inside a tubular passage that splits in three directions.

Zhang turns left, his light fighting a losing battle with the darkness ahead. 'The bridge is that way.'

'Meet back here in thirty minutes,' I say. 'Keep us informed, Engineer.'

Yefremov's already starting down the other passage, which leads to the cryo-modules. I turn to follow, but Price remains in place, her gaze following Zhang towards the bridge.

I blink the command to access her private channel. 'Let him go. We need to check as many modules as possible. The computer may have wrong data if the reporting systems have failed.'

Price is still hesitating. This is a test: if she disobeys, I may have a mutiny on my hands, but at least I'll know where I stand. And how much I can really count on her.

It takes another moment, but finally she moves towards me. 'Yes, sir.'

I let out a breath. No mutiny, at least not today.

We follow Yefremov down a dark passage with dust motes blinking like jewels in reflected light. Powdery flakes swirl in the air, a memory of long-gone technicians who inspected the ship back in the solar system. Ahead, the doctor is already unlocking another hatch. This one opens onto a wide corridor, with metal plating on the surface that once served as the floor. Fluorescent strips mark the positions of cryo-chamber doors, ten on each side. My heart speeds up again. Five thousand people waiting in this cold vastness. Asleep? Or...

Yefremov leads the way, his white suit gleaming ghostly in the beam of my light. He moves to a door with tall, red letters marking CRYO-CHAMBER 356.

My breath catches in my throat as the door slides open, ever so slowly. For a moment I see only Yefremov's back—and then he shifts, revealing a row of pill-shaped pods, all shining with blue cryo-fibres, all indicator lights perfectly green.

They are all right. Alive and well, waiting for us to find them a new home.

I grin, my smile reflected in the glass of Yefremov's helmet.

'This is just one module...' he says softly. 'But it's a good sign, right?'

'Definitely. It means no structural problems, or they'd all be affected.'

'I've got failure logs here.' Zhang's voice joins over the inter-com. 'Thirty-eight in total. Better than expected given how long it's been.'

Thirty-eight out of five thousand. Much better than I dared to hope.

'That's some damn good engineering,' Yefremov says with

approval.

Behind us, Price is already entering the second chamber. 'All green here as well.'

'Split up,' I say. 'Check as many modules as we can. Fingers crossed they match the failure logs.'

The doctor moves out, but my eyes linger on a small figure in the pod in front of me. A woman, her eyes closed, long hair flowing over her shoulders. So peaceful. So trusting.

I reach out my hand, stopping just short of the glass.

That's why I'm here. I can't save Anna. But I *will* save her.

I leave Price to finish the post-mission checks on the shuttle and hurry back to my office. Zhang's figures have been confirmed: only thirty-eight failed pods out of the five thousand, and *Gabriel*'s systems given a clean bill of health. This is great news. Everyone I pass is smiling, the sight so new I fail to recognise some of the faces. I round a corner and float head-on into Kowalski from Operations. Kowalski veers off, both of us flailing for purchase in zero-g, the sight of the big, bearded man cart-wheeling down the corridor sending me into giggles.

I manage to grab a handhold, struggling and failing to keep my face straight. 'Sorry!'

Kowalski laughs. 'That was fun, actually. We should do it more often.'

He pulls down his T-shirt that has rolled up on his stomach. None of the Ops team wear uniforms, probably following the reverend's lead in trying to make the ship feel homey, and Kowalski seems to have brought with him an endless supply of T-shirts. This one has a prism with a beam of light refracted into the colour spectrum—but instead of splitting, the colours emerge pleated, like a hair braid. I'm not sure what this means, but the colours are neat, so I like it.

'I'll remember that!' I laugh. 'Oh, any idea where your

boss is?'

'He was at his desk a moment ago,' Kowalski says. 'Do you want me to call him?'

'No, I'll find him.'

I'd planned to call Sanchez to my office, but this is a better idea. I nod to Kowalski and turn into the side corridor leading to the Operations section.

To manage the crew numbers, the reverend was laden with the extra duty of heading the Ops team, handling everything from the food supply to the cleaning bots. Their 'offices' are really just one room with several service stations and one partitioned space for Sanchez's personal use.

The place is empty when I arrive. Most of the screens are active, though, as if they've only just stepped out. A half-dismantled bot lies splayed on one of the workbenches. I peek into Sanchez's room: empty as well, his wall screen showing machine blueprints I don't recognise. I thought the reverend only managed the support techs—seems he's got some technical knowledge himself.

'Hope I didn't keep you waiting,' Sanchez says from the entrance, his face flushed and happy. 'We've had a spontaneous prayer meeting; everyone's so excited by the good news from *Gabriel*.'

This time it takes no effort to return his smile. 'Yes, it's better than I dared to hope. Sorry I couldn't join you.'

'No, you're not.'

I stare, and he laughs.

'No point pretending. I know back home there's some pressure to keep up appearances, but here? Personally, I'd rather have a tiny congregation of people who want to be part of it than the whole ship showing up and counting minutes. So come whenever you want, but only when you want.' He tilts his head, clearly enjoying the surprise on my face. 'Not what you expected?'

'Nope. But in a good way.'

'Awesome.'

I follow him inside the office, a fraction of the size of mine but with soundproof privacy walls. There's a desk and two chairs, unused while we're still in zero-g. Images of orange, sun-ravaged canyons hang on the wall opposite the screen. American vistas, I guess. Smaller pictures are velcroed by the side of the desk, most showing a solemn, dark-haired woman about the reverend's age. I decide not to ask who she is.

Sanchez closes the door behind us. 'One request, if I may?'

Of course, there has to be a catch. 'Go ahead.'

'I promise to be honest with you, and I ask the same in return. I do what I can for the crew, but it's getting harder. We're light years away from home. Everyone we knew is either old or dead. Hardly anybody got a message since about twenty years into the journey.'

'They didn't?'

'As far as I know.' A grimace tugs at his lips just long enough for me to wonder if the messages he's missing would have come from the woman in the pictures. 'It makes a cruel kind of sense, if you think about it. Any message our families sent would take years to catch up with the ship, and then decades languishing in the memory buffers till we reached Bethesda. Who could keep up three decades of shouting into the void?'

I nod. It does make sense. But that also means that more messages may be coming, a transmission timed to reach us after our arrival. I latch on to the hope even as I know I'm only opening myself to more disappointment and pain. Jason's message might still be making its way to me.

'We expected the communications to wane with time,' Sanchez continues. 'But it's something else to wake up to that reality. It's starting to hit them now. I don't think we've seen the full effects of it yet. When we do... it may be hard. That's why I need you to be candid with me, as much as you can. It will help me help them, especially if there's extra... stress. Either from the mission or the people.'

I look into his eyes, clear and open. I still can't bring myself to trust him, but at this moment he appears totally genuine. It's in his interest for us to succeed, both for the sake of his employer and the flock of five thousand parishioners on *Gabriel*. As long as our goals align, he'll be on my side.

'That's a fair proposal, Reverend. You can start by telling me how they're coping so far.'

Sanchez clasps his hands. 'I can tell you what I know. Of course, this will mostly be about the Americans and the other Christians. I can guess about some of the rest, but when it comes to the engineers...' He spreads his hands in surrender.

'Actually, it's the Americans I want to talk about. Especially Price and her team.'

Sanchez's brows tighten, then he flashes me another smile. 'Price is suspicious of everyone. But isn't it part of her job?'

'She's not just suspicious. She's hostile. And only towards the Chinese crew. Especially the chief engineer.'

'Do you want me to talk to her?'

I shake my head. 'No, I'll do it myself. I thought maybe you knew something that would help me understand. I mean, beyond the politics, the New Cold War, the trade war, all that crap.'

'It's not crap.'

'It's the same for the rest of us. But I don't see you picking a fight each time you see a non-believer.'

Sanchez snorts. 'So you think it's personal.'

'Yes.'

He falls silent, considering. 'There's nothing I know of. Maybe something in the captain's notes?'

'I haven't seen anything in her file.'

Sanchez hesitates. 'I don't mean the official records. But maybe...'

He stops, unsure.

'Go on, Rev. Your turn to show some trust.'

For the first time since I met him, Sanchez doesn't smile. He glances away from me, the corners of his mouth twitching. His index finger taps the top of his clasped hand once, then again. 'I only met the captain once, briefly, in a private meeting just before our departure. He knew things about me... things that were never in my files.' He meets my eye again. A smile fights its way back to his lips but dies halfway. 'He obviously took serious interest in his crew. Maybe he left, I don't know, notes?'

This time I look away. The disappearing link, the strange CCM file that wasn't there. Could that have been it? Hidden behind some encryption that Lim can't crack?

I steeple my fingers, trying not to look shaken. If the captain knew so much about the reverend, what did he know about me? 'I haven't found any notes. But then, I never searched beyond the official files. I'll have another look.'

'Let me know what you find,' Sanchez says, smiling again.

'I will.' The lie comes out smooth as truth. 'Thank you for your help.'

'Of course.'

I start for the door, then stop for another question. 'Has the crew voted on the multi-faith service?'

'Wednesday.' The reverend grimaces, but it's playful rather than disappointed. 'I'm not sure if it's a real preference or just a way to spite me. Well, they'd better show up or I'm changing it back to Sundays.'

He laughs and I join in. It's easy to laugh with him, his voice soft and his smile as warm as a woollen blanket. And yet I can't shake the feeling that this, too, is a tool, finely tuned and precise, like a snake charmer's flute hypnotising me into submission.

But he's given me a new clue, and for this I'm grateful. If the CCM file exists, I must find it. And there's one place I haven't looked: the captain's cabin.

CHAPTER 7

I lean back in my office chair, luxuriating in the feeling of my weight against the soft surface. We transferred into the parking orbit overnight and split the ship this morning: the main deck and the engine section are now on opposite ends of an extended tether, slowly rotating around the midpoint. The resulting 'gravity' is a modest half-g, but it's enough to keep us firmly on the ground. Even Yefremov has stopped complaining.

Price sits on the other side of the table, doing her best not to look annoyed. She must know why I've asked her to stay after the briefing.

I let the silence linger. I may have never been a commander, but I grew up having to read people to anticipate their reactions. Back when it was just Anna and me, alone in the Feidi.

Price stirs, uncomfortable. 'So, what is it you wanted to talk about?'

I smile. 'You. I want to understand you better. In particular, why you hate our Chinese crew so much.'

She snorts. 'Other than the obvious?'

'Yes. There's international politics and national pride, but you knew that when you took this job. You chose to be on this team. And it includes them.'

'Not like there was another option...'

She avoids my glance, her movements cagey and her breathing faster.

'Talk to me, Amy. We're on the same side.'

Her brows rise as if she wants to challenge this notion, but she thinks better of it. 'Have you ever worked for the Chinese?'

'Indirectly, yes. But that's probably true for everyone.' We share a knowing shrug. It's impossible to work in space and not work for a Chinese employer, given their dominance of the sector. 'I did a stint at Solar Explorer, but most of my career has been with Orbital Logistics.'

'Did you do the Europa run?'

Her wide-eyed admiration makes me smile. 'Three times. But really, orbital flying is way trickier.'

'I wanted to go, you know?' Price says, then snorts, embarrassed at the confession. 'Anyway, it didn't work out.'

I pause for a moment, watching her usual swagger return like a defensive shield. 'Have *you* worked for a Chinese company?'

She barks a sharp laugh. 'Yeah. Yeah, I have. And it sucked. Nothing was ever good enough, no matter how I tried. I was just this tool they could push around, like I wasn't even a person.' She clicks her tongue, her mouth downturned as if tasting something bitter. 'It wasn't even that I was American, you know. More like we weren't the same species.'

'We aren't. But that has nothing to do with them being Chinese.'

She cocks her head. 'What, then?'

'For the likes of the people we work for—Chinese, American, or other—to even register as a person, you need to reach a certain numerical value. It's not about your citizenship, it's about the number of zeros in your bank account.'

Price snorts. 'The only zeros in my account come in front of the numbers... But no—I get what you're saying, but it's not just the rich. The way they carry themselves? It's like they deserve everything that they have. Like it was something they did, not just dumb luck that the Two Horsemen went easy on them.'

The Two Horsemen, the almost-Apocalypse.

I don't know if it was luck or foresight that allowed China to emerge the least damaged. My teachers claimed it was due to superior technology and proofing their agriculture against climate change—but that was a Chinese school, back in the Feidi. I'm sure the Americans have their own version of the events, probably depicting China as the source of their woes. The two nations have been at loggerheads for longer than I remembered or cared, each seeing the other as a threat to their existence.

'Honestly, Amy, would Americans be any different if it was you who came out ahead?'

Price opens her mouth in denial but changes her mind. 'All I know is that it's not right. Not a way to treat people.'

'I won't argue with that. Still, I've got a feeling more's going on here. Because you don't just dislike the Chinese crew. You have a personal target.'

She shrugs, then looks at her hands, avoiding my glance. 'I don't trust him.'

'I know that. What I don't know is why.'

Price shuffles her feet, more uncertain than I've ever seen her. I wait, holding back my frustration, careful not to scare her off. I may finally be getting somewhere.

She swallows and looks behind me as if searching for support from the walls. 'I just don't.'

'You're a professional. You don't make decisions that can impact the mission because you don't like someone. You have a reason. And I need to know what it is. I may see things you miss.'

She grimaces, her lips downturned as she nods to herself. This must be something she's considered before. Her fists clench and unclench, and then she makes up her mind and looks up at me, determined. 'There's no proof. And nothing concrete. But just before we left, Williamson, the top boss, he called me for a personal briefing. He said, and these are his words, "There's something fishy about Zhang's resume." He couldn't find a problem with it, at least nothing he could take up with the Chinese company, but he said some things didn't add up. So he told me to keep an eye on him. He said the captain knew, but he wanted me in on it, just in case.'

She pauses, watching my reaction. I stare back at her, my mouth half-open.

'Exactly,' she says. 'The next thing we know, the captain's dead. Coincidence? I don't think so.'

I shake my head, my mind racing. Not a coincidence. Sabotage. Did Price leave me the message? Unlikely, or she wouldn't be so hesitant speaking to me now.

But why would anyone sabotage this ship? Or hide files from commanding officers? The answer must be on Bethesda. What does Zhang know about it that the rest of us don't?

I look away, struggling to focus. I'm a pilot, not a detective. Flight instruments don't have agendas. When you're in shit, they tell you how deep. Sometimes I wish people had gauges.

Price is watching me, a trace of remorse on her face. 'I probably should have told you earlier.'

'A hint would have been useful.' I pause, studying her reaction. 'Especially if you suspected sabotage...'

Price nods, her expression guilty or embarrassed—but only that. 'Yeah. But I didn't...'

'You didn't know if you could trust me. Fair enough. I'm glad you do now, though.'

I keep her gaze, and she nods. 'Yeah. Sorry.'

'It's done. But now you need to do something for me. Two things, actually.'

She leans forward, eager again. 'What?'

'First, back off Zhang. I don't mean stop watching him—I mean, don't let him see we're on to him. If he's really up to something, you'll only make him go deeper. He's smart and he's got access to the parts of the ship where you or I can't go. Whatever he's up to—*if* he's up to anything—you don't want to force his hand. So ease off. Let him feel safe. In the meantime, we'll both be watching him very carefully. But with a friendly smile.'

Half of her mouth twists in a smirk. 'Not my strongest side. The friendly smile, I mean.'

'I'm sure you can manage.'

'Deal. What's the other thing you want?'

'This one's easy: I want to check the captain's cabin. And his personal effects.'

'Right. Of course.'

Her gaze slides past me, not exactly guilty but not innocent either—she's scoured the place already but doesn't want to admit it.

The deceased captain's cabin is officially under security lock, but that wouldn't have stopped her. It wouldn't have stopped me, except she'd get notified and I'd march right onto her 'suspicious' list.

'What are you looking for? Something on Zhang?'

I hesitate. She could be my best ally—she already knows that something's not right on the ship. And then there's that file. It could still be somewhere in the security cache, where she might be able to find it.

Unless it's hidden from me, and she's the one hiding it. Because why else would the computer need to 'configure content' when I inputted my codes?

The possibilities shift around me like quicksand, each move bringing more questions. If Williamson was suspicious, why was Price the only one he called? Why not mention anything to me, the second in command?

I can't trust anyone. Not Lim, and not Price. I'm alone in this mess, and that's only fair. I'm not going to drag anyone with me, not this time. This is my penance.

I look her in the eye, decided. 'Yes. The captain was Chinese. There's a small chance he knew something that he didn't share with Williamson, out of loyalty.'

She tilts her head, sceptical at first, but my mention of Chinese loyalty does the trick. Price taps the table with both hands and gets on her feet. 'Let's do it.'

We walk in silence down the corridors leading to the quarters area. It's empty at this time, almost everyone still busy with the post-split checks. Annoyingly, though, the people we're most likely to encounter are the engineers; the same route leads to the tether elevator that now links the main deck and the engine section. No way around it, though; we just have to hope for the best.

No such luck. We're approaching the captain's cabin, the outermost in the cluster of crew quarters, when Yau Po Li appears on the other side of the corridor, hurrying towards the bridge. The engineer bobs her head as she sees us; her features are a mix of Asian and white, her face heart-shaped, with sharp, angled brows and a pointy chin. Her eyes are a striking grey; a matching silver-grey streak runs through the middle of her hair, shaved bald at the temples.

At my side, Price tenses. I feel her hesitate, wanting to continue down the tether corridor, but that's a bad idea. The tether leads only to the engines, and we have no business going there. Instead, I turn into the side passage, heading towards my own cabin. Price follows in silence till the sound of Yau's steps retreats into the distance.

'Coincidence?' Price whispers as we turn back.

I know what she's thinking. With the field team gone, there are only three engineers left on board. What are the chances we'd run into one at that very moment?

'She was just passing.' I try to sound confident. 'They'd do a better job if they really wanted to spy on us.'

Price grunts, a noise I hope means agreement. She enters the code for the captain's door, and we slide in—but not before glancing up and down the corridor again. Empty.

The captain's cabin is double the size of mine, with shape-shifting furniture that can convert it to a bedroom, a study, or a reception room with a sofa and a coffee table. The air smells of dust, even though I'm sure the cleaning bots still have the place in their roster.

'Where do you want to start?' Price asks.

'His personal items. His wan-kong, his zheping, even—'

'His what?'

We stare at each other, me surprised, she angry, or maybe... offended?

I point to her wan-kong. 'What do you call this?'

'It's a wrist-pad. And this—' She pulls out a zheping from her chest pocket. 'This is a... pad. Or a screen. We have English words for that.'

Oh, that's it. National pride, even here.

I shrug. 'I grew up in Tian-ti Feidi. Also, this tech is Chinese. And the names are better.'

Price steps back, unhappy. I consider reminding her that I'm Canadian and that my father was French speaking, but it's probably a bad idea.

'These are just words, Amy. They all come from some-where.' I gesture to the desk and a transparent container half-filled with just the items I mentioned. 'I'll start with these. Is there anything else?'

She points to an identical container on the floor next to the wardrobe. 'His clothes are there.'

'Go through them. And then check the shelves. And any corners that look like good hiding spots.'

Price doesn't look convinced, but I turn away, back to the box on the desk. Piled on top lie three image frames. The screens light up at my touch. The dead captain stares right at me, from a rock garden, from a mountaintop, in the embrace of a young woman. Daughter? Wife? Whoever she was, she got left behind when he accepted the post. Was he following some inescapable orders? Or running away from something even worse?

The image of the charred pods flashes under my eyelids. I glance at the pictures again, then try to remember the man: short, with a stiff bearing but a warm smile. Someone who'd go to hell for you if you were on his side but stab you in the back if you weren't. I only met him once for a short chat, and then again just before departure. I don't think he even spoke to me then. I certainly did my best to avoid talking to anyone. Everything was still so fresh then: the deaths, my guilt, my exile. Most of what I recall is a blur of faces and empty smiles.

Damn. This box is full of ghosts.

I blink the memories away. Underneath the frames sits a jet-black zheping embossed with Mandarin markings. The first symbols are the captain's name, Chen Xin, then something meaning 'private'.

'Zhang said it was a personal journal,' Price says from behind my back. Of course she's watching.

'He came here?'

'Yes, he tagged along when the rev and I moved the captain's stuff from the office. When you were still in the medical. I couldn't refuse; he's the most senior Chinese officer left, so...' She shrugs, then her mouth twists with distaste. 'I made sure I watched him, but there's no guarantee he didn't swipe anything small, like a file chip.' She points to the zheping. 'He wanted to take it, supposedly "out of respect", but I didn't let him.'

I unfold the pad to its medium size. The screen lights up with a Mandarin inscription I recognise: a password request.

'I never managed to crack it,' Price says. 'But I doubt that'd be helpful. He'd have learned to keep secrets in his military years. I was surprised he even had a journal.'

'He was ex-military?'

'Oh, yeah. A decorated hero or something. Fell out of grace after he retired and started taking corporate jobs. Or so the rumour had it.'

This may be a coincidence. Not the first soldier I'd met, though most of them worked security. And I can't fathom a reason why Chinese military might have any interest in Bethesda. Still, something about the fact makes the back of my neck prickle. Too many questions about this mission, too many coincidences.

I return to the box. The remaining contents are models: stealth aircraft of outdated design, a naval vessel, an orbital transporter, all Chinese. They look handmade, like something one does for a hobby. I take them out one by one. They seem solid, not a cavity or a gap to hide anything. This is useless.

I throw the models back in the box, then the frames. 'Any luck?'

'Nothing here,' Price says in an I-told-you-so voice.

I glance around the room, at the meagre leftovers from what was once someone's life. 'Was there nothing else here?'

'Nope. Unless Zhang swiped it. But it'd have been small, or I'd have noticed.'

If Zhang took it, then he'll never admit it—and I'll never find it, not without access to the engine section. The journal is my only hope. The CCM file won't be there, not in the personal diary of a former officer, but if I can get a clue of what it might have been, that's a step forward.

I slide the black zheping into my pocket. Price says nothing, even though I'm breaking a dozen regulations. We walk out of the cabin and seal the door behind us.

I'm following crumbs, not even knowing what it is that I'm trying to find. But tomorrow, I'll get a big chunk. Tomorrow, the field team arrives on Bethesda.

CHAPTER 8

The airlock fills with the white haze of the bio-cleansers, then lights up in eerie blue as UV lamps cut through the mist, irradiating the last earthy microbes off the field team's yellow ground suits. I watch them wait patiently, their faces calm behind the glass of their helmets. My own breath sounds uncomfortably loud under the VR hood, but at least in my chair back on the bridge, I'm not hindered by the bulk of the suit or the weight of the oxygen tanks. And yet the experience feels disturbingly real, down to the tingling of my skin as I imagine drops of decontaminants sliding down my arms. I *know* it's an illusion, that I'm in a VR compiled from the imager-rings in all the helmets—and yet, as my hand moves to rub my forearm, I wince when my fingers meet warm skin, not the cold, slippery fabric of a ground suit.

The light over the airlock door blinks green, and we move out, trailing single file onto the planet surface. Pebbles crunch underfoot, the sound eerily familiar, like walking on a rocky beach. Thick clouds loom in silver and grey, giving the light a stark blue tinge. Soft gravel covers the ground, in places giving way to bare rock. If not for the total absence of vegetation, this could be Earth. It could be Canada, I realise, or at least what the north looked like after the polar ice had melted but before new plant life managed to get a foothold. The flat, open landscape radiates a primal sort of beauty, like a fire waiting to be lit. The only thing missing is oxygen—but atmospheric content doesn't show up in pictures. No wonder the colonists found the place attractive.

We're only a hundred metres from the southern edge of the settlement, which from here looks larger and more spread out than from the drones' perspective. To the left, I can just glimpse the greenhouse triangles, their solar-glass gleaming in opalescent blue against the grey horizon. To the right, the ever-growing walls of the dome peek above the furthest of the modules. The future that never happened.

I move my head, and the image shifts with perfect smoothness. Four people walk behind me. Beyond them, the base-tent shimmers with the teal of solar-fabric, a flexible if less efficient version of the solar-glass. The puffed-up walls make me think of an air mattress, the entire structure supported as much by overpressure as by the expandable spars of the tent's skeleton. It took the field team five hours to transport the cargo to the site, seven kilometres north of the elevator, and another seven to set up the first stage of the base: the outside walls and the airlocks and filters. They got six hours of rest afterwards, sleeping under blankets on the floor. Yefremov grumbled that I didn't let them sleep longer, but the planetary clock was against us. We have three hours of daylight left, and nobody, not even them, wants to wait another day.

I shift my perspective to the front of the group, the transition momentarily dizzying, but I've played enough sim-games to learn to adjust to the speed-of-thought quality of movement. The first modules are only fifty metres away, the grey walls both familiar and incongruous in the barren landscape.

'We split up here.' Johansson's name pops up in my field of

vision as he speaks. The biologist is the field team's leader. 'Ship, equipment check.'

'We have you all on trackers,' Lim says.

'Life support in the green,' Wang says.

Johansson gestures towards the lake. 'Greenhouse party with me.'

He sets off, followed by two others, their yellow suits banded with coloured stripes over arms and chests: blue for the science team, maroon for engineering, black for security. The names appear as I focus on the figures: Johansson in the lead, trailed by Sheng Jing and Michael Lee.

I stay with the main group, continuing towards the settlement. A tall figure with black bands on his suit takes the point: Moses Miller, Price's deputy. He pauses to indicate something on the ground: a line made of dark stones or pebbles, too regular to be a work of nature.

'City limits?' a female voice asks. Pat Berry, the planetologist.

'Some kind of demarcation, that's for sure,' Miller says. 'It seems to be going around the settlement. On this side at least.'

'Collect a sample for analysis,' Khan says from the lab. 'On your way back.'

We move on, over the 'border' and towards the first of the habitat modules. Up close, the walls are pale with dust and streaked by decades of rainfall. Tall, narrow windows look like arrow slits in some old castle. Miller presses his helmet against the glass. I jump across to the view from his imager but see nothing but the man's blurred reflection.

'One-way glass,' he says. 'Can't see anything inside.'

He runs his hand over the wall. Powdery dust falls under his touch, revealing a darker surface beneath: a layer of solar scales that harvest energy for each module. 'Doesn't seem to have any power, either.'

'Let me try,' a soft voice says. Wu Xiao, according to the name tag.

The engineer presses their hand against the wall, then pulls it back. A faint contour of their glove glows weakly for the shortest of moments before fading to grey.

I gasp. It's still working, after four decades of neglect. 'Is it still providing power?'

'Not enough to maintain the module,' Zhang says. 'But if all the habitat modules are like this, the combined power would be enough to support the hub. They could survive in there.'

So the colony may still be habitable, even now. The implications make my skin prickle. Because if everything worked, if it wasn't some giant technical failure, then what the hell did happen?

The team moves on, deeper into the maze of grey blocks laid out in even rows over the stony ground. Tall white numbers stencilled on the sides peek out from under layers of dust. Two-metre-wide corrugated tunnels snake between the modules, connecting them to the circular artery that surrounds the inner core of the settlement. This is just one of the three habitat zones, each consisting of almost two hundred modules. I've seen the layout in the plans and then again during the drones' flyover —but both failed to impart the true sense of scale. Now that we're deep inside, the modules are all we can see, spreading in every direction like a stone gallery. Dreary monotony has replaced the promise of the open landscape, the mood heavier with every step. Gravel crunches under our feet, the sound echoing in the spaces between the modules where the wind sweeps up grey dust like ashes.

But then, this is not the space the colonists inhabited. Their lives were confined to the insides of these dreary blocks, and the tubular corridors connecting them like the guts of a living organism. I shudder, my breathing accelerating with sudden claustrophobia. And yet, here I am, inside a metal tub of a spaceship much smaller than this colony. You can get used to anything, I guess.

'We're at the first greenhouse,' Johansson's voice says. 'From here, it looks intact. We're going inside.'

I switch the feed to Johansson's team. The image is less responsive, the composite made from only three sets of imager rings, but it's still good enough to lose myself in after only a moment. I'm in an airlock surprisingly similar to the one on the base-tent. A thick layer of dust covers all surfaces, peeling off to descend in swirling eddies as the air-scrubbers kick in. I wait for the puff of the bio-cleansers, but it doesn't come. Yet the light over the airlock door flashes orange, then settles into green.

'Decontaminant spray appears to be disabled,' Johansson says.

Sheng Jing presses her hand—the bionic hand in a specially adapted gauntlet—to the airlock panel. 'No error code. Power levels sufficient. This is not a malfunction but a change in programming.'

'This wasn't mentioned in the reports, but I'm not entirely surprised,' Khan says. 'Local proto-life is inert. They probably just gave up.'

'Commander, we need your authorisation to enter,' Michael Lee says.

They cleaned off any terrestrial microbes when leaving the base. And the greenhouses are self-contained. Even if we contaminate one, the others won't be affected.

I tap my console to log the request. 'Affirmative.'

'Okay, then,' Johansson says. 'We're going in.'

He pushes the airlock handle, and the door swings open. The three of us—of them—slide inside. The picture fogs momentarily as humidity condenses on the imagers' lenses, then clears out again.

'Whoa!' Lee cries.

We are inside a jungle, green and lush, with vegetation

cascading down tall rows of racks in leafy waterfalls. Water trickles softly somewhere out of sight; the fans hum, the foliage rustling in the gentle wind.

Johansson picks his way inside, under a canopy of vines with branches as thick as my arm. He tries to avoid stepping on the plants, but it's impossible. His feet sink into the carpet of large, star-shaped leaves. Something crunches under his boot, and he bends down to fish out a vaguely familiar shape: long, green, and dripping with juice.

'Cucumber sandwich, anyone?'

'How could it all have survived?' I ask. I know the technical answer, but it doesn't seem sufficient, or maybe somehow inadequate, or unjust. How could this life go on when the people who planted it have vanished?

'It's a closed biosphere,' Khan answers, missing the point. 'Water and nutrients are recycled, nothing escapes. In theory, it can last forever. Or as long as the automation works, both the feeding and the pollinator drones.'

'The solar surfaces here were designed to be self-cleaning,' Zhang says. 'Too expensive for all the modules, but the greenhouses were a priority.'

I know all that. I've read the files, even the science briefing. And still, I don't understand. I cradle my wrist, the dull pain returning like a memory. 'What could have happened to them? They had food. Everything works. Then—what?'

Silence. The sound of water and leaves crunching under heavy boots are my only answer.

'The system reports seventy-seven per cent efficiency,' Sheng says after a moment. 'Some filters have failed, but it's far from critical. I'm downloading the logs. The last maintenance report is dated 22 April 2304.'

About the time of the last transmission. That at least makes sense. Something catastrophic must have happened soon after. The central logs may give us a clue. And if we're lucky, there will be personal records as well. Those people didn't just disappear.

'I'm collecting vegetation and microbial samples—' Johansson's voice cuts off as I switch the feed again, back to the settlement.

Miller's group has passed through the habitat and has now reached one of the 'nodes': airlock stations along the central artery that served as transit points between the settlement and the surface. Just like the modules, the solar fabric covering the nodes has lost most of its lustre. Still, the lights blink in response when Miller punches the open icon.

They file inside, and Wu seals the hatch behind them. Dust rises as the pumps engage in a triple cycle of blowing and sucking to dislodge and remove all dust. The last cycle replaces the outside atmosphere with the breathable air inside the base, and then the light on the inner door turns green.

'Decontaminant spray hasn't activated,' Miller says.

'Could be a malfunction,' Wu starts, but Zhang cuts in.

'Most likely it's disabled. That's what they did in the greenhouse.'

I hesitate. Unlike the greenhouses, the settlement is connected into one large network. If we contaminate this passage, we'll contaminate the entire base.

'Wu, is this something you can check from inside the airlock?' I ask. 'If they disabled it themselves, fine, but otherwise we need to restore the cleansers before we enter.'

'We needn't worry,' Khan says. 'There's really nothing to decontaminate here. Nothing the team could have come into contact with on the surface is either toxic or biologically active.'

'At this stage, we shouldn't take anything for granted,' Yefremov says. He's behind me on the bridge, but his voice arrives through my earphones so Khan can hear him, too.

Her answer comes in slowly and with a dry edge, as if she's struggling for patience. 'You misunderstand. I'm not making assumptions. I'm relating facts. I've reviewed all the studies, both from the early probes and from the colonists. Their methodology was sound, and the results are clear. Nothing here can damage or in any way influence human biology, or any biology of terrestrial origin.'

I haven't yet figured out the deal between these two, but I've got no patience for it now. Luckily, Zhang saves me the trouble.

'Commander, it's not a malfunction. We've confirmed that the decontamination system was disabled by the colonists.'

I tip my head to thank him. 'Field team, you are clear to enter the settlement.'

'Acknowledged,' Miller answers.

He swings the inner door open and leads the way into a dim passage. The tunnels looked spacious from the ground side—from inside, they are stifling. The walls would have once provided day-like illumination, but by now the solar fabric has weakened and most light cells have burned out. All that's left is sickly bluish luminescence that makes the dust look silver. A fine layer covers the floor, the powder rising ahead of the team as their footsteps send vibrations through the structure.

'Air composition nominal,' Wu says. 'Low on CO_2, but within parameters.'

Miller raises his hand, and we stop. He points to something on the ground. Footprints. Barely visible, and yet unmistakable. I zoom in for a better view. Most are traces of boots, large and small, but at least one trail, spread out in large bouts of someone running, is barefoot.

'Not that unusual,' Yefremov offers after a moment's silence. 'This was their home. After seven years, they'd think nothing of running around barefoot.'

'Yeah,' I say without conviction. 'It's possible.'

'I'm more worried by the dust itself,' Zhang says. 'It's bad for the equipment, and they knew it.'

Exactly. They'd have had utmost respect for their equipment drilled into them. Without it, they'd all die.

'Look!' Miller drops to his knees, his helmet camera on maximum zoom, following a trail of black drops.

My fingers dig into the armrests. 'Put your headlight on.'

Miller's arm moves, and an instant later a soft yellow beam illuminates the floor. And the drops aren't quite black anymore. They are rusty brown.

'Spokoino,' Yefremov whispers. *Easy.*

'Is it...?' Miller asks, even his voice shaky.

Gonzales, the medical scientist, kneels beside him. 'I won't know till I test it. But yeah, it looks like dried blood.'

My heart pounding, I watch Gonzales and Raji, the pathologist, scoop up a sample of the brown substance into a small vial. They collect another of the 'drops', and then more samples of just the dust, some loose and some from under the footprints. They work in silence, their teammates watching with lowered heads, expressions unreadable inside the helmets. Up here on the bridge, nobody speaks either, even though I'm sure all our minds must be racing.

Gonzales deposits the vials into a sample bag, and they resume their trek, shuffling down the tube in heavy silence. It takes them almost ten minutes to cross five internal bulkheads and reach the hub: a block of twelve over-sized modules that make up the nucleus of the colony, housing its computers, labs, and the medical centre.

'Approaching the ops room,' Miller says.

He rests his hand against the door, and it sways under his touch. Unsecured, as if the place had been abandoned in haste. I feel him hesitate before he pushes it open. The hinges rasp when he finally does. I hold my breath.

The first thing I see is a console ripped from its base, severed wires jutting out like hurricane-torn branches. Dusty chairs form a heap across the central aisle; more lie piled up against the walls. Another console looks like someone tried to pull it apart: the frame hanging on loose screws, the insides strewn across the floor. Scraps that look like fabric, grey with dirt and age, flutter in the gust of air from the opening door. Something round, a cup or a bowl, rattles as it rolls to join a pile of tarnished dishes and tools.

The pressure in my stomach grows heavier. Around me, everyone is deathly silent. This is worse than I imagined. This equipment kept them alive. What in the universe could have made them neglect it, or worse, wilfully destroy it?

'One hour to end of daylight.' Wang's voice sounds like it's coming from the bottom of a well. 'And we have rain moving in from the east.'

I swallow, if only to give myself a moment to shake off the shock. 'Get as much data as you can. You need to be out of there in thirty minutes.'

The engineer is the first to move, heading to the wall of computer equipment at the far end of the room. The two medics disappear into a partitioned office on the left; Miller and the scientists scatter among the consoles, looking for terminals they can access.

I check a sub-screen on the greenhouse team: still gathering samples of vegetation and slime accumulated at the bottom of the hydroponic containers. I'll give them ten minutes and then they, too, need to be on their way.

I signal to Lim to cut the outgoing transmission, then take off my VR hood. My hands are shaking, the pain in my wrist like a constant reminder of everything that can go wrong.

'Any ideas?' I ask as soon as Lim confirms that the field team can't hear us.

'Too early to say,' Khan answers immediately, too quickly for her words to be anything but nerves.

'I don't like any of this.' Price steps towards me, her hands bunched into fists. 'They wouldn't let things deteriorate like that. And it doesn't look like an accident, either.'

I nod in agreement. Those consoles didn't just rip themselves out. 'What would make them do it?'

'Botched-up repairs?' Sanchez tries. 'Like, if something happened to the technicians and the replacements didn't know what to do?'

'This doesn't look like any repair I've seen,' Yefremov says. 'More like wilful destruction.'

'What would make them turn on their equipment?' Lim asks. Her voice is shaking.

I look at the chairs piled up across the central aisle, the ripped-out console next to them, blocking the way. It's not random destruction. It's a barricade.

'Nothing malfunctioned,' Price says slowly. 'No natural disaster. No external threat that we can see. And yet this looks like defences. Which leaves only one option: they were attacked.'

'By whom?' Yefremov asks.

I can't let her answer—because there's only one possibility, and I don't even want to think it, let alone say it out loud.

They were the only ones here. The attack, if it really was an attack, had to come from within.

'We don't yet fully understand the environmental factors,' Zhang says.

Price snorts loudly.

Damn. It was a mistake to ask them. I've let emotions get the better of me, let myself hope they'd refute my suspicions. I should have known better.

I shoot her a hard stare, leaning forward as if that could add weight to my words. 'I agree. It's too early for conclusions.'

'I can say one thing—' Yefremov's voice cracks under forced joviality. 'Myself, I'd go stir-crazy cooped up in that place. I know they were selected for psych-strength, but after all that time I wouldn't put anything past them.'

'I'm in the system,' Wu says from the surface. 'Downloading available logs.'

I signal to Lim to re-establish the link. 'Can you see the date of the last report?'

'Not while we're downloading. We don't want to stress the system—I'm siphoning as much data as I can get in one go.'

I pull my visor down and shift my view to the engineer's position at the end of an extended console, mostly dark except for a couple of indicators blinking faintly. I can't tell if it's because it has so little power, or if Wu chose not to turn everything on at this time.

'The rain's moving in fast,' Wang says.

I check the time. Half an hour to sunset, and it'll be even darker in the rain. 'You need to be on your way out in five minutes.'

'We're good at this end,' Johansson says. 'Proceeding to the airlock.'

'We need more time...' someone grumbles. Gonzales, one of the medics.

'That's not up for discussion,' I say. 'Miller?'

'I'll get them out.'

'Go straight to base. And make sure everyone follows the decontamination protocol to the letter.'

'Yes, sir,' Miller says in the tone that means, *Do you think I'm stupid?*

I make a mental note to thank Price for insisting on sending her people. Someone has to make sure they follow orders.

They're still grumbling as Miller shepherds them towards the exit five minutes later, but it's more out of principle than conviction. Not even the scientists would be reckless enough to make that walk in the dark. Especially not after what we've just seen.

I watch them move into the airlock, and then out of the node, into the fading light of an alien sunset. Only three hours earlier I thought it looked inviting—now the shadows feel razor-sharp and the low clouds stifling. I suck in air, every oxygen molecule precious. This planet is a trap. A lure that turned into a snare and killed them all.

Except... Except it wasn't the planet that killed them, was it? They were the only ones here. Something made them turn to violence, neighbour against neighbour.

I shiver, my mind drowning in questions, each more terrifying than the next. But then one pushes itself to the forefront: if they're all dead, where are the bodies?

CHAPTER -2

6 WEEKS BEFORE DEPARTURE

Down the length of Soko Street, a police cordon futilely tries to manage the flow of hungry-eyed visitors, each with a bulky backpack or a motorised cart filled with the day's spoils. I've forgotten it's kai gou ri, the one day each month when Kenyans from outside the Feidi are allowed to enter the enclave. They come in ever-increasing numbers—whole families clutching their ration cards, faces rapt as if they've found paradise. No wonder, given the state of the rest of the continent. At least here nobody's starving.

I push past a man with two sacks of grain under his arms and a triumphant grin on his face. Several women try to jump the barrier, desperate to reach another market before closing time. I stick to the wall as the police attempt to pull them back in. This is a bad day to be out here—but I cannot wait, not even a day. I look up, searching for the dim holo of The Two Horsemen above the rooftops. Just three more blocks.

The Two Horsemen is one of the bars lost in the liminal place between the business district and the Lower City. I scan the dim interior: fibre chairs and tables of the style that was all the rage a decade ago. A blue-lit bar with a good collection of bottles. The clientele is a mix of better-off Caucasians and Africans, Asians without the right citizenship, and the sprinkling of Chinese teenagers slumming it with home-brew and rationed food while their bodyguards sip lemonade in the corner.

But no trace of the familiar pencil moustache.

My stomach tightens. Maybe he's not here. He could be back on duty, or realised today is kai gou ri and stayed clear of the city. All I have is his name and no other way to find him.

Then a figure bent over the bar turns—and I recognise Jo, the moustache unmistakable but his silhouette transformed now that he's out of the yellow uniform.

He grins as I approach, but then his brows dip into a frown. 'What happened?'

'Is it so obvious?'

'Well, no offence, but you look like you haven't slept since we last met.'

This may be true—or it certainly feels like it.

I plonk myself on a stool next to him. 'I need a drink.'

Jo signals to the barman, a middle-aged, bald man with the thickest arms I've ever seen. The man nods, already busy with the bottle.

'What is it?' Jo says. His face is earnest, not a trace of the fake confidence he put on during our first encounter.

I stare at the line of empty beer bottles behind the bar. No rationing for alcohol. Drink more, talk less. Think less.

My lips tremble and I bite into them. If I start to speak now, I'll just burst out crying, so I say nothing, and Jo doesn't press.

A glass of mnazi arrives in front of me, filled to the brim with the cloudy-white coconut wine. The smell is insultingly cheerful, loaded with memories of long evenings spent with stories and hopes. I snatch the glass and drink in big gulps till a hand lands on my arm, pulling it down.

'Easy,' Jo says. 'Or do you want me to carry you home?'

He winks flirtatiously, but his eyes are full of worry. I'm almost apologetic—but he's the first one, the only one, I don't need to be strong for. I put on the act for Anna and for Stepan; they need it to keep going. Here, all I have to lose is my pride. To hell with it.

I rub my eyes. Suck in a deep breath. And still, I can't meet his eyes. 'My sister... she's dying. And so is the baby.'

Jo swears under his breath. 'So many people are ill. Many more than they admit on the news. And they still claim it's no plague.'

They will recover soon enough, if Huang and the other doctors are right. Unlike Anna. 'We can still save her with the right meds. But I can't get them here. Canada's even worse. And we don't have any other pass.'

'It's the same everywhere. I think by now only China's got stock.' Jo's brows rise in a question. 'Have you...?'

'No chance. I went to the visa office... I couldn't not try, you know? They gave me an appointment for "first hearing" in ten months.' I laugh, the sound sharp and painful.

'I'm sorry.' Jo waves over the barman to refill our glasses. 'I wish there was something I could do.'

I straighten. I've got to try. 'Actually, maybe there *is*.'

He cocks his head, eyes widening in surprise—no, not surprise, something more like apprehension. 'Tell me.'

'I know for a fact that regular shipments of meds arrive in the Feidi. But then they go straight up the elevator to be sold for a hundred-fold in the Yun Ju.'

Jo nods, his expression tentative. 'Yeah, I've heard rumours. It sounds like something they'd do. But if you think I could somehow... because I work in the Tian-ti...'

I tip my head, too breathless to speak.

'Sorry, no way. I don't have access to the cargo side. And they keep it under guard twenty-four-seven.'

I don't let my disappointment show. Of course, they'd have

it under guard, and probably accounted down to a single pill. The Feidi's no Wild West, but the scarcity riots never quite went away, either.

'What I need is information. My boss, up in the Yun Ju, he's a friend. He's been trying to buy the meds for me, but nobody will talk to him. He's not one of them; too many levels below the yun-ying, Chinese or American. But he has contacts in other logistics companies. If he knew who handled the shipments, he could go straight to them.'

I take a sip from the new glass that's arrived in front of me, my eyes on Jo as he rubs his chin, lost in thought.

'I can't get that info myself, but maybe...' He trails off, considering.

I shift to the edge of my seat, not daring to breathe. 'Please, Jo. I don't know what else to do. We can pay...'

He waves the offer away. 'Don't worry about that. Binamu, my cousin, she works in tech support at the Yun Ju. I don't know if she's got access to shipping data, but she's really good at getting into places.' He nods, a spark returning to his eyes. 'Leave it with me. I'll see what I can do.'

I should ask him if it's dangerous, if his cousin could get into trouble—but all I can think of is Anna and the baby. No trouble could eclipse their lives. My voice quivers. 'When... when can you—'

'In two days. She's coming down for her mother's birthday; I'll talk to her then.'

Two days. It seems like an eternity. 'Could you—'

'I must talk to her in person. She'll need some persuading, and anyway, it's not something I can say over a call.'

'In two days,' I say, and try to smile.

Anna strokes Jason's head, her movements laboured, her chest heaving with the effort of breathing. And yet, when it's time to leave, neither of them wants to let go. Jason digs his fingers into her gaunt frame while Anna keeps kissing his forehead as if each kiss will be the last.

I swallow, my voice stiff and metallic. 'Not long now, I promise. We have a plan. Just a couple of days. I promise.'

Anna doesn't look up. She plants another kiss on Jason's forehead, a tear sliding down her cheek. 'I believe you.'

I snatch my wan-kong on the first ring. 'Logan?'

The face staring back at me is two shades paler than Logan has ever been. His eyes are bloodshot and wide with panic. I don't think he's shaved or showered. 'I'm sorry.'

I feel my mouth open, but no sound comes.

'I tried. I think I got to the right distributor.' Logan breaks off. He wipes his nose with the back of his hand. He looks shell-shocked. 'But then I got a visit. In my office. Three guys who... They...'

'Are you hurt?' I hear myself ask.

'No. Not this time. But they said next time they'll come see me at home.' He shakes his head. Pulls in a slow breath. 'I can't, Nat. I've got family. They didn't look like they'd offer another warning.'

'I understand.'

He holds my gaze for another moment, then cuts the connection.

I'm back at The Two Horsemen a week later, this time with Stepan. The place is almost empty this early in the day, only a couple of regulars nursing drinks in the far corner.

The barman waves us over. 'Jo's running late. What can I get you?'

Stepan stops in the entrance, taking in the decor. I hardly

noticed it last time, but the establishment lives up to its name. The walls on the left and right are covered with large murals depicting the Two Horsemen. The one on the left is a blond man in a silk suit and mirror glasses, wads of money sticking out of his pockets. A red automobile disgorges fumes that merge with the black clouds spewed by the industrial complex behind. Next to the man, a skeletal-thin horse tries to feed on desiccated grass. Destitute refugees approach from the edges, one side propelled by desert sands, the other by a tidal surge and hurricane winds.

The second mural shows a gaunt woman standing over the crumpled corpse of the blond man. Her face is hollow and her eye sockets empty. Her fingers beam fluorescent rays on the wretched multitudes around her, sowing death.

'Why is Plague a woman?' I hear myself ask.

Stepan doesn't answer. I'm not sure he even heard me.

The barman follows our glances. 'I used to think these were optimistic. Like, we came so close to the Apocalypse—but we pulled through. We managed.'

'We're still paying for it,' Stepan says. 'Imagine where technology would be now if we hadn't lost a century just trying to survive... What medical advances we could have...'

He trails off, and I say nothing. I ran out of things that could cheer him up a week ago.

We both turn as the door opens again.

Jo rushes in, his lanky frame giving his movements a desperate air. He slumps on a barstool next to me, his face grim. 'I'm sorry it didn't work out.'

I try to shrug. 'Not your fault. The info from your cousin was spot on.'

'Is your boss all right?'

My former boss, because my contract was terminated when I failed to return. 'Let's just say he won't be asking any more questions.'

Jo nods. 'You said you had a new plan?'

I glance at Stepan—no help there, he looks like a ghost holding together just out of stubbornness.

'I was thinking: there must be some weak spot in the system. The elevator's under guard, but somewhere on the way from the port to the loading bay, there must be an opening.'

Jo looks from me to Stepan, then back to me. 'Can you even get to the port? Do you have a visa?'

'I can't leave the Feidi. But there's plenty of Kenyans who can. We just have to find the right ones.'

'That's what I've been saying.' The barman leans on the counter, muscles bulging, a frown scrunching his forehead.

I glance at Jo.

'No worries. Gideon's good people.'

'What do you mean?' Stepan asks, suddenly attentive again.

Gideon crosses his arms, his chestnut skin glistening in the low light. 'People are desperate. If they knew all the meds were going up to the Yun Ju, they'd rip that cursed winch off the ground. The mayor'd better step in or he'll have a revolution on his hands. There's still more of us than there is of them.'

'But they've got better guns,' Jo says, his voice thin.

Gideon shrugs. 'He needs our votes this summer. And anyway, the yun-ying won't let him mess up. The last thing they want is riots by the elevator.'

My heartbeat speeds up as things fall into place. This is it. That's how we'll save Anna and Nadia. And whoever else really needs the meds.

'He's right,' I say, my voice hoarse but firm. 'It's election year. Politicians need votes, and businesses hate disruption. A good crowd of people can throw a spanner in both. That's how we're going to do it.'

CHAPTER 9

The wall of my cabin is the kind of dark brown that on a good day reminds me of rain-soaked savannah at the end of the wet season. Today it looks umber, almost grey, like the stifling sky over Bethesda.

I sit on the narrow bed, staring at my feet, black shoes against a brown floor. Hey, at least I've managed to put my shoes on.

My wan-kong chimes, the third time, even though I've already sent Sanchez a message not to wait for me with the morning prayer. I probe the feeling in my stomach—there's only tightness there, as if I've swallowed a dozen marbles. Just as well, since I'm not going to make it to breakfast.

The screen opposite flicks to standby mode after it announced the arrival of a message burst from Earth. It's the first 'live' update we've received, after the amalgam of yearly updates waiting in the ship's buffers on our arrival. Like all the previous ones, it'll contain a bite-sized update on the world news and personal messages for the crew, if anyone's still getting any.

Not me. I knew I shouldn't have let myself hope, but I

hoped anyway. Just one brief message to tell me Jason was all right. No such luck. The news of my parents' death was the last one I received. The last photo they sent hangs pinned to the wall next to the screen: their faces worn but with the same intensity they'd passed to Anna and me. No photos of Jason.

I don't blame him, really. He was five when I left. If he remembers me at all, it's just a dream overshadowed by the memory of his dead parents. Compared to them, what do I matter? I'm a ghost of his painful past, a thorn from thirty-five years ago. It's better that he doesn't remember. Much better.

I wonder if he looks anything like Anna. Or, if he has a daughter, if she takes after her, if she's got that same restless spark that stares at me from my mother's face. I barely remember her, too.

I wince at the knock on my door. Damn. I hope it's not Sanchez checking why I missed his prayers.

I wipe my eyes, then check my reflection in the mirror. Shouldn't have looked. I'll have to tell him I have a migraine or something. I put on a pained smile, then move to the door.

Tolya Yefremov leans on the frame, his arms crossed and his expression almost amused.

I let out a relieved breath. 'Oh, it's you.'

Yefremov laughs. 'Spokoino. Were you expecting the chaplain?'

'What makes you think so?'

'Your face?'

I snort. I consider trying to look busy but decide it won't fool him. I've missed breakfast, and the briefing is in half an hour. 'Do you want to come in?'

He nods and squeezes past me. 'The reverend's not so bad, you know. I mean, I give him shit any time I can, but, well, that's just part of the game.'

'I'm not sure he sees it that way.' I follow the doctor inside and sit on the bed. 'What brings you here?'

'I guess a friendly visit isn't going to cut it, is it?'

'Not at this hour.'

Yefremov's gaze slides over my modest collection of photos, then he plonks himself down in the desk chair. 'How are you doing?'

I laugh. 'No need for the subterfuge. I feel shitty and you know it. You feel shitty, too. It's all one big mess.'

He nods, his expression unchanged. 'How are *you* doing?'

'What, filling in for the shrink?'

'All in a day's work. Stop deflecting.'

'I'm fine,' I growl. 'Just missed breakfast, that's all. I'll have a ration bar with my coffee.'

'Not so good, then. Is it the news?'

'I didn't get any—' I break off as he tilts his head and his brows knit in a frown. 'What news?'

Yefremov stays silent for a moment. 'So, you didn't get any messages, and that upset you so much you didn't check the news.'

'Bullshit.' I want to scream, or to punch him, or both. I dig my nails into the mattress, my wrist throbbing. 'I didn't check the news because what's the point? It's six years old today; by the time we get back it'll all be history.'

Yefremov leans back in the chair. 'I didn't get any news either. My ex-wife's dead, and my kids... I have no idea. The last message was ten years ago. But honestly, that's what I expected. They'll never see me again, and, well, we were not on the best of terms when I left, so...' He shrugs. 'We're out of their world. We knew that was going to happen, but it's only now becoming reality. Everybody's upset, though they're pretending to be just fine.'

He's right, probably, but this is not the time. I get up. 'I need to get to my office.'

'In a moment.' He doesn't move.

'Listen, I know you're trying to help, but I—'

The doctor waves his arm. 'I'm not trying; I know you won't let me. Still, you're strong, so you're not my worry. Not yet, at least.'

I frown, trying to parse his words into something I can understand.

'But there are two things we need to discuss, and they are related,' he continues. 'First, the entire crew are now going through the same thing as you: realising that everyone they ever knew is either dead or cared so little they stopped sending messages after a few years into our journey. That's a special kind of loneliness, a whole different level. And a lot of tension just looking for an escape.'

'Isn't that the shrink's job? Or the reverend's?'

'They can only help those who ask for it. Most of the crew won't; they're as pig-headed as you are—no offence. They'll just stew in it till something boils over.'

I snort. 'What do you want me to do? Get Price to round them up into the shrink's office?'

Yefremov doesn't smile. He runs his fingers through his hair, and it stands up, bristled with static electricity. It'd be funny if not for the way his eyes narrow and his shoulders hunch.

'What is it?'

He gestures to the blank screen behind him. 'The news today? It was bad. Looks like another war's on the way.'

'What?' I repeat like my own echo.

'Have you read any digests from the last few decades?'

I shake my head. 'I've been too busy to keep up with history.'

'Well, you should. Tensions have been building up for a decade. China's brought the trade war to a whole new level. They want a monopoly on everything space related; they've been cutting all others out. No new leases on patented technology, no leases at all on new inventions. The hydro-growers, all the food technologies that looked so promising when we left?'

He glances at me, and I nod. 'Everything's under embargo now, Chinese management only. The countries that tried to rebel got their supplies cut off. It's scarcity all over again. Europe's descended into riots. It's a matter of time before the Americans decide to take action.'

I stare numbly at him, all feeling gone from my limbs. Another war? Scarcity again? How will the Feidi cope? Is Jason still in Canada now that his grandparents are dead?

Please be all right. Please, please be all right.

I slide down on the bed. I grab my knees, rocking, my breathing shallow and my vision blurred at the edges. Not again. Not now, not in front of him.

I suck in air and force a smile, but I'm not fooling anyone.

'Do you want to talk about it?' Yefremov asks in the softest voice I've ever heard from him.

I pull in another breath, focusing on the coolness entering my lungs. My feet touching the ground. My thighs pressing against the bed. The reassuring pain in my wrist. Breathe in. Breathe out. I'm all right. I can do it.

'This is seriously bad timing,' I say, straightening even as the world still sways around me. 'The news, I mean.'

Yefremov watches me with narrowed eyes. I stare hard at him. *Don't ask.*

He nods, as if agreeing to an unspoken deal. 'Everyone's shaken. And the briefing's going to make it worse.' He rubs his chin, mouth twisting into a grimace. 'It looks like whatever happened in the colony, violence was involved.'

He waits for my reaction, but I can only manage a nod.

'They turned on each other, for whatever reason,' he continues. 'We have this saying: if you want to hit a dog, you'll always find a stick.'

I nod again. 'And we know there was a Chinese contingent down there.'

'Exactly. Foreigners, always the best target.'

Any excuse will do if what you really want is a fight, or a scapegoat; if it's not religion, then it's appearance, or language, or the way someone wears their hair. Anything can be a stick if you really want to hit that dog.

And now the same thing may happen to us. This ship is a wasps' nest—and the news from Earth has just thrown in a burning ember.

I bang my fist against my knee. What to do? I'm no politician and no psychologist. I don't even know where to start.

No more death. Not on my watch.

I must find a way. I can't help Jason, but I won't let this ship turn into a battleground. I need every one of them.

I rise, my legs still shaky. 'I'll talk to Price. I won't have time to talk to Sanchez before the briefing, so you have to do it.'

Yefremov grimaces. 'I'm not sure I hold much weight with the reverend.'

'You're the ship's doctor. That's all the weight you need. Also, you're not giving him enough credit. Sanchez is a politician, but his priorities are in the right place. *Gabriel*'s lives depend on us, and he knows it.'

Yefremov still looks reluctant, but he's out of arguments. I start for the door. This would have been a good moment to ask about the deal between him and Khan—but I've got no right to pry, not after the show I've just given. I guess we'll have to learn to live with all our ghosts.

Price is in the office by the time I arrive. She probably dashed across from the mess as soon as she got my message.

'What's up, sir?'

I close the door behind me. 'I assume you've seen the news?'

She nods. 'Yeah. That's all people are talking about.'

I lean against the desk, my hands clasped and my words

measured. 'We can't let it spill out here. No matter how bad the news gets—from Earth or from Bethesda.'

Price tilts her head. She sucks in her lip, more unsettled than I've ever seen her.

'It's not about you, or me, or Zhang,' I continue. 'It's not even about the dead colonists, or whatever the latest crisis on Earth happens to be. It's about the people on *Gabriel*. This mission is about them. And our team needs to be whole, or we'll be useless. If we splinter, we fail.'

She grimaces, her hands clasped into fists. This is hard for her, and I'm glad—I wouldn't believe her if it seemed easy.

'I'm all for teamwork,' she says. 'But remember what I told you. They warned me for a reason.'

'That's why we'll be keeping an eye on him. But we can't let anyone know. Not even your people.' She wants to protest, but I raise my hand. 'This is important, Amy. People talk, and even when they don't talk, they pick up on each other's moods. You set the tone, and they will follow. And I need you to make everyone believe that you find this particular group of the Chinese blameless. Because they are. They're no more responsible for Bethesda, or the trade war, than you're responsible for the crusades just because you're Christian.'

Price pulls away, surprised or hurt. I keep looking at her, my gaze unwavering. She needs to know I'm dead serious.

'Fine,' she says after a moment. 'For *Gabriel*.'

'For *Gabriel*.'

She marches to her seat at the meeting table while I open the door for the others. Khan and her assistant, Oleg Navrov, are already outside. Zhang and Yau, the grey-eyed, silver-hair-stripe engineer we met on the way to the captain's cabin, arrive from the bridge-side. Sanchez appears moments later, Yefremov trotting behind him.

The table is too small for all of us, so I roll in my desk chair. The mess would be more comfortable, but I want to keep the briefing confidential. They shift uneasily, each eyeing the others while they silently jostle for the best view of the screen. Khan takes her usual seat and buries her attention in her notes, seemingly oblivious. Navrov glances around, then takes his cue from his boss and slides his chair next to her. Yau looks equally confused but more defensive, like a rabbit surrounded by vultures. Price leans back in her seat, a plastic smile on her face. Zhang looks up from his zheping, distracted, then frowns. He probably thinks I've set this all up on purpose, but I'm not that smart. Or that stupid. And yet here we are, a microcosm of the mission.

I tap my wan-kong. 'Lim, open a secure channel to the surface. No access to anyone outside the office.'

'Yes, sir.'

The screen comes to life a moment later. They are all there, the entire field team crowded around a narrow table: the scientists in front; Miller and Lee, back in his baseball cap, standing behind them. All look exhausted, eyes red, hair unkempt, three-day stubble on the men's faces.

Johansson nods a greeting. He's a head taller than the other scientists, lanky and narrow-faced, with pale white skin, grey eyes and fair, almost translucent hair. Scandinavian, judging by his name, because the badge on his uniform shows only the gold stars of the European Alliance.

He taps his hand on the table, calling for attention. 'We've got the initial data, Commander. Nothing conclusive, I'm afraid. The last human-made record in the central log dates to 22 April 2304, the same as in the greenhouse. There's no mention of any problem, either equipment or anything else. The only abnormality seems to be that from about ten days before cut-off, the records had become sparser. Still, everything worked fine: air, food supply, energy levels, all normal. And then it's like they dropped off a cliff. The automatic logs continued for several years, until everything went into standby mode.'

'Did you find any personal files?' Sanchez asks. 'Letters? Diaries? They must have left something.'

'They're not in the central log. That doesn't mean they don't exist; we just haven't reached them yet.'

'Have you found anything useful?' Yefremov says.

Johansson grimaces. 'We don't know what killed them—but we know what didn't kill them, and that's already more than we knew before we got here.'

'Okay, take it step by step,' I say. I didn't expect definitive answers, or they'd have informed me already. But some questions are more urgent than others. 'The stains you found—was it blood?'

Johansson nods to the medics.

'It was blood, all right,' Gonzales says. He's a stocky man with a broad chest that stretches the fabric of his shirt, and a round face with a small red scar under his left eye. 'The samples we collected belong to one individual. The blood loss was probably substantial, but I have no way of telling if it was life-threatening. That's all I can say.'

'Pathology?' Yefremov asks.

'No detectable traces of disease or infection. Again, it doesn't mean there wasn't any—just nothing preserved well enough for us to see.'

'You said it was one individual?' I ask to make sure the others register the fact.

'That's correct.'

Price gets the point. 'So, not a fight. Or at least not there.'

'Nothing in the dust?' Khan asks, looking at her notes rather than the screen.

'Traces of microbial life, pretty much what we'd expect in a sealed environment.'

'What about the greenhouse?' Yefremov asks.

'Thriving.' Johansson takes a deep breath, almost a surrender. 'Humans vanish and the flora seems all the better for it.'

Sheng leans towards the camera, her bionic hand clunking against the table. 'The equipment has been performing above expectation. By my estimate, self-maintenance systems will be sufficient for another two decades.'

I press my fingers to my lips. Everything's working, but the people are gone. Whatever happened, they didn't disappear all in one day. 'You mentioned the logs had been getting sparser—in what way?'

Zhang raises his hand. 'This was my question as well, so I've made an analysis looking at the dates and the frequency. We might be on to something. May I?'

He points to the screen. I nod, my stomach tightening in anticipation. All the others lean forward, deadly silent.

Without a gesture from the engineer, a graph appears on the screen. This is still startling, no matter how often I've seen Mind-Link in action. I focus on the graph; it's an almost horizontal if slightly undulating line, which on closer inspection is made up of multiple coloured strands, like a bunch of wires.

'This is an amalgam of various logs—mostly maintenance, but also things like airlock use, medical, and so on,' Zhang says. 'On average, it's fairly regular, and the variations easy to explain. For example, airlock use drops off each Sunday, which I assume would be a day off for the colonists.' The engineer glances at Sanchez, the reverend's presence enough to explain what he means. 'But then things start to change.'

The graph shifts to the left as the time-arrow extends further to the right. The harmonious bundle of lines splinters into a loose band—still synchronised, if imperfectly. One line, though, arches up and away from the rest, the frequency of logs increasing dramatically till it levels off at the top of the scale.

'What's that line?' Khan asks.

'I think I know,' Yefremov says, but Zhang jumps in before he can finish.

'One moment, Doctor. It's useful to see the entire picture first.'

Yefremov nods. Zhang returns to the screen, where the time-arrow now extends further into the future. The strand of wires no longer resembles anything harmonious—more a haphazard collection of lines, some oscillating rapidly, others zigzagging without any connection to the rest. A date blinks on the edge of the timeline, 22 April, the day of the last report. And one by one, the lines stop, cut mid-dive or mid-turn, some days and others only hours before the blackout date.

'What the hell happened here?' Johansson asks, the feed from the planet popping up in a sub-window on the screen.

Zhang glances at the doctor. From his expression I think he knows the answer, or at least part of it. I shift in my seat, eager to skip the graphs and get to whatever conclusion he's reached—but Zhang catches my gaze and raises his hand slightly as if to say, *Wait.*

'I assume the blue line shows the medical reports?' Yefremov asks.

'That's correct,' Zhang says.

'This matches what I found. A sharp increase in medical interventions not long before the blackout.'

'The plague?' Price asks, the fear always only inches away.

I stiffen. The others, too, are perfectly still, their eyes on the doctor.

'No, that's not it. The reasons for the interventions were all different. And quite odd. José, you've got the details.'

The screen toggles, with the field team now in full view and Zhang's graph in an inset.

Gonzales reaches for his zheping but ends up waving his hand as he changes his mind. 'I've run a report on the codes used—each type of injury or treatment has its own code, so they're easy to track. When the number of interventions started to increase, I expected to see a trend, like what you'd have with an epidemic or a poisoning, or anything with a shared cause. But that's not the case. The spread is as random as someone picking codes out of a hat.'

'So, they are having more and more problems but totally unrelated?' Khan steeples her hands, a note of incredulity in her voice.

'Maybe not totally unrelated,' Gonzales says.

Yefremov said this wasn't a plague. Please, let him be right.

I try to keep my voice steady. 'Explain, Doctor. Concisely, if you can.'

Gonzales pulls in a breath. 'Most codes refer to external injuries: cuts, bruises, hands crushed by furniture, some burns, some frostbites.'

'Could it be related to fighting?' Price asks.

'Frostbites?' Khan snorts. 'More like equipment malfunction.'

'Let him finish.' I raise my voice before the conversation derails.

'There was fighting, too,' Gonzales says. The corners of his mouth turn downward, his face grim. 'But later. Towards the end of what's on record.'

'Do you know who attacked?' Price jumps in again.

'Let him finish!' I glare at her, and she raises her hand in an apology. 'Go on, Doctor.'

Gonzales nods. 'As I said, mostly external injuries. But then I dug deeper into the records and...' He hesitates. 'Well, I don't know how to say it nicely, so I'll just say it. These were all just stupid accidents. Like, all of a sudden, they became clumsy and slow. The same jobs they've been doing for years, and suddenly they can't manage without finding some way to get hurt. And it's not just clumsy—careless, too. Or forgetful. Handling super-cooled liquids without protective clothing. The same with hot stuff. Several cases of people marching out of the airlock without oxygen. One person sliced off their fingers using a laser beam to chop cucumbers.'

Gonzales spreads his arms in frustration. We look at each other, uneasy. People can get reckless when even the most hostile environment becomes the norm. But not *this* reckless.

'Are you suggesting some kind of mental impediment?' I ask.

On the other side of the table, Yefremov nods.

'Yes,' Gonzales says. 'And I think I found proof—in the transcripts of the doctors' voice comments on the critical cases. At first, they are just odd, then increasingly incoherent, down to almost gibberish by the time the records stop.'

'So they've gone mad?' Sanchez is shaking his head, his hair ruffled from pushing his fingers through it too many times.

I open my mouth, but there's nothing I can say to this. Even Khan has run out of comments.

Gonzales looks at his hands for a long moment. 'One last thing. They did fight. But by the time it got serious, I think they were too far gone to merit the question of who attacked whom...'

They lost their minds. Killed each other or got themselves killed through dumb carelessness. It'd be unbelievable if not for the facts.

We put all the effort into making sure the equipment would survive, but it's the human minds that have failed the test. Maybe colonisation can never work; maybe we can't survive away from home, doomed to lose our sanity under alien skies. But if that's the case, then there's no hope for *Gabriel*.

My arms tingle as the numbness returns, the world contracting around me with every shallow breath. No. We're not done yet.

I turn to Yefremov. 'Any hypothesis, Doctor?'

'Loss of cognitive function can have many causes: infections, parasites, poisoning, prion disease. But we've got no mention of those in the logs. They'd have noticed signs before all of them succumbed. Atmospherics all check out, as do nutrition records. We'll keep looking, but...' He spreads his hands to show that he doesn't think it's likely.

'Could it be the confinement?' Sanchez asks. 'I know they'd been pre-selected for stability, but just the idea of being trapped inside those boxes for the rest of your life...'

'Not impossible, but I don't think that's what caused it,' Yefremov says. 'First, they'd survived just fine for several years. Everything worked, they were healthy, things looked good. And the second reason: it happened too suddenly, and too quickly. It points to a trigger, one that both they and their equipment would miss—but I have no idea what it was.'

Zhang stirs. He knows something, I'm sure.

'Chief Engineer?'

Zhang drums his fingers on the table. 'I don't know what the trigger was. But if I run the logs backwards till before things started getting... let's call it "odd", there's one event that stands out.'

He moves his head to indicate the screen. The graph has reappeared, the lines shifting backward in time, returning to alignment—and there, about a week earlier, a red dot appears on the timeline. 'This is when they disabled the decontamination protocols on all airlocks. Apparently, they decided they were unnecessary.'

'That can't be the reason,' Khan says. 'There's nothing on this planet that could cause such symptoms. Or any symptoms.'

Johansson's speaking, too, and so is Yefremov and several others, voices blending into a cacophony of doubt. I stare at the engineer. He looks troubled but calm, secure in his answer.

'I can't say it's the reason,' he says as he catches my gaze. 'But it's the only thing that changed, and the timing is too much of a coincidence.'

The others are still talking, voices raised, faces feverish.

'I'll send you the data.' Khan's voice cuts above the others. She's leaning on the table, almost standing as she glares at Yefremov's scornful face.

He opens his mouth, lip curling, when I bang my fist on the table.

They fall silent, faces turning, some surprised, some grateful.

'This is quite enough. We'll keep looking. Something here did it to them, and if it was the planet or a strain of mutant cucumbers, at this point we'll not dismiss any hypothesis. Is that clear?' I look at Khan and she nods.

'Now, I have another question.' I pause, waiting for them to settle into attention. 'Where are the bodies?'

Johansson rocks his head slowly. 'It's a bit of a puzzle given the chaos near the end. But we've only seen a fraction of the settlement on this one outing.'

'So that's your next target—but only after you finish setting up the base and get proper rest. I don't want you to start making mistakes. Whatever killed the colonists may be in one of your samples. Don't let that slip your mind.'

I shift my gaze from the tired faces of the field team to the focused if bewildered glances from the crew around my table. I won't let them give up or descend into fighting. Prove me right or prove me wrong, I don't care—as long as we find the truth.

CHAPTER 10

That evening everyone is subdued, voices hushed even at dinner, which is our only 'normal' meal for the day. The news is finally hitting, both from Bethesda and the events back on Earth.

The scientists huddle together, arguing in low, anxious voices, then rush off after barely ten minutes, desserts in hands, the babble of conversation following them down the corridor. They and the medics are the only truly international groups. Security is all American, the engineers all Chinese. Sanchez's Ops team is supposed to be international, but they're all Kenyan citizens, and all Christians. That's not unusual—we've all been recruited by the Feidi-based Space Projects, so no wonder they looked close to home. Every national group has a mix of ethnicities: Asian Americans, African Europeans. Yau Po Li clearly has some white ancestry. None of that matters. As long as you've got one nation's flag on your chest, that's where you belong. I wonder if a fully international crew would be more cooperative or make it even harder to focus on common interests. I'll never know.

I chew the bean stew that's today's special, trying to wash

down the bland taste with what passes for apple juice. Yefremov glances at me from the round table the medics have claimed. I give him a wide grin that says: *I'm perfectly fine, and if you try to pry, there will be unpleasant consequences for both of us.*

The doctor snorts in response. Message received.

The Chinese group sidle around my table on the way to the exit. Wang grins at me, and I try not to show my embarrassment at her delight at my existence. Zhang nods a greeting, but his eyes aren't in it. I nod back, hoping my smile looks friendly rather than exasperated.

The moment the door closes behind the engineers, the noise level increases three-fold, the loudest clamour coming from the Americans. Price catches my glance as she tries to speak over them, her smile strained and her expression defeated. It's not working. And it's only going to get worse. Or maybe the next transmission from Earth will bring some good news?

A hollow giggle spills out of my mouth. I cover it up with a cough as all the heads turn towards me. Of all the unpleasant-ness of command, this is what I hate the most. I miss the times when I could sit in a corner, and nobody would give me a second glance.

My wan-kong vibrates with a message. From Lim—finally. I've been wondering what has kept her.

Last night I asked her to unlock the captain's journal for me —I had no choice, I was never going to crack it myself. Luckily, she didn't protest, even though we were breaking a dozen regu-lations. I think by now she realised something wasn't quite right with the ship.

Let's talk when you have a moment, Lim's message says.

My office, in five minutes?

Maybe your quarters? More intimate...

I gape at the display for a good thirty seconds. *More inti-mate?* My office is as secure as it gets on this ship, so that can't be what she means. *More intimate?* Have I given any indication I might be interested in her in *that* way? I'm not sure of anything these days—but no, it can't be. Even if I don't trust myself to notice innuendos from her side—or anyone's side—Lim's not the kind to go after her boss without a clear invitation, and I can at least be sure I didn't do anything explicit. This must be something else. Must be.

I'll see you there, I send, and hope I'm not about to find myself in a really awkward position.

The medical team leaves a moment later. I finish my dessert: a plum and chocolate brownie, or something that once had been one, and carry the tray to the washer. Price casts me an anxious glance from the security table next to the machine. I nod, encouragingly, I hope. Something tells me I may have another visitor tonight—and just the opposite of 'intimate'.

When I arrive, Lim's waiting in front of my door. Her hair falls low over her eyes, but I can see they are red and surrounded by grey circles. When she looks up, her brows twitch in worry or anger.

'Are you all right?'

'I'm happy to see you at last.' She enunciates the words as if they're a secret code.

My mouth opens to ask what this is about, but she puts her finger on her lips. I push the door ajar, confused and wondering if I should be calling the medics, but she reaches across me and pulls it closed instead. She presses her finger to her lips once again, then waves her arm, beckoning me to follow.

Five minutes. I'll give her five minutes, and then I need an explanation. Or she needs a doctor.

We walk in silence along the empty corridor of the quarters section, passing only the puppy-sized cleaning bots toiling over the decking. Lim turns left and then left again, apparently taking the cargo route to the tether. When the ship split, the main deck and the engine section formed slowly rotating counterweights linked by a cargo elevator inside an expandable tether. Two access paths lead to the elevator; the one we're in is wide enough to move engineering equipment but less convenient for personnel as it's farther away from the bridge. If you wanted to access the tether unnoticed, this would be the route to use—though you wouldn't get any farther without Mind-Link-transmitted access codes.

I know Lim has Mind-Link—I've seen her use it. There's no way she has the codes, though. And even if she did, I can't let her take me to the engine section. The entire deck is off limits to everyone but the engineers. I've got enough trouble without antagonising them even further.

Another turn, and the bulkhead entrance to the tether is just ahead. That's it. This has gone far enough.

I put my hand on her shoulder. 'What are you—'

She swings around and puts her hand over my lips. She blinks, her face anguished as if the action causes her physical pain. *Please*, she mouths.

I hesitate—but the desperation in her eyes compels me to trust her. I nod, and we move on, past the bulkhead and into the dark recess of the loading bay. The tether lift is just behind the second bulkhead opposite. Finally, Lim stops. Her shoulders droop, and she leans on the wall, exhaling loudly.

I wait, uncertain. If this empty chamber is our destination, then what on Earth could be so important about getting here?

'I'm so sorry,' she says after a moment. She's trembling, overdosed on adrenaline. 'I couldn't tell you. I'm so sorry.'

'It's okay.' That's not what I'm thinking, but if I express any disapproval, she may just fall apart on me. 'I'm sure you have a reason. Right?'

'Yes. Yes, I have. I think I have.'

My eyebrows rise, and she lifts her arms in surrender. 'You must think I've lost my mind...'

'It's crossed my mind. So just tell me, okay?'

Lim bobs her head up and down, like a bird. 'Okay. Yes. First there's this.'

She reaches into a pocket on the inside of her jacket and pulls out the black zheping of the captain's journal.

'Did you crack it?'

'It wasn't that hard. It's just a personal diary, nothing seriously encrypted.' Her smile fades as she says that.

'You mean, there's nothing there?'

'Nothing I could see at first glance. But I didn't have much time.' She hands me the zheping, then another one, a ship's standard issue pad. 'I've cloned it here, with auto-translation.'

'Good thinking.' This way I can study it in detail without anyone noticing. I slide both pads into my pocket. 'But that's not why you brought me here, is it?'

Lim presses her hand to her chest, her fingers tugging at the seam of her shirt. Her voice takes on a heavier tone. 'No. That file you asked me about, the CCM?'

I nod, her anxiety seeping into my bones.

'I delved into the system looking for it. And why the settings changed when you took command. I kept digging, but all I found were dead ends. So, I decided to try another way, diving into the OS of the main computer, and then finding my way through there.'

'Is that wise?'

'Very tricky, unless you know what you're doing. But that used to be my job, back before. Anyway, I did manage to get into the guts of the system.'

'Did you find the file?'

'I found what's left of it. It was deleted, and the backups scrambled beyond anything I can repair. I also found something else.' She pauses to take a deep breath. 'I still can't believe what I'm about to say. But it's there, I have no doubt.'

The back of my neck starts to prickle. 'What is it?'

'There's an entire higher-level operating program controlling the main computer. One that supervises all its actions. Kind of like watching what the system does, ready to intervene if some trigger is sprung.'

'I don't understand. Intervene, how?'

She lifts her hand to show two fingers. 'Think about it as two different computers. One is what we use as the 'main' on this ship. But it's not alone. It's connected to another system, let's call it a 'spy'. It observes everything the main does. For most actions, it's entirely passive, letting the main do its work—but if there's anything the 'spy' doesn't like, it can override it and do whatever it wants. It can take over the ship.'

I stare, my mouth open, but all I can do is repeat her last sentence. 'It can take over the ship?'

Lim nods. 'Yes. It's designed to take over and enable or disable certain actions.'

'What actions? And what would it do? And what could set it off?'

'I don't know. I couldn't get any deeper into the code without triggering a response.'

I start to pace, circling the chamber like a caged cheetah. If this 'spy' can take over the ship's computer, the very thing we depend on to keep us alive—what will it do? Switch off life support? Send the ship into the sun? And why?

'Are you sure it's not anything normal? This ship's a new design; there could be improvements—'

'No way. I'm as sure of that as I am of my name. This is very far from normal. The spy is watching us.'

Chills run down my back. 'Who would want to spy on us? We are light years away. And we report back everything we discover.'

'Maybe there's something they don't want us to discover?'

My mouth falls open. She's right. If someone didn't want us to find out what happened to the colonists, they could install such a program.

And they'd sabotage the ship to kill the captain.

I lean on the wall but then slide down to sit on the cold floor. *Gabriel*. The frozen woman and the five thousand others waiting for the results of our work. Are they doomed?

'Can you disable it somehow?'

Lim sits on the ground next to me. 'Impossible. Not without destroying the main.'

I put my head into my hands. 'We're at its mercy. And we don't even know what it wants.'

'Maybe we can get some answers.' She leans towards me, her voice low as if sharing a secret. 'Each time there's a reaction, the processing power spikes by a very particular amount. That's something I can monitor. So far there's only one item I'm certain of.'

I look into her eyes, waiting for her words like a sentence.

'It tracks every use of the terms "Si-Lian" or "Mind-Link", in both languages. Not the tech itself, just the words. I have no idea why.'

All the Chinese engineers have Mind-Link, but probably also most of the scientists. Not the reverend or the Americans, or anyone following the religious doctrine that regards the tech as a path to sin. Still, this tells me nothing.

I take a deep breath, the coolness of the floor seeping into my bones while my mind bubbles with questions. 'I don't even know what to think now.'

'That makes two of us.'

I push myself up, my head spinning. 'I assume this place is secure? That's why you brought us here?'

'Yes. The relay system here was damaged in the fire. Also, it can't access our wan-kongs—unless we're transmitting, because it sees everything that goes through the comms.'

'Keep looking, Lim. But be careful. If we have a troll, the last thing we want is to wake it up.'

. . .

I return to my cabin, the back of my neck prickling as I imagine the 'spy' following my every move. What does it want? And how far will it go to get it? I've got more questions and no answers, but at least one more place still to scour for hints: the captain's journal.

I slump into my chair, but no, if it's watching, it may have a hidden camera pointing there. I'm probably paranoid, but the risk is too big. I consider returning to the tether room, but if anybody finds me there, that will only cause more questions. Instead, I curl up on the floor in the corner by the sink and pull out the cloned zheping.

It's a ship's standard issue, not the captain's jet-black pad. I unfold it; the surface locks into the larger size, and the screen lights up. The entries start three years back: mostly family stuff, and an on-and-off affair with a woman mentioned only by name, some sex adventures. Reading it makes me feel nauseous, ashamed for prying into the dead man's secrets. Nothing relating to his work, either, except maybe for some cryptic comments, conversations with people mentioned only by their initials. I flip forward, scanning the notes till I stop on one dated two weeks before our departure.

I'm starting to have serious doubts. The infiltrator has been found, but we don't know how many more have been compromised. So now we're having to change the entire crew, with only weeks to departure. How could they mess this up so badly? After all the work to get the right people through, now we're stuck with this insanity. G assures me things are under control, that they already have candidates earmarked for every position—but this means the crew will hardly get a chance to meet before the launch. I've asked for a delay, but they won't hear of it. Too much is at stake.

They replaced the entire crew? My application went

through ten days before departure, after their first-choice Canadian changed their mind at the last moment. I've heard a few other crew members mention the same story: last minute replacements after the first choice got cold feet. But everyone?

I read the passage again.

The infiltrator has been found, but we don't know how many more have been compromised.

The infiltrator—that points to industrial espionage. Not the first time someone tried to sneak a spy onto a mission, just so they could get a peek at the engines. The Chinese owners got wind of it, and that was that. I've seen this happen before. In any other situation I'd just shrug this off, but now everything is tinged with suspicion. Who *was* the infiltrator? And how come we still ended up with sabotage, even with a new crew? I move on, flipping through the entries till another one almost makes me drop the zheping.

I met my second yesterday. She looks as dazed as I expected, completely unfit for duty. It's barely been weeks since the unpleasantness with her family. I don't know how they expect her to function. I raised my misgivings with the Guardian. No surprise, he ignored me because she's the central piece in the connections matrix—and she's Canadian, which keeps both parties happy. That's all fine, but with her lack of experience and poor mental status, if anything happens to me, the ship will be in deep trouble, and he with it. Of course, his reply was that I was overreacting and that he wasn't going to let anything happen.

I lower the pad, happy that the wall is there to support me. The captain knew about my family—and if he did, so had the others in the company. Did anyone suspect what part I played in the riots? No, that's impossible, or I'd never have got the job.

Still, the captain at least knew I wasn't fit for duty. So, who was that Guardian who overruled him? And why?

I check the previous entry:

G assures me things are under control...

Is 'G' the Guardian? And who is it?

I scroll through the entries, looking for any other mention of the ship, me, or the mysterious 'G'. Then one odd entry catches my eye, dated just a day before our departure:

The archer's arrows are poison. Don't trust him.

Who's the 'archer'? Why such a cryptic entry in a private journal? I shake my head, my temples throbbing with unanswered questions. I look at the words again, then on a hunch switch the text back to the original Mandarin.

Something about the shape of the word looks familiar. The first icon, the snake shape of the sign for an archer's bow. My hands tremble. I know this symbol. I close my eyes and visualise the rest of it.

張. The Mandarin spelling of the name. Zhang.

CHAPTER 11

I pace my tiny cabin just like that lion in the Feidi zoo, the one I took Jason to see on our final day together. The plaque above the enclosure said it was the last lion in existence—probably a lie, but whether there were one or ten of them left, it made no difference. They were doomed to extinction; no hope left.

I grit my teeth at the memory of Jason's rapt face. I tried to make him understand this was all for him. The money would secure his future. I don't think he listened.

My wrist aches, the dull, throbbing pain a constant companion. I can't give up. For Jason, and for *Gabriel*. I have to find a way. My brain's my only tool—it'll have to do.

My pacing takes me back to my tiny desk. I slump in the chair and pick up my zheping, then drop it. *It* may be watching —my screen, or my notes. Only the inside of my skull is secure.

I focus on what I know: the spy, that overseeing computer— somebody installed it to do a job for them. Who? The Americans or the Chinese? Both nations collaborated on the computer systems, so the technology is no indication the way it'd be with the engines.

The fact that it tracks Mind-Link may point towards the

Chinese; it's their tech. But no, it's only tracking *references* to ML, not the thing itself. Which doesn't really make sense —unless...

I bolt to my feet, the chill of realisation shooting like ice through my bones.

Those who have Mind-Link don't talk about it, they use it. Only those who have no access to the technology would need to verbalise their concerns. And they'd certainly talk about it if they suspected it being used against them.

So, if you were using Mind-Link for something insidious, and if you wanted to know if anyone was on to you, programming the computer to track all the references would provide just the warning.

Who, then? Not the scientists, none of them had access to the ship while it was constructed. The two options are the Americans or the Chinese, and only one of them is using Mind-Link. Which means the Chinese are controlling the spy computer.

I start pacing again, slower now as I force myself to be cautious. 'The Chinese' is the easy answer, but it could be just one of them, without the knowledge or participation of the rest.

The archer's arrows are poison.

Williamson warned Price about Zhang. The captain was wary of him, and now he's dead. It *might* be someone else, but why ignore the blazing signs pointing towards that one man? All the warnings? Occam's razor.

I lean on the desk. My legs are shaking, unwilling to make another step. There's an extra computer on my ship, one that might destroy us if it receives such an order. And the most likely person controlling it is my chief engineer, the person involved in all our operations. I must find out what he's after—and how to stop him before it's too late.

For all our lives. For *Gabriel*.

·   ·   ·

The chime from my wan-kong wakes me up. I'm slumped on the floor next to my folded bed. I've missed breakfast, again, but that's for the better as the very idea of food makes my stomach turn.

I splash water on my face and wipe my armpits with a damp cloth. Maybe if I'm smelly enough, they'll leave me alone for a day. The thought makes me giggle, and the next moment I'm laughing uncontrollably, tears streaming down my cheeks. This is bad. I'm breathing fast, teetering too close to the edge. Bad timing for another attack. I lower my head and take ten calming breaths. I've got to keep it together.

The bridge is quiet as I pass on the way to my office; all the lights in the green and only two crew on duty. Lim barely looks up as I enter, slouched over her console. Not likely she got much sleep, either. Zhang's not there, which is probably good as I'm not sure how I'd react. Wang works the engineering console. She flashes me a toothy grin, and this time I don't let myself get embarrassed but grin right back. I could use an ally in Zhang's camp, and the woman I saved from burning alive is the best candidate.

The captain's console blinks with message icons. Most are routine, but one's flagged urgent: Yefremov requesting a meeting.

Come to my office, I send back.

I barely manage to get seated when he arrives, his eyes bright even though the dark circles underneath indicate that he hasn't been sleeping much, either.

'We've found the graveyard! Sanchez and I, we've been studying the logs and comparing them to the maps and drone images.' The doctor winks. 'We're the best of mates now, the reverend and I. Anyway, I'm pretty sure I know where it is. So now they need to go out and dig up some bodies.'

'As soon as they secure the base.'

Yefremov rubs his chin, his beard badly in need of trimming. 'I guess volunteering to shuttle down to help them won't work?' He cocks his head, the question not entirely rhetorical.

'The shuttle's out of the question. We still don't know what happened and I'm not going to risk contaminating it. With the elevator, by the time you got there they'd have dissected the corpses. You'd miss all the fun.'

'Ha! But the fun's only starting. And Khan wants to send someone...'

I slide farther into my seat. My temples throb with an oncoming headache, every heartbeat like a barbed jab inside my skull.

'You may send one more person if you believe that's absolutely necessary. In the elevator. And not you.' I hesitate, but there's no point dancing around the issue. 'Basically, assume everyone you send will die of whatever killed the colonists. And make sure you can still take care of the rest of us here.'

Yefremov squints. 'That's a bit extreme, I dare say.'

'Is it? They had doctors. Plus almost a decade's experience on the planet. And they're all dead.'

He looks away, brows scrunching in thought. I'm not sure if he agrees, but I don't care. 'What precautions are you taking for the post-mortems?'

'A sterile station inside the hub's hospital. All the equipment we need is already there—actually, the medical provisions are much better than I expected.'

I nod. 'Good. The bodies... will they be intact? Considering the planet is sterile, at least according to Khan.'

He laughs. 'The planet might be sterile, but the bodies aren't. We're happy hosts to millions of microorganisms—some of them are actually keeping us alive. So, no, expect the bodies to be decomposed to a mush. But we can still learn a lot from mush.'

'I'll leave that to you, Doc.'

'My pleasure!' He winks, then reaches into his pocket.

'Here. Take two and drink lots of water. And for goodness' sake, try to get some sleep tonight, will you?'

I stare at the blister of pills in front of me. I'm rubbing my temples, I realise. 'Spasiba.' *Thanks.*

He tilts his head. 'Ha! Didn't know you spoke Russian.'

'Just the basics.' The words came out unplanned, but this is the best opening I could have hoped for. I force a smile, desperate to sound casual. 'Not getting much practice, though. I should use it more with you. Does anybody else speak Russian?'

'Only Navrov, as far as I know. But Khan never lets him out of the lab...' He says something in Russian too fast for me to follow.

'On second thoughts... let's stick to English.'

Yefremov laughs as he gets up. 'Save your language skills for Mandarin. Much more useful.'

My smile fades. I'm glad the doctor doesn't notice, already on his way out. Good timing, too, before I could say too much. I'm getting clearer on whom I can't trust, but that doesn't mean everyone else is off the hook. Too many questions remain unanswered, too many games played over the same chessboard.

Both Yefremov and Navrov were in cold-sleep at the time of the accident, so neither could have left me the message. Somebody else here must speak Russian—or at least write enough of it to scribble the warning on my pod.

I crack the blister of pills the doctor left me and pop them into my mouth. More messages blink on my monitor, none of them urgent, and none from Khan. Guess I'll have to do the honours. I call up the comms menu and select her name.

Khan's face appears on the screen a good thirty seconds later. As always, her uniform is immaculate, the name tag perfectly symmetrical, no hair out of place. I'm glad to see her eyes are bloodshot, though. At least I can be sure she's human.

She pinches her lips before stretching them into a half-smile that doesn't reach her eyes. 'How can I help you, Commander?'

I manage not to wince at the title. 'I hear you're planning to send more people to the planet?'

'That's correct. And additional equipment.'

'You should have discussed this with me first, Doctor Khan.'

Her eyes narrow. She leans away from the screen. 'I didn't expect it to be a problem.'

'It isn't. Still, the procedure's there for a reason.' Khan's lips twitch in what I'm sure is going to be a sarcastic comment, so I continue before she gets a chance. 'Like, for instance, when I have to tell other functions why sending more of their people is a bad idea. Helps if we at least appear to be a team.'

Khan takes a deep breath. 'I totally failed to consider that side of it. My apologies.'

She looks sincere, so I nod. 'Who are you sending?'

'Doctor Duangjit, a specialist in organic chemistry. And the equipment to run more tests on the local proto-life.'

I feel myself squint. 'Have you changed your mind about it being a risk?'

'No. I'm positive this is a dead end; the chemistry involved is incompatible with ours. But we agreed not to discard any hypothesis, and as a scientist I can only approve. We'll test it until we run out of ways to test.' She pauses, probably to make sure I notice her perfect attitude. Fair enough—she may be a human icicle, but she's a straight talker and knows her stuff. 'Can I assume you are all right with sending him down? Or should I file a formal request?'

I wave my hand. 'No formal request, just a word of discussion in the future. As for your people, I'll tell you what I told the other party: before you decide, assume everyone you send will fall to whatever killed the colonists. It'd be arrogant to assume our precautions are better.'

'They *are* better,' Khan says, her expression sombre. 'Because we know what happened to the colonists. But I agree, arrogance is the path to failure. I'll send the equipment, but not the man. Thank you for bringing me down to earth. If I can say so, in these circumstances.'

For the first time, her smile appears genuine, even if it's slightly crooked. Lack of practice, I guess. I smile back, wondering how my face looks to her. Exasperated? Overwhelmed? Confused? She'd be right with all those adjectives.

'Thank you. I leave the decision in your hands.'

I cut the connection and check the time. An hour to lunch and no meetings planned till after. I consider going back to the captain's journal, checking for things I may have missed, but this is something I can do from my cabin. There's something else I want to try, and I can only do it here: that extra computer, it must have a physical location. If we can find it, we may be able to disable it.

I tap the menu icon on my workstation. My fingers tremble with the knowledge of the invisible eyes tracking my every move, algorithms analysing my actions against some unknown objectives. But really, it should only be natural for a new commander to check out the specs of her own ship, right?

I select the general systems icon, then ask for the layout of the crew cabins. Innocent enough, and something that might be useful in an emergency. The images pop up on my screen. I turn and enlarge them, mapping the fastest paths to the common areas. The computer responds, following my every command. I zoom out, but the image just gets smaller.

'Computer, show me the ship's blueprints.'

The image appears a moment later, a tangle of lines marking every design detail. I can tell the engineering section by the greyed-out parts, no access permitted. If that's where the spy is hiding, we're out of luck. The main computer is split over several locations, with redundancies in case of damage. I rotate the image, pretending to check the bridge while I scan the connections branching out of there. One of the computing cores seems to be just behind the bridge wall, right next to—

I jump at the sharp knock on my door. Damn, bad timing. And the knock is coming from the bridge-side door. What if it's Zhang?

The visitor knocks again, even louder, and then the door just opens, without permission from me. Lim walks inside, her face so pale she makes me shiver.

She shoots a glance at the blueprints on my screen, then back at me. 'Apologies, Commander.'

'It's all right.' I hold her gaze. She wants to tell me something but can't. 'Have you finished the report?'

'Eh, yes. Yes, I have.' She moves towards my console. 'May I show you?'

I nod and step aside. Lim closes the blueprints, then calls up the keyboard and types: *Stay away from these files*.

She looks up at me to check if I've read the message, then erases it immediately.

'Is it—?' I start, but do not finish. I have a million questions but all I can do is stare at her wide eyes. *Big spike in activity. Don't know more*, she types, then erases.

I lick my lips, suddenly dry. The spy doesn't want me to look at the blueprints. It doesn't want to be found.

'This should fix it now,' she says stiffly.

'Yes, right. Good job. Most excellent. I'm lucky to have you.' The words bubble out of my mouth uncontrolled. But really, I *was* lucky she was at her post when I accessed the blueprints. What would have happened if she hadn't stopped me? Such luck to have someone with her skills on the ship.

The thought wedges itself across my brain, stopping the flow.

She's so good. Almost too good to be true. And conveniently available to feed me information I have no way of testing.

A chill runs down my back. Maybe I'm paranoid—but I'm basing everything on her words. I've got to know.

I motion for her to sit down. She scrunches her brows, puzzled, but makes her way to the nearest chair.

'I need you to tell me something.'

'Of course.'

I hesitate. Could this be another trigger? Something the spy wants to know? But no, the captain and that Guardian knew my past. They probably knew Lim's as well. 'The truth, this time: why did you join this mission?'

She pulls back ever so slightly, folds her hands over her lap. 'As I said, I'm apprenticed to New Horizons. This trip will cover my debt in just months of subjective time.'

I watch her, waiting.

Her mouth curves into a smile, nervous but confident, though a bit too well rehearsed to be entirely trustworthy. 'It's the truth. You have the full record of my apprenticeship in my personnel file.'

'I believe you're an apprentice. Who wouldn't be, at your age? But I don't believe it's the reason you signed up. You're too good. You could have companies bidding to buy out your debt, with premiums. So, I'll ask again: why did you sign up?'

Lim looks away. Her lips tremble, and she licks them with a quick swipe of her tongue. There's a secret there, I'm sure. Something she's afraid of.

She looks at her hands, the silence between us growing heavier with every breath.

'It was because...' she starts, but her voice breaks. She flicks her head to the side, away from me, and rubs her eye. 'Because of the riots. With that fake-plague, remember?'

My body stiffens into a block of ice. As if I could ever forget. Even if it hasn't only been weeks of our subjective time. I force my neck to bend, once, in a semblance of a nod.

'I did something...' She breaks off, hesitant again. Her eyebrows twitch as she seems to be weighing something, deciding how much she can trust me. Then she makes up her mind. 'There were all these rumours about the shipments into orbit, all the drugs stowed away. My cousin, he was part... He wanted to know. Said people were dying, and that they needed the facts. So... so, I hacked the transport ledger. The secure one, from Yun Ju Central.'

She drops her head, the words hanging in the air as if frozen.

I stare at her stooped figure, my heart an icy lump and my body numb.

Lim is Jo's cousin. She's the one who got us the shipping ledgers. Who told us where the meds were held.

She is the one I betrayed.

'You know what happened then,' she says, a tear rolling down her cheek. 'All those people killed. I never thought... I couldn't...'

I want to say something, to comfort her in her despair—but I can't speak, my breath trapped inside me like an accusation.

Lim straightens, defiant, or trying to be. 'I covered my tracks well enough. I *am* pretty good. But they could find it, or someone would talk, whatever. I figured it was best to disappear for a while. A long while. So, this is it. The truth. Are you going to report me?'

I push through my stupor to shake my head. 'You've committed no crime.'

Her eyes widen, some of the anxiety draining from her face. 'You don't think I have?'

'I was there. I know what it was like.' I look away, unable to say any more.

Lim gets the message. She leaves quietly, without a word of goodbye—or maybe she does say it, but I don't hear or see it, my vision shrunk to a grey tunnel.

Binamu. Jo never mentioned her name, only the Swahili term for a cousin. I assumed it was for safety.

Such a coincidence... Almost too much to imagine. But

then, is it really? Most of the crew come from the Feidi, except maybe the scientists and the Chinese engineers. And again, no one signs up to be frozen for thirty-five years each way without a damn good reason. We are all broken; all running away.

What secrets do the others carry? How many more are connected to the events that brought me here? I'm not sure I really want to know.

My hands move to the captain's cloned journal in my inside pocket. I touch the bookmark I made last night, and the screen lights up with the passage:

I met my second yesterday. She looks as dazed as I expected, completely unfit for duty. It's barely been weeks since the unpleasantness with her family. I don't know how they expect her to function. I raised my misgivings with the Guardian. No surprise, he ignored me because she's the central piece in the connections matrix—and she's Canadian, which keeps both parties happy. That's all fine, but—

I stop and return to the line before:

she's the central piece in the connections matrix.

Connections matrix—of what? If I'm a piece, then this is about people. The crew.

Crew Connections Matrix.

CCM.

That's it. A web of connections that link them all to me— but no, it's not about me, it's about the events I was involved in. The fake-plague. The riots.

Most of us come from the Feidi. No surprise the events touched us all. No surprise even that a crew like this would be a collection of escapees, all burdened with secrets. But whoever created the CCM not only knew those secrets—they allowed us to be recruited anyway. Or maybe because of them. Because we were vulnerable. And connected.

I'm pacing again, up to the picture of Earth on the far wall and back around the table. My feet pad against the decking, the sound hollow.

This doesn't make any sense. If mine and Lim's secrets are anything to go by, knowing them doesn't offer any advantage. Blackmail, maybe, if we were still on Earth—but we're years away, in distance and in time. Besides, nobody's tried to blackmail me, and I'm the 'central piece'. So what the hell's going on?

Someone knocks on the door—a loud, strident noise that makes me wince. But this time it comes from shipside, not from the bridge.

'Commander?' Price's voice, followed by another knock.

'Come in.'

The door slides open. Price is there, together with Sandra Russo, her deputy now that Miller's on the planet—a tall, olive-skinned woman with chestnut hair braided into a crown around her head.

Price grins. 'The doctor sent us. We are to escort you to the mess hall and make sure you have lunch. He said we are very much permitted to use force...'

Russo chuckles. Their happy faces seem to belong to a different reality, a wormhole glimpse of a better time. I lean on the table, suddenly dizzy.

'Are you all right?' Price asks, her smile replaced by a frown.

'Yes. You know, the doc's right. I need to eat.' I start for the door, stretching my lips in a semblance of a smile. 'What's on the menu today? Anything special?'

The women laugh behind me. Price says something, but her words drown in the hum inside my ears, and all I can think of is whether our paths crossed in the past, and why it could possibly matter.

CHAPTER -1

3 WEEKS BEFORE DEPARTURE

On Sunday, the churches all over the Feidi are buzzing. It starts with the Kenyan evangelicals, but the last I've heard the Polish Irish Catholics and an Orthodox diocese have joined in. We spread the word, and the local gossip net lit up like the savannah after a dry season. I don't know how many are ill or know someone who is—but I don't care, either, as long as it brings in numbers.

Stepan's group sets off from Kilimanjaro Cathedral; Gideon, the barman from The Two Horsemen, leads a troop from the Lower City. They start small but grow with every church, every street bar, playground, and eatery they pass. By the time the two groups merge, they are at least five hundred strong.

Jo and I watch them through a feed from a drone-cam. Our ops room is a beat-up truck parked on an empty lot inside the ring-shaped accretion of storehouses and repair shops that surround the base of the elevator. The place is abandoned on a Sunday morning; only emergency services and the guards are still on duty, but the nearest post is three hundred metres away, obscured by a row of offices.

'How far still?' Jo asks. He's staring at the screen, his fingers drumming a tattoo on the armrest.

'Twenty minutes.'

I drop the visor over my face and zoom in on the group. They march slowly, postures dignified, their clothes a colourful mosaic of African and European formal: vibrant greens, yellows and reds next to white shirts and blue ties tugged by the morning wind. The faces are mostly black or brown, though at least twenty per cent are non-African.

I toggle the display to the second drone. Its camera points at the steel gates of Deliveries International, a relatively minor player in orbital supplies, but who, according to Jo's cousin, has just received a massive medical shipment. The paperwork she screen-capped showed it was meant for the Feidi—and yet the exact same number of containers were booked for elevator transport. The march today is about getting the media to turn meds shortage into an election issue. If the opposition demand to inspect the warehouse, the mayor will have to listen.

On my screen, a dozen security personnel mill about in the morning sun. I zoom in on the weapons. Stun-guns in every holster, but also some live weapons. Stepan and Gideon will make sure to keep away from the gates, just chanting and flying banners for as long as it takes the media to get there. And given that we're going to call them, it won't be long.

I return to the march. They're only five hundred metres away, singing and chatting as if this were a Sunday promenade. Some wave to the drone as it passes above, while the people counter spins on my screen. One thousand, seven hundred and sixteen protesters. I feel myself grin. Perfect. Just perfect.

'Should we call the *Courier*?' Jo asks.

I'm about to nod when I notice the familiar shape of a police drone. I zoom in on the sky behind it. Police drones always have their media groupies—and there they are, two tiny flyers approaching at top speed.

'No need,' I say. 'The scouts are already here.'

My heartbeat accelerates, my cheeks flush. I haven't felt this good since the day I came down for Nadia's birth. Finally, we're doing something. They can no longer ignore us, no longer lie. It's our turn to be heard—and just in time for Anna and Nadia.

I toggle my displays back to the warehouse camera. The guards are still scattered over the complex, but their relaxed postures have changed to straight backs and alert glances. At least two are looking at their wan-kongs; another waves the agents farthest away towards the gate.

I push the feed to Jo's monitor. 'Keep an eye on the guards.'

The crowd feels the change, too. They're no longer singing, faces solemn, anxious eyes scanning the area. Some seem to hesitate, glancing behind them or up at the police drone now hovering above.

We can't let them lose their nerve. Not when we are so close.

I swing the camera to the back of the procession. Sure enough, the white-and-blue lights of police cabs approach from the city, sirens flaring. They have no right to stop us—but that doesn't mean they won't.

'Call the *Courier*,' I shout to Jo. 'And *Nation* and *Standard*. And *Kenniya Xinwen*. Say police are trying to stop a peaceful demonstration.' I tap my earbud. 'Gideon? Keep them marching. You're almost there!'

'Leave it with me,' he says, his voice hard.

He won't let them give up—his boyfriend's life depends on it, the man as close to death as Anna.

A moment later I see him move to the edge of the road, waving the marchers on. His mouth is moving—opening slowly as if in a song. The crowd picks up the tune, and soon they're all singing, their expressions determined. Gideon and five others wait till the end of the procession passes, then join in at the back. Good. They won't let anyone change their mind.

I return my attention to the drones. The police are almost there—they seem to have slowed down, though, the lights still flashing but the sirens off. Several media flyers track their progress.

'We're live on all channels!' Jo cries, then his voice turns sour. "Unsubstantiated reports of pharmaceuticals withheld from the city's hospitals". "The mayor rejects unproven allegations...""

Of course he would. The Feidi's businesses are his party's biggest donors. I hoped it would take longer, though, give us more time to address the media.

'Messages,' I say. 'Tell everyone to start sending.'

This is our counterattack, something the media won't be able to ignore: messages from all corners of the Feidi, demanding that the reporters investigate the matter.

'Done,' Jo says. 'Now it's their move.'

At Deliveries International, a new person has appeared, a thickset, brown-skinned man wearing a suit rather than the black security uniform. He stands motionless just to the side of the two guards but not acknowledging them in any way. Mind-Link. He's communicating with the higher-ups.

I glance at the procession. They are approaching the gate, the crowd stretched out as some fail to keep up the pace, frail or afraid. Stepan marches ahead of the rest, and just behind him three others unfurl a banner: MEDS FOR ALL—NOT JUST FOR YUN JU.

Media drones dive in to get the best pictures. Further down the road, the police vehicles trail the end of the procession. They're keeping their options open, whichever way the fortune turns.

'Standard's showing the messages.' Jo's voice rings with excitement. 'Habari now demands warehouse access!'

Yes! It's working. It's finally working.

I lift my visor, grinning, just as Jo's smile breaks and his eyes narrow.

'*Courier*'s running a comment piece. '"Foreign agents incite panic..."' He taps on another feed, squinting as he reads the transcript. '*Xinwen*'s the same: "Crowds tricked into disorder." "Rumours campaign to undermine the Feidi".' He looks up at me, his face crushed. 'Tā mā de! What now?'

This is too fast. The comments, the rebuttals. I knew they'd come, but not before we managed to plant the doubt with enough people. With someone with enough power to demand an inspection. But they are ready for us, press releases already written, commentators bribed. I want to scream in anger, but no, that won't help.

Think!

The big outlets are going with the mayor. And not a word from the opposition. Why? I thought they'd jump at a chance to discredit the mayor, but they won't stick their necks out unless they believe they can win.

I sit up. That's what we need: proof, something no one will be able to deny. And right now, while we still have everyone's attention.

'The screencaps. We've got to send them the screencaps.'

Jo swings towards me. 'No way! I promised binamu we'd keep them secret.'

'They're just screencaps. Nobody can trace them.'

'And what if they do?'

I reach for my wan-kong, start typing a message. Jo makes to grab it, but I pull away.

'People are dying, Jo. Really dying. How does that compare to your cousin losing her job?'

'It's not just her job! She'll go to jail for this!'

'She'll be a hero! All the lives she's going to save!'

'How about *her* life?'

I shake my head, determined not to look at him. 'She's a whistle-blower. There're laws to protect such people.'

A part of me questions how I can be so sure, but I don't listen. Anna's life is all that matters. And Nadia's. And all the others. How can anything compare to that?

'We promised her. *I* promised her. She'll never get a job again. We'll destroy her.'

I lower the wan-kong and make myself look at his accusing eyes. 'She won't need to work. We'll pay her salary, for the rest of her life. All the survivors will. I swear to you.'

He scowls but doesn't move. I press send.

Jo doesn't say anything more. He turns away from me, checking the newsfeed. He may hate me, but he's not stupid. That's all that counts.

It takes less than a minute for the screencaps to appear—first on the *Courier*'s drip, then across all the others. Within ninety seconds all public channels are ablaze.

Back at the warehouse, the suited man has finished his conversation. He starts towards the gate, waving the guards to follow. They form a defensive line, hands on their weapons. They're never going to use them—not against civilians safely on a public road, not with all the cameras pointed at them.

Something moves at the edge of my vision. I rotate the camera, sharpening the focus. A bullet-shaped people carrier, black and windowless, rolls through a back entrance. The doors pop open to release eight figures in body-hugging silver uniforms, mirror-visors obscuring their faces, high-tech weapons in holsters on their hips and across their backs. I gasp. Sky Sharks, the elite security forces that guard the homes and the offices of the yun-ying, the orbital aristocracy. My breath catches in my throat, beads of sweat trickling down my cheek. What does this mean?

But no, they won't shoot. It would only prove that they've

got something to hide. They wouldn't be so stupid. Not when the world is watching.

I consider calling Stepan and Gideon. But what would I tell them? They know they must stay clear of the gate. No point making them any more nervous.

'What the hell?' Jo cries.

'What is it?'

'"The Chamber of Commerce confirms that the warehouse manifest has been faked". "Mayor accuses foreign agents of manipulating the populace".' He throws the zheping on the seat. 'Fuck them!'

'They just need to keep reporting,' I say, my voice dead.

I hope I'm right. I must be. Even if the mayor is as corrupt as they say, this is a golden chance for the opposition. They have their own media, as ardent as the mayor's. Someone will question the Chamber's statement, demand access to the warehouse. We just need one voice. One independent—

My heart skips a beat, and the floor feels like quicksand as the realisation sinks in.

Our plan, it's all about pitting the mayor against the opposition, both at each other's throats in the election year. But neither of them owns the media who support them.

Who does? Who owns the *Courier*? Or *Kenniya Xinwen*? Names flash in my memory, the faces of powerful individuals, the yun-ying elite playing us like pawns from their orbital castles.

The very customers at the end of the supply chain we're trying to break.

My grasp tightens on the controls till one of the drones starts a nosedive. I bring it up and set all the machines to hover, sweat running down my back.

They won't let the news spread. They own the media, the very cameras watching us now. Any moment they will—

'Fire at the central hospital. The *Courier* reports an explosion...' Jo's voice quivers. 'It's on all the channels now.'

On my visor, I watch the media drones retreating. Soon it's only the *Standard*'s purple flyer and the cheap buzzers of the independents. Too extreme or too small to count.

Is this how it ends? Is there really nothing we can do to make them listen? I've got no answers, only the bitter taste of bile filling my mouth.

'Call *Standard*. And anyone who's still here,' I say. 'Tell them—'

A loud bang makes us wince. I check the screens, scanning for the source. At the front, the procession resembles tidewaters encroaching on the warehouse grounds, but they're staying well clear, and the guards have not moved from their line on the other side of the fence.

I switch to the second drone: behind the protesters, police cars form a line, lights flashing and the sirens wailing. At least ten agents approach the crowd, hands on holsters. Another *bang* —and this time I see the flare as one of them fires into the air.

The crowd stirs, shifting away from the police, their movements jittery. Some try to retreat, but the only way out is back down the road, through the blockade of the police cars.

Jo gasps. 'What are they doing?'

'Trying to intimidate them. Once they're scared, they'll do what—' I stop.

On the other half of my screen, a small group, maybe ten strong, splits from the main body of the procession, crossing the strip of red soil between the road and the fence. They are a fair distance from the gate, and so far, nobody's paying them any attention. Gideon's in the lead, his movements quick and determined. Is he trying to take things into his own hands? The fence is electrified —no way they can get through. And if the guards see them...

'Call Gideon,' I cry. 'Ask him what he's trying—'

And then I know. Tools emerge from their backpacks: saws and metal cutters. And they are headed straight for the acacia tree closest to the fence.

'They're trying to short-circuit the fence!'

'Will it even work?'

'I don't know. Maybe. Damn it, call them and tell them to stop!'

Jo jabs his wan-kong. 'Not answering.'

I tremble. I've got to make them stop. They'll be walking straight into the guards. Oh, hell. The guards may still hesitate; they are just Kenyans, like the rest of us. But not the Sky Sharks.

My hands shake on the controls. Maybe they'll stop when they see my drones. Maybe the Sharks will hold back if they know somebody's watching.

I swing two drones down in a coordinated dive, zipping low over the fence. I'm almost there, only metres away from the acacia tree already leaning perilously over the wires.

My earbuds screech; my screen blazes with white light. I cry in pain and yank the visor off my head. All the monitors flicker to grey, then black out.

'My wan-kong's dead,' Jo says. 'What—?'

'EM cannon. Everything's cooked.' I throw my gear on the floor and jump to the door.

'Where are you going?'

'I've got to stop them!'

Loud cracks reverberate through the gaps between buildings. Gunshots. I break into a sprint, my feet pounding the baked asphalt in the rhythm of my heartbeat.

Something grabs my arm, pulling me to a stop. Jo. 'You can't help—'

I try to push him off, but he's holding fast.

'There are Sharks there!'

'Imposs—'

'I saw them!'

'What?!' Horror twists his face. His grasp loosens. 'And you didn't warn them?'

'I didn't think...' No point explaining. I pull away from him and his fury and run on, towards the screaming crowd.

Another burst of shots, dry pops like whip cracks. Snipers? The police, maybe trying to intervene? I accelerate even though I can't run any faster, choking on mouthfuls of hot air. Sweat pours down my back, over my face and into my eyes. I stumble, falling headlong, arms outstretched till my hands crash into the tarmac. Something cracks in my wrist, pain blinding me for a moment. I yelp and scramble to get up, my legs shaking, and my trousers ripped at the knees. I limp forward, my wrist sending jabs of pain with every step.

I reach the main road. People rush past me, faces twisted in terror, their Sunday finery covered with sweat and dust. Behind them, the procession has descended into chaos. Groups flee in opposite directions, mixing and colliding. Some shout, some cry, others stand numbly, horrified or dazed. An old woman in a green dress sits on the side of the road, cradling a flower-adorned hat. Next to her, a child in a pink shirt weeps loudly. A man walks past me, eyes vacant, blood staining his forehead.

Then I see the bodies: three people, two women and a child, sprawled on the ground, unmoving. Dust cakes their clothes, their hands, their hair, their bloodstained lips. These are not gun wounds. They've been trampled, killed in the panic. How many? I glance around, the pounding in my ears receding enough to let desperate cries drift in from all directions. The crowd has thinned now, and through the gaps I see more people on the ground, bloodstained and dusty, some unmoving, others struggling to get up or crawling on all fours away from the chaos.

I can't think. My mind locks up, cold and absent. This isn't real. I'm not here. This hasn't happened.

I shiver in the cold. Or am I hot? Where am I?

Stepan.

I've got to find him. I've got to get him out.

I stumble on, some part of my brain deciding that I need to go north, through the stunned, horrified crowd, towards the gate. Somebody tries to stop me, their grasp too feeble to hold. I push through a denser patch, people shouting, waving their dead wan-kongs to catch the signal. The gate's just behind them, past the small group leaning over...

Leaning over bodies.

I recognise Stepan's shirt, still proudly white despite the sprinkling of red dust and even redder stain of blood on his chest. Someone's holding him, lifting his head and shouting for help, more blood dripping from their arm onto Stepan's white shirt.

I drop to the ground beside him, the pain blinding as I land on my broken wrist. 'Stepan! Stepan, please!'

His eyelids flutter. He's alive! He'll make it, I'm sure. We just need an ambulance, and he'll be safe.

'Natty...' he whispers, every sound an effort. 'Don't let them—'

I grab his hand in my good one. 'I'll get you to a hospital. You'll be fine. It's just a flesh wound.'

Behind Stepan, the man holding him shakes his head. I glare. What does he know?

'Go,' Stepan says. He tries to lift his head, but it's too much. His lips move, and I lower my head to his mouth. 'For Jason. Too late for the rest of us. But Jason... Please.'

My tears fall on his face. 'I won't...'

'Jason, Natty... Promise...'

'I promise. I'll take care of him. I promise!'

His eyes close. He gasps, the breath cut mid-rise, his body still.

My shoulders heave. I want to scream, to rip the guards to bloody shreds with my bare nails.

It's my fault. I should have realised this plan would never work. I should have warned them about the Sharks. I should have told them to retreat. I should have saved him.

'Go,' the man says. 'You can't help him.'

I shake my head, numb.

'You can't take care of that kid from jail. Go.'

I'm amazed when my legs lift me and walk me away, my back to Stepan and to all the others I've killed. I limp through the crowd, down the driveway, past our van still standing there, abandoned, doors wide open. I walk on, down a side road, past police cars and ambulances, towards the angry city and the rising cries of spreading riots.

CHAPTER 12

We meet again a day later, with the field team reporting the results of the first autopsies.

There's just the core team in the office, with ample space for the six of us, and yet the atmosphere is as heavy as before, maybe heavier. Price scowls at Zhang whenever she thinks he's not looking; Yefremov and Khan pretend not to notice each other, though in the case of the scientist this might not all be pretence. Sanchez casts me an exasperated glance, but a shrug is all I can manage.

The screen lights up with the image of the field team. They're seated around the same fold-out table, but the space behind them looks lived-in and almost cosy: portable desks and workbenches have replaced metal crates, a drinks dispenser sits next to the food processor on the counter against the wall, spot lamps fill the corners with warm, yellow light. The faces of the people have returned to their normal colouring, though their expressions remain as troubled as before.

Johansson nods at Yefremov and Sanchez. 'We found the graveyard at exactly the coordinates you predicted.'

The image flips to show a flat patch of land surrounded by a low, rickety wall of stacked rocks and pebbles. Inside, knee-high boulders stand in even rows, each carved with a cross and a name.

I gasp. It's not the sight of the graves—that's the part I expected. What makes my breath catch are the colours, a splash of green hues so far unseen in the grey landscape. Not rich and leafy, far from it—more sage-grey and olive-yellow, yet something undoubtedly alive, like the last cry of defiance from the dead.

'The lichen have taken really well,' Johansson continues. 'There's a measurable increase in oxygen level just above the surface.' His mouth twists. 'Another ten thousand years and we can plant an orchard.'

Khan leans back in her chair. 'It's the same genus as what they're using on Mars, I assume?'

'The same genus, but a more advanced species,' Johansson says. 'All the terraforming flora is American-engineered, so I'm guessing the colonists got the best. Better than what the Martians could afford.'

Yefremov taps his finger on the table. 'Could we move on to the autopsy, please?'

Khan shoots him a pointed glance but says nothing as I nod my agreement.

'Of course.' Johansson gestures to the medics on his left. 'Doctor Raji, please proceed.'

The pathologist is a small man with a crown of black hair on the sides of a balding skull that somehow makes me think of a koala. He clears his throat, then casts a hesitant glance at Gonzales. The other medic gives him a tiny nod. Not the usual behaviour from either of them, but then, they've just spent a day dissecting corpses.

'We have analysed four bodies, selected for time of death,' Raji starts. He speaks with a slow, nasal drawl, his Indian accent lost under echoes of other tongues. 'For the earliest, or oldest, we have the exact information on both the date and cause of death from the medical files. This is our "control", if you have it. The other three cadavers come from the beginnings of the "trouble" period, from the first one still recorded in the files to the last one, which didn't even have a marked grave. It's difficult to be entirely sure about the date of death for that last individual as the decomposition process here is markedly different than our standard benchmarks. We studied—'

'Doctor Raji.' I stifle an impatient sigh. 'Do you know what killed them?'

The pathologist draws back, his cheeks flushing ruddy brown. 'Yes, right. I thought the background... Right...' He clears his throat. 'I'm afraid at this moment we cannot provide a definite answer. Or rather, we have a substantial list of things that didn't kill them. We found nothing abnormal in terms of pathogens, toxins, or antibodies that would indicate an immune response. In all these cases, we have some idea of the cause of death, all three apparently the result of accidents. This fits with what Doctor Yefremov mentioned in our last briefing: an unusual number of preventable incidents, indicating potential mental instability, but we did not find anything that would confirm that such instability indeed existed or what could have caused it.'

I glance at Yefremov. I'm sure the pathologist is excellent at his job, but it'd help if we had someone who could communicate with non-scientists. 'So you still believe they've lost their minds but have no clue why?'

Raji flinches. 'Really, that's not a proper diagnosis—'

Gonzales speaks over him. 'We don't know for sure—'

I raise my hand. 'I already know what we don't know. Can anyone tell me something we do know?'

The scientists fall silent, then exchange glances as if trying to decide who to throw under the train.

Gonzales takes one for the team. 'Commander, we'd all like

a quick answer. Unfortunately, the reality isn't cooperating. We've already excluded environmental causes and equipment failure. We can now confirm that it wasn't an epidemic, a poisoning, or any easily identifiable medical cause. The only way we can get to what really happened is by careful elimination of all possible options. This will take time, and that's the truth of it.'

I sigh. 'Fair enough. Did you learn anything at all from the autopsies? Anything you didn't expect to find?'

Raji and Gonzales exchange glances, clearly wavering. Johansson turns to stare at them, surprised.

I lean forward. 'We need to know, people, even if it's early days.'

Raji swallows, then pulls in a bracing breath. 'Please keep in mind that this is preliminary. We need a larger sample to be sure.' He casts another glance at Gonzales, the other medic's face suddenly paler. 'All of the bodies we examined seem to carry residues of brain implants.'

'Mind-Link,' Gonzales jumps in. 'They all had it.'

Mind-Link. The very thing the spy tracks. Is this the secret it's protecting?

I hold my breath, nails digging into the armrest as I wait for the blare of alarm, the hiss of decompression, the boom of explosions. Seconds pass, silent, except for the excited voices of the others around me.

'Is it possible that all five of them came from the Chinese group?' Khan asks.

'Would even the Chinese citizens have Mind-Link?' Yefremov says. 'They were all Christians, right?'

'If they were American, then they wouldn't have Mind-Link,' Price says.

No alarm. No decompression or signal from the engines.

I reach for my zheping and jot a message to Lim: *Is anything happening?*

The answer comes back an instant later. *Nothing I can see.*

I let go of the armrests, easing myself back into the chair. This may be a false alarm. A coincidence that the term the spy tracks relates to the discovery.

On the screen, Raji raises his voice to get the others' attention. 'We know the ethnicity of the first two corpses from the medical records: both American; one of European, the other of African heritage.'

'One more thing,' Gonzales adds. 'We've already noticed the medical facilities here were better than expected. And they include several specialist instruments for deep-brain procedures.'

This time nobody speaks, but all eyes turn to Sanchez. The chaplain shrinks into his seat, unusually silent.

I put my elbows on the table, cutting the distance between us. 'Is there something you want to tell us, Reverend?'

Sanchez examines his hands, avoiding our glances or deciding what to say. His shoulders move in the tiniest of shrugs. 'It was going to come out sooner or later, so it may as well be now.' He leans on the table, lifting his head to face us. 'All the first-wave colonists got Mind-Link. The church elders agreed that it was a life-saving tool for people relying on fast interaction with their equipment. Please remember that we have no objections to the technology itself—the faithful refrain from it only to avoid the temptation of immoral content, ubiquitous on Earth. That wasn't going to be a problem here.'

'Why the secrecy, then?' Yefremov asks.

Sanchez tries a smile, but it comes out exhausted. 'The elders decided to keep it on a "need-to-know" basis. My guess is they were concerned about creating a precedent.'

I can't keep from shaking my head. 'And we don't fall into the "need-to-know" category? The people they sent to investigate?'

Sanchez looks at his hands again, his cheeks turning a deep

shade of red. 'That wasn't my decision. I was instructed not to volunteer the information, but not to conceal it either, should it become necessary.'

'Well, aren't we grateful...' I don't bother to soften my sarcasm. He deserves it, even if he's acting on orders he can't control, the church resembling the military in too many ways to count.

The reverend seems to agree, as he leans back, shoulders hunched, the red colouring spreading up to his hairline.

I let the silence linger for another moment, then ask the scientists to continue the briefing. They move on to the technical details of the many chemical substances they tested and what they revealed. Khan and Yefremov take turns asking questions, but this is miles beyond the scope of my company-funded science education.

I glance at Zhang. He's been keeping strangely quiet. As if he already knew the secret. Or doesn't want to get involved.

Or maybe he's been using the time to communicate with the spy, initiating whatever protocols the machine is about to enact.

Taking control of the ship.

But no, that doesn't make sense. The secret is too trivial to merit such precautions. If we broadcast the news back to Earth, the fact would likely cause the church elders some embarrassment—but only that. Sanchez himself made no effort to conceal the truth. And why would the Chinese be involved? Mind-Link's their design, but it's also a commercially available product.

Which means this is not the explanation, not the reason for the spy's existence.

My heart sinks. I should be relieved, not disappointed. Yet for a terrifying moment I thought I had the answer—now I'm back to the fury of questions and the uncertainty. And still totally, completely, at the mercy of the spy and its masters.

The rhythm of the voices around me changes and I force my attention back to the meeting.

'So, these are the next steps, on top of the work already planned.' Johansson raises his hand and touches his fingers in turn. 'One, for the medical team, three more autopsies; two, search for additional records in the hub's computer and the medical system; and three, investigate the habitat, including individual quarters. Did I miss anything?'

Head shakes all around, and the connection winks out. Zhang is the first one on his feet, the others following one by one.

Sanchez catches my eye.

'Reverend, a word, if you will.'

He slumps back into the seat while the others smirk in mock sympathy. When did I become the evil headmistress?

'You know what I'm going to ask,' I say when the door closes behind the last of them.

Sanchez puts on an apologetic smile. 'I'm really sorry—'

'You did what you had to. I know you had your orders. But the people who gave them are far away. We're here, and so is *Gabriel*. You can't know what apparently "small" detail will make a life-or-death difference to them.'

His face grows sombre, a frown forming on his forehead. 'I didn't think it'd matter. Those on *Gabriel* don't have Mind-Link —it was a one-off, for the first settlers.' He shakes his head. 'I should have told you. I'm sorry.'

'It's done. But I must know if there are any other secrets. No matter what the company or the church told you. This could cost lives, Pete.'

He leans forward, his eyes earnest. 'There's nothing more. Or nothing that I know; that's the only thing I can say with certainty.'

I hold his gaze.

'I'll swear, if you want me to.'

'What I want is for you to come to me if you find anything odd or unusual. No matter how trivial.' I hesitate, not sure how much to say. 'I have a feeling there are more secrets at play here.'

Sanchez's frown deepens. 'What—'

I wave my arm. 'I don't know, or I'd be able to act. But I need to trust my key crew. And you, in particular, Reverend.'

'You have my word, Commander.'

I nod, not entirely sure how much I can believe him. He seemed shaken by my mention of *Gabriel*, though, so he probably never realised that his secret could affect them. Maybe that'll make him think twice about withholding information in the future.

I stand up, the meeting over.

Sanchez gets to his feet but remains at his end of the table. 'One more thing, now that we're talking. Tomorrow's Wednesday. Our first multi-faith service?' he adds in answer to my unspoken question. 'I know it's not your thing, and as promised, I won't bother you on Sundays. This is different. It'll be our first social event outside work. Whatever you think of organised religion, it has gelled communities over the centuries.' He pauses, checking my reaction.

I lean on the chair. 'You mean, when they weren't slaughtering each other over it?'

He doesn't flinch. 'They did good enough jobs of that even without religion. Anything will do, if you want an excuse. Much harder to find things to bring people together. Faith, when done right, can do it.'

'And you hope to do it right?'

'I *will* do it right.' Sanchez moves towards me along the length of the table, stopping an arm's length away. 'Whatever you think about me, I care about this crew. All of them. They'll tear themselves apart if we don't stop them.'

He holds my gaze, firm and open. I may have underestimated him.

'It's worth a try, Reverend. *If* you do it right.'

'So you'll come?'

'Yes. Do you want me to talk to the others?'

His lips curve into a small smile. 'I've been kind of guilt-tripping them into coming after they voted for Wednesdays. I don't want it to feel like it's an order.'

'As you wish.'

He nods a goodbye and moves to the door. I let out a sigh. I hope he's right, even though church duty is the last thing on my wish list. This crew does need a miracle.

I turn to see a message light blinking on my zheping. The text pops up on the screen, and my hands start to shake. It's from Lim.

We need to talk.

Lim's waiting when I reach the tether room five minutes later, her face crumpled with worry. The space is as empty as before, but the air smells of something sharp and metallic, like an industrial warehouse. Someone must have recently used the cargo access. I hope they won't be back any time soon.

I lean against the wall, letting its coolness support me. 'Tell me.'

'When you sent me the question, everything looked normal. But then I found something strange in the power indicators—weird spikes, power diverted from one core to the other without any reason I could explain. It shot off the charts for a few seconds, and then stabilised—but at a slightly higher level.'

'What does this mean?'

Lim leans against the wall opposite me, her hands clasped tightly as if to stop them from shaking. 'It means something's consuming power that didn't do it before.'

I swallow. My voice is a croak. 'It's activated... something? What?'

'I don't know. But I think you're right—I thought the spy was a program, but it's more than that. It must have a dedicated core, separate from the main computer.'

'Because it reacted when I looked at the blueprints?'

She nods. 'The warning system lit up like a Christmas tree. I wasn't sure what it was, but I could see the signal was coming from your office.'

Damn.

'There's a good part to this,' I say slowly, gathering my thoughts. 'If it's got a physical core hidden in some secret compartment, then we can find it and disable it.'

'Maybe. But how are we going to find it without access to the blueprints?'

'It's still just a machine, with cables we can cut and circuits we can smash.'

Lim looks unconvinced. 'If it doesn't have other defences...'

'We need to find it. I don't know how, but we must.'

Another thought snakes its way into my brain. If the ship is hiding one secret compartment, who's to say there can't be more? My head's spinning. It's too much: the sabotage, the dead colonists, the spy computer on my ship. I slump down on the floor, my back soaking up the chill of the metal lining the wall.

Lim mirrors my movement. Judging by the hesitation in her gaze, she's not done with the bad news.

'Did you find anything else?'

'I tried to figure out more triggers, as we talked. We know about Mind-Link and now the blueprints. I found several others which I don't understand: image files that I can't preview without triggering. Links to medical data. And some really odd ones, like tracking the volume and quality of voices. So, not only what we say, but how we say it.' She shrugs. 'I'll let you know if I make sense of any of it. The point is, I don't think any single trigger could set off a reaction. It's like one activates the next, and the next, and only the right combination will result in action from the spy.'

I nod, even though I'm not sure I understand the implications. 'Do you have any idea what that action would be?'

'No. But...' A tremor runs through her frame. 'I don't think it's alone.'

'What do you mean?'

'It's still only a computer. It's not a general intelligence.'

'So, it can flow algorithms but can't think for itself the way a human can.'

'Exactly. It can execute, or even adjust, its own programming, but it can't make decisions on grey issues. And with the number of triggers, and the way they're interconnected...'

She breaks off, but this time I know where she's going. 'You mean it needs human supervision?'

'Yes. Someone on board has the access codes and the knowledge of the spy's objectives.'

Chill naps at my bones. 'Who?'

'I don't know.'

I hesitate. She is half Chinese. My suspicions against Zhang might turn her against me. But I have to know. I pull out the copy of the captain's journal and scroll to the third bookmark.

The archer's arrows are poison. Don't trust him.

Lim looks up at me, not understanding. I switch the text to Mandarin, and watch her eyes widen with recognition. 'Do you think...?'

'I don't know. It *could* be a coincidence.' I force a chuckle. 'Maybe the captain took archery as a hobby.' I let the silence linger for a moment. 'Could you talk to any of the engineers? I mean, you may be—'

She shakes her head sharply. 'I'm not one of them, if that's what you're thinking. I've got a Chinese pa-pian, but I'm half Kenyan—and even if I weren't, I'm not from the mainland. Enclaves are like colonies, only good when the empire wants something from you, not when you want something from the empire.'

She rubs the side of her face, her gaze locked on the floor. Not Chinese enough for the Chinese. I'm sure for the Kenyans she wasn't Kenyan enough, either.

'Lim—'

'Firyali,' she snaps, then her eyes widen in consternation. 'I mean, whichever you prefer, sir. But Firyali is my first name. My Kenyan name.'

'I like Firyali. I'm Nat. Nathalie.'

She sniffs. 'I think I'll stick to "commander", if you don't mind.'

'Somehow I thought you would.' I swing towards her, our legs almost touching across the floor. 'I need you to do something for me.'

'Yes?'

'The fire in the cryo-chamber. I don't think it was an accident.'

'What?!'

'I have no proof. But you know the system better than I. Maybe there's something in the maintenance logs. Or anywhere else.'

She manages a nod, her chin trembling and her eyes wide.

I push myself off the floor. In front of me, the outer bulkhead leads directly to the tether, and through it to the engine deck. I can't even enter the tether without access codes. If that's where the spy is hidden, we'll have a hell of a time trying to reach it unnoticed. Especially if the most senior of the engineers is the one protecting it.

'We've got to find it, Firyali. The spy. We've got to find it and destroy it before it destroys us.'

CHAPTER 13

An urgent noise cuts through my dreams. I spring up, muscles tensing into action. No, it's not the alarm. Just a message. From Sanchez? At this time? I check my wan-kong: 03.00. This can't be good.

The message signal keeps buzzing. I slap the wan-kong on my wrist and reach for the bigger screen of the zheping. 'What's going on, Reverend?'

Sanchez stares at me from the screen: eyes bloodshot, lips cracked from biting, hair dishevelled. I can't see much behind him, but he appears to be in his cabin, lights dimmed and only his face lit with the ghostly glow of his screen.

'I'm sorry to wake you, but... something's come up. I think we should talk.'

'What is it about?'

He forces his gaze to the camera—I haven't turned mine on, so he's looking at a grey screen. 'The logs. They found two personal logs yesterday, the mayor's and the bishop's. Still no answers, but I need to—'

I flick my camera on. Sanchez winces, from surprise or from my glare. I hope it's the latter.

'Why the hell haven't I heard about it?'

'I can explain. Please. Can we talk?'

'My office. In ten minutes.' I cut the connection before he manages to respond. That's the best I can do before I start yelling. If he wants me to trust him, he's going about it the wrong way.

I'm seething when I reach the office. Sanchez waits by the door, a crumpled shirt hanging loosely, something red clenched in his hands. He follows me inside, his mouth pinched in worry.

I lean against the desk. 'I'm listening.'

Sanchez puts the red thing on the table: an American-design data pad, rolled up rather than folded. This one's in cardinal-red with gold trim on the cover. A Bible-pad. I've seen clergy use those before and stupidly assumed that was all they held, the Bible.

He runs his tongue over his lips, then cracks his knuckles, his movements tense. 'The engineers processed another batch of data from the hub. Last night, they found two logs. One was from Mayor Tucker. They're still going through it, but it seems useless. Sporadic entries ending weeks before the blackout. The other is the personal journal of the bishop, Reverend David Cheng. Senior pastor really, for a congregation this size, but since it's the only one on the planet...' Sanchez spreads his arms apologetically, as if I give a damn about the title.

I lean back, my arms across my chest. 'Was that any help? And why the hell didn't they inform *me* about it?'

'It was late,' he starts, but I snort. 'Well, finding the logs wasn't important until we knew what was in them. Johansson was reading the mayor's log, but they weren't going to start on the bishop's until the morning, so I asked Miller to send me a copy. In confidence. The others don't know I have it.'

Blood rises to my face. 'Are you saying you've been making arrangements behind my back? Do you even realise how bad this is?'

'I do, but—'

'No, there's no 'but' that can justify going behind your commanding officer's back and using security to help you. Especially not with this crew. They are already distrustful of each other. You don't want to make it worse.'

Sanchez shakes his head repeatedly, half turned away from me, his eyes on the red Bible-pad. 'I know. But that's exactly why I did it. And I'm glad I did.'

I rub my face, more exasperated now than angry. 'So, what did you find?'

His mouth twitches in a bitter grimace. 'As I said, no explanation as to what caused the tragedy—or rather, plenty of theories, one more outlandish than the next. By the end, the entries are fragmented and barely coherent. The last one just has the word "coming" repeated over and over.'

'So he was losing his mind, like the rest of them.'

'I believe so. He was losing his mind, or had it affected in some way; I'll leave the diagnosis to the doctors. But before that, before he lost control entirely, he recorded everything in great detail. And it makes for a very troubling read...'

Sanchez breaks off. He digs in his pocket for a tissue, then takes a long moment to wipe his forehead. 'It starts with the accidents, just as the medics said. At first, he is worried and bewildered, but then one day it's like he stops caring. He still lists the deaths, sometimes several in a single day, but there's no sorrow in his words, no trace of compassion. And these are no longer accidents. There's violence. Executions... And still he just records each one as if he's counting jars in the storeroom.'

I shiver. The news is not a surprise; we knew they'd caused their own demise in the end. Still, the confirmation is chilling. Executions?

'And that's not even why I woke you up,' Sanchez says. 'It's because of what he claims was the cause of the trouble.'

'And that is?'

'A generation-spanning conspiracy by the Chinese colonists, who, according to him, were never "real" Christians but spies sent to prepare the colony for Chinese takeover.'

'Cāo!' I swear. This is the last thing we need now, especially after the news of China's escalations back on Earth. 'Does he have any support for his theory?'

'Plenty, as far as he is concerned. Detailed schematics of how an undetectable poison gas was released into the air. Pages about food manipulated to make it nutrient deficient. Sort of like causing scurvy, but for the mind. It's all nonsense, of course, but...'

'What did the others think? I mean, the other colonists?'

'From what I gathered, those he considered "real Christians" agreed with him—or at least he believed they did. By then, the Chinese group had their own congregation, but the two had splintered even before the troubles. The American section fractured even further, with talk of heresy and excommunications...' Sanchez wipes his forehead again, his hands shaking. 'It's a difficult read, Commander. Even if you know they were all suffering from... something.' He takes a deep breath, his expression defeated. 'Still, the Chinese got most of the blame. That seems to be the one thing they agreed on.'

My memory returns to the name he mentioned. 'Did you say the bishop's name was David *Cheng*?'

The sound Sanchez produces is somewhere between a laugh and a sob. 'Yes! American of Chinese descent, chosen specifically for his heritage even though his family had left Asia five generations earlier. He'd made an effort, it seems, tried to learn Mandarin... It didn't make a difference. He was American, and this is the age when ethnicity is nothing and citizenship is everything. Any excuse works if all you want is to hate thy neighbour. And that's the only thing we've been consistently good at, over the ages.'

He hides his face in his hands, shoulders trembling. 'These

were Christians, Commander. And they slaughtered each other, down to the very last child.'

He wipes his eyes, not meeting my gaze. This has hit him on some deep personal level, as if a badly healed wound got scratched open. One day I might ask him what it is, if he ever wants to tell me. But not now.

'Pete, they were ill. Something happened to them, warped their minds, and turned them into monsters. That's what we're here to find out.'

'How long before we, too, become monsters? And we don't even have the excuse!'

Right. This ship was a wasps' nest even before the bad news from Earth. And now this. How long before we splinter into hostile factions? Before we end up like the colonists?

'We can't let this get out of hand.' I make my way to the table, my mind racing. Despite my misgivings, the reverend has made the right choice getting his hands on the log. 'Who else knows about the journal?'

'Everybody on the field team, but they won't read it till the morning.' He hesitates. 'Maybe Miller. He did send it to me, so he might have looked inside. And maybe the engineers, when they recovered it.'

I slide into the chair, my limbs heavy and my wrist hurting again. 'If Miller read it, then Price knows the story by now.'

'Possibly. And if so, the rest of the Americans will know soon.'

I try to hope that Price will be level-headed enough to realise the bishop was deranged. But this is just more sparks on dry kindling. She already suspects the Chinese crew—or at least one of them—of trying to sabotage our mission. All it takes is one of her people to believe that where there's smoke, there's fire, and we may have a real problem.

'We must disprove the bishop's arguments—before we even get to the discussion about the state of his mind. We need hard facts. Show there was no "poison gas", and so on. I'll tell the engineers—' I break off. Asking Chinese engineers to disprove a Chinese conspiracy misses the point entirely.

Sanchez nods. 'We can ask the scientists. Or the medics.'

'Good. We need something even the most paranoid can't dispute. I'll talk to Yefremov, and to Khan. You talk to Price. She might listen to you.'

'Might...'

'Tell her it's for *Gabriel*.'

He shakes his head, unconvinced.

'Go. Wake her up. Before this gets out of hand.'

He shuffles to the door when I stop him with one more thought.

'Your multi-faith service today? Get it right.'

I give Khan and Yefremov till 05.00 before I call them in. They appear fifteen minutes later, Khan flawless as usual and the doctor looking like something spat out of the engines. They stand a good distance from each other, each behaving like they are the only one here.

I describe the bishop's revelations, skipping the part on how they came to my knowledge. I expect them to protest, to tell me this is a waste of their time, but the doctor at least nods in support.

'We've already tested the bodies for the effects of toxins, so the "poison gas" theory can be easily disproved, even if no atmospheric traces remain,' he says. 'I'll go through the rest of the bishop's ideas and collate the appropriate data.'

Khan's face is pinched into a frown, her cheeks a pale shade of olive. 'You do understand these accusations are just the ravings of a madman?'

'It doesn't matter what they are if half of the crew choose to believe them.'

Khan waves her hand. 'Oh, I realise that—but I want to know where you stand on it.'

I nod, relieved. 'He wasn't thinking clearly, that's for sure. None of them were, towards the end. So no, I don't believe the accusations—but we still have to disprove them, in case somebody does.'

Khan's shoulders rise and fall, but I don't hear her sigh. 'Strangely enough, the more insane the idea, the harder it is to discredit—at least in a way that will convince its supporters. Still, I'll find you something.'

'Thank you. And...' I pull my lips back in a grimace. 'I hate to say this, but can you get the most devout Christians on your teams to work on this?'

Yefremov laughs. 'And encourage them to share the findings in a prayer meeting?'

'Something like that...'

Khan is not amused. 'I choose my people based on their skills—'

'I know, but—'

'But I'll make an exception and use religious affiliation as the secondary criterion. As much as it displeases me. And as much as it limits the pool.'

Yefremov rolls his eyes behind the scientist's back. I wish I could do that, too, but Khan's been more agreeable than I expected so I still count this as a win.

'One more thing. I'm not going to ask what's up with you two, but we need to act as a team, now more than ever.' I cross my arms, trying to catch their eyes but both have suddenly found the walls very interesting. 'Whatever it is, bottle it somewhere where no one can see it. You can hate each other all you want when this is over.'

Yefremov scowls. Khan opens her mouth to protest.

I raise my hand. 'That's all for now. I'll see you at the service tonight.'

Now they're both glaring at me, but I turn to the zheping on my desk. Maybe they can commiserate.

I check the time. Almost 06.00. According to the roster, Zhang starts his duty at seven. If I call him now, it'll look like I'm panicking—which I may be, but I don't want him to think I give any credit to the bishop's claims. On the other hand, the news may already be spreading, seeds falling on the ground primed and ready.

My reflection stares at me from the blank screen over the desk. I may look better than Yefremov but not by much: ruffled hair, puffy circles under my eyes, worry lines cutting a sharp V between my brows. Hardly the intrepid commander they need right now.

My stomach grumbles. Oh, fuck it. I am what I am. It'll have to do.

I send the message to Zhang, then take a moment to gather my thoughts.

I can't let myself forget that he's most likely the spy's human supervisor. The fact that the discovery of the colonists' Mind-Link hasn't triggered any action only confirms my suspicions: the spy isn't tracking the tech, it's protecting its user. Or users—I have no way of knowing how many others are part of the plot.

Even so—whatever the spy's after, I doubt it includes the rest of the crew turning on the engineers. So at least in this one respect I can be sure of Zhang's cooperation.

He arrives a moment later, entering from bridge-side and looking like he's been up for a while. He nods a greeting, then takes a seat at the table. Expecting a long conversation, then. He must know why I called him.

I take the chair opposite. 'I assume you've heard about the bishop's log?'

Zhang nods. 'The gist of it, yes. Not the details.'

'It's all nonsense, of course, but with the mood as strained as it is, we need to make sure the crew don't take it the wrong way.'

He holds my gaze, his face impassive. 'I assure you my people can control their emotions.'

I scowl. He must know that's not what I meant. Why on earth would *his* people need to control themselves?

Zhang's mouth twists into an ugly smirk. 'Let me guess: you didn't think about how we'd react to the news? The fact that three hundred Chinese citizens were betrayed by the people they trusted, set upon by the thousands-strong majority, rounded up, and murdered?'

Blood drains from my face. No, I didn't consider that. Funny how things change when you switch the angle, truth refracted into perspectives, like light passing through a prism.

Zhang is watching me, his smirk turning bitter.

'They were all ill, Chief Engineer. Or possessed, or deranged, I don't know which. We can't judge them, any of them, by the standards of logic. Not even by the standards of right and wrong. We can't bring them back, either. But we must avoid the situation spilling over here.'

'As I said, I can vouch for my people.'

I stifle a sigh. 'Well, I can't vouch for the rest of them. And they are all my people, including your crew. I don't want any of them hurt, no matter what nationality they carry in their papian.'

Zhang's voice is icy. 'What do you want me to do?'

'We have to prove that the bishop's paranoia was just that— and we have to do it in a way that doesn't require specialist engineering skills.'

He snorts. 'Because they won't believe what we say?'

'That's why it's called paranoia. I've asked Khan and Yefremov to help. Neither of them is happy about the situation, but they understand the need.'

The engineer doesn't answer, his jaw clenched and a vein throbbing in his neck. He's avoiding my glance, probably so he doesn't start screaming in my face.

He may be the traitor, but I still need his help.

'Talk to your people,' I say softly. 'Make them understand. This will pass. It's just really bad timing.'

'Shall I tell them to watch where they go and not talk too loudly? Because if they do, they'll end up like the colonists?'

I push away from the table, sliding half a metre before the chair comes to a stop. 'You say I'm not looking at it from your side? Well, try the reverse. You have complete control of the ship. The rest of us can't even enter the critical areas. Add to it the fact that you can manipulate all the systems without us even knowing. Can you blame the others for feeling vulnerable?'

Zhang clenches his fists, knuckles white. 'Mind-Link's available for everyone. The ship's doctor can install it for you. And you could have it removed by the time we return, if you so wish.'

'That still wouldn't give me full access, would it?'

'You knew the deal when you signed up. Why blame it on us now?'

'I'm not blaming it on you. I'm explaining why some may feel receptive to bad ideas.'

He glares at me but says nothing more. I wait for the lines on his face to relax, but he only averts his gaze, staring straight ahead as if chiselled from ice.

I swallow. 'One more thing: attend today's multi-faith service. All of you.'

Zhang's gaze returns to me, ice turning to fire. 'Do you want us to convert as well? Is that what will keep us from getting slaughtered? It didn't help the people on the planet, did it?'

'It's a multi-faith service, Zhang. I'm not asking you to come on Sunday.'

'What if I don't have any faith? Or choose not to worship the way your reverend finds appropriate? How many ways do I need to bend before you find me acceptable?'

I plant my elbows on the armrests and hide my head in my hands. I'm so tired. My wrist aches; my limbs throb with constant tension. I imagine sneaking out of the office, holing up in my tiny cabin and bolting the door away from the questions, the suspicions, the accusations. Out of the wasps' nest into my own private oblivion.

But no, that would be too easy. I don't deserve easy. Easy lets death win.

And I must yet do my penance.

I pull in a breath. 'You're not doing it for me, Chief Engineer. I don't care what you believe in, if anything. I don't think it should matter. But what I *think* means nothing if we get into trouble. It is what it is. This is the ship and the crew we have to deal with. We can discuss rights and wrongs once this is over.'

Zhang sits in silence for another moment, his expression unreadable. 'Will that be all, Commander?'

'Yes, Chief Engineer.'

I stare at his retreating back and the closing door. There's a steadfastness about him that I can't help admiring. He'd make a great ally—if we weren't on opposite sides. I can only hope he won't turn out to be a great enemy.

CHAPTER 14

Voices spill from the mess hall deep down the corridor. It's still officially dinner time but I've never heard the place so loud. The quality of the voices is different, too: relaxed, almost cheerful. I cross my fingers as I walk. Maybe Sanchez will get his miracle. We could really, really use one.

Lim, no, Firyali greets me in the entrance, her smile happier than I thought possible. She's replaced the uniform with a loose yellow shirt, the hue perfect for her complexion and her thick black hair.

She pushes a zheping towards me. 'Pick a number!'

On the screen, numbers dance in overlapping circles, like a mathematical kaleidoscope.

'What is this?'

She grins. 'I'm not sure. Reverend's orders!'

I groan. Logan once dragged me to a 'team-building session' back at Orbital Logistics. Afterwards, I made sure I was out on a faraway assignment whenever the next one was planned. On any other day, a whiff of anything similar would make me turn back immediately. But then, on any other day I wouldn't even be here.

Next to me, someone laughs. Chao, her grin as wide as Firyali's. 'Go ahead, it won't bite.'

I sigh and press my finger to the screen. The numbers scatter, leaving only a fat purple digit nine.

Chao ushers me in, while Firyali assaults the next arrival. I hope I get to see Khan's face when she appears. That may just make it worth it.

Inside, the place is packed. All the Americans are here, as well as the medics, and the reverend's Ops team. Price flashes me a bright smile from the table she occupies with the rest of the security squad. Yefremov sits stiff-backed and grim-faced at the table next to the wall, the farthest possible from the one Sanchez commandeered as his pulpit. The doctor rolls his eyes as he sees me, his expression resigned.

I glance wistfully at the empty chair next to him. No, that won't do. I need something more up front, where I can grin at the rest of them like I'm having the time of my life.

'Here, Commander. I've kept a seat for you,' Sanchez calls, bright and cheerful.

The reverend points to his table. Kao. 'Up front' doesn't mean I want to sit at the damn pulpit. I scowl, catching Yefremov's delighted sneer out of the corner of my eye. Oh, hell. I hope this won't be long. All in service to the mission.

The moment I lower myself into the seat, the babble of voices fades into silence. Zhang stands in the entrance, his sceptical gaze on Firyali's pad, her chin trembling as she tries to maintain her smile. Tam and Yau appear behind the engineer, faces stiff and postures tense. Only Wang appears relaxed, or maybe just less stressed. She nods as she sees me, and I give her a warm smile.

I watch them pick the numbers from Firyali's screen, then make their way to a table. Zhang catches my glance. I nod in gratitude. His mouth twitches, but he says nothing, nor does he return my greeting. Good, we don't want anyone thinking this is staged. Even though they must suspect as much.

The scientists arrive last, and with disappointingly little fuss. Khan's face has settled in an expression of resigned patience, ready to take whatever life throws at her.

When they're all settled, Sanchez rises and claps his hands loudly enough for everyone to hear. 'Thank you all for coming. This service is a time for us to worship together, no matter by what name we call our God. Or even if some of us don't believe in the existence of one Creator but hope there's more to our existence than just the flesh. This is the time we can unite in our search of truth and empathy. Here, on this tiny ship, alone in the vastness of the universe, we choose to stand together in friendship and solidarity, realising that whatever our divisions, we are all one, all human, all pilgrims on the road to peace and understanding.'

So far, so good. If he doesn't bore everyone to sleep, this is just the message they need to hear.

The chaplain follows up with a prayer, vague enough for everyone to mould into their own belief system. The timbre of his voice is perfectly soothing, rising and falling like the sound of distant rain.

Like the voice of the priest at Anna's wedding.

The memory pierces like a barb, deep and sharp. Anna's smile as Stepan lifted her veil. Their clasped hands, like one ten-fingered limb. I was both her maid of honour and a stand-in for our parents, present only on the screens after their visa applications got rejected. Stepan's mum managed to come, though, and we made it perfect for them. That minister had a great voice, too, warm and soothing, like a chant. Such a beautiful day.

My shoulders shake. My breath catches in my throat. I blink, once, then again, and force my attention back to Sanchez.

He's finished praying; his smile widens as he asks us to stand up. 'Remember the numbers you drew? Now, every number has appeared twice. That means whatever you have, somebody else has that same number. I want you to find them! Yes, that means you have to walk around and talk to people. It's quite safe, I assure you. And you can use the exercise.'

I stifle a groan and shoot the reverend a desperate glance. He winks in response. Great, that's just the encouragement I need. Things don't end well when ministers try to get funny.

The Americans are already on the move, calling out their numbers as they navigate around the tables. Maybe they're used to Sanchez's games. The rest of us range from sceptical to resigned. The murmur of voices rises as we shuffle across the room, culminating in something resembling a schoolyard. The cries of triumph multiply as people find their matches. Some are laughing, too. I've almost forgotten the sound.

My excitement bursts when I discover the other 'nine' to be Tam Chau Yin. Damn. I guess 'leading by example' is on the agenda. At least it's not Zhang.

The engineer forces a smile, his green bionic eyes narrowed in apprehension. 'Hello, Commander.'

Double damn. I'm really not helping things if that's the reaction I get. Though I probably look the same to him: resigned and worried.

We take a breath, probably both realising our trains of thought. He's come here to make this work—and so have I.

'Glad you made it,' I say. 'Though I'm not sure I share the reverend's enthusiasm for this kind of game.'

Tam sighs. 'I agree. The last time I took part in something like this, I ended up lost in a forest for a week.'

I stare, unsure what to say.

His expression stays perfectly straight for a moment, then a 'got you' grin brightens his face. 'Well, maybe it was a day. Or two hours. Anyway, I missed dinner.'

I chuckle, his dry humour totally unexpected. 'Well, I sincerely hope it won't happen today.'

'Sure. Where would we find a forest?'

Now we're both laughing, the initial awkwardness replaced by a sense of shared purpose.

The engineer starts to say something, but Sanchez's voice cuts him off.

'Everyone's found their partner? Good. Now I want you to tell each other three facts about you—nothing too personal, but not something they'd find in your crew profile either. And here's the trick: two of these facts will be true, and one will be a lie. Your partner has to guess which one is the lie.'

'I thought lying was bad!' someone shouts from the other side of the room.

'It's a game, Kowalski.'

'How about other sins, Rev?'

'Don't even think about it.'

More laughs, then the volume of voices returns to school-yard levels. I scan the room, looking at the pairings. Yefremov is with Kowalski, this time in a bright yellow T-shirt with multi-coloured figures holding hands in a ring all around his torso. How fitting. Wang is with Russo, from security. Zhang is next to Navrov, looking relieved. No surprise, the engineer could have ended up with Price. Or with Khan. Where is she anyway?

When I locate the scientist, I have to turn away to conceal an explosion of giddy laughter. Khan stands opposite Price, straight as a stick, arms folded, a frown knitting her eyebrows. A study in discomfort. Next to her, Price is all feigned ease: hands in pockets, a plastic grin on her face, her posture assured, maybe even challenging.

Tam follows my gaze, and then he, too, swings away, his lips pressed tight even as his shoulders shake with laughter.

'This is not going to end well...' I whisper.

He leans towards me, conspiratorial. 'Here's what I think:

Professor Khan will present three bits of scientific information, which Sergeant Price will fail to crack. The sergeant will then punch the professor in the face, and we'll have to carry them both to the infirmary.'

I shake with helpless laughter, my fist against my mouth.

'And you know what's best?' he continues. 'Most people here would probably pay to see that.'

I wipe a tear, breathing hard to control my laughter. Tam is the same, even though he's slightly more successful.

I didn't expect this: not to laugh, not today, not with him. I'm sure he feels the same, his brows raised in surprise as we finally stop laughing and face each other again.

'Do you have your three facts?' he asks.

I shake my head. 'I'm hopeless at this kind of stuff. Care to take the lead?'

'What makes you think I'd be any better?'

'The fact that you can't possibly be worse.'

Tam sighs. 'That remains to be seen. Let's see. One, I'm an excellent cook. Two, as a kid, I used to breed hamsters for pets. And three, I once won an award in a poetry competition.'

He tilts his head, waiting for my answer.

'Oh, that's hard!' I suck in a breath with a whistle that makes some heads turn—not many, I realise, everyone engaged in conversations louder than ours.

I turn to look, forgetting Tam for a moment. Sanchez has got his miracle, it seems. Zhang's laughing; even Khan has cracked a smile. If I didn't know better, I'd think these people were friends.

'This was a good idea,' Tam says behind me. 'I hope we can keep it this way.'

I feel myself smile. Maybe we can get through it. Figure out the spy, find the colony's killer, help *Gabriel* settle, and get home in a better shape than we set off. They are all good people. If they can rise above the circumstances, if they can pull together and focus on what unites us—yes, there's hope for us yet.

My smile widens as I turn back to Tam. 'Let me see. You're too skinny to be doing much cooking, so that could be the lie. On the other hand—'

My wan-kong vibrates. Around me, others frown as they lift their arms to check theirs or pull the zhepings from their uniform pockets. 'A news burst from Earth,' someone says.

My muscles stiffen, blood draining from my face. We weren't expecting another burst. This can only be bad.

Next to me, Tam has closed his eyes, his mouth open in shock at whatever he's seeing on his green lenses.

I look at Sanchez.

He's on his feet, his face pale but his lips curved into a desperate smile. 'Remember, all the messages are years old. By now it may all be different. We've got to focus on our mission here and our work as a team.'

I push towards him, resolved to salvage whatever we can. I swerve past stiff figures, the crowd petrifying into pillars of salt. Someone gasps; another swears.

Behind me, someone curses. An American accent—one of the men on Price's team. 'China blew up the Atlantic elevator!'

Voices erupt in a horrified chorus. The only non-Chinese elevator in existence, the source of American pride and the key to economic independence.

'The fuckers,' someone swears.

'Couldn't take it we were catching up.'

'This means war.'

'How many casualties?'

I crane my neck to see Zhang, Tam, and the rest of the Chinese group slide out the door. Probably better. I reach Sanchez and turn to face the crew. Some are shouting, others read their screens in pale-faced horror.

'Over three thousand dead,' Sanchez says into my ear, his

red pad clenched in his hand. 'And that's just on the elevator site.'

'Are there other sites?'

'Unrest in most of the enclaves, the Chinese pushing out the internationals.'

My heart flutters. 'Kenya?'

'I think so. Haven't read all of it yet.'

Hands shaking, I reach for my zheping. Two message icons flash in burning red: general and personal.

Personal.

I stare at the symbols, mesmerised, frozen, incapable of movement. The voices around me fade, the world constricted to this one light. *Personal.*

I can't look at it. I must.

I know what it is anyway.

My trembling finger makes contact with the red flash of the icon. The screen blinks out for an instant as long as forever, the frozen moment of not-yet-knowing. Then the message appears, sharp black letters carved into a white background:

We regret to inform you that your nephew, Jason Nevsky, passed away on 3 November 2342. We are uncertain as to the exact circumstances of his death, but all evidence indicates that he was killed while refusing to move to the internment facility for immigrant personnel in the Zhongguo Kenniya Fei di.

My vision blurs. A steadying hand grabs my shoulder; a voice calls in my ear. Irrelevant. I drift through the crowd, past tearful figures and angry, swearing ones. Irrelevant. The sound fades as I drift through the door, down one corridor, then the next. Someone shouts my name. Irrelevant. I strain to see through the fog in my eyes, try to breathe through the tightness in my chest. Words pound in my ears, louder and louder: *We regret to inform you that your nephew, Jason Nevsky, passed away on 3 November 2342.*

Jason's dead. I killed him. I left him to die. Like Anna. Like Nadia. Like Stepan.

Death has won his one last battle. Nothing else matters now.

CHAPTER 15

The pounding on my door continues for a while, then fades, replaced by muffled voices. Soundproofing on these cabins is admirable. I can't even tell if it's one person or more. Not that it matters. I tell the computer to turn off the lights. The darkness is soothing, and at least now I can't see Anna scolding me from the pictures above my desk. Though I should probably let her. I deserve every ounce.

Sorry about your son, sis. I should have stayed with him, like I promised. But I was a coward. And a traitor. And now we're all dead.

The pounding returns. I hope they get bored. Forget about me. What use am I anyway? I'll just bring them more death.

I stretch on the floor, the carpet rough under my cheek. My eyes close, and I drift into darkness. Silence, at last.

More pounding.

Go away, I want to scream, but my breath comes out mute. It doesn't matter. They'll be gone soon.

A different sound now: something grating and harsh. A strip of light appears on the floor, then the whole room fills with bright, scratchy incandescence.

'Leave us,' a voice says.

'Are you—'

'Just go.'

Fingers touch my shoulder. 'Nathalie...'

I recoil, searching for darkness. 'Turn it off!'

Silence, then: 'Computer, dim the lights to twenty per cent.'

Not enough. But better. At least he can't see my face, pressed to the floor and covered with one arm.

'I saw the message, Nathalie. I'm sorry for your—'

'Shut up!' I sit up, ready to punch him.

Yefremov doesn't move.

I scowl at him for a moment, then try to lie back down. He reaches out to stop me, so I scuttle away, to the other side of the room.

'Why don't you just leave me alone? Select another commander. You won't be any worse off than with me.'

'You don't really believe that, do you?'

'Fuck off.'

'That's better. Except I won't, and you can't make me.'

'Fine then. Move in here with me.'

His expression hardens. 'Want me to mop up your tears?'

I glare at him with all the fire I have left. He holds my gaze, even if I can see it takes some effort.

'Fine. Just so you know, I promised his dying mother that I'd take care of him. And then I left him behind.'

'Let me guess: you paid for his college?'

I paid for his apprenticeship as well. And started a fund that would set him up for life. Except now he's dead, and no money will help it.

A probing smile appears on Yefremov's lips. 'What, no answer?'

'I'm responsible for his father's death, too. And his mother's and sister's.'

'I don't believe that.'

'I don't care what you believe.'

The tips of my fingers begin to tingle. My chest heaves—but this doesn't seem like another attack. More like the ability to feel returning after hours of numbness. I don't want to feel. I don't want to hurt.

'Damn it, Nathalie.' Yefremov crosses the room and crouches down beside me. 'You didn't kill him. I know who did; I read that message. Internment camps! Those fuckers think they can do anything, and no one will stop them.'

My fists clench into balls, nails into flesh. *Internment camps.* Who else is in them now? Jo? Gideon? Are even the Kenyans free in what used to be their own country?

Despite everything, I'm proud that Jason died resisting. I hope he took some of them with him.

Yefremov's still talking, his words soaking into my consciousness. 'Whatever happened doesn't release you from your responsibility to the crew. You're in command of this ship. We need you to do your job. Or you might really be responsible for more deaths.'

I shudder. I try to hide from his gaze, but he's everywhere, staring me down, pleading, accusing. My chin trembles. 'I can't do it. It's not that I don't want to. Don't you understand? I'm just a jumped-up pilot; I've got no skills for this. I can't do this because I'll fail again, and you'll all die, because of me.'

'Bullshit. You've got all the skills. And the grit.'

I laugh.

'Do you think I'm saying this to make you feel better? Come on. I like you, but I'd be the first in line asking for a replacement if I thought anyone would do better.'

'This crew is already tearing itself apart. I can't stop it.'

'Maybe you can't. But you're the only one with a chance.'

I shake my head. How can he say that? But he won't stop. He fixes me with his gaze, words lashing out of his mouth, unrelenting.

'So, you can sit here feeling sorry for yourself, or you can stop being selfish and help save some lives. Have you forgotten about *Gabriel*? Are you going to let them die? Are you going to lie here and mope while your crew jumps at each other's throats?' His voice quivers, the words hurting him as much as he's trying to hurt me. 'Damn it, Nathalie, I thought better of you. I thought you had guts. I thought you cared.'

I hide my face in my hands. I could kick him or punch him, but I know it's all an act he's putting on to make me angry. It's working, too. Because he's right, damn it. I *am* selfish. I've let my grief erase all else because nothing else matters to me. But I don't matter either, nor my pain. None of it absolves me from responsibility.

Jason's dead. I'll never forget—and never forgive.

But the others, they can live. That woman on *Gabriel*. My crew. My pain versus their lives—it's not even an equation. I must go on, for them.

I can't.

I wipe tears and snot off my face, my hands cramped and shaking. A tissue appears in front of me, and I whisk it from Yefremov's fingers.

'People trust you, Nathalie.' His voice is soft now, soothing. 'Price told everyone how you pulled Wang from the fire. That's the commander they want. They'll listen to you like they won't to anyone else.'

I lean back, my head against the wall, breathing slowly. My body's stiff and worn out, as if I'd climbed a mountain. None of it matters. I close my eyes and look down on myself, small and pathetic. I can't do it. I'm not the person the doctor thinks I am. But I can't abandon them, either.

I can pretend. I can play the part for as long as I need to. For them.

Goodbye, Nathalie. I'll be back with you soon enough,

embracing your pain and your guilt. But I need to be someone else now. Just long enough so I can do my job.

My legs tremble as I push myself up, forcing my will into this strange, feeble body I seem to inhabit. I spread my fingers, frowning at my shaking hands. That'll need fixing.

I bend over the sink and splash water on my face. It won't take away the swelling or the redness in my eyes, but it might cool down the fever. Pushing my fingers through my tangled hair doesn't help much either. So be it.

Yefremov watches me from down on the floor, his expression a mix of curiosity and suspicion. For a moment, his doubt seeps into me. I squash it before it can take root. The new me, it may well be a lie—but it's a lie I intend to live until it takes me where I need to go.

I check the time; somehow, it's late morning already. The field team would be heading out soon. What would a real commander do now?

I grab a clean jacket from my three-hanger wardrobe and seal the velcro on the cuffs. 'Come on, Doctor. We haven't got all day.'

'Where are we going?'

'The bridge. I'm going to address the crew.'

'Are you sure? I mean, great, but you can take some time to rest. It's only—'

'I'm all right, Doctor. I know what I need to do.'

He rocks his head, looking like he's about to challenge me, but I'm already on the way out. He's with me an instant later, probably determined to watch me just in case. It's his job, so I don't protest. Even if I am perfectly fine.

Faces turn as I walk the corridor to the bridge—most anxious, some relieved, all of them upset. And yet they all nod a greeting as I pass, eyes lighting up in hope.

The bridge is quiet, just the usual hum and tart smell of the equipment. Blue and green trajectory data light up the main screen, all numbers within parameters. Firyali and Wang are at their posts, but the engineering consoles are empty.

I take my place in the captain's seat and key in the codes. 'Communications?'

Firyali jumps to attention. 'Yes, sir?'

'Did we receive any messages other than the news burst? Anything from the company?'

'No, sir.'

'Anything for the reverend or the chief engineer?'

'No, sir.' Her voice quivers. 'No personal messages either, except for yours.'

'Thank you. I'll address all crew in five minutes, including those on the planet.'

Nobody else speaks. Their faces are solemn, their postures deferential. Good. I turn to check if Yefremov's still here—he is, loitering by the door as if hoping I won't notice. I give him a nod, then return to my console. The systems are all in the green, no alerts. Perfect.

I close my eyes, composing the message a real commander would give. I've worked with some good ones, read about others. I know what they'd say. I just need to pronounce the words.

'It's time, Commander,' Firyali says.

I look at my hands. They've stopped shaking. 'Open the link.'

'Link opened.'

'This is Commander Hart to all crew. Yesterday's news hit us all hard. However painful, there's nothing we can do about the events on Earth. What happened is already several years old. The war may never have happened or may by now be over. They may be ushering in an era of peace and cooperation. Anything's possible. And by the time we get home, this story will be two generations old.

'Our mission remains unchanged. We must never forget why we came here. *Gabriel*'s passengers rely on us, and so do all other colony ships waiting at their destinations. Thousands of lives depend on us, and that must remain our only focus.

'I've considered restricting distribution of all news bursts from Earth. I won't do that, yet. I trust you and your loyalty to the mission. We can't control the lives back on Earth, but the ones right here are in our hands. I won't hesitate to stop anything or anyone who puts them at risk. I expect you all to do the same. Good luck with your work. Hart out.'

The lights on my console flicker in acknowledgement of the message. This is the moment when they could push back or protest, but I don't think anyone will. I wait twenty seconds regardless.

Behind me, the door closes as Yefremov leaves the bridge.

'Field team departing for the habitat,' Wang says.

CHAPTER 16

The field team divides as soon as they exit the base. Johansson and Wu head back to the greenhouses to check the ones they haven't yet accessed. The others return to the settlement, this time entering through the western access node. There, the group splits again: the medics return to the hub, while Miller and Lee lead the others to explore two sections of the habitat.

With all four feeds playing on my console, I set the VR to Miller's team and put on the visor. When I open my eyes, I'm inside a tubular corridor. Round walls shimmer with faint luminescence, reflecting the beams of our lights. We march in silence, past the first junction, into the middle layer of the habitat modules.

The corridor divides in front of us.

'This one?' Miller asks, then answers himself, 'As good as any.' He turns right, then pauses in front of a metal door. 'Ready?'

The others behind him acknowledge, their voices sharp with tension.

The door groans, opening on a narrow hallway with two doors on both sides. The floor here is softer, a composite carpet cushioning the sound of our steps. Narrow shafts of light fall from dust-covered skylights, too dim to illuminate the interior. I know from the plans that behind each door will be a bedroom with a shared bathroom in between. We leave those for later and continue to the larger chamber at the other end of the module, the communal space for the four families living here. Miller slows as he approaches, as if afraid of what he might find.

The common room lies a step deeper than the corridor and the bedrooms. A patchwork rug covers the floor, maybe a blanket or a quilt. Soft, foldable chairs sit in a circle around a square table, which leans precariously on a stack of boxes in place of a missing leg. Crates and containers make up the rest of the furniture. It should look stark, except every available space is covered with home-made trinkets, crocheted blankets, clumsy paintings, and figurines made of something that looks like clay. Where did those people get paint or yarn? Could it have been made here?

'This certainly looks lived-in,' Miller says. 'But no people.'

'Check that plant,' Khan says. 'Or get the whole thing to Johansson.'

Only now do I notice a metal container with the desiccated remnants of a potted plant.

Berry, one of the scientists, moves towards it with a sample bag in her hand. 'Looks like some herb. Dill, I think.'

'We've found someone,' Lee's voice cuts in from the other side of the habitat.

I switch over to his feed, momentarily dizzy as I find myself inside a tiny room. A narrow window casts pale light on a mattress in the corner of the floor. Two pillows and a thermal blanket lie unmade, as if the occupants had only just woken up. A familiar shape catches my eye: a yellowed bra, crumpled on the floor. Someone gasps. Maybe it's me. This is too real, too personal, too intimate.

And then I see her: a woman, judging from her long

blonde hair and the straps of her thin nightgown. What's left of her body is withered and dried, her skin leathery brown, yellow teeth protruding from the shrivelled skull. She's crouched in the corner of the room, half hidden behind a large metal box. Her head has lolled to one side, as if she's fallen asleep waiting. Her hands rest on the floor, fists clenched. Something clasped in her fingers glistens with reflected light: scissors, the blades pointing outward, like a dagger.

'Looks like she was hiding,' Lee says, his voice too cold.

'Don't touch her,' Yefremov says. 'Leave it for the medical team.'

'Acknowledged.'

Nobody moves, all our eyes on the woman's corpse. Even in death, she looks terrified. What, or whom, did she expect to come through that door?

I force myself to look away. 'Check all the corners and closets. More of them could have been hiding.'

I watch them open the bathroom door and peek into the tiny shower with its water recycler and toiletry containers not unlike the ones above my basin. A towel still hangs on a small hook, hand-drawn petals making it look like a flower.

My finger hovers over the toggle icon, tempted to hop to Johansson's feed. No corpses in the greenhouse. A pang of guilt makes me hesitate, as if watching the intimate details of someone's life could make their death any less pointless.

'I think we found more of them,' Miller says. 'One of the bedrooms is locked from the inside. We're going to force it...' His voice strains. 'Something's blocking the door.'

I listen without changing the feed.

Miller groans with effort. Something thumps, then scrapes.

'There,' he says, exhaling. And then his breath pauses. 'Dear God Almighty...'

I hop to his feed. At first, I can't tell what I'm looking at.

Crates and boxes lie scattered over a mass of... something. I start to zoom in and then stop in horror.

Limbs. Arms and legs, some inside tattered clothes, some in boots, some twisted at odd angles. Not just limbs, though—bodies. Piled up and mangled: six, no, eight heads, eye sockets empty, teeth bared in deathly grins.

'They stacked the crates against the door,' Miller says. 'So they got a bit squashed when I...' He doesn't finish.

Nobody speaks as I stare at the mummified faces, a part of me refusing to believe they are human.

So that's how they died. Hiding in terror till they starved to death.

Raji's voice breaks the silence. 'Don't touch anything. I want to inspect them in situ.'

I'm shaking, darkness smothering my vision. Not like a real commander. I should know better.

I clear my throat, my voice dry. 'Everyone, follow the pathologist's instructions. Before you leave, check for personal records: pads or even drawings.'

I pull off my visor. There's nothing I can do to help, and just watching the dead seems disrespectful.

'I'll be in my office,' I say to the bridge crew. 'Call if you need anything.'

They acknowledge, their eyes on the screens. I wonder if it's easier without the VR. Too late now.

I close the door and slump into my chair, chasing the image of tangled limbs out of my mind. For a moment I can only sit here and stare, but that won't help anyone. I pull the captain's journal from my drawer and scroll through the entries, looking for something I've missed. I find another entry about the 'G', but it only mentions a meeting, not what it contained.

My wan-kong vibrates with a lunch alert. I grimace but close the zheping and hide it back in the drawer. The old Nathalie would have worked through lunch—the commander

Nathalie won't risk losing health or focus. And it will be good for the crew to see me again.

I leave through the door on the ship-side—and almost stumble over a cleaning bot. These things shouldn't be allowed out during daytime. Or at least not where I'm likely to break my legs over one. Maybe they should clean the engines?

I stop. The cleaning bots go everywhere. Including the engines. And the computer cores.

The plan forms in my head as I march towards the mess hall. Pull out the cleaning roster from the maintenance log. Maybe fake a complaint. Check if all the spaces are cleaned. Map all the corners. And see if there are any secret compartments where even the robots can't go.

Wasting time for lunch is excruciating, but I force myself to take a full half an hour, chewing every mouthful of the protein goo with stony determination. I nod a greeting to everyone who enters and respond to their well-meant small talk. Few of the crew approach me, though, preferring a polite smile or a deferential bow. I wonder without amusement when they're going to start saluting. Old Nathalie would be appalled at the idea, but I find it convenient.

Back in my office, I get to work on the plan. Cleaning bots log all their activity, including the paths they take across the ship. Put together, these will add up to a three-dimensional model of the entire vessel, including the contours of each piece of equipment. A de facto blueprint—and one I can create myself, without triggering the spy.

I start slowly, glancing at the cleaning roster, careful to make it appear random. The system could do it for me in seconds—but with the spy watching, that's out of the question. For a moment I wonder how I'll manage without the computer —then I remember what Firyali has told me. The spy doesn't track our personal instruments, only the content we transmit.

No way around it; I'm going to have to hand draw the whole thing and hope I get the numbers right.

I skip the main deck—we can search it ourselves if we have to—and focus on the engine section. Fewer cleaners go there, but there's data from the engineering offices and even some from the guts of the machinery, regularly checked for junk and debris. I draw for hours, letting my mind lose itself in the data.

Sanchez drops in on me at the end of the day. I've requested my dinner to be brought to the office, so of course now they're worried.

'I'm fine. Tell the doctor he doesn't need to fret.'

The reverend's face looks like he's going to protest, but he ends up just shaking his head. 'Can you blame him?'

I rub my face, tiredness creeping in. 'I can't, and I don't. So no need for the appearances.'

'It's not just for you.' He leans against the table, his face serious. 'Everyone's on tenterhooks. The more "normal" we make it look, the better.'

'Does anyone believe this is anything like "normal"?'

'Behaving like it is, is half of it already.'

'You're probably right.' I stretch, stifling a yawn that sneaks into my mouth. My neck is stiff, and my wrist aches after long hours with the stylus. 'How are they, anyway?'

'Coping. Avoiding contact between the groups.' Sanchez pauses. He chews his lip, as if deciding how blunt he can be. 'They need purpose. The mission... They understand the puzzle is harder than we predicted—but unless you're one of the scientists, well, there's little for them to do but sit around and stew in their own juices.'

'What do you suggest?'

'A briefing would help. All hands, catching them up on everything. Make it sound like there's progress.'

I tap the stylus on the armrest. 'That last part will be hard.

But a good idea, regardless. A general meeting, tomorrow lunchtime?'

Sanchez nods. A small smile returns to his face, a shadow of his old cheer. 'Thank you. I'll send out the notice.'

The briefing is like a twisted image of the service we held only two days ago. All the crew are there, this time arranged in stiff layers of function and nationality. They keep their voices low, the tone solemn. At least they're not fighting.

I struggle not to flinch as Zhang's crew walk in. They take a table in the far corner, Zhang's face blank, the others glancing around nervously. Nobody seems to notice them, as if the Chinese were made of air. I avert my gaze, feign indifference the best I can manage. I know I can't blame the engineers for what happened in the Feidi—but every instant my gaze snags on the red and gold flags on their chests all I see are soldiers and guns firing on civilians.

Jason's bloodied body dropping on the ground, red dirt covering him like it once covered Stepan.

And yet they are still my crew.

I manage a brief introduction, then give the floor to Khan and Yefremov. Both sound like they have some actual news, and the crew listen with interest. I didn't realise how much the lower ranks were starved for information. Good on Sanchez for bringing it up. If this gives them some sense of purpose, the meeting is well worth the time.

Firyali gives me a telling glance when we begin to disperse, then heads off towards the long corridor that will take her to the tether room. I wait for the others to leave, then follow, pacing my steps so I don't start to run.

I find her sitting on the floor, her head between her knees.

'What is it?'

She takes a long moment to speak, her voice timorous, stuttering between heavy breaths. 'It's about the accident. Like you asked.'

'Go on.'

'I found the archived maintenance logs. The records for the second cryo-chamber are missing. Deleted. From the night before our departure.'

So, a sabotage after all. The fact registers numbly, no longer tinged with emotion. 'Do you know who—'

She continues, not meeting my gaze. 'So that was a dead end. But there were other records from the same night. The ship logs everyone entering and leaving. So I knew all the ground staff had gone by then. And most of our crew. The only people I can't find any record for are engineers Zhang and Kuang.'

Kuang? The one who died in the fire. The one Zhang was so upset about.

'Are you sure they weren't doing some last-minute checks?'

'Don't know what they were doing. But someone deleted those logs for a reason.'

'That doesn't make sense. Why would Kuang sabotage his own pod?'

I press my fist to my lips, thinking. If anyone wanted to sabotage the captain's pod, they'd have to do it before our departure. They couldn't do it en route—the pods are wired to alert the key crew if anyone woke up during the trip. So they'd have to set up some automated action to be triggered years into the journey. Except it went wrong, and fire spread. This has to be it; I can't think of any other explanation.

The captain suspected Zhang. Did he do it on his own? Was Kuang a victim or an accomplice? The only one, or are there more? Are all the engineers part of some plot to—to do what?

'Maybe I'm wrong,' Firyali says. 'Maybe there is another

explanation. I mean, there must be, right? They wouldn't... murder...'

She doesn't finish, searching my face for a rebuttal I cannot make.

My wan-kong chimes, the high-pitched note for an urgent message. I wince as I glance at the screen. Yefremov, calling a key-crew briefing.

Calling a briefing is my prerogative. He must have a really good reason for going ahead without talking to me first.

I spring to my feet. 'Keep digging. Whatever happened in that chamber, I need proof. A hundred per cent proof. Find it.'

Her mouth starts to open but I'm already out, running down the corridor towards my office.

CHAPTER 17

Yefremov arrives first, then Khan, Price and Sanchez, their postures stiff with anticipation as they take their usual spots around the table. Zhang appears last, the sight of him making me queasy. Still, I need him here, even if I can't trust his answers.

'Your news, Doctor.'

Yefremov's eyes sparkle with anticipation, his fingers twitching in barely contained excitement. 'We've got something. Two somethings, actually. Not the answer, not yet, but...' He hesitates, looking for the right word, then waves his hand.

'First, we've discovered another set of medical logs. At least I think they're medical, as we found them on one of the lab's computers. But all the data there's heavily encrypted.'

'Isn't that normal?' Price asks.

'No. Medical records would be protected, but not to this extent. This is some heavy-duty encrypting. Your people are looking at it now, Zhang. They promised to let us know the moment they crack it.'

Zhang nods, his eyes half-closed. He must be in comms with the engineers on the planet. Or with the spy?

I wonder if Firyali's back at her post. I reach to my wankong to ping her, but Yefremov's next words stop me dead.

'Anyway, I think I know what it's about. We've analysed the corpses from the habitat; they were much better preserved than the ones in the cemetery.' The doctor leans forward, hanging over the table. 'They all had Mind-Link, just as we thought. But not just ordinary Mind-Link.'

My body stiffens. I draw in a careful breath.

'What do you mean?' Khan asks.

'Most of the organic structure's gone, but enough of the fibres survived to show that the lattice had a different design *and* a different connection network. Raji's about to send the schematics.'

This is it. This must be the answer. I don't yet know how, but I'm sure it's connected both to the colonists' deaths and the mystery of the spy.

Get to your post, I send to Firyali.

Khan's asking technical questions, details I don't even understand—but all Yefremov can tell her is that it's too early to say. I glance at the reverend and the engineer. Both are frowning, mouths pursed in dismay or confusion.

I raise my hand, and the scientists fall silent. 'Chaplain, do you have anything to tell us?'

Sanchez turns pale, then red. 'I swear to you, this is all news to me. I knew about the Mind-Link, as I told you. But that was all I knew.'

I keep staring.

'I'm telling the truth. As I should have from the beginning.'

His anguish is too real to be faked. I'll keep my eyes open, but I believe he's telling the truth.

I swing towards Zhang. 'How about you, Chief Engineer?'

The man winces, the question taking him off guard. 'What about me?'

'Do you have any knowledge of a different line of Mind-Link?'

Zhang shakes his head, the corners of his lips downturned in bitterness or derision. 'I deal with engines, Commander. Mind tech's not in my area.'

He's lying, discomfort clear on his face. Even Yefremov raises an eyebrow.

'That's why they went mad,' Price says. 'Because they got to play lab rats for some experimental design.'

'The church would never allow it.' Sanchez's anguish has been replaced by conviction, though it sounds too desperate, as if he needs to persuade himself as much as the rest of us.

Price nods eagerly. She turns to Zhang, her scowl deepening, her fists clasping the edge of the table. 'They wouldn't. It must have been done behind their backs.'

'I don't think that's what caused it,' Yefremov jumps in. 'I mean, it's too early to know for sure, but the timing doesn't work.'

'Explain,' I say, my voice dry.

'The encrypted medical files—I think we can assume they have something to do with this?' The doctor waits for us to nod, then continues, 'We don't yet know what's in them, but we can see the timestamps. Most date from between years two and four of the colony. Then they gradually become less frequent, sometimes months apart. And the last file we found is dated six months before the blackout.'

'What does that mean?' Sanchez asks.

Khan provides the answer. 'It means that if it was some kind of experimental design, then most likely they'd lived with it for years before anything went wrong.'

Yefremov bobs his head in agreement. 'Exactly. And if they'd had the slightest suspicion the new Mind-Link was causing the problem, I'd expect to see more encrypted files from the time the trouble started.'

Zhang leans towards him, his voice tentative. 'So, what do you think they were testing? Even if it didn't—'

'And who do you think those 'they' were?' Price interrupts, her glare fixed on the engineer.

'Enough.' I raise my hand. I don't want to spook him—or the spy. 'Doctor, do you have—'

A message ping cuts me off.

'Aha! This is from Raji,' Yefremov says. He points to my monitor. 'May I?'

I nod, and he pushes an image onto the screen: a lattice of translucent tendrils, like conjoined octopus triplets.

The others turn to examine the image, but I keep my eyes on Zhang. The graphics won't tell me anything I can understand, while the engineer's reaction is another key to the puzzle. He leans forward, a deep frown cutting his forehead in an expression of both curiosity and bewilderment. I'm sure he was lying before—and yet now he seems as perplexed as the rest of us.

My wan-kong vibrates with an urgent message. I lift my arm to check, and freeze.

It's awake.

I jump to my feet. The others stare as I open my mouth—but what can I tell them? I wave my arm in a vague signal to continue without me and rush to the bridge.

Firyali's at her post, typing frantically into the console lit up by explosions of alarm messages.

'What's happening?' I call. Secrecy be damned.

'Something in the transmission was a high-level trigger. An image file?'

I nod, but she's not looking at me, all her attention on the console. 'I know which one. What is it doing?'

'Nothing with life support or controls. But I'm getting error messages from communications...' She scrunches her brows, concentrating on a string of symbols.

Footsteps approach from behind me. Zhang strides to the engineering console, the other four staring in bewilderment from the office door.

'Something's wrong with our radio antennas,' he says.

'How do you know?' I don't hide the accusation from my tone.

Zhang points to his head. 'I get the error reports directly.'

Of course. The Mind-Link is both the truth and the excuse because no one can prove who—or what—is messaging him.

I grit my teeth. More will have to wait. 'Any details?'

'Not yet.'

'A disruption on the outer hull,' Wang says. 'No breach, no loss of integrity.'

I rush to my seat. 'Source?'

Wang shakes her head. 'I can't...'

The proximity alert lights up on the screen—a yellow no-danger icon only, indicating that the object that triggered it is moving away from the ship. What the hell?

'Get me a visual!'

'This is from the nearest camera,' Wang says.

Something small and blurry appears on the screen, a grey smudge against starry blackness at the edge of Bethesda's atmosphere. Wang focuses the image, and it resolves into a conical structure that looks oddly familiar. It's a part of the ship, but what exactly?

'Tā mā de!' Zhang swears. 'Lim, check the transmitter array.'

Firyali taps in a command. 'Not responding. All the transmitters are dead.'

'Look at this,' Zhang says.

On the screen, the drifting object is replaced by two snapshots of the outer hull, both showing the same area but one with a current timestamp, the other from two hours earlier. In the centre of the older picture, a conical structure sits in the centre of petal-like plates. On the current picture, the plates are still there, but charred black and twisted. The conical structure is missing.

'The transmitter array,' Firyali says, breathless.

Our only communication method with Earth, destroyed.

'What does it mean?' Yefremov asks behind me.

'Do we have contact with the planet?' I ask.

'We can't send anything,' Firyali says. 'But we can still receive.'

We're cut off, from the Earth and from the team down on the planet.

Zhang taps his console and the screen switches back to the retreating object, its conical shape clear against the dark background.

'How could that have happened?' Sanchez asks.

'Collision with an orbital object?' Khan suggests.

'No, the proximity alert activated when the transmitter was already moving away from us,' Wang says.

I lean back, leaving the others to speculate. My thoughts are spinning, but for the first time in a while I think I understand what's going on. The spy protects the secret of the new Mind-Link. That's why it monitored the term, waiting for us to discover the new design. Raji's image file triggered the reaction. And by destroying the array, the spy made sure that the secret stays hidden. We've been cut off, not just from the planet, but also from Earth.

Except this is only a short-term measure. We can reconstruct the transmitter, build a new one, or use *Gabriel*'s. That means that the spy's not done. This is only a delay, a prelude to another action. Something that will keep the secret hidden forever.

Will it destroy the ship? No, that would only add to Bethesda's puzzle and trigger more research. What else can it do? Almost anything, to the ship or its crew—but if Firyali is right, it won't do it without instructions from its human minder.

I glance at Zhang. Still busy at his station, apparently oblivious, but I don't believe that for an instant. I can't do anything to stop him, not when he's in direct contact with the spy.

I can't stop him—but I may have a way to delay him.

'Chief Engineer, I want you to inspect the outer hull for damage and potential other malfunctions.'

'I'm preparing the drones,' Zhang answers without lifting his head. 'They'll be ready—'

I stand up from my chair. 'Price can handle the drones. I want you and your people to suit up and check the damage in person. Immediately.'

Zhang swings around to stare at me. His eyes narrow. Probably wondering how far he can push me. We both know my order makes little sense—but he also knows the mood's not right for him to refuse a direct command.

I hold my breath. If he resists, it can only mean that whatever phase two he's preparing is close to ready. I don't dare imagine what it might be.

Zhang waits another moment, then nods, decision made. 'I'll need one person here to monitor the diagnostics.'

That's not what I wanted, but not a request I can refuse without generating suspicions. 'Of course. We're at your disposal.'

He won't ask me or Price, but he might choose Firyali.

The engineer turns to Wang. 'You'll monitor our movements and follow instructions for equipment checks.'

'Understood.'

Zhang casts me another doubtful glance and heads for the exit.

I check the time. Five minutes to get to the airlock, twenty to suit up and leave the ship. Three hours for the checks before they'll need to return. Not much time, but it'll have to do.

I turn to Wang. 'Get the drones out. Check the hull and keep at least two in visual range of the engineers. I don't want anything happening to them. Use security or the ops techs for assistance. I need Officer Lim for another task.'

'Yes, sir.' Wang nods, her gaze uncertain. She may be suspicious, but unless she's part of Zhang's plan, she won't know enough to act on it. At least not at first.

'Lim, Price, follow me. Everyone else, keep working on the new Mind-Link. We'll get back to the briefing as soon as the crisis is over.'

Khan, Sanchez and Yefremov stare as I walk past them, heading back to my office. They must realise something's off, but I hope they blame it on my nerves. No commander should react well to pieces of her ship spontaneously flying away.

'What's going on?' Price asks the moment I close the door. She's frowning, at least half of it directed at Firyali.

I raise my hand. 'Later.'

Price's frown deepens, but she stays quiet. I wave Firyali to my desk and open the cleaning roster. Her eyes widen in question—until I show her my drawings.

'How soon can you finish this?'

She scrolls through the images I've managed to produce. 'Dai sei! How much time do I have?'

I lift three fingers to indicate.

She grimaces. It's not much time, I know. It took me three times as long to map half of the ship.

'Focus on the gaps,' I say, hoping she'll understand.

I leave her at the desk and signal to Price to go with me. At least she doesn't ask questions, just follows silently all the way to the tether room. Even here, she waits patiently while I try to decide how much to tell her.

'Do you know of any ways to block Mind-Link connections?'

Price grins like I've handed her a birthday present. 'There are a few. But I guess you need something ready in three hours.'

'Correct.'

'All of them or just Zhang?'

'I'd prefer all, but I'll settle for what you can give me.'

Price nods, considering. 'Given you brought me here, I assume we can't trust the comms?'

'Assume he hears everything you send, everywhere on the ship.' I gesture at the room around us. 'Almost everywhere.'

'They'll be coming back through the same airlock they left from. That's the best place to set the trap. A short-range disruptor, if I can get one ready in time, or at least a Faraday cage.'

'It mustn't fail, and he can't notice it till he's in it, or we're cooked.'

'I get the point. Who knows?'

'Nobody. But Lim knows what's behind it.' A frown of distrust begins to form on Price's forehead, so I add, 'She's the one who found it. I trust her fully.'

'Fine, then. I'd better get started.'

CHAPTER 18

Wang is with me as we wait by the vestibule leading to the airlock, a square room with racks of EVA equipment and suits. She glances from side to side, uncertain, while I put on a friendly smile and pretend not to notice the scars on her hands as she tugs on the cuffs of her jacket. This is the woman I pulled from the flames. And now I'm about to...

She'll be fine. They all will. I won't let anything bad happen to them. I'm not like those in the Feidi, those who opened fire on civilians resisting internment.

The light above the airlock door switches from green to red as the pumps suck out the air, preparing to open the outside hatch. My heart speeds up. This is the last chance Zhang will have to alert the spy. Once that hatch closes behind them, the Mind-Link will no longer work.

'EVA team entering the airlock,' Firyali's voice says from the bridge.

Then comes the clonk of the hatch closing, the impact reverberating through the floor plating. The warning light flickers as the air begins to cycle.

Behind us, the corridor resounds with heavy footsteps. I don't turn to look, even as out of the corner of my eye I see Wang stiffen. She flinches, and then she's falling, right into Price's arms.

Price slides her stun-gun back in its holster, then checks Wang's pulse as she moves her prone body to the side. 'She's all right.'

I nod in silence. The Mind-Link block works only on the inside of the airlock; Wang might know nothing of Zhang's plot, but I can't afford to take the risk. One message to the spy may be the end of us.

Price moves to the airlock door. The standard procedure is to wait for the EVA team to open it from the inside—but not this time. The moment the light turns green, Price tilts it open. I slip inside, Price and one of her men right behind me.

The engineers freeze in mid-movement of unzipping their suits.

'What is it?' Zhang asks.

I step towards him, the space crowded with the six of us inside the airlock. 'We need to have a conversation.'

'Here?' He frowns, puzzled, then blinks. 'I see.'

'Sorry about the disruptor. I had to make sure no one else is listening.'

Zhang snorts. 'You think I'll incapacitate you with my thoughts? Or are you worried about leaving a record of your actions?'

I laugh. 'Seriously? I'd be happy to send all the records. But I can't do that now, can I?'

'You think I did that? What could I possibly have to gain from destroying the transmitters?'

'I was hoping you'd tell me. You can start by explaining why you killed seven of this crew.'

Zhang winces. 'It was an accident.'

The others around me stiffen. Price shoots me a surprised glance, then shifts closer to the engineer, her hand on the gun in her holster.

'Please. You're not that good at lying.'

The engineer looks away. His face stays impassive as he slowly puts his gloves into the helmet and lays it on the floor. He wipes his forehead with the back of his hand, his hair damp with sweat. 'We can talk. But keep my people out of this. They know nothing.'

Just like the civilians whose only crime was not wanting to be imprisoned?

But no, this is not the Feidi. These are not the people who killed Jason, even if they wear the same flags on their chests. I *will not* go there.

'That may be the case,' I say slowly, 'but I can't take your word for it. The safety of this crew is my responsibility, and you forfeited your membership in it with your deception.'

Tam and Yau look from me to Zhang, bewildered.

'What is this about?' Tam asks.

'Your boss has been keeping busy. Care to explain what you're hiding in your secret compartment, Zhang Min?'

Zhang's eyes widen, but he forces a shrug. 'I can explain my closet. But not here. Not under guns.'

Price laughs. 'Nice try. Can't wait to use that brain web of yours?'

I glare at him. 'Do you deny you have another purpose on this mission?'

Zhang doesn't answer.

'Did you kill the captain?' Tam asks.

I expect a denial, but Zhang says nothing, just stares ahead, his jaw working.

'Nǐ mā de! You did what?' Yau steps in front of him, her chin trembling and her face as grey as her eyes.

'Back off,' Price growls. 'Willard.'

The security man steps forward, retrieving his truncheon. I cringe at the sight of it, but I keep my face straight. We must make it clear we're way past joking.

Tam pulls Yau away from Zhang—but not before she spits on the floor in front of him, muttering a curse I haven't heard before.

'What are you going to do to us?' Tam says. 'We knew nothing about Zhang Min's treason.'

Only days ago we laughed together. Shared hope for a better future. A lifetime ago.

I hesitate. They are still my crew, all of them.

Price squares her shoulders, sensing my hesitation. 'Of course they'll claim innocence. Stage this little show so we keep Zhang and let the rest of them go. And then they'll finish whatever it is they've started.'

She's right. The rest of them might be innocent, but I have no way of knowing, and no time to waste. The spy is awake, waiting for orders any one of them may transmit the moment they step out of this airlock.

'That's a lie!' Yau cries.

Price turns to face her, but I step between them, my arms raised. 'Until I have proof, I have to treat all of you as suspects. And I can't keep you on board, not when you can access the systems from any place on the ship.'

Tam's eyes widen. Yau takes a step back, fear taking hold.

Zhang moves towards me, but Willard pushes the truncheon under his chin. 'Stay put.'

For a moment I freeze, accusation needling its way into my mind. Am I doing the same as the rulers of the enclave? Am I sending these people into my own internment camp?

What choice do I have?

We have no brigs, especially for people with Mind-Link.

Even if we could refit some cabins, it'd take time I don't have, and extra security each time we open the door to feed them. No, this is the best solution. They will be safe and within easy reach of the comms as soon as we fix the transmitter.

I pull in a deep breath. 'I'm going to send you down to the planet. You'll get everything you need to set up another base. If you truly didn't know about your boss's actions, then I hope you will join the field team in their work. Once we complete our mission, you'll be put into cold-sleep, and transported back here for the return journey. I'll let the Earth courts deal with you.'

The engineers scowl, fear mixed with reproach and anger as if they've been dealt a great injustice. Something in me snaps. I want to shake them all, one by one, and shout in their stubborn faces how that's a much better treatment than Jason and others in the Feidi got from their compatriots. And the thousands on the Atlantic elevator site. Would these three do any different if they were there when it happened? Or would they listen to government orders just like the soldiers did? Like Zhang is doing now?

I clench my fists, fighting my fury, and nod to Price. She draws her gun from the holster, her face impassive though a spark in her eyes tells me she's enjoying the moment.

Yau flinches. 'You can't!'

'It's on the stun setting,' I say coldly. 'It'll wear off in a couple of hours.'

'You'll realise your mistake—' Zhang starts.

Price pulls the trigger. The gun is soundless, the ozone smell of electric discharge the only sign of it firing. Zhang's face contorts in pain. His eyes roll back. Price makes no effort to cushion his fall, but instinct gets the better of me and I lunge forward, grabbing him before his head hits the floor.

'Assist the others,' I hiss—but they're already falling, two soft thuds as the engineers crumple to the ground.

It's done.

I call Yefremov to check the engineers before Price's people move them to the shuttle. He arrives with Chao, their eyes opening in horror at the sight.

'What happened?' he asks, crouching by Zhang's limp body. He checks the vitals, then frowns at the impact mark on his neck. 'Stun needle. Care to explain?'

'Not yet. But soon.'

He holds my gaze, then sighs. 'Vse peremeletsya…'

Whatever. Just get on with it.

He checks them one by one, then nods. 'They'll be fine.'

The question returns to his eyes, but I ignore it, turning to watch Price and her people load Wang and the engineers onto an equipment cart.

'Careful with them. They're still our crew.'

Her brow rises in doubt.

'Leave it to the courts, Amy.'

Her mouth twitches, but she nods. 'Crew or not, we don't hurt prisoners. We're not like them.'

I glance at Yefremov as they depart. He whispers something to Chao, and the nurse follows the security people, her face set.

'Will you tell me now?' he asks when they disappear down the corridor.

'I can't. You've got to trust me.'

It takes Price an hour to transport the engineers to the elevator's low-orbit dock, then another forty-five minutes to get back on the ship. Part one done. On to the next.

I'm in my office, looking over Firyali's drawings. The outlines are rough, but even so, the gaping hole not accounted for in the cleaners' routes stands out like a black vacuum over the web of white lines.

'Good work,' I say. I point to a maintenance passage. 'We'll go in through here, and then this way.'

'How about the access codes?'

I shrug. We'll have to force our way into the engine section, but I'm not going to say that aloud, not with the spy still listening.

'So, what—' Sanchez starts, but I raise my hand to cut him off.

The reverend sits next to Yefremov at the other side of the table, both of them wearing heavy frowns.

Yefremov checks his wan-kong. 'They should be waking up soon.'

Sanchez grimaces. His mouth opens again, then closes under my stern gaze.

'We're ready,' Price's voice says from my wan— No. I'm done with Mandarin. My wrist-pad.

'I'll meet you in the same place as last time.' I fold the zheping—the data pad—and slide it into my pocket. My legs tremble when I get up, but only for a moment. It's time to get answers. 'Doctor, Reverend, you'll be safer here, but I won't stop you if you want to join. The choice is yours.'

'And you won't tell us where you're going?' Yefremov asks.

'No.'

The men exchange glances. Sanchez starts to say something, but I'm already on the way out, my fists clenched, and my mind set. Firyali appears beside me, her lips pressed into a flat line, her face pale but determined. I don't look back to see if the men are following, but the sound of their footsteps confirms that both of them are there.

Price and the remaining three of her team wait in the tether room, their glassy black uniforms sealed up and their helmets on. Their holsters are back, each with a truncheon and a ship-safe gun, and this time they've also brought cutting tools and electronic sniffers.

Sanchez glances around, uneasy. 'I must note that accessing the engines breaks several international treaties, if that's what you're planning.'

'The technology's obsolete by now anyway,' Yefremov says.

'We're not interested in the engines,' I say. 'But in Zhang's secret computer that's been spying on us all this time.'

'What?' the two men ask in unison.

'He confessed,' Price says. 'Told us himself he had a secret closet.'

'A *closet*?' Firyali repeats.

I nod to Price. 'Let's go. You'll see the truth soon enough.'

'Okay. You four, stay three metres behind us at all times. Expect booby traps and other deterrents.' Price moves towards the bulkhead and signals to her team. 'Seal up.'

The four of them pull down the mirrored visors on their helmets. I freeze, memory returning with a numbing pain. The Feidi riot police. The fires and the shootings and the deaths. Beside me, Firyali takes a step back, gasping. I know she's thinking the same. It's too fresh still, not even two months in our subjective time.

'Come on,' I whisper towards her.

Price leads the way—at least I think it's Price, the four security figures identical in their obsidian uniforms. The servos of the cargo doors squeak as the bulkhead swings open. Behind it, the elevator platform is a disc about four metres across surrounded by a metal railing. Lights come on above us in two shining columns that extend all the way through the tether, narrowing with distance till they almost meet at the other end.

Price unlatches a low gate in the metal railing. The floor vibrates as we climb on to the platform: first the security, then the four of us sheltered behind them. I push the up button, not sure if we can even get it to move without the access codes. And yet, the structure shudders, and the elevator begins to climb up the tether.

We move in total silence, neither the machinery nor the humans producing any noise. Even our breathing is quiet, as if any evidence of our presence could trigger some ghostly defences. But if the spy is watching, it doesn't seem to mind—yet.

Firyali's question rings in my ear, Zhang referring to his hideout as a 'closet'. According to the plans she drew, the secret compartment, tucked cleverly between two engine sections, is about the size of the bridge. Not something I'd call a closet—but who knows what makes a closet in China?

Three minutes in, I move to the edge of the platform and wrap my fingers over the railing, signalling for the others to do the same. We're slipping from the grasp of simulated gravity— I'm already a fraction of my weight, bouncing on my feet. The others follow my lead—except for the security team, who, I now realise, are wearing magnetised boots. Two more minutes and we're floating, approaching the weightlessness of the spindle, the mid-point of the ship's rotation.

We hold on, ready for 'the flip'. The elevator platform pivots around the central point of the spindle, the motion detectable only in the inertial pull on my fingers. The columns of light become horizontal, then swing back into vertical as what used to be 'up' becomes 'down' and we begin the approach to the engine section.

The lift comes to a stop in a room almost identical to the one we left. The bulkhead here is darker, though, and the air carries an oily, metallic smell.

Price raises her hand as she steps off the platform. We stop, while she slides to the door, soundless. On the lock, Chinese characters spell out a fluorescent warning. Price darts sideways as she presses the pad, as if expecting a shot—but all she gets is a bright red light and a verbal demand for access codes in Mandarin and English.

Price signals to her team. Someone, probably Willard, pulls

out a flat box and attaches it to the control mechanism on the side of the door. It takes twenty seconds, and the bulkhead slides open, the red light flashing frantically.

Yefremov exhales loudly. 'Good job.'

Sanchez flinches at the sound.

'It's all right,' I say. 'Whatever's waiting for us already knows we're here.'

We step out into a dim corridor, black walls lit only with intermittent light strips.

'Which way?' Price asks.

'Right,' I say.

'Wait,' Firyali says. 'I know it's not what we planned, but I'm getting warnings from the security systems. I think it's best if we stay clear from the most restricted parts.'

Price tilts her head. She says nothing, but I know she's suspicious. Firyali's a Chinese citizen after all, even if from the Feidi. And she's got Mind-Link.

'Is it the spy?' I ask.

Firyali shakes her head. 'No, just general security. It shows me the restricted zones, sort of like a colour map. We're in the yellow zone now. Things will get more difficult when we cross into red.'

This makes sense. The system was designed to protect Chinese industrial secrets, nothing more. They'd consider emergency access or other unforeseen circumstances. If we play nice by it, we might avoid triggering the worst blockades.

'We go left, then,' I say. 'Lim, guide the way.'

Price turns to me. My own face stares at me from her visor, mouth flat and eyes narrowed.

'We go left,' I repeat.

Price nods and takes point without another word.

Firyali plots a path through tight corridors between machine rooms and fuel coils. Most doors open without protest, as if the system understands our intentions. Once or twice

Price's man has to use his magic box, but even then the alarm doesn't go beyond the flashing of red lights. It's almost too easy.

And that makes me nervous.

'This is it,' Firyali says, pointing to a wall at the end of another passage. 'Behind that wall. And this is the only access, so the entrance must be here.'

The security team spreads out along the length of the wall. Price aims a scanner at the surface, something like a stylus widening at the end. Ultrasound or an EM sniffer.

One of her people raises their arm. Price approaches with the scanner, then nods.

I slide in behind them.

'A cargo-size door. Metal, same construction as the bulk-heads. Alarmed, but nothing beyond the usual.'

Too easy. I don't know what I expected, but not this. A hidden computer core would need protection. None of Zhang's people were armed. They could have hoped we'd never find it, but still. Something doesn't smell right.

Price has located the opening mechanism, and her man is already attaching his box to the surface.

'Be careful,' I say. 'This is too easy.'

She nods, as if considering the same. 'You think it's a trap?'

'It blew up our transmitter. It wouldn't let us walk in there unless it was prepared for just this eventuality.'

'Makes sense. Let's—'

A cracking noise cuts her off. We stare in horror as a long, vertical fracture forms in the wall in front of us.

'Willard, did you—'

'Not me.'

'Everybody, step back!' Price shouts just as the wall splits, shards of plating cascading to the ground. A wide, heavy bulk-head slides open behind it.

Price reaches for her gun, the others forming a defensive line as they pull out their weapons and their truncheons. The blue light of a cryo-chamber pours from the hidden room, high-lighting seven silhouettes. A tall white man stands in the middle, blond and blue-eyed, his skin ageless-smooth, his silk clothes the most immaculate of orbital fashions. On his left and right, six silver-clad soldiers point heavy rifles back at us.

Sky Sharks.

CHAPTER 19

My chest constricts, every breath an effort. I tremble, fighting the memory of the last time I saw a Sky Shark pointing a rifle, back at the gates of Deliveries International. My wrist throbs with remembered pain, the crack of bone as I drop on the hot tarmac, red dust falling like blood all around me.

Focus. I breathe. *Focus.*

We stand opposite each other in deadly silence for a few seconds, the black line of my meagre security team against the silver line of the Sharks. Our ship-safe guns are no match for the Sharks' armour, designed to disperse such weapons. Can the security suits handle their rifles? Doubtful. No one's supposed to resist the Sharks.

The white man steps forward, ignoring the pointed guns on both sides. He waves his arm, his manner relaxed as if we were meeting in one of the Yun Ju's exclusive bars, about to indulge in designer drinks.

'Hello, Nathalie. What a mess you've got yourself into...' The man's accent is American, his voice deep and with a melodic resonance, like a performer's. He gives me a lopsided smile. 'I hear Captain Chen Xin is no more? Pity. I rather liked the old man. A bit grumpy, but he did as he was told.'

'Who are you?'

'I'm a Guardian. I'll be taking command of this ship. I'm sure you'll be relieved.'

A Guardian. The one from the captain's journal, right here with us.

I push my chin out, determined not to let him see my fear. 'I haven't received any such orders. Until I do, you are intruders on *my* ship. Who sent you and what do you want?'

'Nathalie... I will answer some of your questions, but not here. Later, in my office. Shall we?'

The back of my neck prickles. The man's manner is so relaxed, this is beyond just bravado. He's got firepower on his side, but my people could still hurt him before they got shot down. Which means he's got other weapons, things beyond my control. The spy? More Sharks now converging on our position?

'Don't look so puzzled, dear. There's nothing you can do. The crew won't follow you; they'd never have if they'd known who you were. Most of them come from the Feidi. Many suffered directly in the riots you started.'

Blood drains from my face, then returns in a hot wave of anger and shame. 'How dare you—'

The man keeps talking, waving away my interruption with a flick of his hand. 'Jo Abdi and Gideon Tabo got most of the blame, and prison sentences. But they weren't the real organisers, were they? You were the brain behind it. Yet when things turned ugly, you ran away. You left the city to burn and the others to face the punishment. Unfortunately, truth has a nasty habit of catching up.'

'You did that?' Firyali asks, her face pale.

She knows now. She knows I was the one who gave her screencaps to the media.

'Firyali, I—'

The man interrupts me again. 'Yes, she was the one who sold you out, Ms Lim. You risked everything to help her, and she threw your life away like it meant nothing.'

I move forward, from behind the defensive line of the security team. I've made myself a target now, but I'm not sure I care. Besides, if he wanted me dead, I doubt Price's presence would have stopped the Sharks.

'So that's your plan? Turning the crew against me? Fine, then, how about you tell them the rest of the story? How those who got the plague were left to die because people like you diverted all meds to the stations. For money. I did what I could to save lives. You only did it for profit.'

The Guardian shakes his head, his smirk as sharp as fangs. 'Not me, actually. I had nothing to do with that. Your doctor friend, on the other hand, very much did. Isn't that right, Doctor Yefremov? Why don't you tell Nathalie about the little business you set up to funnel the drugs to the highest bidders? Did you know her sister and niece had the plague? You must have—her brother-in-law called you once, begging for help. But you had the standard line for everyone: there's no plague, only panic. Well, they're dead now. All of them.'

I turn, my knees soft and my vision swaying. 'Did you...?'

The doctor stares at me, mouth gaping, his face red and covered with sweat.

'Did you do it?' My voice is a growl, guttural and vicious.

Yefremov's gaze flickers to the Guardian as if trying to decide if he can pull off another lie. Whatever he finds there offers no help. Yefremov swallows, then shakes his head. 'There *was* no plague. Most of it *was* just panic. I had no way of knowing some cases were real. So many people claimed they had the virus, and every single one I tested proved negative. And the money—I invested half of it back in the hospital.'

The Guardian laughs. 'Your *private* hospital.'

Yefremov spins to face him, his face almost purple. 'Where I treated the poorest for free! This is public knowledge!'

None of this is relevant, even if true. I glare at him, wishing my eyes could spit fire. 'My sister died. Her baby died, only months old. Her husband died trying to get drugs out of that warehouse. You killed them. For money.'

I clench my fists, my body shaking with effort as I turn away from the man who killed my family. This isn't over. I still have the Guardian to deal with. 'What do you want?'

'The same as you: find out what killed the colonists. With a few extra details, which I'll explain later. Shall we?'

The Guardian glances at my security people, their guns still poised, though the resolve is gone from their postures. They probably hate me now, but I hope they'll put duty before their feelings.

'Don't let him manipulate you, Price. He's working for the Chinese.'

'No, I'm not. They had their own plot, so that's a good riddance, but I'm not working for them. Amy, Pascal sends his regards. He was sorry that Deliveries International debacle made you unemployable. Still, the door is open, if you prove yourself again. I could certainly use more Sharks.'

I tremble, my vision shrinking into a bright circle. My throat constricts; I suck in air, but nothing reaches my lungs.

Price was a Shark. She was one of the guards at the warehouse. She was the one who pulled the trigger.

The Guardian's voice booms in the distance, distorted. 'Yes, well, Nathalie's brother-in-law was one of the victims. We'll never know whose bullet hit him, but you gave the order... Personally, I don't blame you. Self-defence, really. But the media had a field day... It was a good move to leave. You did right by your people, bringing them here. I'm afraid, though, you're not going to be popular now that the truth is out. But don't worry. We'll get the job done, and you'll be back with the Sharks when we return.'

The figures around me shift. One of the Sharks opens his visor, then another, their faces obscured by the fog in my eyes.

'Sam?' Price's voice. 'Julio?'

'Surprise!'

Feet shuffle, first one set of footsteps then more. Price and her team move over to the Guardian, to the Sharks. I hear laughter, hands clasped in greeting.

'Amy, what are you...' The reverend's voice, distant and hollow.

I can't breathe.

Feet in leather slippers stop in front of me. 'Oh, poor Nathalie. Another panic attack? It really wasn't fair to push you into this position. Not in your state. But don't worry; now that the pressure's off, you can take care of yourself. You're still welcome to your old post as the ship's pilot. But only if you want it.'

I lift my head up to face him, but all I can see is the outline of the man.

'Go back to your cabin, Nathalie. Take some time off. I'll take care of everything now. And thank you for getting rid of the Chinese. It'll make things so much easier.'

He walks away, towards the tether. Heavier footsteps follow behind him, the Sharks and my security team now together.

A hand touches my arm. Yefremov. I recoil, disgusted. I will not have him touch me. I focus on my feet, the pressure of my body on the floor. The weight of my jacket on my shoulders. My lungs pulling in air in shallow, even breaths.

'What now?' somebody says. The reverend.

Nobody answers.

'We can't let them—'

'What can we do?' Yefremov says. The sound of his voice

makes me want to scream. 'There's twelve of us, medics and scientists. He's got ten Sharks!'

Sharks. The word cuts like it's made of ice.

I pull in a breath. I can do it. I can control it. I'll never give up.

When I open my eyes, Yefremov disappears down the corridor. Firyali casts me a glance full of hate, then shuffles behind him. Only Sanchez is still here, his head low and his eyes moist.

'Are you all right?' he asks.

How to answer? What can I possibly say?

I move past him, into the chamber where the Guardian and the Sharks were hiding. It's spartan: seven cryo-pods against the back wall, a container stacked with field rations. One computer station next to the door. I try the controls, even though I know it won't work—they wouldn't just leave it here if it posed any danger. Red letters stare back at me from the screen: *Nathalie Hart, pilot. No command access.*

I kick the machine, then consider trying to destroy it—but this is useless, this is not the spy or any other system that could hurt them. The Guardian is too smart for that.

'They must have just woken up,' Sanchez says. 'Maybe when the transmitter was destroyed?'

Maybe. Or when Raji sent the image of the new Mind-Link. That's why they are here. To protect that secret. Probably a new phase in the trade war, more profits to be made and empires to be built. That's the only thing that ever matters, to any of them.

'What is he going to do? The Guardian?'

I lean on the wall, thinking. 'He's here for the Mind-Link, so he'll need to find out if it killed the colonists. He's going to continue the mission, just as he said. He'll just make sure to keep a lid on the findings.'

'What are you going to do?'

'I don't know.'

'But you're going to do something?'

My breathing slows, anxiety replaced by something cold and sharp and biting. I turn to Sanchez. 'Yes. Because I don't trust them not to kill *Gabriel*'s passengers the way they killed the colonists.'

'I'm with you. Tell me what you want me to do.'

I examine the reverend, his eyes wide and his face earnest. I've got to know. 'What part did you play?'

He frowns, confused, then seems to understand. 'Nothing to do with the riots. I was at home at the time, in Philadelphia.'

'What's your secret, then? Everyone here has got one.'

Sanchez looks at his feet, his voice broken. 'An affair with one of my parishioners. A married one.'

I keep staring at him, but he won't meet my gaze. 'The truth, Sanchez, or we're done.'

He looks up, his lips trembling. 'It is the truth, just not all of it. I... I'd lost my faith. And started to get vocal about it. Building a following. They gave me the option of leaving or...' He glances away again. 'My family couldn't take the shame. This was better for all of us.'

'To preach a lie?'

'I've kept my doubts to myself.'

I nod. Fair enough. At least he hasn't killed anyone.

I push myself off the wall and circle the room while my mind fights for focus. Open resistance won't get us anywhere. We've got to take a page out of the Guardian's own book.

'Make yourself their best friend, Reverend. Confess to your congregation, say you've found your way, lie if you have to. Make them forgive you, so you can remain their chaplain. Can you do it?'

'Yes. What about you?'

'I'm going to play my part. I'm going to be the Nathalie he thinks I am.'

CHAPTER 20

It is night by the time we return to the main deck, even though the corridors rustle with hurried movements and echoes of lowered voices. I sneak towards my cabin, looking away whenever I meet someone on the way. They avert their glances, conversations pausing mid-word, then resuming in hushed tones as I pass. I try to listen, but the pounding in my ears erases all meaning. When at long last the cabin door closes behind me, I lean against its cold surface, gasping with relief. Then my knees finally buckle, and I slide to the floor, my body shaking even as my eyes remain dry, and my fists clenched in anger. Memories return, faces of the dead staring me down, demanding attention. I chase them away, then cower in guilt at pushing them out so coldly. But I can't help the dead. I must think of the living.

What's the next step? The way the Guardian behaved makes me think he'll assume command as if things were perfectly normal. With the Sharks and our security on his side, there's nothing the rest of us can do, even if he hadn't made sure none of us could trust the others anymore. And our mission hasn't changed. I think he told the truth about wanting to find out what killed the colonists—he'll need to know if the new Mind-Link played any part in it. What he does with that knowledge—and with us—afterwards is a different question entirely.

I make myself get up and dig out an emergency food ration from the bottom of my travel bag. It's almost four decades old—but that's still a long time off the 'forever' claim printed on the wrapper, so I should be fine. The food is chewy and rich, like meat-flavoured toffee. I wash it down with cold water, then sit at the desk, planning my next move.

He expected to find me broken—which I am, no matter how I try to pretend. The old Nathalie, the new Nathalie—that was always a lie, even if it served a purpose. There's just me, broken and hurt. It will have to do.

I'll play my part though, just as I told the reverend. The version of me the Guardian expects would spend a day sulking, so that's what I'll do. Maybe half a day—I can't wait so long to get back in the game. I must gain the Guardian's trust somehow, or at least enough of it to be allowed to move freely over the ship.

I reach into my jacket pocket and pull out the zhep— the pad, the one with the copy of the captain's journal and our hand-drawn map of the ship. A glance at the entries referring to the Guardian tells me nothing new. Except maybe one thing: the man introduced himself as *a* Guardian—so one of many, maybe an entire secret organisation or a cult. I don't know if this matters but decide to keep it in mind.

I scroll through the pages, hoping for something new to catch my eye, anything that would hint at the Guardians' agenda. I stop at the entry the captain made about me:

I raised my misgivings with the Guardian. No surprise, he ignored me because she's the central piece in the connections matrix—and she's Canadian, which keeps both parties happy. That's all fine, but with her lack of experience and poor mental status, if anything happens to me, the ship will be in deep trouble, and he with it.

I want to laugh. It was all right here for me to see, and I missed the point entirely. *And he with it*—I thought that meant financial damage. How wrong I was. I shake my head—but then another thought makes me sit up straight.

The captain was working for the Guardian; the man himself confirmed it. The captain also didn't trust Zhang—and the engineer confessed to killing him.

I was right thinking that the captain's suspicions were the cause of his death—but I thought it was because Zhang was working against us.

What did the Guardian say? *They had their own plot so that's a good riddance...*

Damn. Zhang could have been working *against* the Guardians. If that's the plot the man meant, then I've sent the wrong bunch of people down to the planet. I've banished my only allies.

I spring to my feet and pace the room, five small steps each way. I can't let myself rush to conclusions, not this time. I don't really know Zhang's purpose. He could be opposing the Guardians for even more sinister reasons. My head spins, as much from the whirlwind of questions as from the circles I make inside my tiny room. I need answers.

And I think I know where to look for the first one.

I sit back down and open our hand-drawn map of the ship. Zhang admitted having a secret 'closet'. If it wasn't the place where we found the Guardian, then it must be somewhere else. And whatever's hiding inside it, I must find it before the Guardian.

. . .

By mid-morning, the Guardian sends out his first memo. He's made Price the second in command. He's also made all crew profiles public, 'to stop the gossip'. I stare at the link icon for a long moment. I desperately want to know, never mind how much it's going to hurt. But the knowledge won't bring back the dead; it'll only make my task more difficult. I grit my teeth and put the screen away. The living first. Then the regrets.

I wait till the end of the lunch hour before I leave my room. I look appropriately dishevelled—hair unkempt, face wan, expression anguished—and none of it took any effort to achieve. The corridors are empty now, even though with the Guardian and his Sharks we're at higher numbers than before we sent away the engineers. Before *I* sent away the engineers.

Navrov is leaving the mess when I arrive. He scurries past me, surprise and embarrassment fighting over his face. Inside, three people are still finishing their lunch: Chao, Gintonga the shrink, and El Hussain, a junior doctor. I hesitate. The three of them were Feidi residents. They have more reasons to hate me than anyone else on board, except maybe for Firyali. But I can't run away now, and anyway, there's no place to hide on the ship. I fill my bowl with food, their glances burning into my back. Only when I'm tucked away in the far corner do I realise I forgot the flavouring. Too bad. I'm not going back, no matter how tasteless the food.

I spoon the soup into my mouth, trying to swallow before my tongue can revolt at the taste. It'd help if I felt hungry, but no such luck. At least it takes my mind off the three medics. I shift my head to steal a glance at them and regret it immediately: they're all staring at me with heavy frowns. And yet, it doesn't feel like hate. More like confusion. And pity.

I scoop up another spoonful, then give up. That will have to do or I'll throw up. I take the bowl to the cleaner just as the other three get up to leave. Chao moves towards me, her lips shaping around something that doesn't look like a curse—and then the door behind me opens, and she slams her mouth shut, her scowl returning.

A Sky Shark stands in the entrance, fully suited and with the visor down as if we could burn them with our glances. I bite down a sarcastic comment. Not fitting for my desperate image.

The medics slide out of the mess hall, keeping as far from the Shark as the door allows. I wait just long enough for the sound of their footsteps to retreat down the corridor, then follow them out.

One junction down, I turn towards my—the Guardian's—office. At least this part of the ship is empty. Alas, my luck doesn't hold. I round the corner down the final length of the corridor and almost walk into Price.

She stops, surprised, then a lopsided grin crawls onto her lips. 'Hi there.'

I stifle a gasp, a cold wave squeezing my chest. I'm not ready for her. The Guardian I can take; he's a stranger and the enemy. Price was a friend. Or at least an ally. Until she turned out to be a traitor and a murderer.

I glance behind her as another Shark crosses the corridor but turns in the other direction. There's no escaping this; it's just me and her, and the ghost of Stepan.

She ambles towards me, her eyes narrowing even as the stilted smile sticks to her face. 'I know you must be pissed—but I did what I had to do.'

I grit my teeth. I need her as much as I despise her, especially now that she's the second in command.

'Of course.' My voice is cold, but at least I manage to keep it steady.

'They'd have won anyway. Our weapons are no match for theirs. And they're part of the company.'

'Is that so?'

Price's grin falters, but then she stretches her lips again, though I can see the effort. 'Who else could have put the pods on board?'

I don't answer. The Chinese could have done it; they built this ship. She knows that well enough.

'The Guardian's American. From the Yun Ju, but American. He let me read his chip.'

'That's reassuring.' It comes out bitter. Damn, I need that man to trust me, and she can turn him against me. 'Did he tell you why they were hiding?'

Price bobs her head. 'Because of the Chinese! The Americans suspected they were experimenting with Mind-Link, so they sent the Guardian to investigate.'

This *could* be true; it fits the patterns of the trade war. The captain could have been a spy working for the Americans, and that's why Zhang killed him. It's possible. My gut says it's not true, but my gut had me send Zhang to the planet. This time I *will* keep all options open.

I manage a small smile. 'Good we got rid of them, then.'

'Right on!' Price returns my smile, but then it breaks on her lips. 'Listen, about that... that shooting in the enclave...'

I shake my head. 'I don't want to talk about it. I won't lie and say it doesn't matter. But at least you were doing your job. Not like...' I break off, unable to say the doctor's name. I make myself pull in a slow breath. 'At least you didn't do it for profit. And anyway, there's no bringing those people back. But *Gabriel*'s still here. That hasn't changed.'

'That's my thinking, exactly.' She nods, her features relaxing.

I wonder if she wanted absolution or simply to gauge how much trouble I'd be. Whatever it was, I hope she has bought my spiel.

I pull down my jacket, feigning concern for my appearance. 'Do you think the Guardian will talk to me? I... I want to be useful, you know?'

Her face opens in a grin. 'Of course! Come, I'll take you to him.' Her mouth twitches as if she belatedly realises how patronising she sounds, but I pretend not to notice.

She types into her wrist-pad as we walk, pre-warning the Guardian or avoiding more conversation, either are fine by me. As we near the door, she gives me a reassuring nod. I bite my tongue before I say something I'll regret. This is a game, and we're only starting. A game with *Gabriel*'s lives as the prize.

The Guardian meets us at the door, his expression a study of patient concern. 'Come in, Nathalie. I'm glad to see you're better.'

My smile must look strained at best. I hope he blames it on my distress, not on the fact that I'm trying very hard not to kick his perfect teeth out.

He turns to Price. 'Thank you. I'll take it from here.'

She stiffens, uncertain or just curious.

'It's all right, Amy,' I say. 'I'm not planning a one-person coup.'

Which wouldn't even be a coup given that he's the usurper, but I won't point out the obvious.

The Guardian chuckles. 'See? I'm perfectly safe.'

I can't see her reaction, but a moment later the door closes, and the Guardian shows me to the table.

'Take a seat, Nathalie.'

'Thank you. I see you've made some changes.'

The room has transformed more in the half day he's been here than during my entire time in residence. The desk is gone; the conference table now stands in the middle, surrounded on all sides by screens interspersed with images of Earth as seen from the Yun Ju stations. I wonder if that's the only way he's ever seen our planet. Has he even been to the surface?

He takes the seat opposite. 'Well, yes, it suits my needs better this way. I don't need the interface, you see.'

He points to his head. Mind-Link. I shouldn't be surprised

—he's from the Yun Ju, after all—but his accent has tricked me into thinking he was more American than orbital.

'Of course.'

He glances at one of the images, his brows scrunching as he turns something over in his mind. When he looks at me again, his expression is serious, almost pained.

'I'm sorry, Nathalie. I know an apology must seem inadequate after what I've done to you, but... well, that's all I have.' His smile returns for a moment, but it's small and uncertain. 'It was the only way to avoid bloodshed. I had to get Price over to my side quickly. Before she got trigger-happy again.'

I try not to wince, my back straight and my lips pressed tight even as I feel the corners tremble.

'Damn, I'm doing it again...' The Guardian grimaces. 'Not the best way to convince you that I'm sorry...'

I say nothing. I force my thoughts away from my pain, focusing on the man in front of me. Apology is the last thing I expected. He looks sincere, too, leaning over the table with all that worry in his blue eyes.

I've never been good at mind games, but I'd better catch up quick because here I'm facing a master.

'Why didn't you recruit someone you could trust? Why this whole charade, the CCM and such?'

The Guardian spreads his arms in surrender. 'We tried! We had a hand-picked crew ready, but at the last moment we discovered that the Chinese agents had sneaked in a spy. We had to rush to plan B, and that was the best one we had.'

His smile is probing and almost shy. He must mean it, or at least has convinced himself that he does. It's not that strange—only psychopaths enjoy hurting people. All other assholes find a way to believe they're doing the right thing.

'Why are you here?' I ask.

'To find out what killed the colonists, just as I said. We couldn't risk the same happening to *Gabriel*'s settlers.'

'That's what we were doing.'

'True, but without the necessary information. I realise we made your work harder, but we couldn't risk letting them find out that we knew about the new Mind-Link.'

'Them?'

'The Chinese, of course. That's what they were doing here. Experimenting on the colonists.'

Possibly. Or just as easily, this could have been an American attempt to design their own version. It's a growing business, despite all the religious misgivings. Bethesda would have been an ideal field test, light years from home and in secrecy imposed by the church.

Something in my expression must reveal my doubts because he leans towards me, his voice earnest. 'Did you wonder why your engineers have 'failed' to crack those encrypted files? That shouldn't be so hard. If they ever actually tried...'

Good point, though they'd only had them for a short time. 'Can your people decode them?'

'I'm afraid not. They're skilled in combat, but not much more.' His smile turns apologetic again. 'But Price got her men on the planet to secure the server. We'll bring it all up here and see what we can do. In the worst case, we'll just take it back home with us.'

Right. And in the meantime, Price's people will keep it locked away from all sides. Smart move, and with perfect deniability.

'What do you think it does, that new Mind-Link?'

'No idea. But nothing good would be my guess, or why would they test it all the way out here?'

I nod several times, as if chewing on his words. In fact, I'm wondering why he's giving me all this time, all this fake concern. Why does he care if I believe him?

Because it makes his job easier. If he has to lock me up,

others may start asking questions. He needs them to cooperate, at least the scientists.

'Nasty business,' I say at last. 'Still, the doctors don't believe it was the cause of what happened here.'

He waves his arm. 'I've heard that. But until they give me a hint of another reason, I remain unconvinced. Especially as the flow of information between the medics and the scientists has been... how shall I put it... compromised?'

I blink. Khan and Yefremov pretty much hate each other, but I didn't think it interfered with their work. Was I wrong?

The Guardian's pained expression returns. 'You don't know?'

I shake my head, bracing for the news.

He grimaces, apologetic again. 'That's why I made the profiles public, you know... I thought it was better if you knew the whole truth at once. Anyway, better you find out from me than... in a more public space.' He pauses for a small sigh, then continues, 'Khan's an epidemiologist. She was the chief scientist on the Second Pandemic report. Basically, she's the one who declared the plague was a fake. She was an acquaintance of Yefremov's, so it's possible she inspired his little enterprise. And now he blames her for his downfall, even though it was all his own doing.'

His words cut me like the barbs they're meant to be. My shoulders quiver. I look away, hiding from his concerned gaze and his pity.

I won't let him see me break.

I can't bring back the dead. And I won't let him sabotage my mission.

I wipe my eyes to make him think I'm crying. I'm not sure I could cry anymore, even if I wanted. My pain is different now, colder and duller, and so much a part of me that I'd miss it if it vanished.

The Guardian stays silent for another moment. When he

speaks again, his tone is resigned. 'I wish we'd had more flexibility when putting this crew together. But the only way we could get high-calibre candidates was if they were, well, tainted in some way. People who had to leave rather than wanted to, if you get my meaning.'

Oh, I get it. I get it perfectly.

I resist the urge to wipe my hands on my trousers. I'm hot, a bead of sweat trickling down my back. *Fuck you and your trade wars. I don't give a damn if you're working for the Americans or for the Chinese. I'm not here for either. I'm here for* Gabriel.

Time for Act Two. I put on a nervous smile, troubled, but not too timid or he won't buy it. 'What do you want me to do?'

He leans back. 'You could go back to being a pilot, if you wanted.'

I snort.

'There's no disgrace in doing the job you were hired for.'

There's curiosity in his gaze, and expectation. He's weighing his options. My next move must be just right, or he'll know I'm trying to play him. But I'm a quick learner, and he's already given me a lesson: half-truths make the best lies.

I lean towards him, my eyes on his. 'I'm not going to lie and say everything's fine, no hard feelings. It's very much not fine. I hate what you did and how you did it, even if you really had no choice. But I'm not here for you. I'm going to swallow my pride and do it for my crew, and, more importantly, for *Gabriel*. There are five thousand people there, and I'd never forgive myself if I didn't do everything I could to help them. If that means working for you, so be it.'

He holds my gaze for a moment, then leans over the table, shrinking the distance between us even further. 'You know what? I believe you. I thought I'd find you a wreck and the crew in disarray—but you've pulled through, and I'm glad because this makes my work easier. So I'll let you stay. The crew respect you, so you can help bring them along. As you say, we have the same objective.'

He pauses for the tiniest of moments, then his voice turns steely. 'But remember this: unlike you, I'm not running away. I left a good life to spend decades in the freezer because what I'm doing here is important. I'm not going to let you, or anyone, get in my way. If I have the slightest suspicion you're plotting against me, you're going straight into cold-sleep. Am I clear?'

I hold my position, our faces uncomfortably close, his breath warm on my cheek. I have no doubt of his commitment. Or the amount of money he's getting for his time in the freezer. Or that he'd rather kill me than let me get in the way.

'Perfectly.'

'Good.' He pulls away, easing into his chair.

I do the same, my muscles stiff.

'You'll be wasted on the bridge,' he says, his manner relaxed again. 'But if you really want to help, I could use a liaison with the science team. If you can bear it. That woman makes me regret my life choices.' He chuckles. 'I don't know how you could stand her, even before you knew who she was.'

Can I bear it?

I can. Whatever it takes, I'll do it.

I lift my chin. 'For the colonists. For *Gabriel*.'

The Guardian grins, and this time the expression doesn't seem to have a hidden edge. 'I'm glad you see it this way. It makes it easier, for all of us.'

He gets up and reaches out his hand. I manage to keep my face calm as I shake it, not too enthusiastic, but not hostile either.

I got what I wanted. I'll have access to the research and some freedom of movement around the ship. Enough to start looking for Zhang's files.

Let the games begin.

CHAPTER 21

Khan meets me at the entrance to the lab. She's her usual prim and proper, but her eyes are bloodshot and her fists clench and unclench inside her uniform's pockets. She leads me in, walking tall and straight between workstations and screens scrolling columns of numbers or symbols I don't understand.

'The *Guardian* has just messaged me.' Khan enunciates the word like an insult. 'Does he have a name? Anyway, I'm glad not to have to deal with him.'

We enter a small office in the corner of the lab, perfectly square and arranged with geometrical precision. Two interactive boards face a polished desk, where a single data pad lies exactly in the middle. Symmetrically arranged stacks of reading pads and instruments sit on a shelf opposite the entrance. The air smells of disinfectant, though I might be projecting.

Khan points to a chair opposite the desk, then moves hers minimally to the right to maintain symmetry. Her jaw is tight, her hands deep in her pockets. She moistens her mouth with a flick of the tongue that makes me think of a snake.

'Do you want to talk about it?' Her voice is coarse, but she looks me straight in the eye.

A wave of heat rises to my face, the pain dulled but unrelenting. And yet I'm grateful for her candour. 'No. Let's leave the past in the past, at least till we're done dealing with the present.'

She nods, though I can't tell if she's relieved or disappointed. Maybe she was hoping for a chance to explain and earn forgiveness. No such luck, for either of us.

'The present, then.' She reaches for the pad and taps the screen. 'What do you want to know? No, forget that. Tell me first how you see your role. With the *Guardian*.'

She lowers the pad and looks at me expectantly. She must know he may be listening. Even without the spy, the main computer would do the job if the Guardian requested it.

'Our mission hasn't changed,' I say. 'I intend to find out what killed the colonists, and make sure the same doesn't happen to *Gabriel*.'

I hold her gaze, hoping she'll understand. I have no idea if she can help me, but it's good to know she doesn't trust the Guardian.

She returns my glance. We remain silent, staring into each other's eyes like some doomed lovers.

'We're still analysing the data from the habitat. Most of the actual work's being done on the surface, of course. We just help them crunch the numbers and search for patterns.' Khan pauses, holding my gaze for another moment. 'Though the bandwidth we have to deal with at the moment is less than optimal.'

I nod. We've been using the shuttle radios for communication—hardly the best arrangement. 'I'm told the replacement transmitter will be ready by tomorrow.'

'I hope it will.'

We spend another thirty seconds staring at each other—until I realise that she did, in fact, tell me something new, or rather something I didn't fully understand. The real research is done on the surface. They decide what, and how much they tell us.

I do some quick math: including the engineers, we have thirteen people on the planet now, and only two from Price's security. There's no way they can monitor everything, even if they understood the science. If we could establish a covert link, we'd be able to control what the Guardian knows.

Easier said than done. Firyali's not talking to me, and the engineers aren't likely to cooperate. And I still know nothing about Zhang's agenda. Damn.

I rise slowly, my chair scraping the floor. 'Thank you, Doctor. Please keep me informed. Especially if there's anything we can do to help the field team.'

A tiny smile breaks Khan's lips. 'Of course.'

This time I access the tether through the personnel entrance, the one closer to the bridge. I won't run into the engineers anymore, and if someone does see me going, my explanation will sound more convincing if I don't look like I'm trying to hide. My cover story is investigating what else the Chinese conspirators may have been hiding, which is a perfect pretext in that it's actually the truth.

The personnel lift is faster, and the direction flip in the spindle more stomach churning. I emerge on the opposite side of the corridor where we arrived yesterday. Not even twenty-four hours ago—and an entirely different universe.

I turn right, towards the guts of the engine—or at least as far as I can get before the alarms set off. The first door opens without so much as a red light, and so does the next. I hesitate. Too much good luck makes me nervous. I push on, slowly now, my footsteps stirring puffs of dust in the dim, warm interior. Blocks of machinery stretch deep on both sides of the walkway, most of them dark, some blinking an occasional light like a machine breath.

I stop. That I've been able to get this far can only mean that the alarms have been disabled. So much for the Guardian's claim that he isn't interested in the Chinese technology. Maybe that's even what he's really after. Or at least a side benefit, a chance to finally get their hands on the propulsion tech. Whichever it is, if they've been here before, the Guardian or his people could be back at any moment—and even if they believe my cover, I can't let them find Zhang's hideout before I do.

I glance around, my gaze sliding over metal guts, prying into crevices between equipment towers. This feels wrong. Zhang wouldn't hide his 'closet' inside the machinery. It's not like he'd be walking around here with a wrench. No, it will be in a place he could access without a need for excuses.

I retrace my steps back to the tether, then check my map of the deck. We based the plans on the cleaning drones. The thickest lines correspond to the most frequented paths. The cleaners go where there's stuff for them to clean—and on a spaceship, humans are the main source of mess.

I follow the lines into a corridor branching off to the right. The space feels different here, brighter and more hospitable. I pass a picture pinned to the wall, a green, hilly landscape with a Chinese description. More posters appear, like clues in a quest game. The engineers came here to work, not to hide. This was their true home, away from the rest of us.

A narrow door on the side of the corridor stands ajar. I peer inside to find a desk and a screen station. Could it be Zhang's? Unlikely: the way the chair and the instruments are stowed makes me think the space hasn't been used since we were in zero-g. I move on, passing similar offices till I arrive at a large chamber with workstations arranged in a ring around a pillar of screens. Most of the monitors are live, some showing numbers, others graphs or up-and-down bars annotated with Chinese characters. Consoles and desks line the perimeter wall, the chairs pushed back as if expecting the occupants to return at any moment. A teacup, plastic but painted in a flowery design that's nothing like the ship-issue, sits on one of the desks next to a half-eaten bowl of protein soup.

I circle the room, looking for anything that would point to Zhang. To the left, a door opens on a square room with a meeting table and a desk, a diminutive version of my office. This one must be his.

The door creaks as I enter. I move past the table, towards the desk. A faded photograph sticks to the wall next to the chair, its corners frayed. On it, two young men stand in front of a giant machine, laughing as they point at some part of it. The faces look vaguely familiar—but only when I lean closer do I realise that one of them is Zhang. He's younger here, but that's not what makes him almost unrecognisable. His relaxed posture, his wind-blown hair, his happy, open smile—everything about the man in the image is unlike the Zhang I know.

I wonder if he'd think the same if he saw a picture of me from before... Before.

I pull away, annoyed. None of this matters; I'm wasting precious time. A reading pad sits on the desk, a general issue, not any of the specialised engineering devices. The screen lights up at my touch with a page from a Chinese news burst. A moving image shows a tall building engulfed in flames with the headline screaming about American aggression. So the New Union retaliated. No surprise there. It was probably in our news as well, I just didn't read that far after—

I push the memory away before it overwhelms me. I'll never get over it, but I can control it now, and that's all that matters. I scroll through the pages, but it's just more pictures of crumbling buildings, barren fields and food shortages, and more sabre-rattling about stopping American imperialism. Not a word about how the Chinese started it, but that's no surprise, either.

I navigate to the root menu, but the whole pad is just news. The drawers and the cabinet next to the desk yield only engineering manuals and odd-looking instruments. One drawer is locked—I force it open but find only more pictures: some of what seems to be a small town, others of Zhang and the other man, his face somehow familiar even though I'm sure he's not any of the engineers.

My timer buzzes. Thirty minutes to dinner. Can I pull off another sulking session and skip it? No, I'd have to be in my room then, in case they decided to check. Besides, I'm a crew member again. A bit worse for wear, but they need to see me try. I glance around, biting my lip. He said a 'closet'. Where would he hide one?

I try the walls, then return to the main room and try everything there. Nothing. The timer buzzes again. Ten minutes. Damn. It's not going to be today. I take a deep breath and head back to the tether.

The Guardian's not in the mess, so that's a relief. He kept Price, too, maybe as personal security. The others gather in function circles, their conversations subdued—except for the security team, now ten strong, joking aloud as if they're having the best time. Maybe they are—or maybe they're trying to convince everyone else. The Sharks are still in their silver suits. They've removed the helmets but are keeping them at the ready, probably in case we start a food fight.

They quiet for Sanchez's prayer, then resume chatting the moment it's over. The reverend gives me a nod before sitting down with his people. He looks frail, his perfect smile gone, his body hunched and somehow older. But his people are talking to him, and everyone has followed his prayer. He may yet be forgiven. I hope.

When I return to my cabin after dinner, Yefremov waits by

the door. I push past him, ignoring the pain in my chest and the stinging under my eyelids.

'Nathalie...'

I don't look at him as I press the lock-pad. I thought I could let bygones be bygones. I can't. Not with him.

'Nathalie, please. We need to—'

I swing around, my fists clenched and my breath hot. 'I didn't think it was possible to hate a human being as much as I hate you. Go away and never, ever talk to me again.'

I slide past his stunned face and close the door behind me. Eventually, my breathing quiets. I don't think he'll bother me again.

And tomorrow I'll find Zhang's hiding place.

CHAPTER 22

I return to the engine section just after lunch and spend all of my allotted two hours checking the disused service rooms along the entry corridor. My frustration is growing with every room I visit, but they are all the same: a desk, a chair, a dusty workstation that hasn't seen action since before our departure. When my timer rings, I want to keep going, but that's just asking for trouble. Someone's going to notice my absence.

The next day is no better. I try the central room and Zhang's office once more, but that's useless. The area would have people coming and going, too many to sneak in unnoticed. I consider the machine compartments again, but that's unlikely —I know little about engineering, but I've seen mechanics at work, and they never venture into the machine guts alone. The 'closet' has to be somewhere nearby, somewhere Zhang could get to without going out of his way and without raising suspicions. It must be in the offices, I just have to look harder. Much harder.

I come back on the third day determined to search under every floorboard and every wall panel. All the offices look identical: a console, some shelves, and a chair, all securely stowed.

But something about the third one seems different—too neat, as if the chair restraints have only just been fastened. I move closer, my heartbeat accelerating.

Behind the chair there's only a wall of composite panels, identical to all the rest. Yet when I touch it, the structure gives under my fingers, as if not properly secured. I tap it gently, then try the other walls—the sound is definitely different. I'm on to something.

I start by pulling the edge of the panel. No good. Pushing doesn't work either. Do I need tools? I don't think Zhang would be coming here with a toolbox each time he wanted access.

I take off my jacket, my heart pounding. I slide my fingers along the edge of the panel, pressing gently. Nothing on the left, or on the top—but on the right, a different sound, like a mechanism catching. I push and hold the pressure—something clicks, and the edge of the panel pops out just enough for me to slip my hand underneath. There, a catch. My finger hooks on the release, and the panel swings out like a trapdoor.

I pull it open to find only the grey aero-carbon that makes the ship's base structure. A dead end.

Gao shenme? But no—why a door if it leads to nowhere?

I touch the wall, and it swings inward. It's not a wall but another, larger door, its edges out of view so it appears solid. I slide into a dark, dusty room, the air stifling with the heat of electric circuits. I wait for the lights to come on, but nothing happens. Damn. On a hunch, I reach behind me and pull the outside panel closed, then the inner door. The lock clicks, and the room fills with soft yellow light. That's more like it.

The space is tiny—just a computer station and a chair, so close that I reach it with just one step. The walls are bare; a ship-issue squeeze bottle and two cups sit on the floor, forgotten. A data pad lies on the seat, dark green with black lines embossed into the surface. The screen lights up, requesting a passcode. Shit! No way I can crack it. Maybe Firyali could, but she hasn't so much as met my gaze since she found out who I am.

I put the pad aside and try the computer. More luck this time: the monitor comes to life, showing a menu. It's in Mandarin, but I can read enough to tell these are dates—and the most recent one only from yesterday. I frown. How come? Zhang's been gone for four days, so it's not something he created. I slide my hand over the touch-board to select the last entry, then groan with disappointment when the link opens on a submenu of news outlets. Another damn news burst! I return to the root menu but it's all the same: listings of news feeds logged under different dates.

I rub my chin. Is *this* Zhang's secret? What's the point?

I look around, searching for another hiding spot. There's nothing here, just the computer and the chair. Maybe a hidden compartment? No, I'm already inside a damn hidden compartment.

I chew the inside of my cheek, thinking. Zhang must have had a reason to keep this place hidden. So, if these are the same news bursts we've been receiving, then why are they here, on a secret computer in a secret room, concealed from the rest of us?

I go to the most recent entry and select an outlet. Chinese state news. The images show a construction site, then a city, Shanghai, I think. The commentary's about an engineering breakthrough in rice growers. I flip to another outlet, with news on land reclamation on islands submerged by the sea level rise. More channels, more news, none of it remotely relevant. Except maybe for one thing: the absence of burning buildings and cries of American aggression. Maybe I caught them on a good day.

I drum my fingers on the edge of the touch-board. This is getting me nowhere. And soon it'll be dinner time and I'll have to go back, empty-handed and more frustrated than ever.

Back in the list of outlets, I scroll through the options. My heart stops when I see the Feidi's news drips. No, I'm not ready for them. Besides, what will they show me but more death? If they're even allowed to report on the internment camps.

Further down the list are the American channels. I select one at random and let it play. A report from the Thanksgiving parade, happy citizens marching and singing like they're already in Paradise. A trade agreement with the European Alliance. Rationing lifted for the holiday season. Developments in compound agriculture. A lucrative, hard-currency contract for a relay station for inter-orbital transit. A debate on—

Wait. I wind back to the relay station.

The construction will use orbital assemblers, but the aero-carbon components will come from ground-based American manufacturers, increasing the pressure to add capacity to the Atlantic elevator.

I play the fragment again, then check the date. This can't be. The Atlantic elevator was destroyed two weeks before the date of this article.

I return to the menu and bring up the news from the day after the attack. This should be headline news—but I find nothing, not even a mention of the elevator. I check the date again, try the day before and after. Nothing. No disasters. And no Chinese attack.

This is impossible. I'm missing something. Why would Zhang store alternative news? How did he even get these? Or did he create them? No, there are decades' worth of weekly reports here, much more detailed than our news bursts.

I lean back in the chair, my head spinning. Our news bursts —how do we get them? Some were already on the system when we arrived, received in the decades we were en route. The most recent ones came in 'live' with only six years light speed delay. Received by the ship's antenna straight to the comms system.

No, that's not true. Everything we receive goes through the main computer. And possibly, the spy.

Two versions of news. And yet only one of them can be true. Which?

Follow the money. If you don't know who's telling the truth, check who benefits from the lie.

I try to decide what Zhang, or anyone, would gain from making us believe his version of the news. Chinese citizens would have avoided the blame—but if that'd been his purpose, then why keep the messages hidden? Why not send them to the main computer for everyone to see?

On the other hand, the news we did receive benefits no one. The war impacts us all: the Americans, the Chinese, the Kenyans, even the ji-gong, the internationals. Everybody hurts.

And everybody blames everyone else. The Americans for the attack on the elevator. The Chinese for the burning buildings. The Kenyans for the internment camps. The news has split us apart.

And there's one person who has already benefited: the Guardian.

I stand up, the tension in my limbs too much for this cramped space. I rock on my feet, wringing my clammy hands. Could this be it? Were our news bursts just a delusion created to fracture us and prepare for the takeover?

I close my eyes. The last news burst was the unscheduled one, on the day of the service. The day we learned about the elevator, and I learned about Jason.

The day we were beginning to get along.

And then, after we were already divided along the national lines and the Chinese crew banned to the planet, the first thing the Guardian did was expose our secrets, so we splintered even further, refracted into individual beams, person against person.

I was right thinking we were all here to escape our dark secrets. We were recruited that way. The Crew Connection

Matrix, the Guardian's insistence on having me on board despite the captain's protests—it was only to make us vulnerable, kindling ready for the flame. This is the 'plan B' the Guardian mentioned.

But who would go to such lengths? What ends could possibly require such means?

No, this can't be true. I've latched on to this idea because it lets me believe that the Atlantic attack didn't happen, that there was no violence, no internment camps. That Jason might still be alive.

I slide back into the seat. My hand shakes as I select the entry for Feidi's *Courier*. This is a mistake, I know, and yet I can't resist. A lump grows in my throat at the sight of the familiar vista, the Feidi glorious in early December, with streets decorated for Jamhuri Day parades. Kenyan flags hang together with Chinese banners; the stalls are laid out for the annual feast —scantier than I remember, but festive regardless. A reporter interviews passers-by, black, brown, and pink-skinned. All complain about food shortages, but that's not new. They still smile and joke as if life were normal. This is not the picture of a city under siege.

I switch the screen off and hide my face in my hands. I thought Zhang's secrets would give me answers. They've only given me more questions.

The Guardian is the key to all of this, and the new Mind-Link.

If Zhang was still on board, I could talk to him and maybe, somewhere between his lies and the Guardian's, I'd glimpse the truth. But that's no longer an option. I'm on my own.

And somehow, I've got to figure it out.

Next day after breakfast I signal Sanchez to stay behind. He looks tired, his formerly perfect face crumpled and grey. But his smile is still there, warm and welcoming even if frayed at the edges.

'How have you been?' he asks as I approach.

'Fine.'

'You're not supposed to lie to a minister. Not even to a failed one.'

I give him a small smile. 'At least your humour hasn't failed you.'

'Deflecting, I see. That's a good sign.'

I snort, then cock my head. 'How are they?'

'Better than I thought they'd be. Price's people are fine, of course. I tried talking to her but...' He shakes his head. 'She's chosen her side. The scientists are letting their work distract them. The others... I hope one day they'll forgive me. At least they haven't tried to stone me yet. Though that may be due to the lack of stones.'

He tries to laugh, but the sound comes out broken. His gaze flickers to the two security men lingering by the door. They appear to be chatting, but they've been following our every move.

I give Sanchez a tiny nod. We'd better keep this short. 'I need to know something: when was the last time anyone received a personal message? I mean, from someone they know, not an official letter like...' My voice breaks, but I push on, 'Like what I got.'

Sanchez frowns. 'It's been a while. Actually, I'm not sure anyone got much after two decades into the journey. It's not that surprising, though, is it?'

That's what I used to think. 'Listen, ask Firyali to check the logs. I need to be certain.'

'She's still not talking to you? Do you want me to—'

'No. Don't tell her it's for me, either. Okay?'

'Sure.'

I glance at the two security men at the door. Jeff Willard

stands next to a Shark, still suited and with the confident air of someone calling the shots.

'I'd better go.'

I put on a sad smile and slide away looking appropriately subdued.

A message from Khan arrives just as I reach the corridor. *Come see me. Yefremov's found something.*

I accelerate towards the lab, trying hard not to run. Yet when I reach the door, Khan's stepping out, her mouth pursed and her brows tight, the Guardian right behind her. He's wearing a new set of clothes: loose trousers and a silky buttoned-up jacket, both in steely grey reminiscent of the Sharks' suits.

He grins when he sees me. 'Nathalie. Come to my office. We deserve to hear the news together.'

I glance at Khan. She says nothing, but by now I know her well enough to realise she's fuming. He must have intercepted her message—and he's not even coy about the fact.

We march in silence, crossing two junctions before meeting up with Yefremov. He nods a greeting, but I don't return it. If the Guardian wants us to hate each other, in this case I'm happy to oblige.

Price is already waiting by the office door, accompanied by the Shark from the mess hall—white, tall, and broad shouldered, with a square head and straight brows over narrow grey eyes. Price nods, her back stiff and her shoulders rigid. She's not happy with the Shark's presence.

'This is Major Donahue, for those who haven't met him,' the Guardian says.

From the curt nods Khan and Yefremov give the Shark, that's all of us. I wonder why he's here. The Guardian may be trying to drive a wedge between him and Price, just in case either of them gets too comfortable.

We file into the office. There's a moment of consternation as the others stare at the table, figuring out their places in the new power balance. I know mine. I move past them to the seat at the far end of the table, the one Sanchez used to occupy. The Guardian takes the head, with Price and Donahue at his sides. Khan and Yefremov take the next two seats, which puts them on my half of the table.

The Guardian steeples his fingers. 'Doctor, please bring everyone up to speed.'

Yefremov clears his throat. 'Well, we found a well-preserved body inside a food freezer. No apparent external injuries other than, obviously, frostbite. If we're lucky, we'll get a full brain scan.'

'Do we know why they were in the freezer?' Price asks.

'Nothing's certain, but he appears to have been hiding, like the people in the habitat.'

The Guardian nods. 'Will this help you study the new Mind-Link?'

Khan answers slowly, choosing her words. 'It depends how well the organic parts have been preserved. We already have the wire-work from previous autopsies, but the amount of decomposition made it impossible to say anything about the connections.'

The Guardian wrings his fingers with a loud crack of his knuckles. 'Are you going to scan it?'

'We have to thaw the body first,' Yefremov says. 'Our equipment won't differentiate the organic parts of the Mind-Link from the brain itself. We didn't anticipate working with frozen bodies—or with Mind-Link. And defrosting is tricky. If we go too fast, the external tissue will start decomposing before the inside is ready. Back home we have ways to do it safely, but here all we can do is go slowly, with temperatures just above zero.'

'By slowly, do you mean hours? Or weeks?'

'Days. Assuming the freezer's temperature control is good enough.'

'It's worked so far, hasn't it?' Donahue asks, his accent

American with the hint of a southern twang. He folds his arms across his chest, his brows rising.

'Nobody's touched the thermostat for four decades, Colonel,' Khan says, her accent at its most British.

'Major.' Donahue's voice is stone cold.

Khan puts on a pleasant smile. 'My mistake.'

I almost laugh—but the moment bursts when I notice the Guardian's studious gaze, watching us like a culture under his microscope. He has us exactly where he wants us—fighting each other and forgetting that he's even here.

'Have the engineers checked the freezer?' I ask.

'Zhang has,' Price says. 'When he first discovered it.'

I frown. 'I assume he wasn't alone at the time?'

'He was.' Price grins. 'He's been in the hub on his own ever since they got down to the planet.'

'What do you mean?'

'His people kicked him out for killing the captain and all the others.'

'Chinese people don't take treason lightly,' Donahue says. 'That's one thing we agree on.'

'As I understand, he has everything he needs to survive,' the Guardian says. 'Frankly, he's lucky the engineers are unarmed, or I doubt he'd still be alive.'

Blood drains from my face. 'This is a disgrace.'

All eyes turn to me, and I remember that I'm supposed to hate all the Chinese and Zhang especially. I don't know what I feel anymore—and my feelings don't matter anyway. Even if he is responsible for seven deaths, this is vigilante justice at best; at worst, they are condemning the only man who can give us a clue to this puzzle. But I can't tell them that.

I spread my hands in feigned frustration. 'We've done everything to prevent contamination. Zhang living there, breathing, eating, defecating—it's thrown all that effort out of the window.'

'Unless whatever got the colonists gets him, and then we'll have a fresh corpse to dissect,' Price says. It's supposed to be a joke, but nobody laughs. Even Donahue produces only a snort.

The Guardian sighs. 'I tend to agree with you, Nathalie, but nobody asked my opinion. And Amy's right, even if I wouldn't put it so crudely. *If* there's something in the hub we've missed, we'll find out soon enough.'

I force myself to nod. Next to me, Khan's olive skin looks almost green and Yefremov's ghostly grey.

I've got to talk to Zhang. I must know his side of the story. And if Price's prediction is right, I may not have much time left.

CHAPTER 23

I manage to hold it together till I reach my quarters. By the time the door closes behind me, I'm shaking. I slide to the floor, my strength crumbling under remorse and regret. If Zhang dies, it will be my fault. Guilty or not, he doesn't deserve to die like that, without due trial. It makes no difference that I didn't mean it to end this way. I didn't mean for Stepan to die when I didn't tell him about the Sharks. I didn't mean for the protests to get out of hand. I didn't mean for the riots to kill so many.

I swore I wouldn't let death take anyone in my care—and then I pushed another person right into his hands.

My tears return like a long-missed friend. I press my fist to my mouth. All the fighting, and I only keep making things worse. How can I face the Guardian if I can't get anything right?

But this is still my crew. Even Zhang. I owe it to them. And if I have to go down to the planet to talk to him, then that's exactly what I'm going to do.

I push myself up to my shaky feet and reach for the pad. The zheping. Whatever. I can't do this alone. The others may hate me, but they know we must work together or we'll all go down.

I type a message to Firyali, my fingers clumsy with tension. *We need to talk.*

The reply arrives within seconds. *Stay in your room.*

I frown. How does she know where I am?

Another message pops up on the screen. *Who do you trust?*

She told me the spy can see what we transmit. So either she's managed to make this connection secure—or she hates me so much she's decided to work with the Guardian.

No, not Firyali. She might hate me, but she would never expose the others.

Now, who *do* I trust? Nothing's been proven, and I still don't even know who left that message on my pod. It's a gamble, but all I have to go on is my gut.

Sanchez, I type. *And probably Khan.*

Yefremov?

No.

Fifteen minutes.

Nothing more comes. Fifteen minutes what? She told me to stay here, so that's what I'll do.

I glance around. The place is a mess: the 'immortal' ration bars strewn on the floor among empty wrappers, dirty clothes in another corner, unchanged towels on the floor by the wash-basin. I haven't noticed it before. The room probably stinks, too, even though I can't smell it. Cleaning's the last thing on my mind, but I can't let them think I've totally lost it.

I sweep the ration bars and other detritus into my travel bag and dump it in the closet. Dirty clothes join the towels in the hygiene unit, the door shut. The air recycling on a cooling cycle should take care of the smell. Better. As long as nobody opens any doors.

Eight more minutes. I sit in the desk chair, trying to wrap my mind around what I'm going to tell Firyali. I can't tell her about Zhang's files, not before I decide what to make of them. She'll think I'm falling into his trap. No, it's better—

A knock on the door makes me wince. It's six minutes ahead of time.

My knees tremble as I move to open. She could be early. Or they've found us out.

Khan stands on the other side, her expression puzzled. I breathe with relief and wave her in.

'That woman, Lim?' she starts, and I nod. 'She said to come here. And that your room was secure.'

'I don't know about the latter. But if Lim said so...'

I show her to the chair, the only one in the room. Khan raises an eyebrow.

'It's okay,' I say, and slide to sit on the floor.

She glances at the chair and the layer of crumbs on the surface. So much for making an impression.

Khan moves to the wall and leans against it. 'What is this about?'

I start to answer when another knock makes us both flinch.

It's Sanchez. He enters, his eyes widening at the sight of Khan.

'It's okay,' I say. 'I'll explain when Firyali gets here.'

She arrives two minutes later. It's the first time we've faced each other since she learned who I was. Guilt turns my knees into jelly, but somehow I manage to stand straight and look her in the eye. She returns my gaze, though I can tell it takes some effort. She seems exhausted, her face pale and her eyes surrounded by grey circles.

I pull the door closed. 'That's all of us. Did you say we were safe here?'

'We have thirty minutes,' Firyali says, sliding to the floor next to Sanchez. 'The spy still monitors everything. The trackers are inactive, but the Guardian can listen in on any

space. I've put in a hack for here, but any longer and they may
see it.'

'The 'spy'?' Khan asks.

I raise my hand. 'Wait. What do you mean, they're
inactive?'

'The whole thing was set up to trigger a response. Once that
happened, its job is done. It still listens, but all the action is left
to the Guardian.'

'What do you think his goal is?' I look at Firyali, then at the
others.

'At first I thought it was the new Mind-Link, like he said,'
Khan says. 'But I don't believe that now.'

I lean forward in surprise. 'Why?'

'We have no Mind-Link experts on board, neither on mine
nor on Yefremov's teams. This wasn't something we expected to
deal with. The Guardian would have known that—so if his
mission were to investigate the Chinese experiment, he'd bring
someone qualified to do it.'

'Unless the experiment isn't Chinese,' I say slowly,
watching their faces.

Khan snorts—not with derision but in a way that seems to
say *I haven't considered that.*

'The spy tracked references to Mind-Link. And it woke up
the Guardian when we discovered the new design,' Firyali says.

'I think you need to explain that 'spy' if you want us to
contribute,' Sanchez says.

We catch them up, jumping over each other to compress the
information into the least amount of time. Khan frowns;
Sanchez shakes his head in disbelief.

I leave them to digest the facts and turn to Firyali. 'Did you
get the question about the messages?'

She nods. 'You've got something there, I think. We effec-
tively stopped receiving personal messages six years after departure. There were a few more, increasingly impersonal, and then

nothing at all for the last fifteen years. Sure, time passes—but not even a single birthday card or Christmas greeting? Why do you think that is?'

I look at my hands. Damn, this is tricky. 'I have a reason to suspect that not all the news we've been getting is... accurate. In that case, personal messages would have to be withheld so they don't contradict the news.'

Sanchez shakes his head again. 'Do you mean they fabricated it all for us? And sent it years in advance just so it could reach us now?'

'Wouldn't be the first time someone used the news to manipulate people,' Khan says coldly. 'The question is, to what end?'

'What do you think?' I look from face to face. I'm not trying to challenge them, only to test my own thinking.

'The only thing the news has done is put us all on edge,' Khan says.

Firyali snorts. 'That's an understatement.'

Of course, she, too, has family in the Feidi. The news about the internment camps has touched all of the Kenyans.

'I'm sorry,' Khan says. 'I didn't mean to trivialise the events.'

'I don't believe it,' Sanchez says. 'Who'd go to such lengths just to get us to distrust the Chinese? We never trusted them to begin with.'

Firyali cocks her head. Sanchez catches her gaze, and his cheeks turn red.

I have to stop this before we waste the rest of our time offending and apologising. 'How about us, then? Isn't it a perfect coincidence how we're all connected, and just in a way that would make us hate or at least distrust each other?'

The three of them stare at me. Sanchez's mouth opens and closes without a sound; Khan takes a deep breath.

Firyali drops her head. 'Shit.'

'But why?' Sanchez says after a while.

'Divide et impera,' Khan says. 'Divide and conquer. The tactic of choice of dictators and tyrants. Make us so busy pointing fingers at each other that we miss the bigger game.'

'Then, what *is* the bigger game?' Sanchez asks.

I shake my head. 'It must have something to do with the Guardian—who he really is and why he's here. And how it's connected to the new Mind-Link.'

They look away, each chasing their own thoughts. I check the time. Ten minutes left.

'What do you want to do?' Firyali asks, startling the others back to attention.

'I've got to talk to Zhang. I thought he was behind all this. I'm no longer sure.'

'You think he's innocent?' Sanchez asks, a tremor in his voice. 'That we sent him—'

'Not 'we'. I. I'm responsible.' I stare into his eyes until he nods, then continue. 'I don't know if he's innocent. But he knows something—and even if he lies, he may still help me get a better picture.'

'What did you find on the engine deck?' Firyali asks.

I stare. 'How did you know?'

'I've been tracking your wan-kong.' She shrugs the embarrassment away. 'I needed to know. And good I did, or you'd have triggered the alarms.'

'You turned them off?'

'Who else?'

'I thought...' I wave my hand. 'Never mind. I found news—other news. Where the destruction of the Atlantic elevator never happened, nor the internment camps. I don't know if any of it is true—but I also don't know it isn't.'

Khan rubs her face, more distraught than I thought possible. 'I've got a million questions, but we're running out of time. So, how do you want to talk to him? Can we arrange a secure connection?'

Firyali shakes her head. 'Here, maybe. But not on the other end.'

'So—how?'

'I've got to get down to the planet,' I say. 'It's the only way.'

They all start to talk, but I raise my hands to silence them. 'Zhang may not last long. I've got to go there—I just need an excuse so the Guardian lets me.'

'A medical emergency?' Khan suggests.

'No.'

She narrows her eyes. 'You can't avoid the doctor forever.'

I make my voice hard. 'No.'

'It's a moot point anyway,' Firyali says. 'We can't engineer an emergency from this end. They'd need to inform us about it, and that's not going to work.'

'What, then?' Sanchez asks, but nobody answers.

We sit in silence for a moment—and then I know. There's a way—the only way.

'I'm going to steal the shuttle.'

They all speak at the same time, eyes wide and heads shaking.

'Shénme?'

'How?'

'They won't let you.'

'You're going to get yourself killed,' Khan says. 'And then we'll be in real trouble.'

'It's the only way,' I repeat. 'Firyali, can you check the security?'

She chews her lip for a moment. 'I can check, but I can't disable it, not with the Sharks on board. They're damn good. Changed all the codes and got the critical systems wired directly to their own alerts. I can't touch those.'

'I'll find a way,' I say, sounding more confident than I feel.

Khan checks her wan-kong. 'It's time.'

'One last thing,' I say as we get up. 'We can't appear too

friendly. Best to maintain current levels.' I glance at Khan and then at Firyali, and they both nod. 'If there's anything urgent, talk to the reverend.'

Firyali leaves first, then Khan three minutes later. When it's just me and Sanchez, he leans against the door, eyeing me with his arms crossed.

'Are you sure it's the only way?'

'Got a better idea?'

He sighs. 'I wish. Because I don't like yours in the least.'

I snicker. 'Frankly, nor do I...'

'Do you have a plan?'

'I'll think of something.'

He snorts, then checks the time. He turns to go but stops for another moment. 'How come you trust me now? Is it because I've lost my faith? Has that made me trustworthy?'

'No. But it made you human. Fallible, like the rest of us. And if it makes you feel better, I hope you find your faith.'

He considers my answer, then smiles, satisfied.

I make my way to the shuttle dock the next day. We have two, one on either side of the main deck. The spread makes sense for safety, but it's going to make my work harder. Stealing one shuttle won't do me much good if Price can come after me in the other with a squad of armed Sharks. I have to disable the other one and do it in a way that won't raise suspicions.

I nod to the few people I meet on the way, mostly Sanchez's ops crew who store their equipment here. Kowalski and Auma nod back, both meeting my gaze for the first time since the Guardian's arrival. I move on, wondering how quickly someone from security is going to catch up with me. The floor here is lined with metal plating, as if someone had planned on making my footsteps ring like an alarm bell. I make it to the vestibule unobstructed. At one end, a bulkhead leads to the EVA airlock, the very same where we intercepted Zhang and his team. How fitting.

I head to the shuttle lock. The light above flashes a happy green, the vessel docked and pressurised. I put in my codes, half expecting to have them refused, but the pad chirps confirmation. Good, at least the system still has me as the pilot.

I barely manage to pull the door open when I hear hurried footsteps from down the corridor, breaking into a run. Their owner catches up with me inside the airlock, just as I reach the inner hatch leading to the shuttle. It's one of the Sharks, a dark-skinned man with yellow hair.

His hand rests on his gun as he leans inside. 'What are you doing?'

'My job?' I try to sound casual as I shoot him a half-smile. 'I'm the lead pilot here. And I finally have time for the inspections. Should have done them earlier, I know, but...' I shrug. 'Better late than never!'

The man scowls, unsure. I pull the hatch open, then take off my jacket and throw it over the hatch—just in case he failed to notice that I'm not dressed for extravehicular activities.

I slide inside, breathing in the scent of composite and stale air. Dashboard lights blink as if to say hello. Man, I missed this place.

The Shark moves in behind me, so close I can feel his breath on my neck.

I walk to the console and slump into the seat. 'The nav-systems should have been recalibrated. Call me old school, but I don't rely on the locators. That's asking for trouble.'

I activate the navigation panel and check the settings. Everything perfect. Damn.

'What trouble?' the Shark asks. He's looking at me, not the console. I really hope he's got no clue.

'Normally, the shuttle can navigate using the locators on established objects. At home, that's all we use, but the number of orbital objects is way higher.' I look at the man: he nods, but his eyes are glazing over. Good.

I type in some innocuous requests as I continue. 'Here we have our ship, the elevator, and *Gabriel*. This should be enough. But you know what they say about shoulds... If they fail, then we have nothing to guide the shuttle. When you do it old school, you calibrate for orbital data. That's tedious and needs to be redone each time we shift or our orbit changes, but if you keep current, you'll never end up with a shuttle that can't find its way home.'

The man's no longer listening. Good, because that last part was some high-calibre nonsense. He walks back to the hatch, where another Shark's head has now appeared. The two chat in hushed voices, then the man steps out to continue their conversation, though I can still see his hand on the hatch, as if in confirmation of their surveillance. Never mind. This has gone exactly as I hoped. I want them to get used to me coming here day after day, doing boring piloty stuff till my presence in the shuttle will no longer raise an eyebrow—and no one will check what it is I'm working on.

I spend twenty minutes recalibrating systems that nobody ever uses and verifying perfectly set settings, then leave the shuttle, looking appropriately grumpy.

The two Sharks are still there, the man now joined by the only female Shark, lanky and pale-skinned, with bright green bionic eyes that seem to be of the same model as Tam's.

'That's half the work done,' I announce, stretching. 'Now the other one...'

I grab my jacket and shuffle away, two sets of footsteps trailing behind me like echoes. They follow all the way to the second dock, though by the time we get there, the woman has peeled away. I repeat the routine inside the other shuttle, and when I'm finally done, the Shark looks thoroughly bored, his eyes half-closed as he watches something over his lenses.

I wipe my hands on my trousers as if I'd just done some serious maintenance. 'That's it for today. I'll be back tomorrow. About the same time, if you need to babysit me.'

The man nods, expressionless. I'm sure they'll send Price here to check after me, but she'll find only calibration routines in mid-run.

The Shark departs without a word when we return midship. I turn towards the labs, sending Khan a meeting request as I walk.

Navrov greets me when I arrive. He's a big blond man with a surprisingly gentle manner for his bulky frame. He speaks in a soft baritone with a melodic Slavic rhythm. 'The boss's on the way. She was just talking with the Guardian.'

I try not to frown as my suspicions return. But no, if she was snitching on me, I'd already have all the Sharks here with their guns pointed.

On Navrov's screen, a 3-D model of a brain rotates slowly, encased in a lattice of multicoloured wires.

'Is this the Mind-Link?' I ask.

'Right.' He points to the monitor, where a green lattice appears over the brain. 'This is the common Mind-Link. And this is the new one.' He touches the screen, and a network of yellow and red lines appears on top of the green ones. 'The yellow wires are where we think it mirrors the standard design. The red ones are a puzzle. I'm modelling possible connections to see what makes sense.'

'And? Any ideas?'

'Not yet,' Khan's voice answers behind me. I didn't hear her enter.

'Doctor Khan. How was your meeting with the Guardian?'

'Splendid.' She points me to her office. 'How can I help you?'

The room looks exactly like it did the last time. Khan waits for me to sit, then moves her chair so it balances mine on the other side of the desk, like a counterweight.

'Something I wanted to get back to,' I say. 'The research of the native pathogens.'

Khan sighs. 'There are no pathogens.'

'Just like there was no plague?' I don't know why I say it, but the words are out before I manage to stop them.

The woman winces. She swallows and takes a slow breath before she answers. 'There *was* no plague. Or pandemic, as is the proper term.'

I glare at her.

Her shoulders move as if she were trying to shrug but didn't quite manage. 'Check the research data if you doubt me.'

'I can show you the data. I have their pictures on my wall.'

Khan leans back. Her hands are shaking, and so are mine. If he's listening, the Guardian must be delighted. Fine. We're playing our parts, even if the emotions are all too real.

'We may have underestimated the effects on the vulnerable populations. Or rather, the numbers of those most vulnerable— the malnourished, chronically ill, or immuno-compromised. But it doesn't make the research wrong. That was no pandemic, far from it. Just as there are no pathogens on the planet.'

I hold her gaze for a long moment. 'Fine. Still, you agreed to run the research. So how is it going?'

'We've rerun all the tests the colonists did before us, with the same results. What we're doing now is checking the local prions for possible interactions—'

'Wait. Prions, like in prion disease?'

Khan scrunches her mouth. 'Very much not like that. We call them prions because they are bits of oddly folded proteins. But they're tiny, just fractions of protein chains. Proto-prions is probably a better name.'

'So, they won't cause prion disease?'

'No. They are entirely incompatible with our biology. We're

testing them now not on human cells, but on the bacterial life present within the human body. You may be aware we have millions of microorganisms living inside us.' She tilts her head in a question.

'The doctor's mentioned something to that effect.'

'Right. They are much simpler organisms, so we're testing if there might be any interaction there, something that could produce undesired side effects.'

'This sounds like something we should have considered before.'

Khan grimaces. 'Except we never picked up any hints of such interactions. The prion proteins are too different from anything that evolved on Earth—human, plant, or bacteria.'

'So you think it's a dead end?'

'Yes. But I'll run all the tests I can think of anyway. It's my job. I always try to find the truth, even if it contradicts my initial judgement.'

She stares hard at me. I know she's not talking about the planet, and all I can manage is to look away, avoiding her gaze before my anger flares again.

'We have our guinea pig out there,' I say after a while. 'I guess we'll find out.'

Khan takes a deep breath. 'I've had a chat with Yefremov. If it's really something to do with the environment, we should expect to hear very soon.'

'How soon?'

'From the doctor's analysis, the colonists experienced the first symptoms—as in, the first instances of carelessness and accidents—within days after the decontamination systems were disabled.'

'Days?'

'Yes.'

Khan holds my gaze. Zhang's been in the hub for three days already. The clock is ticking.

Footsteps approach from outside the office, then the sound of voices exchanging greetings.

Yefremov bursts in, the pad in his hand covered with scribbles of chemical structures. 'Amal, look at this—'

He freezes at the sight of me.

I jump to my feet. 'I'll see myself out.'

'Nathalie...' Yefremov starts, but I'm already out, rushing past Navrov's yellow-lined brain and out into the corridor.

One day I may be able to face the doctor—now I need all my focus on the task at hand. I thought I had days to prepare the shuttles and dull the Sharks' attention. Zhang may not have that much time.

I must leave tomorrow.

CHAPTER 24

I take my time over breakfast and even manage to chat with Navrov as he invites me to his birthday celebrations later today. He pulls in Sanchez and Kowalski, who today is wearing a black T-shirt with the image of the Milky Way and a place-marker saying, 'You are here'—except it's crossed out and another one inserted right next to it saying, 'Actually, here.' We brainstorm ideas for hacking the food processor to turn the 'soup' into something resembling a cake. I throw in a couple of suggestions, then make a show of checking the time.

'Got to go?' Sanchez asks.

'That's it, exactly. I've got to go.' I hold his gaze till the corners of his mouth twitch and I'm sure he understands. 'So much to do *today*.'

'Good luck, then. I'll see you at the party.'

'Yes. I'll see you.'

He returns to the others, frowning as he struggles to focus on the conversation. He'll need to pass the message to Firyali, and soon. I don't know if she can help, but I'd rather have her on the bridge, just in case.

I make my way back to the shuttle bay, retracing yesterday's route. The yellow-haired Shark catches up with me before I reach the vestibule.

'Right on time,' I say. 'Hope you've got something to watch because it's going to take a while.'

The man doesn't answer, stone-faced and indifferent. *Suit yourself, mister.*

I whistle as I pass through the airlock. Just as yesterday, I hang my jacket on the hatch, leaving it half closed as I enter the shuttle. I hope he doesn't follow me inside—if he does, my plan will get a whole lot more complicated. But he stays behind, though he keeps his hand on the hatch, holding it open for as long as I'm close enough to try to reach it. This could be a problem—but not just yet.

The dashboard lights up as I slide into the pilot seat. The menu screen shows the default options—not the navigation submenu I left it on. So, they did send Price in to check. I feel myself smile. How predictable.

Now to work. This is going to be tricky. I could have a ball if I could access the hardware, but that's guaranteed to get the Shark's attention. So I have to disable the shuttle in a way that won't trigger alarms or show obvious error codes, get there using only the dashboard interface—and do it all in one go, instead of the three days I planned for it.

I pull up the system menu, then dig into the settings. Back in training, our most hated teacher was 'Sergeant' Schmidt, a grey-haired, stiff-backed orbital pioneer, whose favourite trick was finding the most ingenious ways of disabling our craft. We'd waste hours toiling over the engines and the avionics only to discover a chain of tiny alterations to secondary settings, none of them enough to trigger a warning, but combining to render entire systems deaf and blind. *It's no trivial system if it can kill you*, he used to say. I thought he was wasting my time—now I'm hoping Price's teachers were less pedantic.

The Shark is still there when I leave the shuttle an hour

later. His hand returns to the hatch as I approach, but it's not as fast as before. I have a chance. I just need to time it right.

I crack my knuckles and pull on my jacket, then try whistling again as I start towards the second shuttle dock. The sound breaks on my lips, my breath too ragged and my throat too tight. I hum instead, hands in my pockets, determined to appear casual.

This time I hang my jacket on the inside of the hatch. The Shark's hand appears on top, as if to make a statement. Fine, as long as he doesn't keep it there. I don't think I could win a tug-of-war.

I keep humming as I slide into the chair and start to work. Just like before, I go through the systems and adjust the settings —only this time I'm not planting an error, I'm preparing for manual control at a moment's notice. My hands shake as I wonder if the Guardian can monitor my work remotely, or if he will send Price to check on the other shuttle and find it unresponsive. No time for finesse. I'm committed. I have to trust my luck, and maybe Firyali's foresight.

Twenty minutes later, I'm ready. The first shuttle took an hour, so that's what the Shark will be expecting. I slip out of my seat and tiptoe towards the hatch. I can see the shadow of the man on the airlock wall, but his hand's not on the door. A drop of sweat trickles down my back. I lean forward, my arm reaching for the handle, fingers stretching...

The Shark jumps to attention as footsteps thunder down the docking bay. His hand grips the hatch. I recoil, snatch my arm back and flatten myself against the wall, my heart pounding. Did he see me? Did he notice my hand?

'Is she there?' a familiar voice asks.

Yefremov. Fuck!

My fists clench as I sidle back inside the shuttle. It's not all lost yet. I just have to get rid of him and hope the Shark will go back to his bored reverie.

'Can I help you, Doctor?' the Shark asks.

'Just need a word with her. Nathalie!'

Yefremov's head appears in the hatch just as I make it back to the pilot seat.

'What do you want?'

'We need to talk. Right now.'

'I've got nothing to say to you.'

Yefremov flings the hatch open, pushing his bulk inside. 'Damn it, Nathalie, we can't stay stuck in the past. We have real lives at stake here!'

'Like the lives you took were any less real?'

Yefremov's mouth snaps shut. He's inside the shuttle now, his hand on the hatch, right next to the Shark's. He takes a deep breath. 'Okay, let's have it, then. Get it out of your system. Maybe that'll make you feel better.'

I move towards him. I'd spit in his face, but this is not the time. 'Fuck off, Doctor. Fuck off, and fuck away, and don't come back or I'll hurt you. And not even the Sharks are going to stop me.'

'Go on, then. Because I'm not leaving.' He turns to the Shark, his face red and his eyes manic. 'Excuse us. We need a moment.'

The Shark snatches his hand back, his action instinctive as at the same instant his eyes narrow in suspicion. Too late. Yefremov slams the hatch closed, then turns the lever to seal it.

'Now,' he says. 'I'm going with you.'

I stand frozen for a moment. 'Why?'

The Shark bangs at the hatch, his shouts echoing through the metal.

'I know what happened. Go!'

'Fuck you, Yefremov, if it's a trick...'

I rush back to my seat and initiate the systems. Outside, the alarm blares as the airlock prepares for decompression. Ten seconds and the Sky Shark will be a Space Shark, sans air or helmet.

The man gets the message—the banging stops, and the alarm drops to a low buzz as the airlock doors seal.

Yefremov climbs into the seat next to me.

'Get your straps on now,' I say. 'Because I'm not going to give a shit how many bones you break.'

The engine light flashes readiness just as a sharp beep brings up the warning: *Docking clamps secured.*

'What is it that you're doing, Nathalie?' the Guardian's voice asks over the PA. 'You know I can't let you go.'

I grin. 'I'm sorry. I really do need to go.'

My fingers tap the commands. The engine pulses to full power.

'The shuttle's stuck, Nathalie. You can't—'

I push the power slider, and the shuttle peels off its moorings. I rotate, flopping us upside down and accelerating away from the ship at top speed.

Next to me, Yefremov grunts, hanging by the shoulder straps that dig into his flesh. I'd love to keep him there, but we're out of the centrifugal gravity now and my trajectory doesn't allow for frivolous acceleration just to make him suffer. I roll out of the turn, and we both settle into weightlessness.

'How did you do that?' the doctor asks.

'The shuttles have a few tricks. Including emergency release. Which I'd prepped for. Now shut up and let me work.'

I activate the flight plan I've prepared. The departure went perfectly, but landing will be rough. I've handled worse, but only in sim. That's the drawback of being an orbital pilot—you get really good at docking, but never have enough landing practice.

Now, pray that Price doesn't fix the other shuttle anytime soon.

I glide out of the seat, towards the emergency equipment

lockers at the back of the cabin. We have four suits, not full EVA but enough to keep you alive for an hour or two in case of a hull breach. Down on the planet, temperature and pressure pose no hazard, so oxygen supply will be our main concern. That and Miller and Lee's willingness to shoot.

I pull out one suit and run the safety checks. It helps that I've got a suit-liner under my uniform—it's not strictly necessary, but it'll make changing easier. Yefremov watches me with a deepening frown. I wonder if he even considered needing a space suit. From where he sits, he can't see if we have more than one. Good.

'That was impressive, Nathalie,' the Guardian's voice says, his tone tired or disappointed. 'One day you'll have to tell me how you did it. But first, do tell me why.'

I return to the dashboard and press the intercom button. I make my voice small. 'Sorry I had to do it this way. I was afraid you'd refuse if I asked.'

I pause, but he stays silent.

'I can't let Zhang die. I sent him there. I wanted him to stand trial for what he did. This is not right. I won't have another death on my hands.'

'You think you can help him?'

'I don't know. I hope so. At least we'll try, the doctor and I.'

'I wish you'd talked to me. I did mean what I said to you. And I have information...' The Guardian breaks off, his voice strained. 'Well, too late now. You're on your own. Good luck.'

Oh, the bastard. Always dangling the carrot, playing me to the end. Still, if a part of him believes I've got no agenda beyond placating my conscience, it might just come in handy.

I return to the back of the cabin and hook my feet into supports as I start to undress. I pull off my shirt and leave it floating next to me, then start on the shoes.

'What information do you think he has?' Yefremov asks.

'All kinds. Like what the fuck he's really doing here. But he's not going to give us anything useful, you can bet on that.'

Yefremov nods, somewhat hesitantly. 'Will they come after us?'

'Of course. It's just a matter of how fast they can do it. And how persuasive Price is towards her pals down on the planet.'

'Chert,' he swears. His eyes widen, as if he's only now realised this isn't exactly a school outing.

'Second thoughts? Too late for that.' I swing towards him, one shoe in hand. 'So, what the hell are you doing here? And who told you?'

He hesitates. 'Sanchez. I told him... that I needed to redeem myself.'

I laugh. 'And he bought that?'

It's possible. He's a chaplain after all, with or without faith.

Yefremov starts to answer, but I can't stop myself, a volcano spitting out anger like lava. 'You think you can martyr your way out of this? Play a hero until everyone forgives and forgets? Well, I'll never forget, and I won't let them. I'll remember till your last day, your last breath. I'll be there, watching, with the picture of Anna and Nadia in my hands.'

His head drops. 'I didn't think—'

He doesn't finish, and that's better or I might punch him. I pull off my other shoe, then send them both gliding back towards the lockers.

'Zhang started hallucinating,' Yefremov says.

'What?'

He turns to look through the viewport, the silhouette of the ship lined in silver by Bethesda's sun. 'Can they hear us?'

I hesitate, then push myself back to the dashboard and switch off the transmitter entirely. 'Do you really know what happened?'

His mouth twists. 'I don't *know*. I have a hypothesis, and

some data to support it. Khan agrees, but she wouldn't tell you until she had proof. Flexible as a brick, she is.'

I bite my tongue before I start yelling again. The fucking pair of them.

'Do you think you can help him?'

'If my idea is correct, then potentially, yes. That's why I'm coming.'

I snort. 'Spoken like a true doctor.'

'Cut it, Nathalie, you're not helping.'

I laugh. 'And I'm supposed to feel bad about that?'

His face changes colour from white to red like some deranged chameleon. His knuckles stay white though, clasped tightly on the armrests. He lifts his head, his mouth open and wet. 'I made a mistake! They told me there was no plague, that we had a surplus of meds, that it was all just panic. I didn't know people would die. I thought... I thought it would all be fine.'

His voice drops on the last line. He stares at me, waiting. For absolution? He's got to be kidding. But then, he probably thinks *everything* will be fine, a happy end to every story, forgiveness for every sin. Not this time.

I turn my back on him and return to the lockers. My hands are shaking. Damn it, no time for this now. I focus on my breathing as I stash my shoes into the carry sack, add my shirt and jacket, then take off my pants and throw them in as well.

Yefremov scrambles out of his seat, floating towards the lockers. I pull out another suit and toss it at him. His lips twitch in an aborted smile. He grabs a handhold and starts unzipping his pants.

'Only your jacket and shoes,' I say. 'You need an under-layer.'

I slide into my suit, the liner making the fabric glide as if oiled. Boots come next, both the suit and the boots adjustable to fit most sizes. I prepare the gloves and the helmet but won't put them on till the last moment.

Behind me, Yefremov is struggling to fit his trousers into the suit legs. Fuck this. I'm tempted to leave him to it, but I know I'll just have to help him later. I somersault to bring myself head-first towards his feet, then wrap the fabric of his pants around his calves and pull the suit up like an oversized pair of stockings. I let go when he's knee-deep in and let him fumble with the rest while I search for suitable boots and gloves.

'So, what's your hypothesis?' I ask.

'When we tested for interactions with local prions, we included only naturally evolved life. Humans, plants, bacteria— it's all inert, as we thought. But the organic components of Mind-Link use synthetic proteins based on D-isomers. The way the prion proteins are structured, it's possible that they can 'cheat their way', as it were, into the ML cells, and start to—'

I raise my hand. He's lost me two sentences prior. 'So the prions mess up the Mind-Link? Is that why they went mad?'

Yefremov grimaces as if he wants to deliver another lecture but ends up just nodding.

'Can you reverse it?'

'I can kill the Mind-Link cells in Zhang's brain. But I don't know if that will be enough.'

And if it's not, then Zhang will end up like the other colonists.

I've got plenty more questions, each more urgent than the next, but they'll have to wait. I check the seals on his suit, then return to my seat. Putting the shuttle in emergency mode means I can't rely on automation. I check the glide path, then reconfirm the heat-shield status. Good to go.

'Strap in, Doctor. It'll get a bit bumpy.'

Yefremov's back in his seat just in time. He's still scrambling for the harness when the atmosphere hits us like a fist to the underbelly.

The temperature indicators jump into oranges and then reds within moments. The viewports turn black as the cameras retreat into their shells. The one actual window, small and only on the pilot's side, shows the tail ends of orange flames. The shuttle shakes and rattles like an old tin can. These things were never designed for atmospheric flight. They don't have to like it, but they can take it, and that's all that matters.

Gravity takes hold, pushing my body firmly into the seat. Yefremov is holding the armrests like his chair could turn into a flying carpet. I allow myself a sardonic smile, then focus back on my dashboard.

The navigation display shows our glide path. The settlement has two landing sites: the one by the lakeshore was the colony's initial landing point. The second one is next to the dome—a tiny strip used by the assemblers in their mindless toil to finish the city for the dead. That's where I plan to land—the lake strip is bigger and more convenient, but I'm guessing that's where Miller and Lee, the only armed people on the planet, will expect me to go. If I'm lucky, they've forgotten the second strip exists at all. We'll have to face them sooner or later, but I'd prefer the 'later' option.

I come in steep towards the lake, adjusting the shuttle's geometry for lower airspeeds. The wings expand, drag slowing us down as we teeter on the stall line. To anyone watching, this must look like I'm heading for the lake strip. I pull the nose up, bleeding off airspeed till the frame starts to buffet like an ancient aeroplane. Then, as the wing dips, I throttle up, zooming past the shore, past the settlement, towards the dome. With just enough airspeed to get us there, I cut the power and swivel the thrusters into vertical. We swoop towards the dot of the landing strip. When we cross the threshold, I pull up airbrakes and power up just enough to cushion the fall. The legs extend, and the shuttle plonks down on the ground with a disapproving groan.

'Come on.'

Yefremov follows me to the emergency airlock at the back of the shuttle. This is slower than using the hatch, but I'd rather preserve the air. We may yet need it.

Four air packs sit next to the exit. I clip one onto my back, then the other to piggyback on top of it. The connections are foolproof, but I check Yefremov's anyway. Looks good.

'Seal up.' I lower my helmet and watch him do the same. 'Ready?'

The doctor nods.

'Speak up, let me hear your radio.'

'Ready.'

I open the hatch, and the airlock inflates into a small tent like a tumour on the side of the shuttle. We scramble inside and seal the exit behind us. The walls collapse as the air begins to drain—but when there's just enough space for us to move, the pumps reverse, bringing in outside air to equalise the pressure.

The clock in my helmet visor shows three minutes since touchdown—not enough for anyone to have made it here from the base or the other landing strip, if that's where they were waiting. If we're lucky, we'll reach the hub before we meet the others. That's all I have for a plan—get inside and buy enough time to talk to the field team. I don't know how the loyalties are split, but I do know that out of the thirteen people here, only two have guns.

The light on the airlock bubble blinks green and the lock clicks open.

'Follow me. Run.'

I dash out onto the tarmac still hot with the blast of our arrival. The sky above is grey and infinite, the absence of walls disorienting. I look down, focusing on my feet and the rhythm of my run. The visor overlays a map with green arrows pointing to the nearest node, three hundred metres away. Yefremov's breath syncs with mine.

So far, so good—nobody here, no sound or sight of the field team. I glance around, readjusting to the idea of open space. To my right, the gossamer structure of the dome stretches up like the masterpiece of some giant spider. To the left, the grey modules look like granite blocks, their colour perfectly matching the natural landscape even as their design defies it.

Ahead, the node looks like the knuckle of a bent finger, the airlock door right in front of us. Yefremov pants, the sound of his footsteps receding further behind me. Not far now. Another moment and I'm at the airlock, tapping the entry command. The light flashes green, and the door swings open just as Yefremov catches up with me.

I seal the lock behind us. The air cycles, dust swirling in shadowy circles into the filters. The walls glisten red, reflecting the warning light above. We stand motionless, our breaths subdued as if we are afraid to wake up the dead.

The light blinks out, drowning us in momentary darkness before the door opens and the light from the corridor fills the space. I step out, Yefremov two paces behind.

'Hello there,' Lee's voice says. 'Welcome to Bethesda.'

I turn—and stare at the nozzle of a gun pointed at my chest.

CHAPTER 25

Lee walks us at gunpoint through the winding pipe-corridors of the habitat towards the hub. A few times, when we cross a junction or make a turn, I consider running away—Lee's behind Yefremov, the doctor's large frame shielding me from the gun. But there's nowhere to go; even if I avoid Miller and the other gun, in a few hours I'll be out of air and back at their mercy. I was always going to face them; I was just hoping I'd have more control over how and when it happened.

Five suited figures wait in the main room of the hub, its dusty workstations and overturned furniture vaguely familiar from my VR visits. Their names appear on my visor even before I get close enough to see their faces. Johansson and both doctors are here, all three standing stiffly in the middle of the central aisle. Miller watches them with his gun drawn. I can't see his expression, yet there's something despondent about his posture, his back straight but his shoulders hunched.

The last figure leans against the wall furthest from me, arms crossed, maroon stripes on the suit marking it as engineering. My throat tightens with shame as her name pops up on my visor: Wang You Yan, the woman I saved and then banished.

'What's going on?' Johansson asks. 'Why did you hijack the shuttle?'

We're close enough now that I can see his face through the helmet: brows furrowed, mouth pinched in doubt or confusion. I didn't expect him to side with security, but then, he hasn't been on board. All the information the field team has is what the Guardian sends them.

I take a slow breath to calm my voice. 'I'll explain. But can we have a normal conversation around a table and without guns pointed at us?'

'No way,' Lee says. 'We're not taking you back to base.'

'Why not? What do you think I'll do?'

Johansson waves his arm impatiently. 'Why did you come? Do you think you can help Zhang?'

I glance at Yefremov. Beads of sweat cover his face, his hair plastered to his forehead. His breath steams the visor, too hot and fast for the filters. 'The doctor has an idea. We don't know if it's going to work, but—'

'Why do you care?' Wang asks, her voice cold.

I can't tell them about the doctor's theory, not when we're on the intercom and everyone, including the Guardian, can hear us. 'I care about *Gabriel*. If we can cure Zhang, then we have a chance to save the rest of them.'

Johansson shifts on his feet. 'What's your hypothesis, Doctor?'

Yefremov begins to answer, but I cut him off. 'We can't tell you. Not while they keep the guns pointed at us. What guarantee do we have they won't use them when we're no longer useful?'

'Come on, you're not suggesting...'

He hasn't seen the Sharks. He doesn't know it was these very people, Price's team, who opened fire on the civilians in the Feidi.

I point at Lee. 'If you think it's just for show, then tell them to give you the guns and see what happens.'

Johansson glances at Lee, then at Miller. His brow twitches, nervous or impatient. 'I know we need discipline—and she shouldn't have hijacked the shuttle and such. But come on, she's got a point. Why don't you put those things away?'

Lee doesn't move. 'We've got our orders.'

Johansson frowns, the reality finally breaking through to him.

I look at Lee. 'Orders from whom? Price or the Guardian?'

Lee doesn't answer.

'It's the same, isn't it?' Miller says.

I nod. 'It is now. But what if Price hadn't flipped? She'd likely be dead, shot by his Sharks. Who would you be following then?'

'The Guardian wouldn't have killed her,' Lee snarls. 'He's an American.'

Johansson snorts. 'Like that explains everything.'

Lee opens his mouth but ends up shrugging. He avoids my glance, though, so I must have touched a sore spot. Loyalty matters to them, and I'm their former commander, one that Price has betrayed.

I consider my next move. I'm walking a dangerously thin line. If I somehow manage to turn them against the Guardian, he will know. Bad move when we need to get back to the ship. The Guardian won't hesitate to leave us behind if he feels we'd cause a problem.

I raise my arms and make my voice brighter. 'Listen, we're on the same side. Even the Guardian. We all want to find out what killed the colonists, we all want to save *Gabriel*. Can we at least agree on that?'

Lee keeps his mouth pursed but gives me a curt nod.

'Why did you steal the shuttle?' Miller asks. He sounds hesitant, as if he, too, is trying to decide how much he can say.

'Because I felt guilty. I sent Zhang here. I mean, I hate the bastard, but I'm not one for the death penalty. If he dies, I'll blame myself.' My voice breaks. None of this is a lie, as much as I'd like to pretend that it is. 'So, okay, I used the shuttle without permission. I'm sure there are disciplinary procedures for that. Something not involving guns?'

Miller nods. Lee's scowl has lost its edge. They're with me, at least for now.

'Well played, Nathalie.' The Guardian's figure shimmers into existence on the other side of the room, ghost-like. It's just a projection on our visor screens, but solid enough to make us all wince.

Miller and Lee jerk to attention, expressions guilty. The tips of their guns lift towards my chest.

The Guardian strolls across the central aisle, the projection eerily realistic. Only the absence of a suit and helmet betrays that he's not really here.

He takes a deep breath, his face drawn in an almost mournful expression. 'I thought I could trust you. I thought we were on the same side. I'm sorry this is not the case.'

He knows I'm lying. He's read through my game. No point pretending, then.

I step towards him. 'Depending which side that is. Because I'm with my crew and the colonists. Not with someone who takes over my ship and won't even give me his name.'

He holds my gaze, the sadness in his eyes too deep to be entirely staged. 'My name doesn't matter, Nathalie. I thought you understood that. It's not about me, never was. I never wanted any of you to get hurt. But I won't let you stand in my way. We are all pawns in a bigger game, I'm afraid.'

'Then why won't you tell us what it is?'

The Guardian ignores me, his eyes narrowing as his face grows cold and distant. His lips move, but no sound comes, at least not through my speakers.

Next to me, Lee tilts his head to one side, listening. His jaw tightens, and his scowl returns. Miller frowns, then the two men exchange a nod.

I glance at the Guardian—but he's gone, the projection vanished as suddenly as it appeared.

'We're heading back to base,' Lee says. 'You two will stay here. If you can cure Zhang, then you can cure yourselves.'

They want to leave us in the hub. Yefremov's theory is only that—a theory. If he's wrong, and it's not about the prions and the Mind-Link... Our tanks will only last a few hours. And then we'll have to breathe the same air that turned the colonists' brains into mush.

I shiver, the vision of the habitat's tangled corpses flashing under my eyelids. I swallow, my throat dry.

Yefremov sidles closer. 'We need more time. Even if I can cure him, it won't happen immediately. And if I'm wrong, we'll both die.'

'You should have considered this before,' Lee says.

Yefremov sucks in air, but Lee cuts him off before he can devise an answer.

'Enough. Back to base, everyone.' Lee waves the others on, his movements jerky with tension.

I stare at Johansson. 'Are you just going to let them do this?'

The scientist glares at Lee, then back at me. 'What choice do I have?'

Wang's already at the door. Johansson turns to follow. They're not going to put up a fight, not against men armed with real weapons. Only the two doctors remain.

Gonzales pushes his chin out as he looks up at Lee. 'I want a word with Yefremov. In case I have to finish the job.'

'You can do that from the base.'

'But I'd rather—'

Lee flashes his gun. 'Move!'

I wince. Yefremov inches towards me, for protection or

defence, either option equally ridiculous.

Gonzales drops his head and shuffles away. Raji stands frozen in place, his gaze following the barrel of the gun as Lee waves it towards the exit. Another moment, and he, too, staggers towards the door. Lee and Miller stomp behind them, the thud of their footsteps fading with distance until all I can hear is my ragged breath and the boom of my heartbeat.

I stumble, then catch my balance. My legs tremble, all my muscles twitching with released tension. Some of it is fear, but not all. Anger rises in my throat, the taste sharp and bitter. Not at the Guardian even—he at least has played a consistent game. I'm furious at Price, and Lee, and Miller—the same people who shot at Stepan now betraying me all over again. And at myself, for always lagging one step behind the Guardian.

Fuck it. This is far from over.

I glance at the readouts at the bottom of my visor. Two hours of air left in this tank, four more in the spare. If we follow Zhang's pattern, we have four days of breathing the habitat's air before we start losing our minds.

'Come on,' I say to Yefremov.

He stands frozen stiff, face pasty white and wet with sweat, his whizzing breath loud in my ears. If I had time to waste, I'd laugh. He thought he'd play a hero, only to realise he may have to die as one. Forgive me if I don't cry.

'Pull yourself together, Doc. You need your head on when we find Zhang.'

He meets my eyes, his gaze unfocused. I wonder if he's heard me.

I call up the map of the hub. Sanchez said Zhang had taken over the space behind the life-support equipment. I start walking. The sound of Yefremov's breath follows me through the intercom, then his steps shake the floor behind me.

The machine hall sits on the outskirts of the hub, in a ribbed extension chilled by the icy wind and water pumped down long ducts from the lake. The place will offer little comfort, but at least it's far from the habitat and its corpses. And at least here Zhang can watch over the equipment keeping him alive.

Keeping *us* alive.

I accelerate, chasing the arrows on the map. Yefremov falls behind, his footsteps muted in the cold, dim passages. Not far now. I turn the corner and open a narrow door.

Zhang stands leaning on a faded chair with a missing castor. He seems almost naked without a suit, his chest moving as he breathes the colony's toxic air. Bloodshot eyes stare at me from a pale, bloated face, sharp cuts of wrinkles digging into his skin. Behind him, the consoles blink with dim green lights. Four chairs and a desk stand by the wall on the right; on the left, a sleeping bag lies crumpled on a foldable bed, its head positioned next to the narrow slit of the only window.

I stop, unsure what to say. Apologise? He admitted to killing seven people—a crime for which his own crew exiled him from the safety of the base. And his 'news' may still be a lie, another trap waiting to be sprang.

Zhang meets my eyes, his gaze as sharp as ever. His hand rests on the back of the chair, fingers twitching in a tic I never noticed before.

'How are you?' I manage to ask.

Zhang snorts. 'I'm not sure how to answer that.'

Yefremov arrives behind me, his breath still heavy but less ragged now. He pushes past me—then stops at the sight of Zhang.

The engineer laughs. 'Come on. It's not that bad. Most of it is tiredness anyway. I... I've been busy.'

'We need to go to the medical,' Yefremov says. 'The equipment there—'

'—is what they're using to dissect the corpses,' Zhang says. 'It can wait till I'm one.'

Yefremov straightens, his voice clear and insistent. He's a

doctor again, even if broken. 'We have several rooms to choose from. And more than one set of equipment. What we don't have is time.'

'Very true, Doctor. So I suggest we don't waste it arguing.' Zhang shuffles to a crate on the floor by his bed. He groans softly as he leans to rummage inside it, then pulls out something that looks like a screwdriver. 'Come here, both of you.'

'Why?' Yefremov asks.

'To get us some privacy.' Zhang waves his arm impatiently. 'Sit on the bed so I can reach your helmets.'

He's going to disable our imagers. It won't help much; most rooms have security cameras, and everything we hear or say goes through the suits' radios, but those watching us will no longer have access to full VR.

'Do it,' I say to Yefremov.

I sit on the bed and lower my head towards the engineer. He jabs the circle of cameras one by one, each cracking with a dry pop inside my helmet.

Zhang pulls back to inspect his work. 'Not the most elegant, but effective. Your turn, Doctor.'

Yefremov doesn't sit but bends low to let the engineer reach the top of his helmet. The eight lenses make tiny bumps on the surface, protruding just enough to provide the optimal recording angle. A larger bump at the top of the helmet holds the comms' transmitter.

I point it out to Zhang, but he shakes his head. 'It's too deep. Can't break it without making the suit leak. Anyway, don't worry about it. Follow me.'

He walks towards a small door next to the consoles on the other side of the room. I start behind him, but Yefremov catches my arm.

'We've got to get him to the medical immediately.'

He's right, but even so I'm determined to get my answers before he starts poking in the engineer's brain.

'Soon.' I try to move, but his grip tightens on my arm.

'You don't understand. I can't wait. I must get to work now, before I run out of good air and start second-guessing my every thought.'

'You don't have Mind-Link. So...' My voice breaks. I try again, holding back my desperation. 'So, if your theory is correct, we should be immune, right?'

'*If* it's correct. It's still just a guess.' He shifts, glances at the door then back at me. 'I won't know till I've examined him. And I need time to set up the equipment. I've got to start now.'

I hesitate. I don't trust him farther than I can spit, but I doubt he can talk himself back into the Guardian's favour. Still, he's desperate. He could sell out Khan or Firyali.

Yefremov huffs. 'For God's sake, you still don't trust me?'

I glare at him, my mouth pursed.

'Fine. So come with me. Your chat can wait, but I won't be able to work when my air runs out and all I can think of are the prions I take in with every breath. I'm not strong enough. Do you understand? *I* don't have the time.'

He holds my gaze, his chin trembling, then looks away in embarrassment.

I still don't trust him, but I believe his shame. He'll do everything to cure Zhang, if only to save himself.

My hands shake as I reach for the spare tank on my back and unclip it from its holder. Four extra hours won't make a difference to me. But if he can't cure Zhang, then we're all dead anyway, Mind-Link or not.

Yefremov's eyes widen as I pass him the tank. His hands shoot out to grasp it. He seems to want to thank me but changes his mind under my stare.

He turns to the engineer instead. 'Zhang Min, I want you in medical in an hour. Please?'

'We'll be there,' I say.

Zhang says nothing, watching us both with a lopsided smile.

CHAPTER 26

Zhang leads me through a storage room full of metal crates, some in neat rows and too big for one man to have handled, others smaller and piled about haphazardly, maybe by the engineer himself. He continues to another door, narrow and with a wiry mesh stapled to the grey surface. A low light comes on as he enters, intensifying as I follow him inside.

The moment I cross the threshold, alarms ring on my suit systems. The AR overlay on my visor flickers, then disappears. My earbuds fall silent, my hearing reduced to what can penetrate inside the helmet. Around me, metal mesh covers the walls, floor, and ceiling, though a bunch of wires snake out from an opening in the far corner to a multi-socket on the floor by a 'table': a broken panel laid over empty crates.

'You've built a Faraday cage?'

Zhang nods as he closes the door. He moves to one of the two chairs next to the table and leans on its back, his gaze focusing on me. 'Why did you come?'

'I need some answers.'

'And you think I can help?'

Obviously. But we're circling the issue, both unsure how

much we can trust each other. Best to get right to it. 'Why did you kill all those people?'

Zhang's head drops. He looks at his feet, his expression defeated. 'The way the fire spread... it was an accident. We only wanted to kill the captain. He was working for the Guardians.'

I notice the plural in the Guardians. But first things first. 'Who's "we"?'

Zhang doesn't answer. He shakes his head, then slides into the seat. 'Have you found my room?'

'Yes.' I lean on the other chair, looking down at the engineer through the glass of my helmet. I'd prefer to be at eye level, but the life support pack on my back won't let me sit. 'I found your "news". What is it?'

'News bursts from Earth. The real ones.'

'Then what about all the transmissions we've been receiving?'

'Not transmissions. Pre-recorded files released by the tracking AI based on some triggering algorithm, all run from a secret server. I assume that's what you were looking for when you captured me?'

'Yes. I thought it was your doing.'

Zhang's lips crack into a sad smile. 'Did you find it? The server?'

'We thought we did—but we found the Guardian instead.'

'Right. Let me guess—he then used your past to set the rest of you against each other just like the 'news' had turned you against us?'

My hands tighten on the back of the chair. 'How do you know?'

He shrugs with just the tops of his shoulders as if the question doesn't merit a full gesture. 'It's a tactic they've been using for centuries. Find an "other" and blame them for whatever's wrong. It's never failed to work, so why stop now?'

'But fabricating the news? All this just to manipulate us?'

I start to shake my head—but is it really so far-fetched? For all the years in cold-sleep, we got only digests. Maybe ten hours put together—and that included sports news and trivia. Much less than what Zhang had in his files. Our last burst was more extensive, but it was precisely the stuff that turned the crew against the Chinese—the news of the Atlantic attack. It could have easily been pre-recorded, just as the reports of the American retaliation. The timing was certainly impeccable, each blow delivered exactly when the crew was starting to get along. And then there's the absence of personal news.

And yet...

My doubts return as I push away from the chair and pace three steps to the mesh-covered wall. I already suspected exactly that, so why waver now? Is it because it's Zhang, his words, his files, his explanations?

I study the man's face for a moment, the sight shifting from the tired face of my chief engineer to that of a Chinese operative, someone I blamed for Jason's death, even if only by proxy.

If this is about manipulation, then it's worked better than I'd like to admit, the prejudices woven too deep into my consciousness to separate truth from preconceptions.

Focus on the facts. Consider who benefits and how.

I return to the chair and turn it to sit astride, my elbows on the backrest. 'If that's true, then how did you get your news? The comms are all wired though the main computer.'

'The main antenna, yes. But we managed to install a secondary system before we left. We had people in the dock-yards... Then Kuang Jin and I got it running on the last inspection. The captain was there, and we thought he'd noticed. That's why... We couldn't take the risk...' Zhang looks away again, the apple in his throat moving as he swallows.

Kuang. The engineer who died in the fire. Maybe the very person I didn't—couldn't—wouldn't save. Suddenly I'm hot again, shrinking under the memory of the flames and limbs thrashing in a smoke-filled pod.

I realise something else now, too: the pictures in Zhang's hideout, the other young man—that was Kuang. They were friends. Partners. Co-conspirators. And Kuang died in the fire they started.

I recall Zhang's anguished face back on the bridge, after the accident. He said Kuang'd been a friend. But he'd been more than that.

'Did you leave the message in my pod?'

Zhang turns back to me, his eyes moist but his face dry. 'Yes. I needed you to know that something was wrong. Or maybe I wanted to get caught and punished for what I'd let happen. He was so sure he could control it. And I believed him.'

He looks away again, his jaw tight and his lips pursed. He'd helped Kuang set the fire that killed him. I can't even imagine how that must feel. Maybe something like not telling your friends about the Sharks' guns pointed at them?

I clench my fists, my hands clammy inside the gloves. 'I'm sorry. I couldn't...'

Zhang meets my eye again. 'You saved one. That's more than I can say.'

My mouth opens, but no sound comes. I'm out of words, out of regrets. But this is all a distraction, and our time's running away.

Focus on the facts.

'Let's get back...' I stop at the expression on Zhang's face.

He's staring at something behind me, eyes wide, lips parted in shock. His fingers bend, digging into his flesh.

I start to rise, turning to glance behind me.

'There's nothing there,' Zhang says through clenched teeth. 'I know. It will be gone soon.'

He's hallucinating.

'Are you...' I swallow the question. Of course he's not all right. 'Can I do anything?'

'No.' The engineer's face relaxes, and his eyes turn to me. He breathes in slowly. 'I can still tell when it happens. I don't know for how long, though.'

I nod. He doesn't have much time. And if Yefremov's wrong, then I can expect the same in only four days.

'Go on,' he says, impatient again. 'What were you saying?'

'I need to start from the beginning. Who are the Guardians?'

Zhang nods, his voice gaining strength as he proceeds with the explanation. 'An orbital organisation, a sort of executive arm of one of the yun-ying factions.'

He throws me a questioning glance and I shake my head. The yun-ying are the orbital elite, the richest of the rich, but that's all I know.

'The yun-ying are split into factions with conflicting philosophies and interests. Ostensibly, they are business collectives, but they're more than that.'

'This I know,' I interrupt. 'The stations are always fighting, especially now when the Americans are trying to get a foothold with their new...'

I stop as Zhang shakes his head.

'That's just games. Something for the masses, for Earth media to spin stories around. These are not the real factions, nor the real leaders.'

I frown. I'm not sure I understand, but nuances can wait. 'Okay, so the Guardians work for one of these factions. The Americans, from what he says. And he's investigating the new Chinese Mind-Link—'

Zhang leans back, his brows scrunched into a thick line. A hiss escapes his mouth, angry or disappointed.

'What? You say it's not Chinese?'

'I'm saying you're missing the point entirely.'

'How so?'

'You're thinking how they want you to think. The Chinese, the Americans, the Canadians. None of it matters, not in orbit. It's a distraction they maintain to keep the rest of us blaming each other while they do what they want.'

I cross my arms. 'It may not matter to them, but we still live with the old borders. Any new technology will benefit the nation that produces it.'

'That's insignificant.'

'Insignificant?'

'Yes, the factory workers will get their pittance, but that's nothing compared to the profits. Take Mind-Link: the tech is Chinese, and that's where most of it is assembled. But the rest of the supply chain? The organic parts are grown in northern Europe, because it's cooler and cheaper. The wiring comes from South America—yes, despite the embargo. They reroute it through subsidiary companies till it becomes untraceable—which isn't that difficult since it's in nobody's interest to expose it.'

'I don't believe you. The Americans would never agree to that.'

Zhang laughs. 'Oh, it gets better. Supposedly, the Americans oppose it for religious reasons, right? Well, that's nonsense. Blocking entertainment use would be a minor adjustment. They oppose it because the biggest donor to the church and the American government is the Liberty faction, direct competitors of the Sunrise group who own most of Chinese manufacturing, including the entire Mind-Link supply chain.'

I take in a breath. 'What does this even mean?'

'It shows you that the people the Guardian works for don't care about our divisions. The nationalities, the New Cold War, all that. It's a smokescreen to distract us from seeing how every year Earth's getting poorer and they're getting richer.'

'How do you know all that? And why should I believe you?'

Zhang leans forward, his hands on his knees. 'You came here because you thought I knew something you didn't. Well, I'm sorry if it's bigger and uglier than you expected. I can't "prove" anything, not here, without any of my files.' He pauses and tilts his head, hesitating. 'Except maybe for one thing. Your sister's son, his name's Jason, right?'

I sit upright, my muscles tensing. 'What about him?'

'He's been sending you messages all these years. None of the personal stuff makes it through the buffer, did you notice? In case it contradicts the pre-recorded news.'

My heart pounds so loudly I barely hear his words. 'The messages... have you read them?'

Zhang's lips twitch in embarrassment. 'Some of them. Sorry. I thought they might come in useful. But it's just domestic stuff. He got married, has a daughter, I think. Worked in the Feidi for a while but then moved back to Canada.'

I lean forward, tilting the chair till I almost tumble at the engineer. 'When did he move?'

'I don't remember. A while ago.'

'Before...' I'm not sure how to ask, or what to believe anymore. 'Before the internments?'

Zhang shakes his head. 'That never happened. Nor the Atlantic attack, or the revenge strike on Shanghai. All lies, as I told you. There are tensions and innuendos, but no more than when we left.'

I'm not listening. I pull myself up, the chair dropping to the floor with a muffled bang. I don't know what to think, what to believe. A part of me screams with joy that Jason's still alive, that he hasn't forgotten me, that maybe, maybe one day he'll forgive me. But what do they say about things that seem too good to be true?

Zhang could be lying. He knew enough about me to scribble in Russian on my pod's door; he could easily know about Jason. This could all be part of a Chinese plot, just like the Guardian said.

Focus on the facts. Consider who benefits and how.

Zhang confessed to killing the captain—and that has made his own people denounce him. What would he gain from lying to me now?

Conjectures pop into my head, each challenged by another set of questions. I won't think my way to the truth, not with so many unknowns.

I lift the chair and sit down, sideways this time and a bit further from the engineer, who's watching me as if I were a wild animal.

'Okay, let's assume it's as you say. The Guardians are the henchmen of some orbital faction. What does this have to do with Bethesda?'

'They were developing something here. Destiny—the faction the Guardians serve—has been consolidating power. They're also the most secretive. So, when they suddenly became active when Bethesda went silent, we knew it had to be something big. And now we find a new design of Mind-Link and a medical lab with encrypted files.'

The files that the Guardian was so keen to 'secure.'

I shake my head. 'So it's all for the Mind-Link? For what—competitive edge? It doesn't even make sense! Not with the costs and the time frame. Why not run the test on Mars, if they wanted secrecy? Or buy a city somewhere if they needed guinea pigs? Plenty of desperate people around.'

'You are right—which only means they're playing the game at the highest level. When one faction wants to hide something from the rest of the yun-ying, nowhere in the solar system would be secure enough. And you're right, too, that it makes no *commercial* sense, not in the short term. Which means this is something much bigger.'

'Like what?'

'Your guess is as good as mine. But I'd ask myself what it is that the rich and the powerful always want.'

'You mean, they want to get even richer and more powerful?'

Zhang shrugs with just his eyebrows as he pushes himself up from the chair. 'The rest will have to wait. We've been here too long already.'

He starts for the exit, but I put my hand on his arm. 'I still don't know what this means for us. All I want is to save *Gabriel*. And this crew, if possible.'

'That may be trickier than you think. Especially the second part.'

'Why?'

He pulls in a long breath. 'Because if I'm right, there's no way they'll let us return.' He pauses, the intensity of his gaze making me shiver. 'We must find out why this Mind-Link is so special. That's more important than us—more important than *Gabriel*. Whatever happens, we must send the message home.'

He moves to the door while I stare at his back, something sharp and heavy settling in my stomach.

CHAPTER 27

We're returning to Zhang's quarters back in the machine hall when my air alarm beeps. Half an hour left. I've been expecting this, and still the sight of the flashing icon makes sweat pour out of every pore in my body. I shouldn't have given my spare tank to the doctor. Now I've got too little left, and I must keep some in reserve. If I ever want to get off this planet, I'll need the rest of my air to reach the shuttle.

I clench my fists. No, Yefremov needed the air more than I do. And one more hour won't make a difference. It's obvious what I must do—even if all I can think of are the corpses of the colonists, killed by Bethesda's air.

I hope that damn doctor is right. I hope those without Mind-Link are immune.

I reach for the clip at the back of my life-support pack and close the air valve. Within seconds, the suit's CO_2 warning starts flashing. No point delaying. I force my hand to release the visor. The screen rolls back till it forms a narrow display strip at the top of my field of vision. It's done—yet my lips remain sealed till I can take it no more, my body demanding oxygen in whatever form it may come. I suck in air, warm and stale, smelling of dust and sweat.

If Yefremov's wrong, I have only days of sanity left.

'Let's go,' I say.

The engineer nods in confirmation or approval—or maybe just appreciating the lack of glass between our faces. He doesn't comment, though, and I'm grateful for that.

We find Yefremov next to a wall-sized console at the far corner of the medical bay. The set-up is a large-scale version of what we have on the ship: movable panels divide the space into niches, some with treatment beds, others with lab or diagnostic equipment. Most haven't been used in decades, yet only a thin layer of dust covers the chairs and beds.

Closer to Yefremov's position, four of the niches on the left have been joined together, the equipment arranged in a circle around a semi-opaque tent: the sterile lab where Gonzales and Raji have been dissecting the corpses. I speed up, picturing human remains splayed out on the examination table. Zhang's walking faster, too, both of us staring firmly ahead as if a sideways glance could wake the ghosts. Or remind us how close we are to joining them.

Yefremov looks up as we approach. His eyes widen at the sight of my raised visor. He seems about to speak, lips parting, then collapsing into a tight line.

'Where do you want me, Doctor?' Zhang asks.

Yefremov straightens. 'Right there.'

He points to a contraption on the right side of the room, a narrow bed with a raised back, sitting atop something that looks like a sarcophagus. A translucent cupola hangs over the head-rest, with spiky extensions protruding inward, like a cactus turned inside out.

Zhang frowns. 'Are you trying to cure me or kill me?'

'Neither, for now. This is just a scanner.' Yefremov's smile dies before it reaches his eyes. 'Gonzales and Raji are on the way. There's been some... discussion about that, but they need to see the results and I refused to share anything over the comms.'

He glances at me, holding my gaze as if there is something he wants me to understand. He's stating his allegiance, even if it makes little practical difference. Every word they speak over their suit comms, every sight their cameras register—it all goes up to the ship anyway.

The doctor's helping Zhang with his jacket when the doors at the far end open, admitting four suited figures. The names appear on my visor's display strip: Raji and Gonzales in front, fast, jerky steps betraying their agitation. The lanky figure behind them is Johansson, long arms dangling at his sides. Miller brings up the rear, his back straight and his movements assured—but his gun is holstered, even if in easy reach.

The medics join Yefremov positioning Zhang inside the contraption, then lower the glass 'cactus' over his head. The spikes come to life, wriggling and stretching as Yefremov guides them into position on the engineer's skull. I catch Miller's glance as he shifts his gaze between the scientists, watchful as much as uneasy. His lips twitch when our eyes meet, almost apologetic, as if he regrets having to wave his gun at me. Maybe he does—but it makes no difference, not for as long as he keeps the weapon handy.

I saunter to the other side of the room, still in sight of the scientist and Miller, who repositions himself immediately to the best viewing—and shooting—angle. My mind's still spinning from Zhang's revelations, still unable to decide how much I believe him.

I lean against a console, my arms crossed, determined to keep my mind cool. Someone using Bethesda to develop or test secret technology is the only theory that fits all the facts: the two sets of news, the lack of personal messages, the captain's notes, the way we were hastily recruited after the original, 'hand-picked crew' had been infiltrated. And if that's the case, then Zhang is right—this is not some trivial field test for a new product. It's too large, too clandestine, something that only the most powerful could manage.

The orbital elites, the world's super rich. They already own most of the industry and the land. What else could they possibly want?

My breath catches, my knees soft like I'm sinking into the floor below me.

There's still one thing they don't own: our minds.

And what they're working on is Mind-Link, a technology operating inside human brains. One that turned thousands of peace-loving settlers into bloodthirsty monsters. Even if this was an unwanted effect, a reaction to Bethesda's prions, the fact that Mind-Link could do it at all chills me to the bone.

I swallow, the weight of the realisation settling on my shoulders. Whatever the cost, we must find proof of what they are up to. We must send home a warning, before it's too late.

We are all pawns in a bigger game, the Guardian said.

Indeed. But some pawns intend to fight back.

The three doctors have shifted to a large monitor, pointing at the display and commenting in loud, fervent voices. I'm sure the Guardian's listening. He's probably summoned all the remaining medics to help him understand. I wonder to what lengths he'd be willing to go if they refused. Somehow, I'm sure that whatever he decides, Price will happily oblige.

I watch them, trying to figure out a plan. I have to find a way to brief the scientists or the doctors, explain the situation to them. Tell them to find proof, something no one on Earth will be able to refute. And we'll have to do it without the Guardian realising what we know, or he'll make sure the message never gets out.

Easier said than done. The Guardian can hear our every word, see our every move. I have to cut his link to us, that must be the first step. How? Even if I could reach the hub's transmitters, destroying them is not an option—we'll need them to send a message to Earth. I've got to find a way to disable his connection while keeping the rest of the system going.

I squint, trying to remember the set-up. There are five local transmitters and two—

Don't react. The text scrolls across the display strip on my visor.

I freeze. Someone's sending me a message. Firyali.

Shark engineer fixing shuttle.

An engineer? Damn! I should have realised they'd bring brains on this mission, not just muscle.

K says trust J, the message on my visor continues. *What need? Go to display @ 35 deg.*

I glance towards it: a single light flickers on a station thirty-five degrees to my right. My heart's pounding as I put on a bored expression and stroll to the console. I roll two chairs together so I can sit sideways on one and let the other take the weight of my life pack. Miller's watching me, but he turns his attention back to the scientists as I stretch my legs and half close my eyes. I wait fifteen seconds, then reposition slightly, resting my arm on the desk. I can only hope Firyali's disabled any cameras facing this way. They'll still see me in the VR composited from the helmet imagers—but none of them can see the monitor, nor my hand as I place it on the keyboard.

Hurry, appears on my visor.

I type with the tiniest moves of my fingers. *Must cut off G.*

Impossible. 100% chance detection. Will do if must.

Damn. I need her there, even if it's good to know that she's willing to expose herself if there's no other option.

From here? I send.

Difficult. Multiple relays, hub and base. Will send plans.

I bite my lip, then remember to look bored. Miller's still

watching the others, but their suit cameras have me in plain view.

I close my eyes again, typing without looking. *Be ready.*

I'm glad she doesn't ask what she needs to be ready for because right now I have no idea.

Copy.

I shift my hand, then consider one last question: *Who is this?*

Next time more intimate?

I bite down on a smirk. It's Firyali all right. No one else has seen that exchange and my obvious discomfort.

On the other side of the room, the doctors have moved to yet another console. Johansson's with them, all four agitated as Yefremov points to something on the screen. I push off from my chair and stride towards them. Miller spins to face me, his hand twitching, but his face still wears that uncertain expression.

I give him a half-smile as I pass, heading for the doctors. 'What's the verdict?'

'We've got a plan,' Yefremov says.

'Do you think you can cure him?'

Yefremov bobs his head in a gesture that's not quite agreement. 'We've confirmed that the synthetic proteins in the Mind-Link are affected. I don't know if they are the only ones impacted, mind you, or if they're just the first to succumb. If it's the latter...' He breaks off, fright creeping back on his face. He shakes it away. 'For now, we're working on the assumption that it's only the Mind-Link.'

I'm glad he doesn't dwell on the other option. His fear has told me all I need to know.

I follow him towards the machine. Yefremov touches the controls, and the cupola rises, the spikes retreating from the engineer's head.

Zhang rubs his face, now even paler than before. 'Your diagnosis, Doctor?'

'We need to kill all the Mind-Link cells and all the connections, and do it as quickly as possible. It's not dangerous in itself, but we'll have to put you in an induced coma until—'

'How long?' Zhang interrupts.

Yefremov frowns. 'What?'

'How long will I be in a coma?'

'No longer than two, maybe three days.'

Zhang shakes his head. 'I'm not doing it.'

'You must,' Gonzales says from behind me. 'It's gone further than we thought. If we don't do it now, it will kill you.'

Zhang looks at me, his lips curving into a broken smile, almost apologetic, as he swings his legs down and starts to get up.

He's going to sacrifice himself to finish his work. To find out the secret of the new Mind-Link and send the message home.

And I thought he was a traitor.

My mind scrambles for arguments, something to persuade him to get treatment. And then I see the opening. This is my chance to talk to Johansson. Zhang can provide just the distraction—if he agrees to play along.

I make my voice hard. 'I'm afraid I can't let you refuse.'

Zhang scowls.

I hold his gaze, urging him to understand. 'This is not about you. If we can cure you, then we can save *Gabriel*.'

Zhang glares, betrayal in his eyes. 'Get yourself another guinea pig. I'm not doing it.'

I wave at Yefremov. 'Get a sedative, Doctor.'

'We can't... not against the patient's wishes,' Gonzales stutters.

'Then take it up with the ethics committee.'

Zhang tries to rise, but I put my arm on his shoulder. He's not fighting me, not yet, and he's probably too weak to do much anyway.

I peer into his eyes as I dig my fingers into his flesh. 'Don't fight me, Zhang. This is not about you or your crazy theories. Think about *Gabriel*! We need to know why the colonists lost their minds. Your brain is the answer!'

Zhang's eyes widen. At the edges of my vision, Yefremov and Raji shift their gazes to stare at me.

Luckily, Yefremov catches on. 'She's right. Your symptoms are different. We can learn the truth from treating you.'

Good—but I need more from Zhang. I dig my fingers deeper into his flesh until he winces.

'Stop fighting me!' I shout, leaning into his face.

Zhang's eyes narrow for an instant, and then he shoves me away, scrambling to get up.

Thank you.

I try to grab him, making a show of it while the scientists watch us, baffled. 'You have to have the procedure!'

Zhang gives me the tiniest of nods, and I breathe with relief before pushing him back on the bed. 'Moses!' I cry. 'Help me!'

Miller rushes in, even as his lips move in acknowledgement of some other order he's receiving. He pins Zhang down with one easy move, while the engineer kicks and struggles.

'A sedative, Doctor,' Miller says.

The medics exchange glances, unsure.

'Do what he says,' I say. Then, as Yefremov moves to a supply cabinet, I pull Johansson's arm. 'Come with me.'

I start to walk, my hand wedged under Johansson's elbow, dragging him along as his face brightens with understanding. I catch Zhang's glance, too, and the engineer kicks again, straining to slip away. Miller glares as he notices me go—but his choice is between holding Zhang or chasing after us, and he knows we can't get far, not inside a base studded with security cameras.

That's my gamble: that he'll choose to hold on to Zhang, and I'll get a moment to talk to Johansson. But as I stride towards the door, I realise the other possibility. He can shoot us. The Guardian may order him to. Or Price.

I speed up, pulling Johansson with me, walking as fast as I can without breaking into a run. My back tingles with the expectation of a bullet. But nothing comes, and for now I don't care if it's Miller's restraint or the Guardian's mercy. I push the door open, then swing to the right, behind the shelter of the wall.

Johansson's breathing fast, a puff of vapour appearing on his visor with each exhalation. 'Where are we going?'

Good question. We don't have much time—Miller will come after us the moment Zhang is sedated. I lower my visor, the augmented reality projecting the map over my field of vision. The ops room lies right ahead, but it's too big and too exposed. I shift my head, checking the projection till I notice a chain of offices on the other side of the hub—small, secluded, and not important enough for full surveyance.

'This way.'

I rush past the first office and dive into the next: two by two metres, with a desk and two chairs, a dead plant in the corner and shattered picture frames on the floor. I push the door closed. Luckily, it opens to the inside.

'Help me!'

We shove the desk against the door. It's not much, but with the weight of the two of us, it should buy us a few minutes.

Next, the cameras—there's one, in the corner facing the door. I scan the room for a tool to smash it. The picture frames. I pick up a shard and hop on a chair, then jam it into the camera. The fibre shatters in my hand, but the lens barely cracks.

'Tā mā de!'

'Wait!' Johansson digs into his belt and hands me a stylus.

I drive it into the lens with all my strength. The glass shatters as the stylus digs into its guts. That will do.

'Put your suit into reset,' I say as I hop down from the chair.

Johansson focuses his gaze on his visor's menu. 'Done.'

I do the same with mine. We have a minute before the suits —and the comms—come back online.

'Everything you know about the new Mind-Link,' I say.

'The Guardian doesn't know, but we've started on the freezer cadaver. We found two extra links in the areas of the brain that stimulate compulsive behaviour and the reward system. We think it's for gambling. Like on-demand addiction. It'll make somebody a lot of money, that's for sure.'

My breath catches in my chest. This is it, the answer. This is what they're trying to do.

'It's not for gambling,' I say through a lump in my throat. 'You can do much more when you control compulsions and rewards. You can make people happy about doing things they might otherwise not like. Work. Fight. Obey. You can turn them into slaves and make them happy about it.'

Johansson's eyes widen, his long, thin face grey in the cold light. 'Mind control? But that'd require...'

He pauses as comprehension dawns. Whoever has the resources to test such technology on a colony light years away from home will have the power to put it to full use. 'Who'd do it?'

I wave my arm. 'Later. Don't say anything aloud. The Guardian can't find out that we know, or we're all dead. Discover some bug in the Mind-Link, anything to buy us more time. We need to warn Earth. Who's on our side?'

'All of my people, and I think the doctors. Don't know about —' He stops as his gaze flies to something on his visor.

I see the same on mine: the icon flicking into green as the suit's systems come back online. We could run another reset, but the thud of footsteps echoing down the corridor makes me reconsider. I've told Johansson as much as he needs to know; I've got nothing to gain from antagonising Miller any further. I don't want to push him to use force or lock me up somewhere away from everyone.

'In here!' I motion for Johansson to help me remove the desk.

He frowns but seems to decide that I must know what I'm doing. That makes one of us.

We're sitting on the desk when Miller's bulky frame appears in the doorway.

I put on a smile. 'Sorry about that. Needed a chat away from the doctors.'

Miller shakes his head. He's not buying it but doesn't seem to care, either. 'Don't do that again.' His tone is heavy with worry. 'I mean it.'

He waves his arm to shepherd us out. I'm glad to see he's not happy in his role—but it's clear, too, that ultimately his allegiance remains with Price.

We're entering the medical bay when a new message appears on my visor: *Three probes sent. Something's happening.*

I start to wonder about the purpose of the probes when Johansson stops. A shadow runs over his face, his gaze unfocused as he listens to something on his private channel.

'What is it?' I ask as Miller's heavy hand lands on my shoulder, urging me on.

'They've downloaded all our research files. All the raw data. Plugged directly into our server.'

Shit. So far the Guardian's been playing nice with the scientists because he needs them to do the research. Once he realises they've started on the freezer corpse and lied to him about it, he may decide he no longer needs them. Or the rest of us.

We all stop as the Guardian's calm voice sounds in our suit speakers. 'I really *was* hoping to settle this without incident. But I can't let you sabotage my work and I've got no resources to watch your every move. I'm sorry, Nathalie, you've forced my hand. What comes next is on you.'

The connection breaks. We stand frozen for a moment, Miller frowning, Johansson staring at me with his mouth half-open and his brows rising.

'This can't be good,' he says.

The probes. You can do more with those than just gather data. You can smash them into things.

'What's going on?' Miller asks.

Firyali said they had sent three probes. One for the transmitter, so we can't send a message to Earth. The second for my shuttle, to ground us here. The third?

What comes next is on you. The words cut through me, but I keep my focus. He's trying to kill us. He can't do it with one probe, not when we're scattered over the settlement. But he can destroy our supplies—and the base.

'Get them out of the base,' I shout to Miller, then press my intercom button. 'Everyone, suit up and get out. Now!'

CHAPTER 28

We're running when the probe hits. The floor shakes under my feet, the vibration resonating through the walls with the chilling groan of overstretched metal. Johansson stops, but I push on, back through the maze of the hub's passages. Miller has pulled ahead, faster than either of us.

Johansson catches up with me in a few strides of his long legs. 'What was that?'

'Do you have contact with the base?'

'No. I've got no comms at all.'

We round the corner into the corridor leading to the medical. Miller is ahead, walking towards someone approaching from the opposite direction.

'What the fuck's happened?' Lee asks.

Right. He was probably already on the way after I rushed off with Johansson.

'You need to get everybody out of the base,' I say. 'Take a doctor—'

'What have you done?' Lee marches straight at me, his eyes wild, his hand on the gun, like some evil reincarnation of the man I once saw pinning badges to his baseball cap.

'I'm not the enemy,' I say calmly.

'The fuck!' Lee pulls out his gun and points it at me. 'He didn't do it for no reason. You made him do it!'

Miller steps between us. 'Easy. She hasn't done anything.'

Lee glares, his anger shifting to Miller. 'You with her now?'

'Not a chance. I'm with our people.'

They face off for another moment. Lee's jaw is working, his mouth tight and his brow scrunched into a painful line.

'We may have wounded,' I say softly.

Lee considers me for another moment, then finally holsters his gun. 'We'll go see.' He nods at Miller, then points a finger at me. 'Don't fucking try anything, or I'll make sure you're not a problem to anyone ever.'

'I need to check the shuttle. If they—'

'Do not get out of the hub or don't bother coming back.'

I want to protest, but Lee's glare gives me little hope.

Johansson pulls my arm. 'We'll wait here.'

I grit my teeth. 'Fine. Go with them,' I say to Johansson. 'Make sure they check on the engineers.'

'Will you—'

'I won't go out. I promise.'

Johansson rushes off behind the security men, and I turn back, heading to the hub's operations room.

Along the central aisle, system consoles stand in rows like pews in a church. Some are toppled and lifeless but many still function, standby lights blinking dimly.

Gonzales is here, bent over a screen at the far end of the room, his brows scrunched in frustration and worry. 'We've got a breach on the south side of the habitat, but it's contained. The hub's holding, I think. But the comms are all error messages.'

Together, we go over the systems and check their status. The long-range transmitter's gone, as I expected, and the impact has knocked out the extenders that make our radios work inside the metal framework of the modules. But the hub's holding, and most of the settlement appears to be intact except for the damage at the south edge that Gonzales mentioned. Probably debris from the base, but we can't say for sure, or have any indication of how badly the base itself has been hit.

Seven people unaccounted for. I hope they got my warning.

I'm at the comms console rebooting the extenders when someone shuffles in from the side entrance—Yefremov, his shoulders hunched and his face weary.

'How's Zhang?' I ask when he joins me.

The doctor lifts his arm as if to rub his forehead, then grimaces as his hand hits his visor. 'We've mapped the lattice and injected the toxin. His Mind-Link should be dead by tomorrow. Then his brain can start healing itself. We can't help him with that, not with the tools we have here.'

'Right.' I stand motionless, not daring to ask the next question.

Yefremov answers anyway. 'I don't know. It's still the best theory I have, but I won't know for sure till he's either healed, or not.'

Makes sense, even if it's not the answer I hoped for.

To my left, a console pings.

Gonzales springs over to check. 'Airlock Five activated.'

'Can you see how many are in there?'

'No way to tell from here.'

I glance at the comms console. The extenders should have rebooted by now. 'Hart to security. What's your status?'

No answer. It's either the comms, or Lee and Miller are trying to decide if responding means they accept my command. For fuck's sake.

'Do you need help?' I repeat.

'We've got everyone,' Miller answers. 'Some bruises but nothing major.'

'We managed to put our suits on just in time,' another voice says. Wang. 'Thanks to your warning.'

Seven lives. Good. 'How's the base?'

'Bad. One section burned, the rest punctured in too many places to fix.' Miller pauses, then comes back, hesitant. 'They've busted the recyclers. We won't be making any more air.'

I gasp. That means hub air for everyone, even those with Mind-Link.

'Can we get the colony's recyclers working?' Gonzales asks.

I ponder the question—but don't voice my answer. Because the Guardian would have considered this option. He's targeted our recyclers because he wants us to panic—and to focus on getting air instead of preparing for the next stage. Because this is far from over.

'How's the shuttle?' I ask instead. I'm sure that's where the third probe went.

Someone starts to laugh, the voice rough and tinged with nerves. Lee. 'The assemblers saved it. Well played, I've got to say.'

What the hell? I frown, trying to make sense of the words. Then I get it: the dome defences. The assemblers would have built-in lasers or something to protect the dome from random impacts, debris, or anything that could threaten the structure. And I've parked the shuttle on the edge of the strip, right next to the dome.

I consider telling them it was just dumb luck but decide against it. I can use a boost in the ratings, and if this gets me on Lee's good side, I'm happy to live a lie. 'Very well. Get everybody to the medical. We need to talk.'

Ten minutes later we're all in the med-bay. Yefremov and the other doctors take positions next to Zhang's 'sarcophagus,' where the engineer's still figure lies under a canopy of blinking lights. The scientists line up three chairs like they're an audience in some symposium. They sit together, brows tight, glances flitting, fists clenched or held tightly in their laps.

The Chinese group, five strong, push away the partition

walls on two of the niches and prop themselves against the treatment beds. Some look shocked, others suspicious, all of them worried. I'm the one who banished them from the ship—and now another anti-Chinese commander has destroyed their air supply. I'm surprised they're holding it together at all.

Lee and Miller watch the gathering from further down the aisle, their faces set, and their arms crossed—ostensibly not part of the group, but at least no longer pointing their guns at us. I'll take what I can get.

I step to the middle, taking a brief moment to look at every face. 'We don't have much time. But now that the Guardian can no longer hear us, I can tell you what I know so you can make up your minds about where you stand.' I glance at Lee and Miller and continue, 'Bethesda was a laboratory for a new type of Mind-Link—one designed to influence the behaviour of everyone who used it. Yes, I'm talking about mind control.'

A murmur runs through the others. Heads shake in disbelief; brows furrow or rise. They're not going to take my word for it, so I ask Johansson for his report. He repeats what he told me, adding just enough details to get the scientists and the doctors nodding.

Questions follow, but I cut them off. 'We can discuss this later, if we're still alive to do it.' This gets their attention instantly. 'Just know that it *can* be used for mind control. The mechanism is there.'

'Is it the Chinese?' Miller asks, and the room falls dead silent.

'No. And not the Americans, either. It was made by the people who really run the world—through business empires, not national borders. That's who the Guardians work for. And that's also the reason why they had to do the work here, far away from their competitors, if only because they, too, may one day be the target of the new Mind-Link.'

Voices rise like the buzzing of insects; heads shake or nod, sometimes both.

Lee crosses his arms. 'I've heard some crack theories in my life but this...' He makes a move as if to spit, but his visor is in the way.

'Then you'd better keep listening, because this is just the beginning.' I tell them about the news, about the Atlantic elevator and the strike on Shanghai. About the reason why all personal news has stopped. About how we were recruited and manipulated.

They are silent when I stop, their faces a mix of incredulity and shock.

'Prove it,' Lee spits.

'I don't have to—the Guardian's already done it. What's the first thing he destroyed?' I pause, watching the realisation hit. 'The transmitters. First on the ship, then here. To stop us from warning Earth. Why would he do it if he were on an official mission?'

Lee doesn't answer, nor does anyone else.

'He can't allow the information to get out,' I continue. 'And that means he won't let any of us return or fix the transmitter. The only reason they're not here yet is because I've sabotaged the second shuttle. But they'll fix it, sooner or later. And then the Sharks will come down here and finish the job he started.'

'Do you mean... they're going to kill us?' Pat Berry asks, wide-eyed with horror.

'They will try to, yes.'

More stunned silence, then Tam steps out of the circle of the engineers. 'We can't resist them.' He points at Lee and Miller. 'Even if they decide to help, their guns won't hurt the Sharks.'

'That's why we won't fight them directly.' I try to sound confident, but I'm not sure it's working. 'We've got to figure out how to use this base to help us. You're the smartest people I know. We'll find a way, but first I need your commitment. Are you with me?'

The doctors and the scientists all raise their hands, then Wang, and then the rest of the engineers. I look at Miller and Lee, still at a distance from the rest of us, their faces closed and uncertain.

'Moses?'

He hesitates, beads of sweat shiny against his brown skin. 'Does Price know?'

'I don't think so. Most likely she still believes she's helping thwart a Chinese plot.'

Miller nods, his shoulders twitching. He glances at Lee. 'It makes sense.'

Lee looks away, silent for another moment, then nods without meeting my eye.

Not enough. 'Michael?'

'Fine. Unless it turns out that you lied.'

I stare hard at him. 'Make your mind up, Michael. You can't second-guess every decision I make. Either you're with us or with the Guardian.'

He slaps his hand on the Cross and Stripes on his suit's chest. 'My loyalty's to my country. I won't swear allegiance to anything—or anyone—else.'

We scowl at each other across the length of the medical bay. If I push him, he'll walk away. Maybe even take Miller with him. I can't afford that.

'Don't do this for me. Do it for the five thousand Americans on *Gabriel*. By attacking the settlement, the Guardian's put all of them at risk. Do you agree?'

This hits a nerve. Lee winces, his hands clenching into fists. 'Yes.'

That's all I'm going to get, so it'll have to do. I move back a few steps, looking at the others again.

'One more thing,' Yefremov says. He joins me in front of the group, his visor steaming up with hurried breaths. 'Which of you have Mind-Link?'

Shit. Right. With filtered air running out, they're the most at risk. If his theory's right, of course—otherwise we're all equally screwed.

All five of the Chinese raise their hands, and so does Raji. Berry's arm twitches, but she keeps it down, her face ashen. She's American—revealing that she's got Mind-Link would end her career. Beats being dead, if you ask me, but it's her choice.

'If I kill off the organic parts, you should be safe,' Yefremov says. 'But I need to start immediately.'

'Will you have to sedate us?' Tam asks. 'Like Zhang?'

'Not for as long, no. Just a few hours.' Yefremov grimaces. 'And you'll probably be a bit dizzy afterwards.'

The engineers exchange glances—and probably opinions in the secrecy of their Mind-Links.

'Then we won't do it,' Tam says. Yefremov opens his mouth, but the engineer raises his hand, his tone matter of fact. 'Our minds are all we have to defend ourselves.'

The doctor glances at me. He licks his lips, working himself up to something. A drop of sweat slides down his face as his hands move, slowly and shakily, towards the life-support pack on his back.

'The rest of us are almost certainly immune,' he says, as much to himself as to everyone else.

I watch him, incredulous. He claims we're safe—but he can't be sure, or the gesture would be a no-brainer. Has the doctor finally found his conscience?

The others hold their breaths as Yefremov unclips his air tank and hands it to Tam.

'You need it more than I do,' he says through shaking lips. 'And we need you more than you need me.'

The doctor steps away, pale and spent. This has cost him all he had. And yet, it's just one shitty air tank.

I follow the glances to Gonzales, as he, too, removes his life-pack, his face stiff and his gaze vacant, as if distancing himself from his own actions. For a moment I think he'll hand the tank to Raji, his fellow doctor, but he passes it to another of the engineers, then shrugs as he catches my eye. Probably right: if we don't get through this, no doctor will help us.

Johansson is next, and the last. He pulls off his tank but doesn't give it to anyone, just puts it on the ground next to a console. Nobody else moves, the others glancing at their feet as if wanting to stay alive was a reason for shame. Only Lee stares ahead with jaw-tight defiance.

'Okay,' I say, my voice hoarse for some reason. 'We'd better get to work. Wang and Raji—go back to the base and see what can be salvaged. Air's the priority, then water. The rest of us, split into teams. Lee and Miller, take whoever you need. Figure out likely attack scenarios and how we might defend ourselves. The rest, start thinking how we can use the colony to help us. Don't underestimate the Sharks. They are the best of the best.'

Heads nod, as eager as they are scared.

Lee strides forward, finally crossing the distance to join the rest of us. 'How much time do we have?'

I've set good traps in the shuttle's programming—but none of them are insurmountable, not to an engineer. They might already be on the way. But that knowledge won't help anyone.

'Not more than a day,' I say over a lump in my throat. 'But most likely hours.'

CHAPTER 29

I call a check-in two hours later. Johansson, Gonzales, and two engineers, Tam and Sheng, march with me down the central aisle, past rows of consoles facing the large screen at the end of the room like some damn funeral procession heading towards an altar.

Lee and Miller wait for us by the screen, now displaying the map of the colony and the two landing sites.

'What have you got?' I ask.

Miller points to the lake-side landing strip. 'They'll come in here. After what happened to the probe, they won't land on the dome side.'

I squint at the map. 'So, that means airlock three or four, right?'

'They won't use the airlocks,' Lee says.

'Why not?'

'Because that's an easy trap. We can control them remotely, and the walls are too thick for them to cut their way out. I wouldn't do it, so they won't, either. The risk's not worth it.'

I freeze for an instant at the reminder that these two once used to be Sharks, the very Sharks who...

Irrelevant. Only the living count.

'Then how—' I start.

'They'll cut directly into the internal passage pipes,' Miller says. 'Between the bulkheads, where the structure's soft enough to do it quickly.'

'These are the most likely places.' Lee touches the screen, leaving red marks on the maze of passages inside the settlement.

'That's a lot of possibilities,' Johansson says.

'Twenty, and that's just the *best* places to cut, not all the *possible* places,' Miller says.

'We can discount the spots too far from the landing pad,' I say. 'Unless you think they'll expect us to do that?'

'No, they won't waste their time. They're not afraid of us, beyond walking into obvious traps.' Lee swipes the glass to remove the marks on all but the easternmost part of the settlement. 'They'll come in at one of these six points. Two, actually, because they'll split into two groups.'

Shit. I thought defending one entry point would be next to impossible.

Tam shifts closer to the screen. 'If we scatter as well, they'll take a long time to find us. It's a big place. They may run out of air.'

'Then they'll send for more,' Miller says. 'They have the ship to help them.'

That could be an opening. 'I can immobilise the shuttle, if you get me to it.'

Miller shakes his head. 'Not a chance. If they've got any brains—and believe me, they do—they won't keep the shuttle on the ground. They have better equipment and better endurance. We won't outrun or out-hide them. Our only option is to come up with something they won't expect.'

'Like what?' Gonzales asks.

Silence follows.

'We need weapons,' Miller says eventually. 'Explosives.

Anything with firepower. Once we know what we have, we can figure out a trap.'

I turn to the scientists. 'Any luck?'

'We found several chemicals we could use for explosives,' Johansson says. 'But the quantities are too small to cause serious damage. The only thing we have plenty of is hydrogen from the fusion tanks.'

A grimace twists Miller's face. I'm sure I look the same. Hydrogen is explosive all right, but unwieldy in the extreme.

'Keep looking,' I say. 'If you can't give me explosives, then find something else—corrosive, paralysing, or some damn glue trap.'

Johansson nods, but there's not much conviction on his face.

I look at the engineers, but Tam only shakes his head.

'We've mostly been discounting options. The assemblers, the construction machinery—nothing remotely useful, not in the time we have. We'll keep searching, but we still need to figure out how to make your guns work against the Sharks.'

Right. Miller's and Lee's weapons are 'ship-safe'—unfortunately, that also makes them Shark-safe. 'How is that going?'

'We have some ideas,' Sheng says. 'But we can't do anything without examining the actual weapons.'

She looks at the security men. They've been reluctant to hand in their guns—even without the lingering distrust, the last thing they want is for the attack to happen when their only weapons lie in pieces on an engineer's table.

'One of you, give her your gun,' I say. 'Sheng, make sure you can give it back fully functional with five minutes notice. These are the only weapons we have.'

Miller and Lee exchange glances—and yet it is Lee who reaches for his holster. 'Be careful with it, will you?'

'I promise,' Sheng says, and hurries back to the corner of the room the engineers have turned into their workshop.

I rub my eyes. My wrist hurts again, the pain dull and familiar. Two hours gone and we're no closer to a solution. How long till the Sharks are here?

'Okay, let's talk again in an hour. Let's find something, people, we're running out of time.'

Tam and the scientists depart, leaving me with the two security men.

Miller shifts, his fingers drumming on the console. 'I have an idea. If you agree.'

'Tell me.'

'There's a code we use, something all Sharks know. Line of sight, laser signals. We could send them a message that we'—he points at Lee—'that the two of us are on their side. Maybe they'll bite.'

'And what if they do?'

Miller shakes his head. 'I won't betray you, if that's what you're asking.'

'It's crossed my mind. But the question stands; they can pretend to play along only to lure you away from us. They'll still kill us all. We know too much to be allowed to return to Earth.'

'That's exactly what they'll try to do,' Lee says, his face hard and his mouth twisted.

I cock my eyebrow. His change of heart is unexpected. 'There's something you're not telling me.'

Lee looks away, his jaw working. 'I've talked to Price.'

Miller scowls, indignant. 'What?'

'How?' I ask.

'The security channel. It goes up the elevator.'

I grit my teeth, furious neither of them told me about its existence. Too late now. 'How much did you tell her?'

Lee snorts. 'Nothing. I asked if it was true that the Sharks were coming to kill us. She said, "Not if you kill her first".'

Her. Me, of course. But they wouldn't stop at that. 'And?'

'I asked, what if I didn't? She said, "Then you're on your own".'

Miller swears. 'She sold us out, the dust-fucker.'

'Yeah,' is all Lee says, his tone bitter.

'The Guardian's turned her,' Miller says.

'That's not how it works.' I stare hard at them. They should know better by now. 'She makes her own choices. All of us do. You, me, and them.' I gesture at the others. 'Forget the labels. It's the actions that show who you are.'

I pause, stunned by the irony of my words. I made my choices, too, back in the Feidi. I let my actions speak as I led others to their deaths and then ran away from the fires I started.

I'm no better than Price.

But now I'm here. And they need a leader, and at the moment I'm the best they have. So, I will keep on trying, for as long as it takes.

'Prepare your message,' I say to Miller. 'Do what you think is right.'

I have no time to register their responses as their eyes turn to the door at the far end. The room falls silent, as if everyone has stopped breathing.

Wang and Raji pull in a transport crate, its squeaky wheel and their heavy footsteps the only sounds.

I stand on my tiptoes, straining to see inside the crate. My breath catches in my throat. Only six air tanks.

Wang and Raji stop in the middle of the hall, their faces grim. The others approach from the corners, gathering around the crate like mourners at a funeral.

'That's not going to last long,' Yau says, her voice sharp and breathy.

We have ten people still on bottled air, most of them close to running out. Six people with Mind-Link—seven, if I'm correct about Berry.

I walk towards them, glancing at Yefremov as he approaches from the other side, hoping his expression will give me some reassurance even though he told me it'd take at least a day before he could draw any conclusions from Zhang's condition.

The doctor stares gloomily at the six bottles, his mouth downturned. No help there.

I turn to the engineers. 'Can we get the colony's production back online?'

'It's a matter of time. And priorities,' Tam says. 'Getting the bio-filters installed and reconnected will take—' He shakes his head and points at the bottles. 'Longer than this will last. And that only if we abandon everything else.'

Damn. Not much use to the air if we're all dead. Even if those without Mind-Link are immune, we need the engineers if any of us are to survive at all.

'People with Mind-Link should get all the air,' Yau says. She steps into the middle of the circle and closer to the air tanks. 'We're the most at risk.'

A ripple spreads through the others, anger or defiance. She's right, but even so I can't order anyone to give up their air. We need them all—even more, we need to stay united.

Raji joins Yau in the centre, his face moist and his hands twitching. 'She's right. You can survive without it. We can't.'

'Well, screw you,' Lee says.

Raji's voice is breathless. 'You're not at risk yourself.'

Berry steps closer to the cart, not quite joining the other two. 'We know nothing for sure.'

'We know what the doctor said.' Yau turns her back on the others and reaches for one of the bottles in the cart.

'Put it down,' I say slowly.

A shudder runs down Yau's back—but she continues, reaching out to the nearest tank and pulling it into her embrace. Raji's next, already lifting a bottle. Berry glances around, uncertain, while Sheng inches her way to the cart, her eyes wide.

'Stop it, right now!' I yell.

Yau recoils, Raji scowls—but both stand their ground, each with a tank clasped in their arms.

'This is a death sentence,' Raji croaks. 'I've seen what happened to the colonists. I don't want to die like that!'

No more death. The drowning feeling waits at the edge of my consciousness, poised for a chance to grab me. Not this time.

I point my finger at him and Yau. 'We don't have enough air even for all the Mind-Link people. And what we—'

'You need engineers,' Yau cuts in. 'Not pathologists.'

Raji flinches, his whole body shuddering as if hit by a gust of wind.

'Nobody's taking this air,' I say. 'Is that clear?'

Yau pushes out her chin, about to protest, but instead she swings around to stare at Tam and the other engineers. They've formed another circle, faces agitated and arms waving even though their mouths remain closed. So, this is what an argument over Mind-Link looks like.

Yau breaks the silence. She shouts something too fast and too accented for me to understand, her arms wrapped tight around the bottle.

Tam steps towards her, his face red and his fists clenched.

'Wèishéme shì nǐ?' Yau shouts. *Why should it be you?*

This has gone on long enough. I nod at Miller and Lee. They move to the cart, their postures menacing. Miller still has his weapon—but where's the other?

I gasp as I see it—the other gun, clenched tightly in Sheng's bionic hand, the woman one step behind Raji and Yau. Her arms are still at her sides, but her shoulders inch up in preparation of a move.

How fast can she be? Is the hand for engineering work only —or will it improve her reflexes?

Our eyes meet, her face contorted by regret and fear.

Miller has noticed it, too. His shoulders hunch, like a

predator ready to pounce. His fingers twitch—but he's holding his nerve.

One wrong move, and it'll end in bloodshed.

'The air won't help you when the Sharks get here,' I say as softly as I can. 'This is a battle we must fight together, or we all die.'

For a long moment she stands motionless, as if chiselled from ice and fear. I hold my breath. Everyone around me is deathly still.

Sheng's head drops. She relaxes, relieved or resigned. Tam stands behind her, and she lets him take the gun. And then she turns to Yau and reaches for the air tank the other woman still clasps to her chest. I can't tell if they're communicating over Mind-Link, but Yau tenses, then relents, all fight gone from her body.

Sheng hands the tank to Miller. 'I'm sorry. I... I got scared.'

The silence lingers as Tam walks to Lee, returning the gun.

Lee reaches out to gab it, his face set—but something in it breaks. He pauses, his eyes on the engineer. His hand shakes. 'Do you promise to keep it safe?'

'As much as I can.'

Lee considers the answer for another moment. 'Keep working on it.'

I watch him, stunned. But he's right, not just about needing to make the gun work—there won't be another reason to start a fight. No more air is coming, and killing the rest of us won't save anyone from the Sharks. They all know it now.

I move towards the cart. 'We've got to stick together, people. That's the only way. Yefremov, Gonzales, you're responsible for distributing the air based on people's condition. If you have to choose, prioritise for the mission.' The doctors acknowledge, and I turn to security. 'Miller, Lee, make sure everyone shuts off their tanks with no less than fifteen minutes of air reserve—we may have structural damage, we'll need it to get to safety.'

'Yes, sir,' Miller says. Lee only nods.

'Now, can we all go back to trying to survive this? Because the Sharks' bullets will kill you faster than this air, Mind-Link or not.'

Some heads nod, others still stare at the tanks, eyes glazed over. Slowly, they return to their stations, and the buzz of conversation resumes.

I hope they stay strong. I hope they'll hold their focus. All we have are our minds, and precious little time left to use them.

CHAPTER 30

It's early morning when Firyali's message arrives, patched to my visor from the shuttle's receiver. I knew she'd find a way.

Launch in progress, is all it says. It's enough.

'It's a go, everyone!' I yell into my helmet radio. 'They're coming!'

Those around me jerk into action, sleepy faces transforming into wide-eyed readiness.

'Cāo!' Tam swears over the intercom. 'We need another hour!'

'Same here... Damn!' Sheng's tired voice responds.

They are in the eastern passages preparing the gas traps. They must be done and out of the blast zone before the Sharks get here, or the plan won't work. We never discovered any new explosives, or a secret cache of weapons hidden under the floorboards. We're back to the only option the scientists had found: hydrogen. Risky as hell. We have only one chance—and it depends on the Sharks following exactly the route Miller and Lee have predicted.

'You have twenty minutes before they're in position.' I stop myself before I tell them what will happen if they get it wrong—or don't get away in time. As if they don't know.

I listen for another moment as Tam shouts hurried commands, his voice breathless and raspy with exhaustion.

'I've got contact,' Johansson says from his post. The colony's radar has survived, and the engineers managed to connect it to my shuttle's sensors.

'That's it, people,' I say. 'Get your suits ready, but wait with the air till my signal.'

I can almost hear them snort from the corners of the hub. They've been breathing the settlement's infected air for hours now—all except Tam and Sheng, chosen by the other engineers to get the extra tanks. Everyone else has fifteen minutes of air left, and that solely because of my orders. If the hub is breached, this is all we'll have to get to safety.

'Bearing zero-eight-four degrees,' Johansson says.

I pull the visor down over my eyes. The shuttle's coming low, keeping just over the water line. Approaching from the lake side—but that means nothing because I came that way as well, only to throttle up and land on the dome strip.

I wonder who's at the controls. Price, most likely. She's their best pilot—and as I remember from our trip to *Gabriel*, surprisingly good.

'They'll go for the lake,' Miller says calmly, for my sake or his own.

'Are the drones ready?' I ask. They were ready two hours ago, but it doesn't hurt to check. We've hidden cameras along the route, but nothing beats an aerial view.

'Ready and waiting,' Wang says, her voice tinged with nerves.

I zoom in on the shuttle, but the visor's magnification is rubbish. Still, I catch the moment when the wings' geometry changes and the air brakes deploy. Going straight in for the landing—no recon, unless they launched a drone we missed.

The clouds are thicker than ever, so they aren't getting any intel from orbit.

'No probes,' Johansson confirms. He's thinking the same. They're too confident to bother with recon. Good: confident means cocky. And cocky means we've got a chance.

'They're landing. Lake strip,' I say as the shuttle's exhausts swoop to vertical thrust. 'Deploy the drones.'

'Drones out,' Wang says.

The image on my visor sharpens with the data from the drones' cameras. The shuttle is touching the ground, its legs extended but the engines powered through bleed nozzles. The cargo doors open before the craft settles. Six figures in silver suits jump out in fluid movements, weapons poised, breaking into a run the moment their feet touch the ground.

'They're all here,' Miller says. 'He sent all the Sharks.'

Which means the Guardian trusts Price's people enough not to worry about his personal safety back on the ship. By now, that shouldn't be surprising, but it still comes with a pang. Damn.

The shuttle lifts off again as soon as the Sharks clear the blast radius. An instant later, its engines roar above our heads, sending the module walls into momentary resonance. The floor vibrates, metal plates groaning with a nauseating rasp. Three seconds later it's gone, the thunder retreating into the distance.

My gaze returns to the Sharks. They're nearing the edge of the landing strip, running in pairs of stooped figures with bulky supply packs on their backs. One lifts up their arm, sending out a flash of light.

'Drone one down,' Wang says. 'Drone two holding.'

Lee hisses with admiration. 'That was a good shot.'

As if anyone needed to hear that.

'Proceeding according to plan,' I say by way of encouragement. All our surveillance comes from the second drone and the hidden cameras. That first machine was meant to be shot down. They'd expect us to launch one, so we did. And we made it an easy target, only to reassure them of our incompetence. I hope it's working.

'Miller, your message?' I ask.

'My drone's out... now.'

I can't see it from the angle of our camera, but a change in the Sharks' gait tells me they're receiving the message. Two heads turn to face each other, communicating. The next moment, one of them swings around, a flash of light erupting from the nozzle of their gun followed by the shadow of debris tumbling to the ground. The Sharks haven't stopped or slowed down, proceeding along the previous path as if no interruption has occurred.

'I guess that's a "no"?'

'Well, I did manage to send a "fuck you, too" before they shot it,' Miller says.

'It was worth a try,' I say, not quite believing it. I'm glad the rest of our plan didn't hinge on this.

The image on my visor jumps as the feed moves to the next concealed camera. This one has a higher angle, showing the Sharks steadily advancing towards the eastern airlock, the one closest to the landing strip. The farthest out from the settlement, this was the colony's main transport route for the strip, the greenhouses, and the processing stations by the lake. It's also the most direct access to the 'circular' surrounding the hub— but, as Miller pointed out, not as direct as just crossing the distance over the ground.

We need them to continue. If he's wrong and they enter here, they'll turn off the circular before they reach our traps.

I watch them, my heart pounding. Even Miller has stopped breathing.

'It's a decoy,' Lee says. 'They'll split up about... now.'

Nothing happens for three more strides, then the line of

Sharks divides in the middle, the two groups angling north and south.

I let out a breath. So far, so good. But we're very far from success.

The image jumps again, just as they pass the stone circle that marks the border of the settlement. I split my feed in two, watching both groups slide along the modules. They're slower now, heads turning left and right as they scan the surroundings. They speed up again to cross the twenty metres dividing the habitat's six groups, now clearly following the paths to the ES and EN nodes on the circular.

'Hart to engineers. What's your status?'

Nobody replies for so long that I stop breathing, my mouth open as I lean forward over the console. Someone on the channel gasps—then something cracks like an old-fashioned channel switch, and Sheng responds in between loud intakes of air, as if running.

'Finishing the 38-A junction. 25-A needs another ten minutes. The backup positions are... not optimal.'

'Focus on the main targets. You have five minutes.'

She gasps in response, and we leave it at that. I hope we at least get the main positions ready. If the Sharks decide on an alternative route, we're toast.

They are approaching the circular now, so far following the path Lee and Miller predicted. The hub will be the initial target —they'll want to secure the ops room so they can control the bulkheads and life support. Most of all, they'll want to deny us that control. They'd be cutting their way in here directly if they could—but the ops room lies at the centre of interconnected, thick-walled modules surrounded by a ring of engineering equipment. The most time-efficient access is through the EE node—or, if you are two groups wanting to maintain separation in case of ambush, the EN and ES nodes. And that's what we're praying they'll do.

I track their steps, imagining the crunch of gravel under each heavy footfall. Seconds roll on my visor's clock. My throat's parched dry; my fingers drum an annoying rhythm. I force myself to stop even though nobody's paying attention. They may not even hear it over the pounding in their ears.

Fifty metres to the nodes. Forty.

If they go past them, if they choose a different place, our plan won't work.

Twenty metres. Ten.

They slow down.

I hold my breath, lean forward into the image on my visor.

The lead Shark in each group reaches for their supply pack. They drop it on the ground just as all the Sharks come to a stop.

These are the wrong corridors, farther out than we expected —but still on the target nodes. As long as they follow the shortest paths to the ops room, we're good.

The Sharks pop up mobile airlocks, similar to the tent I used on the shuttle, only five times bigger. They slide inside, cutting equipment already in hand.

I swallow hard. Decision time. 'All teams, abandon backup positions. Full focus on prime targets. Prepare to engage in five minutes.'

That's it. Now we can only pray that the plan will work.

I switch my feed to the monitoring camera inside the corridor. The wall's already glowing; seconds later, the sparks of the cutter pierce through the darkness.

'They're fast,' Tam says. 'We'd better—'

'Start pumping. Everyone, seal your suits. Get away from the target.'

The Sharks breach the wall in less than three minutes. We've fused the controls on the inner bulkheads, but that's only a minor delay. Those were never meant as defences, only as seals, with simple lids on the control mechanism. It takes the Sharks less than two minutes to cut through the bolts.

I watch them jog down the corridor, their steps assured. They hesitate only an instant when the first bulkhead closes behind them. Nothing abnormal, a forced seal reasserting itself. They move on, opening the next bulkhead even faster. Heads turn, as if they are responding to a sound, a soft hissing of air passing through overhead ducts. Nothing to worry about. Two more bulkheads and they'll be inside the hub, on the way to the ops room and full control of the colony.

Another bulkhead closes behind them, just as the first. They hardly notice it now, not until the whizz of flowing air intensifies and the air around them condenses into mist. They pause, movements uncertain. I can't see their faces, but I can imagine their hesitation. They'll be checking their instruments, but those won't tell them much: a slight decrease in temperature and a momentary fluctuation in pressure.

They make up their minds, both groups moving towards the bulkheads almost simultaneously.

'I suggest you stop now,' I say on the general channel.

They pause, then a familiar voice responds. Donahue. 'And why would that be?'

'You've noticed the flow of air, haven't you?' I pause for a moment, then continue. 'Except it's not 'air.' You're standing in a fifty per cent air-hydrogen mixture. Highly combustible, I might add. Any spark from your cutting equipment and we'll be scraping you off the gravel outside.'

Silence. Then: 'It would take you out as well.'

'Er, no. We've run the math. The hub can withstand it. And we're all safely far away.'

That last part is a lie—some of the engineers may still be within the blast radius, but he doesn't need to know that.

More silence follows. The condensation has cleared by now, and I can see them again, their postures stiff and their movement cagey.

Donahue speaks again, his voice gruff. 'What do you suggest?'

'Put down your weapons and your equipment. Move back the way you came; we'll open the bulkhead for you. We'll keep the air mixture in the explosive range till you clear the space. Once you're out, we'll open all the bulkheads leading to the habitat. You can wait there till we get the rest of this mess sorted.'

He snorts in response, part anger, part scorn. 'And what if we don't go?'

'Then we'll wait till your air runs out. You can try breathing hydrogen... You know, I never did ask the doctor, but I'm sure he'd focus on the deficiency of oxygen in the mix.'

A smile stretches my lips. I'm enjoying this. I shouldn't. If they try to push it, they will die.

No more death.

Fuck them.

No response comes—but they're not putting down their gear, either. They turn to face each other, their movements cautious, aware of the electronics in their suits. Any spark, any overheating circuit could set off the blast. If I'm telling the truth. Because I could be bluffing.

They straighten, resolved. Decision made.

'Don't do it,' I say. 'I'm not bluffing. The colony was powered by hydrogen. They had plenty of stock—'

A blast shakes the ground. My visor greys out for an instant. When it returns, half of it has lost signal. The feed from junction 38-A, gone.

'Heavy damage to circular, sections thirty-five through thirty-nine,' Tam's voice quavers. 'Minor damage to neighbouring sections. Hub integrity holding. Bulkheads holding.'

'All crew, med check-in,' Yefremov says.

I touch the sensor on my neck and watch as signals come in from the others—but not from all. Sheng's icon remains blank, and Yau's comes in orange, requesting medical attention. Damn.

'I'm going to check—' Tam starts.

I cut him off. 'Stay at your post. Yefremov?'

'Raji and I are on the way,' Gonzales responds. 'We're closer.'

I switch back to the general channel, my voice trembling with fury. 'That wasn't necessary. Half of your team are dead, for nothing. Will you cooperate now?'

It takes ten seconds before the answer arrives. A different voice, higher and edgy. Not Donahue. 'What are your instructions?'

I repeat what I said before, then watch them lay down their equipment and weapons.

Donahue's gone. The deaths feel more real now that I can put a name to them. It doesn't help to know that they did it themselves. Was it pride? What lies did the Guardian make them believe that they were willing to risk everything?

'We're ready,' the Shark says.

'Proceed to the habitat.'

On my signal, Wang opens the first bulkhead, then the next, closing each one as soon as the Sharks pass through. It'll take them ten minutes to reach the habitat. We can't keep them locked up there forever, but we're not done yet. The biggest challenge is only about to start.

I push myself up. 'Away team, proceed to the shuttle. Time we paid the Guardian a visit.'

CHAPTER 31

I cut through the ops room, then out through the hub towards the western airlock, the closest to the dome strip and my shuttle. Lee and Miller join me when I reach the circular, each carrying a pack of tools and weapons scavenged from the Sharks.

'Only from the one group,' Lee says. 'The other won't have anything left to salvage.'

'Or free of guts,' Miller adds. Neither of them is laughing.

Tam and Wu approach from the other direction.

'Sheng got caught in the blast,' Wu says.

'Is she...?'

'The medics are with her,' Tam says, but their expressions are grim.

I clench my fists. 'Let's go.'

'Wait!' a familiar voice calls.

I spin. Zhang hobbles towards us, dragging a bulky ground suit. Yefremov is behind him, frustration scrunching his face.

'I'm coming with you,' Zhang says. He stumbles forward, his movements jerky. He looks hot, cheeks flushed, and hair plastered to his forehead. But he's up, walking again even if it's clearly an effort. His eyes are bright, too, alive with determination that shines stronger than fever.

My chin trembles, the joy at seeing him catching me unprepared. 'Zhang Min... you're in no shape to help us.'

'I can talk and think, that's all you need from me.' He glances at the others, hesitant. 'I've got some... tricks. Ways to handle the ship.'

'Then you'd better tell us now.'

'Not possible. It'll only work with my codes.'

I start to shake my head, but the engineer leans in to me, his eyes burning.

'How are you even going to get in? They'll have Price waiting for you. Or they'll block the airlocks and leave you out in the cold.'

'We'll find something.' My voice is shakier than I'd like. I'm counting on Firyali to find a way to help us, but that's by no means certain.

'You need me,' Zhang says.

'You're probably right, but I still can't take you. Not while you're... infected.'

'Then you're kidding yourself. You're carriers as well by now, all of you. This stuff's on your skin, in your every exhalation. The moment you set foot on that ship, all of them will be exposed.'

That can't be. I glance at Yefremov.

'He's right. You or he, it makes no difference.'

A chill runs down my back. Some of the scientists on board have Mind-Link. And what if Yefremov's theory is wrong and Zhang's remission is only temporary? We'd be taking Bethesda's plague to everyone on board. Still, we must get back to the ship —and before the Guardian finds a way to annihilate us from orbit. We must send out a warning. Even if it's a death sentence to the entire crew.

Sanchez. Khan. Chao.

Freedom of billions against death of a few.

Jason is still alive. The thought makes me ashamed, the idea that I might choose for my own kin, not for the billions of strangers. And yet...

'We're going.' My voice is as hard and dry as the gravel outside the walls. 'You may come with us, Zhang Min, but you've got to hold your own.'

'I understand.'

I cast another glance at Yefremov. Still frowning, and yet he nods, something between encouragement and approval.

'Good luck,' he says, then spins around and hurries back into the hub.

With the six of us inside, the shuttle's heavier than I'd like. No problem for the engines, but every kilo means more fuel to take us into orbit. Especially with the extra manoeuvring I'm sure we'll be forced to make. I check the gauges as we lift off. We should have enough. Should.

The moment we clear the clouds, Price is on us. She dives in from above, approaching almost vertically at full power, her engines thundering till the air shudders with a sonic boom.

I used to play this game, too, back in flight school. And then I taught the response manoeuvre to our recruits, just so they could beat the crap out of competition pilots in sim games. It's the old chicken game—and just like with playing chicken, it only works if you're ready to go through with the threat. No way Price will sacrifice herself for the Guardian. She's going to pull up at the last moment, creating kilotons worth of down-thrust, and, if she's good enough, angle it in such a way as to send me into a spin. At this altitude, uncontrolled spin could kill us—if I let it get that far. I'm not planning to.

I power up, ready for my response. For a moment I wonder if Price could possibly be one of the recruits I once trained, now planning a surprise tailored to the moves she knows I'm going to make. Too late now. Either it works, or this will be a very short trip.

I slide the power to maximum and sweep the wings back. I'm a rocket now, cutting through the air on thrust only, like a bullet heading straight for her. Separation numbers roll down to where she'll have to pull out of her dive or we'll collide—and just as she does, I flick the rudder to rotate, presenting my thinnest side to the tornado of Price's exhaust as it passes above me. The frame rattles, the shuttle moaning with effort as we tear through the storm. Our altitude plummets as the very air we're in sinks down under the punch. Next to me, Tam grabs the armrests. Someone groans, the sound barely audible above the high-pitched whine of the engines at max capacity. Another couple of seconds and we're out, the air smooth again and the shuttle climbing unhindered.

'That was... unpleasant,' Zhang says from behind. 'But then, I never liked flying.'

'You picked the wrong job!' Lee's laugh bubbles with relief. Ever the manly man. I'd better not tell him how dangerous that really was or he might start a comedy routine.

On my sensors, Price's shuttle pulls up ahead, heading on full burn back to the ship. Smart move: she can't outfly me, but she can do much more damage waiting for me on the ship. At the moment, she's barely a minute ahead, but she'll gain time if she goes full burn.

That's the problem with stealing a shuttle: they're never parked with a full tank. And orbital mechanics hardly ever plays out the way you want it. I run the fuel numbers again and swear. We don't have enough to chase the ship around the planet; we'll have to park in a higher orbit and wait till the position is right for a quick burst to get us to rendezvous. That will give them plenty of time to prepare for us, but there's absolutely nothing I can do about it.

I glance at the comms screen. Nothing from Firyali. And our oxygen levels are dipping way below comfortable. Shit.

My stomach lurches, struggling to reacquaint itself with weightlessness as I release the seat restraints and float to the others. 'Okay, if anybody's got a brilliant idea, feel free to share.'

'Can't we send the message from *Gabriel*?' Miller asks.

I shake my head. 'It's still at geostationary. We don't have enough fuel or air to get that far. Our ship's the only option. I'm heading for dock number one. If they block the airlock, we'll try the maintenance hatch. I'm betting they'll let us in just so they can dispose of us.'

Miller snorts. 'That sounds like what Price'd do.'

Lee's voice is bitter as he raises a Shark's gun, silver-sleek and streamlined, just like their suits. 'We have better weapons now, but we're still two against four. Against five, if the Guardian counts. If we take them head on, we have no chance.'

'Dock at the engine deck,' Zhang says. He pushes himself off his chair and floats to the seat next to me, currently occupied by Tam. 'May I?'

Tam scowls as he removes the straps, then glides away without a glance at Zhang.

He's still the 'captain-killer' for them. I never managed to clear that up. I should, before it gets us in more trouble—but not right now.

'If we do that, we'll be trapped,' I say. 'There's only one way to the main deck, down the tether elevator. Unless you have a way to send a message to Earth from the engine deck?'

'I'm afraid not.' Zhang says nothing more. He types commands into the engineering system, biting his lip as if it were a challenge.

'Then why would we go there?' I ask. We're wasting time. Zhang's probably too drugged to be of any use.

The engineer doesn't reply, typing with concentration

worthy of a first-year recruit. He mumbles something, a slurred complaint about 'clumsy fingers.'

Shit. Of course—he's doing manually what he'd normally do with his Mind-Link. It must be decades since he's had to do that.

'You're right that the tether is a trap,' Zhang says finally. 'If you go on the inside.'

I know what he's thinking. Still, it won't work. 'There're maintenance cameras on the outside. We won't get far before they see us.'

Zhang's lips twitch in a laborious smile. 'Not if someone disabled the security feeds...'

Now we're talking. I lean towards him and have to grab the armrests so I don't float away. 'Can you do that? Won't the spy notice? I mean, the other computer?'

'I don't think it will. It was programmed to a narrow set of triggers, and most of those were used up when it woke up the Guardian.'

I nod. This echoes what Firyali said before. 'So it's dormant now?'

'Not exactly dormant—just never designed for this. But the Guardian can still activate it, and then it'll overrule any block-ades I put in. I'm hoping to buy you some time before they realise that they've been hacked.'

They will know we're outside—but if they don't know where... 'Can you keep us hidden long enough so they don't know which way we've entered?'

'We'd have to time it perfectly.'

I bite my lip, considering. Without the cameras, they won't be able to discount the tether. They will have to split to secure all entries. That could give us just the advantage.

'We can't use the comms,' Tam says. 'Or they'll be able to track us.'

Right. Any transmission would give away our location. And

we'll be out of visual range of the shuttle for most of the climb up the tether.

Zhang nods. 'As I said, we'll have to time it perfectly.'

A gamble, then. Still, I see no better option, and from the others' expressions, neither do they.

'One more thing,' I say. 'Some people there may still be with us. Let's see if we can talk to them.'

I go through the motion of pretending to approach dock one before rolling away and heading for the emergency dock at the engine deck. Not a moment too soon—the shuttle's already showing CO_2 warnings, and most of us have only fumes left in our tanks.

We are perched at the far end of the spinning counter-weight, next to the engine nozzles. Lee and Miller slide out through the passenger hatch into the small airlock that leads to the tether. Tam and Wu follow. They start by disabling the cameras, first inside the airlock then inside the tether corridor. They return carrying two fresh air tanks, their own already changed.

We're ready a minute later. Zhang gives me an encouraging nod as he and Wu settle behind the controls and we seal the cockpit. The pumps engage. When the pressure is just above zero, Miller pops the cargo hatch.

'Start the timer,' I say, then switch off my transmitter.

Lee jumps out first, disappearing into the vacuum outside. I'm next, sliding down the ramp onto the scaffold that covers the 'roof' of the engine section. This is the segment that will slot under the floor of the main deck when the ship reconnects. From close up, all I can see are jagged ridges of the ship's inner frame and spikes of ducts cut off from their main deck's endings. The sight draws cold sweat on my forehead. We had no time to look for magnetised boots or even a safety line. Every minute is precious. I follow Lee down a narrow path of greasy metal slabs laid out for service access. For now, we're still under the simulated gravity of the ship's rotation so we can simply walk, just like on the inside. Except here, if one of us stumbles, there's nothing to stop us sliding off the path, into the metal spikes below or the empty space beyond. Best not to think about it.

I watch the digits roll down on the timer. Not good. It takes us seven minutes to reach the tether, two more than planned. We're already behind, with no way of letting Zhang know.

The tether extends up like a mighty pillar, wider and taller than I've ever imagined from the inside. I know its dimensions by heart, but this is different. I lift my head, for the first time daring to look at the main deck, a silver shadow two hundred metres above us. Shit.

We start up the service ladder, the rungs slippery under my boots. I'm breathing hard, my muscles cramped with exhaustion after the sleepless night and all the stress. Sweat trickles down my back. I'm slow, too slow. Lee's pulling ahead, but even he's slower now. I glance down. Tam is further below, Miller right behind him.

I check the time. Fifteen minutes. Fuck.

We're halfway to the spindle when the structure shudders under my feet, the entire tether vibrating as something pushes inside it. The elevator, activated by Wu at the agreed twenty minutes mark. And we're not even halfway across.

This is bad—we counted on splitting them up by having at least some of Price's people wait for us at the elevator, only to find it empty. Now they'll have the time to regroup. They'll know we're up to something, and there are only so many options.

I hold on to the rungs as the elevator passes inches behind the hyper-carbon wall. As soon as it's gone, we move again. We're lighter now, closer to the centre of rotation. It makes the climb easy, but even more dangerous because of that. It's tempting to let go and fly several steps in a single push—except the Coriolis effect would snap the ladder away and leave you with nothing but empty space under your feet.

And yet, that's not what gets us. We're at the spindle, rotating to make our legs point to the new 'down,' when Tam loses his grip. Lee and I are already on the other side, starting our descent. I watch in frozen horror as the engineer's attempt to rotate turns into a somersault, his fingers peeling off the ladder. He reaches out with his feet, struggling for purchase, but the momentum pushes him out and there's nothing to stop him drifting away from the ladder, away from the ship. Our eyes meet, his mouth opening in the moment of realisation. I reach out my hand even though I know I can't help him; nobody can.

But then another figure smashes into the engineer, Miller's bulk propelling both of them forward, towards the upper deck—no, right into the tether's path as it rotates towards them. They fly over my head, hands outstretched, hoping for a chance to connect with anything they can grasp. They're coming close—but it won't work, they'll overshoot by a couple of metres.

I push myself off the ladder, hooking on to the rung with only my feet, almost perpendicular to the tether. I reach out, my arm stretching till I feel the fabric of Miller's suit against my hand and clasp my fingers to grasp it. I've got them—but they keep going, the momentum of the two men pulling against my grip. I clench my fingers. My muscles cramp, burning, the shoulder about to tear out of its socket.

I should let go. It's not worth it. Not for me, not for the mission. I hold on.

My arm throbs; my wrist is on fire; the ladder digs into my feet. I'm a stretched piece of string, about to snap.

I hold on.

I'm risking my life for the man who might have killed Stepan.

An American, risking his life for a Chinese engineer.

I hold on.

The pain is dagger-sharp—and then it's gone, and so is the pressure, as the two men get hold of the ladder. I keep on holding, my feet free now as Lee pulls us all towards him. We huddle together, muscles trembling, eyes wide with understanding how close we came to losing.

I throw my head back, desperate not to scream—in both relief and in anger, because that was stupid and the mission is more important than any one of us—and still knowing that it was the right thing to do, no matter what.

Enough. I motion them to go on, and we resume our climb. Nothing's changed—the worst is still ahead. And yet, nothing will ever be the same.

CHAPTER 32

We're on the main deck, crossing a mirror version of the service path when a message appears on my visor: *Price and Guardian on bridge, all airlocks fused.*

Firyali. At last. Is Zhang in contact with her? I can't count on that. She's seen us arrive just like everyone else, and she may have only now got the chance. The message itself is what I expected. When they found the elevator empty, they knew we had to be outside. They're spread too thin to protect all airlocks; fusing them makes sure our attempt to get in will either be futile or clearly visible, and most likely both.

Luckily, we were never planning to use the airlocks.

We approach our target over twenty minutes later than planned. Twenty minutes the Guardian and Price have had to prepare. I can only hope Zhang, too, has managed to do his part.

Tam stops at a metal square, slightly raised and thicker than the plates that make up the service path but otherwise inconspicuous. Reinforced bolts secure it to what lies beneath: an emergency access duct, one of seven over the entire ship, each leading to some crucial bit of the super-secret Chinese technology. I found out about their existence only an hour ago. Nobody else knows about them—except for the engineers, of course.

Tam drops to his knee and proceeds to unscrew the bolts. I glance around, half expecting a drone to swoop down on us any moment—Zhang can fool the cameras, but I doubt he can stop the drones. They're probably already out there, looking for us around the airlocks. Not long before they decide to widen the search.

When the last bolt is out, Tam twists four tiny knobs on opposite sides of the hatch, then looks up at me. Time for the signal. I nod to Miller. He aims his arm towards the engine deck, now high above us, and the corner where I can just about spot the tiny pimple of the shuttle. He makes a tiny circular motion, the laser in his suit's cuff pointing at the shuttle. Our radios crack an instant later—an innocuous enough signal, and one that won't betray our position. Message received.

Tam slides down first, then Miller, Lee, and myself at the end, dropping into a chamber so tiny I have to wriggle to fit between Miller's and Lee's bulky frames. Tam turns a lever in the ceiling, and an iris-like seal closes over our entry point. Another lever opens a hatch in the floor, with a narrow chute and a short ladder fixed to the side. We climb down, our footsteps sending soundless vibrations through the metal structure.

The next chamber is hardly bigger than the first, but this time with four pressurised doors on all sides, each with a code word marked in Chinese characters. Tam signals for us to stand clear, then punches a code into the opening panel. A red light appears above, flashing urgently as the door trembles, then whips open. Air rushes inside, condensing into fog with low pressure. For a moment I'm blinded, lost in milky whiteness pulsing with the blood red of the alarm. Then the sound arrives, a thin bleat settling into the familiar blare of the decompression alert. My visor clears, and we move on, into a dim, narrow tunnel, past bits of machinery that could as well be alien. The alarm withers, then dies, the pressure equalised.

All bulkheads sealed, appears on my visor.

That's what we predicted they'd do—try to isolate us in a space they can control. But the fact that they've deployed *all* bulkheads means Zhang has managed to confuse them enough that they can't tell where the breach has occurred.

I check the clock: four minutes since we signalled the shuttle. For once we're on time.

We're through the maze of the engine and approaching the first bulkhead when my pre-recorded message starts.

'This is Nathalie Hart, your lawful commander. The Guardian's true objective is to conceal our findings from the people on Earth; this is why he destroyed the transmitter. He's not working for the Americans or the Chinese, but for a secret organisation of the yun-ying—they used Bethesda to develop mind-control technology to turn us into their slaves. If he wins, those on Earth will never get our warning. To security: I know you believed you acted in service of your country. Now you know the truth. The future of—'

The recording cuts abruptly. Still, it lasted longer than I expected.

I cross my fingers as we reach the first bulkhead and Tam punches in the override codes. If the spy is awake, it can block us. But the panel chirps, and the door slides open. I let out a breath. Either the Guardian hasn't reached the spy, or the Chinese override settings are hardwired into the system. I never thought I'd be thankful for the trade wars.

We file into the next corridor, halfway between the ops workshops and the bridge. The space is deserted, but that's to be expected with decompression protocol.

Everyone on bridge. G's trying t—

The message cuts mid-word. I wait, hoping Firyali got interrupted, but nothing more comes. Maybe they're watching her. I try not to think what would happen if she got caught.

Three more bulkheads and I'll know.

'This is the Guardian,' the soft voice says over the PA speakers. 'Nathalie and her people are infected with Bethesda's plague. I'm afraid they're already exhibiting the symptoms that led the colonists to annihilate each other: paranoid suspicions and conspiracy theories. This is tragic, especially as I don't doubt that they're sincere in their delusions. They are ill. We may be able to help them, and we'll certainly try, but my priority has to be keeping the rest of you safe from the disease. Wherever you are, lock the doors and avoid all contact with the infected. No heroics—let security handle the problem. I'll update you as soon as it's over.'

We exchange glances as we listen, fear growing like a tumour in my chest. He's outsmarted me. I expected denial, arguments to prove me wrong. I should have known better. By invoking the plague, in one move he's rendered my accusations irrelevant and made us a threat to everyone on board. We're the enemy now. The lunatics consumed by the plague. No one will listen to anything we say.

I stop. It's over. What little was left of our plan depended on planting a doubt with the security people. With Miller and Lee on my side, they might have wavered. If we could talk, we had a chance. Price herself might have switched sides again when she saw how things were panning out. Not anymore. We are outgunned and outmanoeuvred.

Miller swears under his breath. Lee punches his fist into the palm of his other hand. I'm sure he'd punch the wall if he didn't have to be quiet. As if there is still any point.

Ahead, a workshop door tilts open, then closes rapidly. The dry snap of the lock stings like betrayal. We're on our own.

The others are watching me, faces grim and hesitant.

No, this isn't over. I don't know how, but we will try.

I straighten and let a sour smile twist my lips. The men respond, all three of them nodding in agreement.

'Let's go,' I say aloud. Screw the surveillance. They'll see us in person soon enough.

Tam marches to the next bulkhead, his head high and his steps assured. The panel flashes green when he puts in his codes. The door slides open, revealing two waiting figures.

Pete Sanchez stands in the middle of the corridor, hands in pockets. Kowalski leans on the wall three metres farther back, his posture hesitant.

'You took your time.' The reverend puts on a sly grin. 'I'm coming with you. Don't know if I'll be of any use, but I'm coming anyway.'

I swallow, lost for an answer.

Kowalski folds his arms over a smiley face on his orange T-shirt. 'Is it true? About the plague?'

'Yes. We're infected, or at least carriers.'

He shrinks a bit, then nods, resigned. 'So be it. Reverend says you're right about the other thing, so we gotta stop it.'

Lee pulls out two guns from the supply pack—the old ship-safe guns, not the Sharks' weapons they now carry. He hands one to Kowalski. 'Do you know how to use it?'

'Not a sharpshooter, but I know which way to point.' Kowalski checks the gun with an ease that makes it clear he's handled weapons before.

'Reverend?'

Sanchez shakes his head. 'No. Sorry.'

'It's self-defence,' Miller says.

'I know. But I won't. That's final.'

Miller wants to argue, but I wave them on. 'Come on, we've got to move.'

We pass another door that snaps locked at the sound of our footsteps.

Lee appears at my side, the gun in his hand. 'Take it. Even if you've never used one.'

I glance at the gun, but all I can see is the red stain on Stepan's shirt while the gunshots crack like distant whips.

No more death.

My hand shakes as I slide the gun into the pouch on my belt. I don't know if I'll be able to use it, but I can't cheat guilt by avoiding weapons.

We stop at another bulkhead, the last one before the bridge.

I glance at Sanchez as we wait for Tam to open the door. 'Thank you.'

He smiles. 'There'll be more.'

My brows rise in question, but then the door opens, and I see what he meant. Three people are waiting behind the bulkhead: Khan, prim-faced and stiff as ever, Navrov with a research pad under his arm as if he were heading to a conference, and Chao in a medical coat and a first-aid pack over her shoulder.

'I tried to address the crew,' Khan says. 'But the comms are locked.'

I push through the shock of seeing them there. Of course. That's what we need. They'll listen to her. She's the head of science, and she's not infected. They can't accuse her of insanity.

We need the comms. I look at Tam, but he shakes his head.

'I've tried. It's not respon—'

He stops as the comms light flashes on Khan's wan-kong.

Her eyes widen. 'How—?'

Zhang—or Firyali. I don't know, and at this moment, I don't care.

'Do it,' I say to Khan.

Khan lifts her arm. 'This is Doctor Amal Khan. We have mapped the structure of the new Mind-Link. Commander Hart is correct: the technology can be adapted for mind control. Yet the Guardian has prevented us from sending any messages, to the company or to any government, including the Americans.'

I leave her talking and start towards the last stretch of the corridors leading to the bridge. Miller and Lee are behind me. We are nine strong now, and half of us armed, but we're still no match for Price's team of highly trained shooters in protective armour and with a free supply of ammunition.

We turn the corner, our footsteps beating like a war drum. The door to the bridge is right ahead—polished metal with a web of carbon veins reinforcing the structure. I've never seen it sealed—and never realised how narrow the passage was. Two people can fit abreast, but they'll make easy targets for the defenders.

'I'll go in first,' someone says. Sanchez, moving around Lee and Miller to walk beside me.

'No way, Reverend. If it goes how I think it will, they'll shoot first and talk later.'

'That's why I need to go in first.'

'You're not even armed,' Lee says. He turns to me. 'Miller and I go first, then Kowalski and whoever knows how to shoot. You stay behind till it's clear. You need to survive this to send the message.'

'Khan can send a message,' I say. 'Or Zhang.'

'It must be you,' Miller says. 'You're the Canadian.'

Damn. After everything, we're back to this?

We stop just short of the door. Tam moves to the control pad, waiting for my signal.

'Listen to me,' Sanchez says. He pulls in a breath, searching for words. 'If you go in shooting, they'll shoot back. You might win, but most likely you'll lose. And you can't lose. The stakes are too big. So, we must stop them from shooting.'

'How?' Lee asks.

'By letting them kill me.'

'What?'

Sanchez looks into my eyes, his gaze calm. 'You know why. And you know why I must do it.' He smiles, his face almost cheerful. 'I thought I'd lost my path. But this was all planned. He knew where He needed me. And now I'm here, ready to do His will. It's what I've been born for, Nathalie.'

My mouth opens—in rebuke, dismissal, or pity. But he's right. If anything can stop the bloodshed, it's Price's people, all Christians, mistakenly killing their reverend. Still, I'm not going to let him sacrifice himself, not even if he thinks it's his God-given destiny.

I lift my chin, my voice firm. 'You can come in behind me. Miller, Lee, you go in low, then me, then the reverend. Don't shoot until they open fire. That's an order.' I turn away before they get the chance to protest. 'Tam, the door.'

The engineer punches a long string of numbers into the pad on the side of the silver and black door, the metal glistening through the fog in my eyes.

I don't think I'll survive this. But maybe the reverend's right. Maybe it's my destiny. A small price to pay for Anna, and Stepan, and all those people I led to death in the Feidi.

I just wish I knew for sure that Jason was alive.

Tam nods. Lee and Miller crouch at the sides of the door, weapons drawn.

I take a deep breath. I'm ready.

The door slides open, reluctantly as if in slow motion. I lift my foot and step forward—

—but a hand on my arm shoves me back till I tumble onto the people behind me.

'I'm sorry,' Sanchez says, and walks inside the bridge.

Four shots fire in quick succession, then stop.

The reverend's body drops to the ground in deathly silence.

I rush forward, past Miller and Lee, into the red puddle spreading under Pete's body. I grab his hand. His mouth twitches and his eyes blink, one last time.

'Pete!'

Someone's next to me, brown fingers reaching for his neck and checking the pulse.

'He's gone,' Chao says in a voice so distant it seems frozen.

I look up at the suited figures, their visors opaqued with bulletproof coating. 'You killed him!'

They stare, unmoving, as if they were just empty suits. I search for the Guardian—he lurks behind them, brows furrowed, lips pursed: a tactician, planning his next step.

Then I notice the lump on the floor: Firyali, a bloody bruise on her face, hands tied behind her back, crumpled next to the comms console. My heart stops for an instant, but she blinks, her head shifting. She's alive.

Inside me there's only boiling fury, rising like a sea of lava. I return my gaze to the soulless visors. 'He wanted to talk to you. And you killed him. For what? For him?' I point to the Guardian, my hand red with Pete's blood. 'Talk to me, Price. Is this what you wanted?'

One of the suited figures moves their arm to open the visor: Sandra Russo, Price's second in Miller's absence. Pain twists her lips. 'This is wrong, Amy. We were wrong.'

The person behind her swears. Price. 'For fuck's sake! This is what they wanted. They pushed him in so he'd get killed.'

'Nobody pushed him.' Chao rises, tall and straight. She points to me. 'He did it to save her. Because she's right, and you've chosen the wrong side in this fight.'

'Bullshit! Did she tell you how much the Chinese were paying her?'

I stand next to Chao. All the others are now on the bridge, their presence like an advancing front. 'Make up your mind, Price. Are we insane, or are we working for the Chinese? Because it can't be both.'

Another figure opens his visor—Willard, his face anguished and pale.

'Fuck you, Judas,' the fourth figure says. 'She'll have us all executed.'

'But what if she's right? If it's really mind control?'

'That's what it is, exactly.' Navrov appears beside me.

For an instant I wonder where Khan has gone, but my attention returns to the Guardian. He's been too quiet—not arguing, not spurring them on.

'I can show you the data,' Navrov continues. 'You can see for yourselves.'

Price replies, but I'm no longer listening, my eyes on the Guardian. He's up to something. What?

His face twitches, eyes narrowing with effort. Mind-Link. He's doing something over the connection.

'Zhang, can you—'

A different voice comes from my helmet audio, strained and broken. 'He's... trying... the main engine.' Wu groans. 'I can't... stop him...'

He's trying to kill us all. If he starts the main engine while the ship is split and rotating, it will tear us apart.

I fumble for the gun, my fingers slipping off the unfamiliar shape. 'The Guardian!'

I raise the weapon, hands shaking, no time to think, no time to question. I must stop him.

On my flanks, two figures move, fast like pouncing cheetahs.

I pull the trigger.

Something cracks—two, three cracks like whips or firecrackers.

A suited shape in front of me raises a gun, then all I see is a blur.

The Guardian stumbles, face twisting, mouth opening in slow motion.

He falls, our eyes meeting one last time.

My chest bursts with pain.

I'm falling, floating, crashing.

Darkness.

CHAPTER 33

'There, there,' a warm voice says, smooth and comforting like a blanket on a cool Sunday morning.

'Five more minutes,' I groan, and try to pull the covers over my head.

Needles of pain shoot up my arms. I can't move, my limbs crushed under something sharp and unbearably heavy. I gasp, but that only brings more pain, a knife stabbing my chest from the inside.

'Easy, girl,' the voice says. Chao. She's leaning above me, her round face creased with worry. Red lips part in a smile. 'Hello there.'

My memories return, blurry at first, then sharpening into focus. 'What... The Guardian?'

'He's gone. It's over.'

'It's over?' I wait for relief to wash over me, but nothing comes. I stare at the furrows on Chao's forehead, the pinch in her smile, the tension in her muscles as she checks my IV. I try to remember, but it's all a blur. 'What happened?'

I want to sit up, but a spike of pain makes me fall back on the pillow.

Chao puts her hand on my shoulder. 'Don't move, you'll make it worse. There.'

She adjusts the bed to bring my head up—not quite a sitting position but at least I can look around me now. I'm in one of the med-bay cubicles, like where I woke up from cold-sleep. The panels are drawn together, only a small gap allowing a peek at the rest of the medical suite. I glimpse a tall figure in a white coat, probably El Hussain, the junior doctor who is now in charge.

'How is everyone?'

The nurse glances behind her. 'You've got visitors. They'll tell you everything.'

She moves away, her face morphing into an older, more tired version of herself the moment she thinks she's out of my sight.

'Don't make it too long,' she says as Lee and Miller appear in the narrow entrance to my cubicle, then pull the panel closed behind them.

They're back in the black security uniforms, though neither has buttoned up his jacket and Lee's baseball cap is back on his head. Both look like they haven't slept for a week. They shuffle towards me, faces uneasy. I probably look even worse.

'Good to see you, too. Now, tell me what happened.'

Miller pulls up a chair. 'How much do you remember?'

The image flashes in front of my eyes: Sanchez's body on the floor, his eyelids fluttering, then closing. My hand covered in blood. 'Pete's dead... isn't he?'

Miller nods. 'Yeah.'

I squeeze my eyes shut for a moment. This pain is deeper than the wound in my chest—but it's not time to grieve, not yet.

Then I remember the Guardian: falling, his gaze boring into me, the gun in my hand... 'The Guardian?'

'Dead,' Miller says. 'He was trying to start the engines. I mean, we didn't know, but it was clear you wanted to stop him.'

'Did I...'

The men exchange glances, then a small smile breaks Lee's lips. 'You got the comms console. But don't worry, Tam says it'll make it.'

He cocks his brow, unsure of the joke.

I drop back on the pillow. The Guardian's gone. We did it.

'Price then tried to shoot us, but Sandra pushed her, so she missed and hit you instead,' Lee says. 'We got her, though.'

'She's alive,' Miller adds, then snorts. 'Thanks to Sandra, too. She'd be dead if Sandra hadn't pushed her.'

I close my eyes, replaying the broken images in my head. My shaking hands as I fire the gun. The figures moving at my flanks—Miller and Lee, obviously. The blur of motion in front of me: Price shooting and Sandra pushing her away. The Guardian falling.

His eyes drilling into me as if he's trying to tell me something important. Too late.

Lee and Miller keep talking, something about the others coming to their senses, or giving up. Their joy at learning I wasn't quite dead yet.

I exhale, letting the relief sweep over me like a cool shower on a scorching day. We've done the impossible. Now we can fix the transmitter and send the warning.

Except... My eyes pop open again. We've won one battle, but there's still Bethesda's plague, and we've got *Gabriel* to worry about.

'Any news from Yefremov? How's Zhang? And the others?'

'We didn't ask too many questions. The medics are busy enough.'

I don't like the way Miller says this, his voice flat and his gaze fleeting, as if he'd rather talk about anything else.

'Tell me.'

'Khan got one of Sanchez's bullets, right in the chest,' Lee says. 'They worked on her for a few hours. Chao says she'll make it.' He shrugs, the gesture more bravado than conviction. 'The people with Mind-Link are having it killed, here and on the planet. Yau's wounded, and Sheng... she's dead. Killed by debris from the explosion.'

Dead. The confirmation cuts through me, even though I expected as much back on the surface.

But there's more they're not telling me. Lee's looking at his feet; Miller checks his nails. They're hiding something.

'What else?'

'Zhang's relapsed,' Miller says. 'They say it's not the plague, but...'

'It's not,' Lee insists. 'It's just his brain not coping. He pushed himself too far, that's all. Not the plague.'

They glance at me expectantly, as if I can offer reassurance. I'm not even going to try.

'How long have I been out?'

'Just over a day,' Miller says.

'I need to talk to the medics as soon as they have a moment. And I need a line to Yefremov.' I try to pull myself up, my arms unsteady as pain drills into my bones.

'One more thing,' Lee says. 'Price claims she's got a message from the Guardian. That it's urgent. I think it's a ruse, but...' He shrugs. 'Your call.'

My brows knot. That's got to be a trick. But he's right; I risk nothing by listening to her. 'Is she here, in the infirmary?'

'She got patched up already.' Miller gives me a lopsided grin. 'We've turned the reverend's office into a brig. Left all his photos there, just so she had something to look at.'

Lee makes as if to spit but stops himself just in time. 'We voted to get rid of her. Dump her on the other side of the planet with a week's supply of air.'

I scowl. 'You voted?'

'Security. Her old team.' Miller nods, not quite meeting my gaze.

'You voted?'

They say nothing for a while. Then Miller turns towards me. 'Do you think she deserves better?'

'Probably not. But it's not your decision.'

'That's the only reason she's still here,' Lee mutters.

'Good. Because nobody's getting dumped anywhere.'

They frown, either at my lenience or their democratic vote being ignored.

'Why do you care?' Lee asks. 'After what she's done?'

I manage to smile. 'You have it backwards. I don't give a hyena's turd about Price.'

Lee's eyes widen. He bites his lip as he looks for an answer, surprised at not finding one.

'Go now. Get my office set up, and then find a free medic to untangle me from this.' I lift my arms to show the IV tubes and sensor wires emerging from under my hospital gown. 'And get me some clothes.'

It takes another day before I can bully the doctors to discharge me. I'm in my office with Chao adjusting my wiring when Yefremov finally pings me from the surface.

I reach for the terminal, my arm burning with the effort. 'Can you—'

Chao doesn't look up. 'Nope.'

I scowl.

'You were going to ask me to up your painkillers, weren't you?'

'And you refuse?'

'The pain's there to stop you from doing too much. You do want to get better?'

I consider a protest but change my mind. I'm not winning this one.

'Stay here,' I say as she starts for the door. 'You may as well hear this.'

Chao's face grows solemn. She pulls the sides of her coat together and slides into a chair within line of sight of the screen, as much to see as to be seen.

Yefremov's face appears on the monitor: his hair in oily tangles, his cheeks feverishly pink, and his lips grey.

I swallow, the question stuck at the tip of my tongue. We've come too far to let the plague defeat us now. 'And?'

The doctor rubs his cheek with a brown-stained hand. 'I think we got it.'

This time, the relief is so palpable I can taste it. I lean back, the pain forgotten as the sweet wave rolls over me, soothing and calm. It really *is* over.

'I grew a sample of the infected tissue from Zhang's brain,' Yefremov continues, oblivious. 'It's as I thought. Bethesda's prions have just the right structure to bind with the D-isomers in Mind-Link. And the result becomes—'

'So if you kill the Mind-Link, everyone will be safe?' Chao cuts in, her voice trembling.

'Yes. If it's done early enough.'

I sit up again. 'Are we early enough?'

'Most of us. Yes.'

'Except for Zhang?'

Yefremov looks away, his gaze heavy. I clench the armrests, waiting for his answer.

'If he'd stayed here, he'd probably be all right. But...' The doctor rubs his cheek again. I wonder if the brown stains are blood. And whose. 'He's not gone yet, that's all I can say.'

My hand trembles as I bring it to my face—but my eyes are dry.

We wouldn't have done it without Zhang. He knew what it would cost him, and he made his choice anyway.

Yefremov breaks the silence. 'I've killed or removed the Mind-Link of everyone here. Including the Sharks.' He smirks.

'They started cooperating once they got to breathe the local air. Not sure what they'll do when they realise they're no longer in danger.'

Right. I still have the Sharks to worry about. They've got no weapons, but I don't trust them not to have any tricks saved for when they get back on the ship.

'We'll bring you all up as soon as you're ready. Sedate the Sharks. I want them back in the pods with big padlocks on, the sooner the better.'

'My pleasure.' Yefremov nods, then leans forward a tiny bit. 'And how are you doing?'

My mouth twists. If he thinks we can be friends again, he's got another think coming. 'I'll see you on board, Doctor. Thank you for your work.'

I push the icon to disconnect. A grin pours on to my lips as I swing my chair towards Chao. 'We'll be all right. And so will *Gabriel*. Go, tell everyone.'

She nods, her grin mirroring mine, her face bright with relief as she heads to the door.

One thing left to do. I touch the intercom button. 'Bring her in.'

Price saunters into the office, her nonchalance too desperate to be persuasive. She cocks a smile, her eyes not quite meeting mine. She's wearing civilian clothes: brown slacks and a loose cream shirt with an open collar. The corner of a healing patch pokes above the neckline. She lifts her hands to push a strand of hair behind her ear, a security tie binding her wrists.

Miller walks in behind her, his mouth pursed and his body tense. I could tell him to unbind her, but I'm not in the mood for charity. I stay in my seat, watching her for a long moment.

Price straightens, as if to repel my gaze. She snorts, or laughs, the sound tinged with nerves. Still I say nothing. Even

Miller is uneasy now, shifting his weight as he leans on the door.

Finally, she's had enough. She turns away, then back to me, exasperated. 'What was I supposed to do? If the Sharks hadn't got me, you'd have flushed me out of the airlock after you found out who I was. Not just me, all of us. Because we were all there.' She points behind her, the gesture awkward with her hands tied. 'He was there, too. And Lee. All of us at that warehouse, doing our job.'

Heat rises up my chest and over my face till my cheeks burn and my eyes sting. I glance at Miller, but he averts his gaze, the corners of his lips twitching. It could have been his bullet that killed Stepan.

Price turns to Miller, her mouth curling. 'Let's see how she changes her tune now that she no longer needs you.'

'Don't go there, Price,' I say slowly. 'They made the right choice when they realised it wasn't just about them.'

'Like you're all "forgive and forget"? Are you going to tell me you'd have let us be if the Guardian hadn't forced your hand?'

'That's beside the point.'

'No, it isn't. What I did was survival. For me, and for my people. Protecting them from your vengeance. And your dirty conscience.'

I wince. I should've stopped her before it got this far—but now that she's planted doubt in Miller's head, I have to let it play out. 'I wasn't the one who did the shooting, Price. I wasn't the one who killed unarmed civilians. You were.'

'You brought them there. You knew we'd have defences. You knew there'd been looting. We had strict orders to protect—'

'They were stealing medicines meant for the hospitals! Letting people die so they could get rich! That's what you were protecting. If you'd had any decency, you'd have...' I break off. I'm breathing hard, my fingers clenched so tight all my muscles hurt. I bang my hand on the armrest, then brace myself for the pain in my wrist.

It doesn't come. The pain's gone; it's been gone since that moment on the tether when I held on to Miller and I knew...

I take a slow breath. 'I'm done, Price. I'm not going to play your game. Nobody's getting punished. Not the doctor, not any of your people, not even you. You're going in the pod until the courts on Earth have their say about what happened. Moses, take her away.'

'Wait. There *is* a message. I wasn't lying about that.'

I cock an eyebrow, almost sure it's just another ploy. Almost.

'In your files,' Price says. It's her tone, subdued and defeated, that tells me she's telling the truth. 'You must listen to it before you do anything. Then you'll know why he did it.' She puts on a sad smile. 'You talk about decisions. Well, the toughest one's still ahead of you.'

The door closes behind them with a dry click. I turn to the screen and stare at the icon marking my personal files. I could ignore the message. Why should I give him more time? It'll be only tricks and deception.

A chill runs down my body, as if a cold wind has replaced the heat of Price's accusations. I must know.

I touch the screen, then sit back, ready for the storm.

The Guardian's cream-white face has acquired a greyish tinge; thin lines of wrinkles fracture the corners of his eyes. He looks straight at me, his gaze intense even as a smile breaks on his lips.

'Hello, Nathalie. If you're listening to this, you've done the impossible and managed to get control of the ship. Congratulations.' He draws a deep breath and flashes another smile, sad but surprisingly sincere. 'As odd as it sounds, you almost have me rooting for you. Because if you succeed, then you and your team will have beaten all the odds, transcended all the barriers and tricks we used to control you. Impressive. You almost make me believe in humanity again.'

He laughs or snorts, his expression a mix of amusement and disbelief. Then he grows sombre again. 'If you do win, this message is all I have to make you understand what this has really been about. I know you hate me now, but hold that hatred back for a moment. Before you send that warning to Earth, you must understand the truth. Then you can decide if I really am the villain you think me to be.'

He steeples his fingers, his face drawn. 'I'm a member of an organisation of sorts; we call ourselves Destiny. We came together two centuries ago, when it became clear that our civilisation would not survive the transformed climate. The changes came too quickly, too violently, and we were too slow to adapt. Even as the sea levels were rising, we kept arguing about who to blame. The plague changed all the equations for the worse—but, in a cruel way, it saved us. By the time it hit, our agriculture couldn't feed more than eighty per cent of the population. The first scarcity wars were just starting—and would have become much, much worse. The plague did the culling for us, and we had only nature—or God—to blame. That's easier for a society to endure than neighbour turning on neighbour, believe me. Read history if you need proof.'

He pauses, glancing towards the door that's just off camera. He's in this office, I realise with a shiver, sitting in the same chair I'm sitting in now. The image flickers, then returns—recording paused and restarted.

The Guardian leans in to the screen, his voice urgent. 'So now you're wondering what this has to do with Bethesda. There's something few people dare to say out loud: we've never recovered. The plague got the population numbers to match our resources. But the climate hasn't reverted to pre-warming status. The crops haven't adapted. The most fertile lands are now under water or in the middle of expanding deserts. Our technology gets better every year, but robots won't replace soil. And that's the problem: the population's growing too fast for our resources. We're almost back to where we were before the plague. Except now there's no act of God to get us through this. All models point to the same: we're reaching the tipping point. Once the infrastructure starts to unravel, the nations will follow. Hunger is a terrible thing. It will turn neighbour against neighbour. Anything to survive. Total war.'

He pauses, looking at the camera. A chill runs through me. I want him to be wrong, but the shadow on his face tells me he believes every word.

'So this is where you come in, Nathalie. Yes, Bethesda was a field lab for the new Mind-Link, and yes, it's about mind control —but this is where your predictions stop being correct. Because it was never about profit or political manipulation. It was created to help us survive, to avoid war. Of course, we could just tell people to live more sustainable lives, waste less, give more to their communities. Do you think they'd listen?' The Guardian shakes his head. 'For an intelligent species, we are surprisingly dumb. And as much as I'd like to, I don't believe that this time the outcome will be different.'

He stops, pushes his hand through his hair. He looks spent, older now and tired. 'So, this is it, the truth. The third Horseman is on his way. Humanity is heading for total war. Mind-Link is our only tool to prevent it, to get people to do what they must in order to survive—and be happy about it. And don't lecture me about free will! It's not your free will to eat or not. To feed your children or watch them starve. The voice of reason will always drown under lies because lies are easier, and we so desperately want to believe. When applied to the masses, free will is what will take us all to hell. Where's the choice then?'

He takes a deep breath, regaining his composure. 'We could spend days discussing the morality of this. It's irrelevant. It's not about morals; it's about survival. If we agree that humanity's survival is the ultimate good, then everything that prevents our annihilation must somehow be good as well. That's what I believe. What we believe.

'I'm not going to lie and say this is easy. It's damn hard, but it's the only way. That's why I left everything and came here. Only now I'm dead, and the decision is in your hands. I beg you, consider the consequences. It's easy to take the high ground when it's others who'll suffer. But it's real lives, Nathalie, real pain. Your nephew, Jason—he's still alive. If not him, then his children will live through it. Or die through it. You decide.'

He looks at the camera, his face open and his gaze earnest. 'Our future's in your hands. Be strong, Nathalie. Make the right choice. Goodbye.'

The image flickers, and then he's gone and I sit alone, staring at the dark screen, trying very hard not to scream.

Some of it may be lies—but not the part that matters. I know it in my blood, in the marrow of my bones. The tipping point is coming, again. That's the only way this plan could have ever gained support. The Guardian, Destiny, they believed it. That's why he tried to destroy the ship rather than let us send the message.

Images from history lessons flood my mind, the record of the world on the brink of apocalypse, when all rules collapsed, and survival was the only purpose. Pictures of starving children, hollow-eyed and skeletal, wading through the marshes of former cities. What use is free will if all it gives you is pain?

It's up to me now. I have to decide if I let humanity descend into famine and war—or leave our minds at the mercy of whoever happens to own Mind-Link technology.

I push my fist into my mouth as my shoulders heave in a soundless cry. Jason is alive. I did it all for him. I can't let him die in a senseless war. I can't let him watch his children starve. Anything's better than that.

Even Mind-Link.

CHAPTER 34

Gabriel's crew stare at us with grim faces. We've woken only five of them: the captain, chief engineer, chief of security, the doctor, and the reverend. We're still in the medical bay, this one much larger than what we have back on our ship. Perched on chairs we've rolled in from all the corners of the bay, Yefremov, Miller, Tam, and I wait patiently as they digest the news.

Captain Feng shakes his head, his mouth pinched, his pale face covered with black stubble. He seems about to speak, only to shake his head again. What do you say to learning that five thousand of your future neighbours have perished? That the thriving colony you expected to join is a ghost town littered with corpses?

'Are you sure we'll be safe?' Wilson, the security chief asks, his eyes shifting between Miller and Yefremov.

'Positive,' Yefremov says. 'Provided we remove everyone's Mind-Link. Am I correct assuming only your engineers have it?'

'The engineers and a few senior officers, including myself,' Feng says.

Yefremov nods. 'It won't last too long, then. A week at most.'

'It will take some getting used to,' Tam says to Feng and

Sun, the engineer. 'But we'll help. We've been developing some workarounds.'

From what I've seen, these will be very much needed. Our engineers took the loss of their Mind-Link hard. For most of their tech, the manual interface was only designed as emergency backup, with half the functionality. It took them a day to even set up the team's communications, with much arguing and the most creative swearing I've ever heard in Mandarin.

Sun nods, then they fall silent again.

'We'll stay as long as you need us,' I say. 'Our people know the settlement pretty well by now.'

Miller leans forward. 'This is a tragedy, but it also gives you time. The base is already set up. With *Gabriel*'s modules, you can double the living space. Lower the restrictions on having children. And with the number of assemblers you now have, the dome will be ready much sooner. As much as I hate to say it, there are advantages.'

Reverend Davis pulls in a deep breath. He's a stout white man with a mane of grey hair despite not looking older than thirty. 'We need to make the best of it, for sure. Focus on the positives. But...' He pauses, searching for words. 'It's one thing that they died. A tragedy, of course, but no one expected colonisation to be easy. We, too, might die if things go wrong. But... it's what happened before that bothers me. The fractures. The accusations. The divided communities. Even before the infection. How could that happen?'

He looks at us, then at the others around him, their faces equally pained.

'You know that it did happen,' I say softly. 'You can learn from that. Keep your eyes open for the signs.'

'We'll need to integrate,' Wilson says. 'One community, and make sure everyone speaks English, so we can communicate.'

'No, it doesn't work like this.' Miller shakes his head with sudden vehemence. He leans towards Wilson. 'It's not about forcing *them* to become like *us*—or forcing *us* to become like *them*. It's about learning to respect *them* even if they are not like *us*. Do you understand?'

The other man frowns, but then nods, and so do the others. Tam's nodding, too, and so am I, I realise. So much to learn. They have their future in their hands. It's up to them how they shape it.

My chest heaves, my stomach constricting with pain. I'm about to shape the future of the rest of humanity. I'm saving them from war. From hunger and suffering. I'm making the right choice.

Or am I?

I get up, my eyes moist and my hands trembling. I haven't been sleeping well. Or at all. 'Take your time. And use our resources for everything you want.'

'Anything you need from us?' Captain Feng asks.

I feel the others' glances bore into me. *Gabriel*'s transmitter is functional—but I insisted that we don't tell them the whole truth just yet. Yes, the Mind-Link and the prions that turned the colonists mad. But nothing about the Guardian or the new design. It was the shrink's suggestion, actually. Dose out the bad news, he said, give them time to digest it step by step. I was only too grateful.

'We'll let you know if there's anything,' I say, and start for the exit.

Chao is all smiles as I enter the medical. If we ever run out of fuel, we could probably run the ship just on this woman's warmth. And yet, even this is not enough to chase the chill from my bones.

I contort my face into a grin. 'Is he awake?'

Chao doesn't notice the heaviness of my voice. 'Yes, he is! Awake and talking. Better every day.'

She leads me towards the corner cubicle, the only one still enclosed within privacy panels.

'That's good to hear,' I say, because I should say something.

'The brain's a miracle. And so is Tolya's surgery.' She knocks on the side of the panel before pulling it open. 'Hello again. You've got a visitor.'

Zhang Min looks up from the bed. His hair's gone; his face has lost all colour. He's thinner, too, his cheeks hollow and his arms gaunt in the loose hospital shirt. Yet his eyes are as bright as ever, maybe even brighter now against his pale, lean face. He's sitting, his head high and a zheping in his hand.

'Hello,' I manage.

He smiles with half of his face, the muscles on his left barely twitching. His left arm stays immobile as he motions with his right towards the visitor's chair in the corner. I pull it closer, wondering what to say next. There are a million things I want to tell him: about the Guardian, the truth, and my decision —but he's suffered enough. Anyway, I know what he'd say. What he'd urge me to do.

And that's exactly why I'm not going to ask.

I point to his zheping. 'What are you reading?'

He gives me a guilty grin, then glances at the door. Chao's gone, but still he leans in closer, his tone conspiratorial. 'Maintenance reports...'

I chuckle, then force a frown. 'I really should tell on you...'

'I'll deny every word.'

Tears well in my eyes, catching me off guard. 'It's good to have you back.'

'I'm not displeased myself.' He smiles his half-smile, his speech slurred but his pride shining through. He's done his job. He set out to save humanity and...

'I'm sorry. About what I did. Sending you to the surface...'

He waves his arm. 'You made the right decision when it mattered.'

I grit my teeth. He's right. I've made the right decision. Even if he doesn't know...

It's for the better, I repeat inwardly, the words my new mantra. Because I can't condemn them to war and suffering. I won't.

Zhang is watching me, his eyes burning with conviction. I blink the tears away, hoping it will chase away the doubts. *It's for the better*.

'The zheping, did you bring it?'

'Yes!' I pull out the green pad I found in his hideout, grateful for the distraction.

'Oh, good. It's got all the dispatches. The real news, and the personal messages.'

He puts the pad under his left arm, using the stiff limb to hold it in place while he taps the screen with his good hand. 'Damn, this was easier with Mind-Link! I bet Lim could crack it faster than I can type... There.'

He hands the pad back to me, relieved.

I push it into my pocket and plaster a smile on my face. 'I'm sure the crew will be grateful.' I get up, ignoring the disappointment on his face. 'There's something else I brought you. I hope...'

I show him the image I pulled off his wall, the one with him and Kuang laughing in front of a giant machine.

Zhang snatches the photo from my hand as if it were oxygen. His eyes widen, then fog. His chin trembles. I turn away, embarrassed by this invasion of his privacy.

'We've stopped them,' he says as I reach the exit. 'That's what counts. That's what he died for. He, and Reverend Sanchez, and Sheng Jing. We stopped them.'

I stay at the door, unmoving, my back to Zhang.

His voice is soft as he adds, 'Thank you.'

I turn slowly, facing the engineer, so small now in his thin white shirt against the bulk of medical equipment behind him. 'No. Thank *you*.'

I stride out before another word shatters me into pieces.

Firyali meets me outside the med-bay. She seems to have grown a head taller since I gave her a field promotion to my 'chief of staff.' Not even a function on the company's roster, but I need help with the crew still reeling from the events—and I could hardly promote her to reverend.

'How is he?' she asks.

'Better. You should see him when you have a moment.'

'I will. As soon as the work's done.'

This almost makes me crack a smile. 'You're allowed a break. The ship won't fall apart without you.'

She casts me a sideways glance that's almost her former shyness, but then she laughs. 'Ai-yah! And what if it does?'

I hand her Zhang's green zheping. 'It's got all the news and personal messages. Put it in the system and inform the crew.'

Firyali's eyes grow large with hunger as she snatches the pad. She wants nothing more than to run to her quarters and check her messages. I would, too, if the prospect didn't scare me to tears.

She pockets the zheping, a slight frown marking her resolve. 'I'll put it in the system, but—with your permission—I'll wait on announcing till after the transmitter shakedown. It's a tricky procedure... better to avoid distractions.'

Transmitter shakedown. The replacement system will be ready by the end of the day.

'Is that all right?' Firyali repeats. She's watching my face with her head tilted and lips parted in an impending question.

'Yes. Of course. It makes sense. Anything else?'

'No, sir.' She glances up at me, eager and worried, sensing something is off even if she can't name it. Her trust in me won't let her.

I walk away, the queasiness in my stomach settling into a
dull throb.

It's for the better. It's for the...

Is it?

I push the comms button on my wrist-pad. 'Doctor Khan,
can I see you for a moment?'

Amal Khan's office is as pristine as it's always been: terminals
arranged symmetrically on the desk, a ship-issue zheping on one
side and the lab terminal on the other, the stylus resting in the
exact middle. Only her seat has been replaced by a wheelchair,
the tracks already worn into the carpet.

Navrov is there as I enter, the two of them studying the
screen in his hand.

'Good news, Commander. We've nailed the theoretical
basis to Tolya's hypothesis.' Khan cracks a smile. 'I'd ask Oleg to
explain it, but I don't want to put you to sleep. Unless you
insist?'

'Er, no. I'll take your word for it.'

Navrov feigns a sigh. 'If you change your mind...'

'I'll remember that when we run out of sleeping pills.'

I stay by the door, holding it open till he gets the hint. He
nods and heads out, and I pull the door closed.

'Have a seat,' Khan says.

She's in her uniform, though the jacket's draped over one
shoulder, her arm in a sling over her chest. Her hair's been cut
short, and her skin has lost its coppery glow.

I slump into the seat. Khan's lips twitch, and she reaches for
the controls of her wheelchair.

'Wait.' I rise again and slide my chair to the right, exactly
opposite hers. 'Is this good?'

Her chin trembles. She stares at me, eyes wide, blinking
repeatedly before she finally manages to nod.

I sit back down. 'There's something I'd like you to hear. It... won't be easy.'

'What is it?'

I pull out my zheping and lay it on the desk. 'A message. From the Guardian.'

Khan's brows rise, but she doesn't say anything. I touch the screen and watch her face as she listens, her expression a mirror of my own emotions. By the end of the recording, her fingers clench and her lips part as if she wants to scream or cry. She leans back, not looking at me for several seconds.

When our eyes finally meet, her face is hard again, calculating.

'He's right, you know.' Her voice is cold, but a slight tremor betrays her emotions. 'There was talk of the tipping point long before our departure, both from the economists and the environmentalists. Papers got published but never made it beyond the science journals. And then funding got pulled from those who published. As if muzzling the scientists ever changed the facts.' She gives a tiny shrug, then winces at the pain in her shoulder. 'Is that what you wanted me to tell you? If his predictions are correct?'

'No. I know he's right.'

'What are you going to do?'

I lean back, turning my gaze to a picture on the wall to the right: a mountainous landscape with sharp, snow-covered peaks. 'With Mind-Link, they can stop violence. They can teach people to use resources sensibly. To share. We could avert the tipping point or survive it without bloodshed. In peace and harmony. Isn't that a glorious vision?'

Khan nods. 'Glorious indeed.'

'If we send the message, everything will go to hell. And we'll be responsible.'

'True.'

'If we don't, we'll hand all the power to the privileged few—

to Destiny or whoever takes over from them. And as much as I don't trust humanity to do the sensible thing, I trust *them* even less.'

Khan gives me a lopsided smile. 'I'm afraid that's a correct diagnosis.'

'We'll plunge Earth into war.'

'Maybe not. Maybe they'll learn. And if not, then at least it'll be a war of their own doing. And a new peace they'll forge later. That must be better than eternal slavery in the hands of the orbital masters.'

I glance at the snowy peaks again. I wonder what snow feels like. Is it as soft as it looks, or is that an illusion, icy shards masquerading as down?

'Do you believe in good, Doctor?'

She sniffs quietly. 'I believe in truth. I used to think it was enough.'

I wait. Khan looks away, her gaze lost on whatever snowy peaks rise in her mind.

'Yes,' she says after a while. 'Yes. I believe in good. And in forgiveness. And in trying to be your best, and failing, and learning. We must be free to do that.'

'Thank you, Doctor.'

I get up. I'm lighter now—not happier, but at peace with my decision. It'll haunt me forever, yet I will always know it was the only right one.

CHAPTER 35

We watch the first of *Gabriel*'s modules descend to the planet ten days later. Only four, with the core crew whose task it will be to prepare the habitat for the others. We've already cleared most of the corpses, the colony's graveyard now as big as the hub. It will be an orchard one day, Johansson's assured me. I hope he's right.

Miller sits on the other side of my office table, his hands clasped in front of him. He looks different in civilian clothes, no less imposing but somehow softer, like a brother I never had.

'Are you really sure you want to stay?'

'Yeah. It feels right.'

Captain Feng offered the opportunity to all my crew but no one else took it up. I can't say I'm surprised. Most of us can't wait to get away from this place, no matter how uncertain our own futures.

I sigh. 'You have two more days to change your mind. You can return any time, no matter what Feng says.'

Miller smiles. 'He seems like a good boss. They'll have their hands full trying to get everything going. They can use any help they can get.'

That's an understatement. *Gabriel*'s passengers were expecting to find a thriving colony, not a ghost town full of corpses of its former occupants. They know the truth now, all of it, and will have to live with that weight.

'Your replacement?'

'Michael Lee, if you agree. Russo's better qualified, but given the circumstances, he's better placed to bring everyone together.'

'Agreed.' I get up and reach out my hand to shake his. 'They're lucky to have you.'

'Thank you, sir.'

I hold his warm hand in mine. 'Keep them together, Moses. No matter what happens. Don't let them blame "the other", whoever that may be. We're all one. Bright and stupid, scared and brave, angry and generous. All the same. Don't let them forget that.'

'I won't.'

My eyes itch, so I start to laugh. 'Go now or I may hug you.'

'That would be dangerous indeed...' He salutes with an exaggerated flair, but even his eyes are moist and his brown cheeks unusually rosy.

The door barely closes behind him when Firyali's message pops up on my wan-kong. *We're ready.*

I start for the exit when the woman herself appears from the bridge-side entrance, her uniform buttoned up and her hair clipped in an official do.

I grin. 'Lead the way, Officer.'

She blushes ever so slightly, the old Firyali still there under her newfound confidence. Or maybe she's Lim again, Lim Firyali, both parts of her finally united. I hope so for her.

We head out ship-side, crossing the corridors in silence on the short walk to the mess. Everyone's here, except for Price and the three Sharks, already secured in the cold-sleep pods. The room buzzes with conversation—some excited, some uneasy.

The medical team is on the left, with Yefremov at his usual spot next to the food dispensers. Khan has lost her sling, though she still keeps her arm at her chest as she and Johansson lean over his pad. The engineers have a table in the right corner, Tam smiling at me from the seat next to Zhang's wheelchair. Next to them, Sheng Jing's seat remains empty. The security team seems split in the middle, Price's former allies watching the others with sombre expressions. Miller is still here, he and Lee counting pins on their baseball caps according to the new tallies. In the centre of the room, Kowalski, in a red T-shirt, looks up from the table reserved for the ops team, with one empty seat in the middle. Sanchez's.

I push to the front, ignoring the sting in my chest. 'Thank you for waiting. I know you're all hungry...'

They groan theatrically.

'I know. Life is hard. But this is something we must do together.' I pause, taking a moment to look at the gathered faces. 'We saved *Gabriel*. And now we send our message home to tell them what we've discovered. That's all we can do; they must handle this knowledge themselves. We can only hope they will choose right—but at least we can be sure that the choice will be theirs.'

Firyali approaches with a zheping. The screen has only one button, a bright green *SEND* waiting to be pressed. We've spent days crafting a message that will speak to all the nations on Earth as one people. It'll go to all governments and all media, repeated over the ten days left before our departure. There will be many who'll try to block it—but it takes only a few good journalists, a few uncorrupted politicians or activists to spread the message far and wide, until the truth can no longer be denied.

They nod, the weight of the moment settling in on them. We're heading home to a place we may not recognise by the time we get there, a place our own actions may have plunged into a bloody war. Who knows what welcome we are going to get. And yet, nobody here is trying to stop me.

The room is perfectly quiet as Lim holds the pad for me to touch. But it's not up to me. I whisk it from her hands and carry it across the room to the far corner, where the chief engineer sits in his wheelchair, a crumpled photograph in his hand.

'Will you do the honours, Zhang Min?'

He says nothing, his arm shaking as he reaches out his hand. I hold the zheping as his finger hovers above the green button, then lands softly on the glass surface.

In total silence, the quiet ping of the signal rings like a victory bell.

'Hell, yes!' Lee shouts from the other side of the room.

The others cheer. The buzz of voices rises like a wave, cresting in bubbling laughter. I share a smile with Zhang, then with the other engineers. Chao hands me a glass of something, and then Kowalski passes me a cake, a leftover from Navrov's birthday that never happened.

I linger by the door, watching. They're good people. A small miracle, given how we started. I guess it's all down to choices.

My eyes find Yefremov cradling a bowl of something in the far corner. He still looks tired, his hair ruffled and his beard in urgent need of trimming. He catches my glance, his eyes widening in question. I don't smile but do not avert my gaze.

I'm not ready. Not yet. But maybe soon we'll be able to talk.

Back in my quarters, my personal zheping waits on the bed. I haven't checked my messages, haven't even dared to see if there were any.

I hold my breath as I slide to the floor and pick up the pad. It's time. Whatever the truth, I can face it.

The screen fills with date logs, one, two, three pages long. Ninety-two messages in total, with dates starting just after my departure. The most recent one has a title: START HERE.

My hand shakes. It takes all my strength to touch the icon to get it to play.

Stepan's face looks at me from the screen—older than Stepan, though, and with Anna's blue eyes and cheeky grin. A brown-skinned woman with a bright smile sits next to him, a toddler in her lap.

'Tetushka! They tell me this is the message you'll get when you arrive. So I want to introduce my family. This is my wife, Maia, and this here is your grand-niece, Anna Nathalie. Wave to your auntie, Anna!'

He reaches for the toddler, and I hear the three of them laugh but I can no longer see anything, my tears raining on the screen in heavy, happy drops.

GLOSSARY

Most of the Mandarin-derived terms in the novel have entered the common vocabulary and became 'anglicised' (or adapted to other languages). For them, a simplified spelling is used, without diacritics. Pinyin spelling is used for lines of dialogue spoken in Mandarin, to reflect the actual pronunciation. Hanzi characters were used where the characters would experience the information in this form.

GENERAL TERMS

di shang de / 地上的 / dìshàng de
'grounders'; Earth-bound people

Feidi / 飛地 / Fēi dì
Enclave; short for the Chinese enclave in Kenya

Huanying lai dao Kenniya de Zhongguo Fei di / 欢迎来到肯尼亚的中国飞地 / Huānyíng lái dào Kěnníyǎ de Zhōngguó Fēi dì
Welcome to the Chinese enclave in Kenya

ji-gong / 際工 / jì gong
an international worker with residence permit

kai gou ri / 开购日 / kāi gòu rì
open shopping day

Kenniya Xinwen / 肯尼亚新闻 / Kěnníyǎ Xīnwén
name of newspaper (Kenya News)

laowai / 老外 / lǎowài
a non-Chinese person

pa-pian / Pa片 / pa-piàn
passport chip

tian-ti / 天梯 / Tiāntī
sky ladder; a common term for the space elevator

Tian-ti Feidi / 天梯飛地 / Tiāntī fēi dì
the space elevator enclave

tian shang de / 天上的 / tiānshàng de
general term for all the people living in the orbitals

wan-kong / 腕控 / wàn kòng
a wrist-pad/controller

Yun Ju / 雲居 / Yún jū
Cloud Residence: orbital stations inhabited by the super-rich and their
staff

yun-ying / 雲英 / yún yīng
the elites; the super-rich business and political leaders inhabiting the
orbitals

zheping / 折屏 / zhé píng
a folding data pad

Zhongguo Kenniya Fei di / 中國肯尼亞飛地 / Zhōngguó Kěnníyǎ Fēi dì
the Chinese enclave in Kenya

zhu-yuan / 助員 / zhù yuan
the support staff of the yun-ying

DIALOGUE

Dai Sei! / 抵死! / dai2 sei2
Damn! [Cantonese]

Fashengle shenme? / 发生了什么？ / Fāshēngle shénme?
What happened?

Gao shenme? / 搞什么？ / Gǎo shénme?
What the hell (is going on/are you doing)?

Hai la! / 係啦！ / hai6*2 laa1
Indeed! / That's right! [Cantonese]

Shenme? / 什么？ / Shénme?
What?

Weisheme shi ni? / 为什么是你？ / Wèishéme shì nǐ?
Why is it you? Why you?

Zou kai! / 走开！ / Zǒu kāi
Go away! Get out of my way!

wou kao / 我靠 / wǒ kào
ta ma de/ni ma de / 他媽的/你媽的 / tā mā de/ nǐ mā de
cao / 操 / cāo
various expletives

Si-Lian (Si Wei Lian Jie) / 思连 (思维连接) / Sī lián (Sīwéi liánjiē)
Mind-Link

A LETTER FROM THE AUTHOR

Dear reader,

Huge thanks for reading *Refractions*, I hope you were hooked on Nathalie's journey. If you want to join other readers in hearing all about my new releases and bonus content, you can sign up for my newsletter.

www.stormpublishing.co/mv-melcer

Or sign up at mvmelcer.com/newsletter

If you enjoyed this book and could spare a few moments to leave a review that would be hugely appreciated. Even a short review can make all the difference in encouraging a reader to discover my books for the first time. Thank you so much!

Some books have journeys as complicated as those of their characters—that was the case with *Refractions*. The novel was conceived just before the start of the Covid pandemic, which made the mentions of the 'plague' in the novel both prophetic and unwelcome, since few people wanted to hear about a fictional plague while the real pandemic was raging. The worsening relationship between the USA and China also seemed uncomfortably prescient.

In *Refractions*, I wanted to tell a story about a person trying to do her best in a hopeless situation; about failing and trying again and again, because you refuse to give up hope, refuse to stop believing that despite the odds you can make a difference. This belief is what keeps Nathalie going, and what gives her strength to succeed in the end.

Refractions is also a story about weaponised prejudice—about people manipulated to turn against each other while the real villains run unchecked. This is a story as old as ages: the powerful manipulating the populace into blaming the 'other' for all the ailments of the society they control, fabricating conflict through lies and prejudice so we're too busy fighting our neighbours to notice who really benefits from the discord. I wrote *Refractions* hoping that, just as Nathalie, the reader may pause on hearing demagogues pointing accusing fingers at the 'others': those who look differently, talk differently, dress differently, love differently. They are not the enemy. They are a smokescreen behind which the Guardians hide their lies.

Thanks again for being part of this amazing journey with me and I hope you'll stay in touch—I have so many more stories and ideas to entertain you with!

M V Melcer

mvmelcer.com
Bluesky: @mvmelcer.com

facebook.com/m.v.melcer
x.com/MVMelcer
instagram.com/mvmelcer
tiktok.com/@mvmelcer

ACKNOWLEDGEMENTS

This book has been a long project and so many people have helped and encouraged me on the way—so many, in fact, that as I'm sitting down to write my thanks, I'm sure I'll fail to mention someone and then I'll want to disappear in shame. If it's you I've forgotten, please forgive me!

My big thanks go to Robert T. L. Chang, who developed all the Mandarin vocabulary and dialogue, and provided advice and authenticity checks through the many versions of the story. I am grateful for the depth of thought that went into the creation of the terms—most of which I could only glimpse in the translations Robert T. L. Chang provided. Alas, only a fraction of the work made it into the final edits, and to the glossary. Thank you for helping me build this future!

Big thanks to the entire team at Storm, the publisher, for bringing this novel to the readers. I'm especially grateful to Kathryn Taussig for believing in the story and my treatment of it, and to Amanda Rutter, for her insightful edit.

Big thanks to Lisa Rodgers, my agent, for all her advice and persistence. To Brady McReynolds, who helped when help was needed, and the entire team at Jabberwocky.

Thank you to the Elementals, my wonderful critique group, beta readers, and counsellors: Laurence Brothers, L. D. Colter, M. E. Garber, S. L. Harrison, Sandy Parsons (alas, no Sandy in *this* novel!), and Lettie Prell. Honestly, you are the best!

To all the folks from the Menagerie, for their humour, wisdom, and support.

And to all the other beta readers and mentors who provided feedback on the text or offered advice and encouragement along the way: Anatoly Belilovsky (with thanks for the medical advice and Russian terms), Robert Dawson (for science help in figuring out how to trap the Sharks!), Adam Jackson, John Jarrold, Leonid Korogodski, Yoon Ha Lee, Grayson Morris (as well as Jeff, Matt, Steven, and Marion from Villa Diodati 19), Barbara Newman, Erin Tidwell, Emma Maree Urquhart, and Heidi Wainer. To Codex, for existing.

To the people who provided sensitivity/authenticity reads (whose names I won't mention because if anything is wrong, that's on me, not them)—you have my gratitude.

To Mary and Emma, again, for holding my hand through this.

Lastly, to my family: my husband, Jan, for all the help and support. Without you, this book would never have happened. Thank you, dear. And to Earl Grey, the cat, for letting me use the keyboard and not throwing up on the manuscript this time. Keep it up, buddy!

Made in the USA
Columbia, SC
29 October 2023